MW01675059

David

The Life and Times of Bertrand Du Guesclin

Vol. 2

SALZWASSER VERLAG

David F. Jamison

The Life and Times of Bertrand Du Guesclin

Vol. 2

Reprint of the original, first published in 1864.

1st Edition 2022 | ISBN: 978-3-75259-510-9

Verlag (Publisher): Salzwasser Verlag GmbH, Zeilweg 44, 60439 Frankfurt, Deutschland
Vertretungsberechtigt (Authorized to represent): E. Roepke, Zeilweg 44, 60439 Frankfurt, Deutschland
Druck (Print): Books on Demand GmbH, In de Tarpen 42, 22848 Norderstedt, Deutschland

THE LIFE AND TIMES

OF

Bertrand du Guesclin.

THE

LIFE AND TIMES

OF

BERTRAND DU GUESCLIN:

A History of the Fourteenth Century.

By D. F. JAMISON,

Of South Carolina.

IN TWO VOLUMES.

VOL. II.

MDCCCLXIV.

CONTENTS OF VOL. II.

PAGE

CHAPTER I.

Triumphal progress of Henry from Toledo to Seville. Sir Matthew Gournay at the Portuguese court. Henry discharges the Free Companies . . . 1

CHAPTER II.

Edward the Black Prince. He warmly espouses the cause of Peter the Cruel. Negotiates successfully with Charles the Bad, the king of Navarre, for crossing the Pyrenees at the Pass of Roncesvalles. Makes ample preparation of men and money for the expedition into Spain . . . 9

CHAPTER III.

Henry prepares to resist the invasion of Castille. Bertrand du Guesclin returns to France for additional troops. The Prince of Wales commences his march across the Pyrenees. The Count de Foix . . . 22

CHAPTER IV

The Black Prince crosses the Pyrenees into Spain. Henry resolves, against the advice of Bertrand du Guesclin, to give battle to the invaders. First successes gained by the Castilians. Battle of Navarrete, or Najaro. Defeat of Henry. Bertrand du Guesclin is taken prisoner . . . 38

CHAPTER V.

Trial of the Maréchal d'Audeneham, for the breach of a military oath, before a jury of knights. Cruelty and bad faith of Peter after the battle of Navarrete. Quarrel between him and the Black Prince. Edward leaves Spain in disgust. Henry escapes into France obtains aid from Charles V., and returns to Castille . . . 54

PAGE

CHAPTER VI.

Bertrand du Guesclin is released from captivity on payment of a large ransom. He collects troops, and assists the Duke of Anjou in taking the town of Tarascon, in Provence. He crosses the Pyrenees with five hundred lances, and joins Henry at his camp near Toledo 71

CHAPTER VII.

Battle of Monteil. Defeat and death of Peter the Cruel 87

CHAPTER VIII.

Charles V. is anxious to provoke a quarrel with the English. He entertains an appeal of the nobles of Gascony, who refused to pay a tax imposed on them by the Black Prince 96

CHAPTER IX.

Charles V cites the Black Prince to appear before the Chamber of Peers at Paris, on the appeal of the Gascon nobles. Irritation of the Prince on receiving the summons. Charles declares war against England . 108

CHAPTER X.

A change in the fortunes of Edward III. The death of Sir John Chandos. Bertrand du Guesclin is recalled from Spain. His first exploits after his return to France 118

CHAPTER XI.

The sack of Limoges by the Black Prince. Bertrand du Guesclin is created Constable of France 131

CHAPTER XII.

Bertrand du Guesclin, upon assuming the office of Constable, collects troops and marches against the English. The battle of Pontvalain 140

CHAPTER XIII.

Results to the French of their success at Pontvalain. The Black Prince leaves France and goes to England. The siege of Mont-

PAGE

paon. Successes of Bertrand du Guesclin in Poitou and Auvergne. Death of Tiphaine Ravenel, wife of the constable 149

CHAPTER XIV.

Sea-fight off Rochelle. The English are unsuccessful both on sea and land. The king of France orders new levies of troops. The constable marches into Poitou, and takes the strong castle of Montcontour. St. Sevère is carried by storm 161

CHAPTER XV.

Voluntary surrender of the city of Poitiers to the French. Capture and imprisonment of the Captal de Buch. Important conquests of the French in Poitou, Saintonge, and Angoumois. Surrender of Rochelle 178

CHAPTER XVI.

The constable takes the castles of Benon, Marant, and Surgières, near Rochelle, and the town of Fontenay-le-Comte. Secret negotiations between the Duke of Brittany and the king of England. The constable lays siege to Thouars. Unsuccessful attempt of Edward III. to relieve it 193

CHAPTER XVII.

The constable invades Brittany. Campaign of 1373. Battle of Chizey. Defeat and capture of Sir John Devereaux. The constable takes Niort. Flattering reception of the constable, by both king and people, on his return to Paris 204

CHAPTER XVIII.

The king of France resolves to drive the Duke of Brittany from his duchy. The constable invades Brittany with a large force, and compels the duke to take refuge in England. The sieges of Brest and Derval 217

CHAPTER XIX.

Invasion of France by the English, under the Dukes of Lancaster and Brittany. The king of France adopts a policy wholly defensive. Fruitless results of the expedition 230

PAGE

CHAPTER XX.

Efforts of the Pope to make peace between the kings of France and England. Success of the French under the constable in Gascony. The Duke of Brittany obtains troops from Edward III., and returns to his duchy. Narrow escape of De Clisson and other Breton lords 241

CHAPTER XXI.

The legates of the Pope prolong the truce between France and England for another year. Death of Edward the Black Prince. Charles V. prepares to invade England by sea. Death of Edward III. Coronation of Richard II. Success of the French arms in Picardy and Aquitaine 259

CHAPTER XXII.

Charles V. resolves to drive the king of Navarre out of his possessions in Normandy. Assassination of Evan of Wales. Unsuccessful attempt of the English to invade France, under the Duke of Lancaster and the Earl of Cambridge. The constable lays siege to Cherbourg 273

CHAPTER XXIII.

The king of France resolves to annex the duchy of Brittany to the domains of the crown. He obtains a decree of the Parliament of Paris against the Duke of Brittany. Opposition of the Bretons to the measure 291

CHAPTER XXIV.

The king of France entertains suspicions of the loyalty of the constable. Indignation of the constable at the imputation that he was an adherent of the Duke of Brittany. He tenders to the king the sword of his office. He is sent to the south of France. His death 306

CHAPTER I.

Triumphal progress of Henry from Toledo to Seville. Sir Matthew Gournay at the Portuguese court. Henry discharges the Free Companies.

THE passage of Henry into Andalucia was a triumphal march. At Cordova he was received with great demonstrations of joy; and the preparations for his reception at Seville were on so grand a scale, that, although he arrived very early in the morning at the gates of the city, so great was the crowd assembled from all quarters to do him honour, that it was past three o'clock in the afternoon before he was able to enter the palace. The example of Cordova and Seville, in their manifestations of respect and submission, was followed by all the other towns of Andalucia, and even Mohammed, the Moorish king of Granada, the friend and ally of Peter, sent to offer willing terms of peace.*

Henry hearing, while at Seville, that Peter had entered the kingdom of Portugal, was anxious to know upon what terms he had been received at the Portuguese court; whereupon he was advised by Bertrand du Guesclin to send an envoy to Lisbon, and learn, from the king of Portugal himself, if he designed to give aid to Peter in the pending quarrel. This suggestion was adopted; and Sir Matthew

* Ayala, *Cronica del Rey Don Pedro*, p. 421.

Gournay, an English knight in the service of Henry, was, at his own instance, appointed on the embassy. Gournay made speedy preparations for the expedition, and set out, with a retinue of ten persons, for Lisbon. Upon his arrival at that city, he learnt from his host, at an inn, that Peter the Cruel had already passed through Portugal into Galicia, and gone to seek the aid of the Prince of Wales. Sir Matthew, however, repaired to the palace, where he was recognised by a squire attached to the court, who had served with him at the battle of Poitiers, and who introduced him to the king. He found the latter making preparations for celebrating the nuptials of a noble knight with one of his own kinswomen. At this interview the king opened the conversation by a kind inquiry about Bertrand du Guesclin, the Begue de Villaines, and the Maréchal d'Audeneham; and expressed the opinion that Peter had been wrongfully driven from his kingdom. The English knight maintained the contrary, and then exposed the object of his mission, which was to know if the king of Portugal designed to aid Peter in his contest with Henry for the crown of Castille. To this inquiry the king replied that he had determined not to involve himself in any war, or to mix himself in Peter's affairs.

Sir Matthew, having expressed his satisfaction at this resolution of the king, was seated at table, where he was very courteously treated and served. At the sumptuous entertainment which followed this interview, his more cultivated taste being offended at the noise made by the musicians, Sir Matthew Gournay said to the king, with a smile:—

"The minstrels in France and England are not so merry as these."

"I have two minstrels," quickly replied the king, "the like of whom are not to be found in the east. The king of

Bel-Marin has often begged me to send them to him ; but I will not part with them on any account."

The king then ordered the minstrels to be summoned into his presence. They soon appeared, with much ceremony and ostentation ; each attended by a servant bearing a dulcimer* at his neck. The minstrels, at the king's order, began to play ; when Sir Matthew, who had heard their skill so much vaunted, could scarcely suppress his mirth at their performance.

" What do you think of them?" asked the king, evidently much pleased.

" Such instruments as your musicians play on," replied the Englishman, who appears to have been a blunt soldier, " are only used in France and Normandy by blind people or poor beggars ; and, therefore, they are called there the beggars' instruments."

The cool contempt of the English knight for his music greatly offended the king ; and, although he drove the musicians from his presence, with a positive order not to return, he never forgave the affront. As the festivities were to be continued by a tournament on the following day, the king, in a sneering manner, said to Sir Matthew, that he had heard that the English were good jousters, and that they

* Cuvelier, at verse 10,050, says :—

" Et s'avoit chascun d'eulx après lui i. sergent,
Qui une chiffonie va à son col portant.
Et li ii. ménestrez se vont appareillant ;
Devant le roy s'en vont ambdui chinfoniant."

The instrument of music here alluded to by the chronicler as the *chiffonie*, which in the " MS. of the Arsenal " is termed *cyphonie*, is probably no other than the *symphonie*, mentioned in the French translation of the Book of Daniel, ch. iii. 5 and 10, as *symphonia ;* in St. Jerome's version, which is translated in the Douay Bible as *symphony ;* and in King James's version as the *dulcimer*. And see *Lexique Roman de la Langue des Troubadours*, by M. Raynouard ; and Du Cange, Gloss. voc. *Symphonia*.

claimed that one could know nothing of chivalry unless he had been in England; so that he would witness with pleasure how the English bore themselves in the lists, as he doubted much that he had heard of them. The Englishman, colouring deeply at the ill-tempered remarks of the king towards his countrymen, replied that he knew no knight so valiant, that he would not joust with him; and he went on to boast of what feats he had performed himself, on land and sea, without ever having been vanquished. The king then said to the knight that he was anxious to be a spectator of his feats of arms, and that he would order a prize to be prepared for the following day, of a mule worth one hundred marks, with an ivory saddle and a chanfrin of gold.

The lists, accordingly, were erected near the palace; and early the next morning five hundred ladies, as spectators of the approaching conflict, were seated on the benches around the lists, or within the splendid chambers of the palace. The jousts were appointed to commence at sunrise, on account of the heat of the weather; and, already drawn up in two ranks, prepared to commence the day's pastime, were sixty knights: for none but knights jousted on that occasion. In the *mêlée*, a promiscuous combat, which first took place, many lances were shivered, many shields broken, many heads unhelmeted, and many horses prostrated on the plain. In that conflict of arms Sir Matthew Gournay approved himself so good a knight, that both horse and rider went down before every thrust of his lance. The success of the English knight was witnessed by the Portuguese monarch with intense feelings of mortified pride, and he exclaimed, in much passion:—

"Honoured Virgin! shall this Englishman go away thus from my court! How he will boast, when beyond sea, that the Portuguese are worth nothing!"

Then, calling to him La Barre, a Breton knight distinguished for his prowess, he asked :—

"Are you bold enough to dare a joust with him?"

"Should he slay me with a sharpened lance," promptly replied La Barre, "I will joust with him, if you wish it."

The Breton was then speedily armed and mounted, by the king's order; and he rode into the lists and offered battle to the English knight, who had already overthrown twelve opponents. The challenge was readily accepted by Sir Matthew, who supposed that La Barre was a Portuguese knight, and that he would probably have as easy a conquest as he had already achieved over the others. Both parties then put spurs to their horses ; and, upon the shock, it was seen that La Barre had aimed his lance so well, that the point, piercing the helmet of Gournay, had carried away the visor, and, striking full against the body and breast of his antagonist, he overthrew both horse and rider. The Englishman was stupified by the fall, and on recovering his consciousness he fainted through pain, when it was discovered that one of his arms had been broken. The king exhibited a very unbecoming exultation at the discomfiture of the English knight, by clapping his hands and shedding tears of joy. When Sir Matthew had recovered from his swoon and had his arm bandaged, the king asked him, with malicious satisfaction :—

"Chevalier, tell me, are there any good knights of our nation?"

"Sire," said the Englishman, "I may justly praise you, as I have a brave present from them."

The king now had his revenge, and he offered the richly-caparisoned mule to Sir Matthew, who accepted the present ; but when he learnt from a squire, on leaving Lisbon, that he had been vanquished in the lists by a Breton, instead of a Portuguese knight, he returned to Seville, heartily cursing

Peter the Cruel, on whose account he had been sent to Lisbon, and the whole Portuguese nation.*

The flight of Peter, and the almost entire submission of the kingdom to the government of Henry, induced the latter to take immediate steps to deliver Spain from the Free Companies, as they seemed no longer necessary for his purposes; and he was now anxious to get rid of them, not only on account of the great cost to his treasury, but on account of the irritation among his people, caused by their repeated and lawless depredations. He accordingly paid and discharged them, sending them away well satisfied with his bounty. He retained, however, Sir Bertrand du Guesclin and the Bretons of his company, with Sir Hugh Calverly, and some English knights and squires, amounting in all to fifteen hundred lances. The Count de la Marche and the Lord de Beaujeu, whose sole motive in joining the expedition into Spain was to avenge the death of their kinswoman, Queen Blanche, before taking leave of Henry, demanded that Juan Perez de Rebolledo, the alleged murderer of the queen, should be delivered up to them. The unhappy wretch was accordingly put into their hands, and was hanged by their order.†

* Cuvelier, vv. 9877, 10,237. "Matthew Gournay," says Fuller, "was born at Stoke-under-Hambden, in this county (Somersetshire), where his family had long flourished, since the Conquest, and there built both a castle and a college. But our Matthew was the honour of the house, renowned under the reign of Edward the Third, having fought in seven several signal set battles."

After mentioning where and against whom the battles were fought, he continues:—"But it added to the wonder that our Matthew, who did lie and watch so long on the bed of honour, should die in the bed of peace, aged ninety and six years, about the beginning of King Richard the Second. He lieth buried under a fair monument in the church of Stoke aforesaid, whose epitaph, legible in the last age, is since (I suspect) defaced."—"Fuller's Worthies," vol. iii. p. 100.

† "Which was poor satisfaction" (que fué pequena emienda), as

Galicia was the only province that still adhered to Peter, where a small, but active body of men, under the command of Don Fernando de Castro, kept up a show of opposition to the new government. Henry, deeming it an easy conquest, after a residence of four months in Seville, set out for that province, in order to reduce it to subjection; but De Castro shut himself up in the strong town of Lugo; and Henry, after a fruitless siege of two months, hearing that the Prince of Wales was collecting troops to aid Peter in recovering his kingdom, returned suddenly to Castille, and assembled the Cortes. That body was convoked to obtain the means of resisting the threatened invasion of the Prince of Wales; and but little eloquence was necessary to excite the fears of its members, in order to oppose, by every means at their command, the dreaded return of Peter to power. They therefore granted, without hesitation, a very liberal aid, which yielded that year nineteen million maravedis.*

Peter the Cruel, degraded by his vices and stained with blood, abandoned his kingdom, without a struggle for its possession. He embarked at Corunna for Bayonne, as has been mentioned, in a single vessel; but an adverse wind drove him back, and he was forced to re-enter the fortress. While bewailing the malignant fortune which still pursued him, he took the advice of De Castro, who yet faithfully adhered to him,† and sent messengers to Edward, the Prince

Ayala dryly observed, in alluding to the death of Juan Perez.—*Cronica del Rey Don Pedro*, p. 423. "And for which," says the anonymous author of the *Chronique de Du Guesclin*, "they were blamed by some honourable knights, who maintained that he did not deserve death for obeying the orders of his prince."—Ch. lxxvi. p. 43.

* Ayala, *Cronica del Rey Don Pedro*, pp. 423, 427. The maravedi is something less than a farthing sterling.

† Peter probably owed the attachment of De Castro far more to the hatred of the latter towards Henry than to any love for himself: for that nobleman, assigning as the cause of his revolt, as well the attempt

of Wales, to know if he would receive him, and give him his powerful aid in recovering his kingdom. The Black Prince treated the messengers of Peter kindly; and, after a careful perusal of the letters which they brought, he deliberately weighed their purport, before calling to his aid Sir John Chandos and Sir Thomas Felton, the most trusted of his council. When they came, he read the letters over to them very carefully, and then asked their advice as to the course he should pursue. The two knights looked at each other without reply, when the prince somewhat impatiently said to them, "Speak! speak out boldly what you think of it!" They then advised him to send a body of men-at-arms to Corunna, and bring Peter back with them to Bordeaux, that, upon a conference with him, his wishes and necessities could be better known. The prince adopted their counsel, and ordered Sir Thomas Felton, with several other knights, and a body of men-at-arms and archers, to embark at Bayonne for Corunna; but, just as they were leaving the port, Peter, whose impatience would not suffer him to await the answer to his letters, arrived with a small retinue, bringing with him the treasures which he had saved.*

of Peter to slay him without cause at a tournament at Valladolid, as the dishonour of his sister, entered so warmly into the league of the year 1354, against Peter, with the brothers Henry and Fadrique, that he formally denaturalized himself, and renounced his allegiance to his king, for which he was rewarded by the hand of their sister, Donna Juana; but as the marriage was annulled, on the ground that it was within the prohibited degrees, and Donna Juana was wedded to another, De Castro became the implacable enemy of Henry, not only during the reign of Peter, but for life.—Ayala, *Cronica del Rey Don Pedro*, pp. 135, 171, and 182, and note (4).

* Froissart, liv. i. part ii. pp. 507, 508. Froissart has been relied upon for most of the incidents at the court of Edward the Black Prince, as he must have been much better informed of them than Ayala, who probably joined Henry on his march from Burgos to Toledo. See *Cronica del Rey Don Pedro*, p. 410.

CHAPTER II.

Edward the Black Prince. He warmly espouses the cause of Peter the Cruel. Negotiates successfully with Charles the Bad for crossing the Pyrenees at the Pass of Roncesvalles. Makes ample preparation of men and money for the expedition into Spain.

THE Prince of Wales was then in the prime of life. He was distinguished for all the chivalric virtues of that warlike age. He had been successful in all his enterprises, and he was then somewhat impatiently reposing on the laurels acquired at the great battle of Poitiers, which he had gained under the direction of Sir John Chandos, not only one of the bravest knights, but, confessedly, one of the greatest generals of his time. Ten years of comparative inactivity had passed since the day of Poitiers. It was therefore very natural, when the prince received the letters of Peter, imploring his protection and aid, that he should exclaim, in showing them to Chandos and Felton, "My lords, see what grand news has come to us from Spain!" This was an adventure of no ordinary character. The situation and claims of Peter were calculated to draw forth every sentiment which he professed as a knight: for the suppliant monarch was an ally of his father, beseeching aid to recover a kingdom wrested from him through the treason and violence of a bastard brother. He was accompanied, too, by three helpless daughters, whom

Edward was bound, by his knightly vow, to protect; and, moreover, it was whispered by some, that "the prince was jealous of the fame acquired by Sir Bertrand du Guesclin, in conquering the whole kingdom of Castille, in the name of king Henry, and making him king." *

Edward, therefore, did not await the arrival of Peter at Bayonne, but left Bordeaux with a large retinue of knights and squires, to meet him on his way and do him honour. No knight or gentleman of his time possessed in a higher degree the virtues of courtesy and condescension than the Prince of Wales. On every occasion he treated Peter, in word and deed, with every mark of respect and deference; he placed the humbled king always above himself, and he never would consent to do otherwise. Before the arrival of Peter, certain lords of England and Gascony had advised the prince to be cautious in espousing the cause of a king whose character was stained by the vices of tyranny, cruelty, and infidelity; but Edward, whose sympathies were with the prince rather than the people, and who, at that early day, had pretty well-defined notions of the rights of kings, replied, that he was well informed "of all such charges against Peter, but that he had been moved to aid him, because it was not proper nor reasonable that a bastard should hold a kingdom, and put out of his inheritance a brother and an heir by lawful marriage; that all kings and sons of kings should by no means suffer it: for it was a great prejudice against the state royal." Edward, moreover, had his weaknesses; and when Peter, in imploring his aid, said that he came to him to complain of the ill-treatment which he had received, he came "to complain to honour, prowess, and complaisance; to virtue, the flower of chivalry; to the sword of the valiant, where every one resorts; to him who, by right, bears the

* Froissart, liv. i. part ii. p. 514.

dominion, the key, and mastery of all knights—prowess, hardihood, largess, and courtesy," the prince could no longer resist the entreaties of the king, and he promised to replace the crown of Spain on his head, though it cost him all he was worth, and even life itself, in a well-ordered field of battle. Peter did not, however, entrust his cause to words alone. He distributed the thirty thousand doubloons and the jewels which he brought with an unsparing hand; and, as promises cost nothing to a prince of such bad faith, he made them, without limit or reserve, to both Edward and his people.*

Among the presents distributed by Peter was a magnificent table,† elegantly wrought, and composed of the most costly materials, which he gave to Edward as a present for his consort.‡ The princess had received Peter with all

* Froissart, liv. i. part ii. pp. 509, 510; Cuvelier, vv. 10,577, 10,605. Peter gave to the Prince of Wales the province of Biscay, with the town of Castro de Urdiales, and the villages of Vermeo, Vilbare, and Queyte, and promised to pay him and the leaders of his army 550,000 florins of the coinage of Florence, besides 50,000 florins of his exchequer to the prince alone. For the performance of these promises, he left his three daughters, with other persons, as hostages.—Ayala, *Cronica del Rey Don Pedro*, p. 433, and note (2). See *Carta Donationis Regis Castellæ terrarum principi Walliæ Concessarum*, in Rymer, vol. iii. par. ii. p. 802, and *Obligatio super Expensis Solvendis*, ibid. p. 805, in which Rymer states that Peter promised to pay, in addition to the 550,000 florins mentioned by Ayala, the expenses already incurred by the prince.

† This was the same marvellous table described by Cuvelier, at verse 9093. It was made of gold and precious stones, and, among these, was a carbuncle of such dazzling lustre, "that it restored at night the light of the sun."

‡ The Princess of Wales was the dowager Countess of Holland, before her intermarriage with the Black Prince, in the year 1361. She was the daughter of Edmund Earl of Kent, and "was commonly called *Joanna the Fair*, by reason of her great beauty."—Barnes's "History of Edward III.," p. 251; and Rapin's "History of England," vol. i. p. 437.

outward demonstrations of respect and courtesy; but, like a true woman, she could not overlook the incidents of a reign which had only been marked by guilty passions and blood, and especially by the cruel death of his innocent and unhappy wife. She therefore set but little value on a gift coming from such hands; and, coldly replying to the knight, who informed her that he came to present it on the part of the king of Castille, she said:—"Put it down; it is really a beautiful present, but it will cost us dear."

Edward was waiting for the return of the knight who carried the table, to know what his wife thought of the splendid present; and when he came, the prince anxiously inquired what she had said about it. To which the knight answered, that she made no account of it, for she was grieved at the coming of the king to them. The prince, who was quick and passionate, and, though he tenderly loved his wife, bore impatiently any opposition to his wishes, even from her, hastily replied:—"I see well that she would constantly have me hanging about her bedside; but it is unbecoming in me, and I will not do it. He who would acquire the name of the brave and valiant must often seek the rain and the battle-field, as did the bold Roland and Oliver, Ogier the powerful, the four sons of Aymon and Charlemagne, Duke Lyon of Bourges, Guion de Couruans, Perceval the Gaul, Launcelot and Tristan, Alexander, Arthur, and Godfrey the Wise, of whose deeds the troubadours made those noble romances. By St. George! I will restore Spain, and all that belongs to it, to the rightful owner, before the year ends."*

Edward, although he had fully determined to aid Peter in the recovery of his kingdom,. adopted the recommendation of his special counsellors, to call a general parliament of his government, to consider the expediency of undertaking the

* Cuvelier, v. 10,670.

expedition into Spain, and devise the means of carrying it on. Whereupon, at his summons, there assembled at Bordeaux, "the counts, viscounts, barons, and all the sage men of Aquitaine, as well as those of Poitou, Saintonge, Rouergue, Quercy, and Limousin, and those of Gascony;" and, after a deliberation of three days, they advised the prince to send messengers to England, and learn the wishes of his father, before he undertook the expedition; and, after obtaining the response of the king of England, they said that they would reassemble and advise him to the best of their ability. The prince adopted this counsel, and despatched, immediately, four knights to Edward III., whom the envoys found at his palace of Windsor. The king, as soon as he understood the purport of the letters from his son, repaired to Westminster, and there assembled such members of his council as could be speedily brought together, to consider the application of the Prince of Wales. After mature deliberation, the king and his council concluded that it was proper for the prince to undertake the expedition, and replace Peter on his throne; and, accordingly, letters to that effect were despatched to the prince and the barons of Aquitaine. The Black Prince, upon the reception of the favourable response to his wishes by his father, reassembled his parliament at Bordeaux, when the barons readily promised to obey the commands of the king and his own; but, with an evident distrust of Peter and his unreserved promises, they wished to know beforehand who was to pay their wages: for no one, they said, takes men-at-arms from their homes to make war in a foreign country without pay. "If it were for the interests," they continued, "of our dear lord your father and yourself, or for your honour or that of our country, we would not speak of it before doing it." The prince then turned to Peter, and said:—

"Sir king, you hear what our people say; it becomes you to answer them, as it is your business."

"My dear cousin," replied Peter, "so far as my money and the treasures which I have with me will extend, which are not by thirty times as much as I have at home, I will give and divide them among your people."

"You say well," rejoined the prince, who would suffer no obstacle to baulk his purposes; "for the balance, I will make my debt to them, and lend you all that you may need until we are in Castille."

"By my head!" replied the king, "you do me a great favour, and great courtesy."*

There was one obstacle, however, which it was necessary for the Prince of Wales to employ means to obviate, presented by the famous pass of Roncesvalles, lying between Guienne and the kingdom of Navarre, and which could only be removed by the consent of Charles the Bad. This pass, made memorable by the defeat of the rear-guard of Charlemagne's army, under the famous Roland, by a party of marauding Gascons, led by Lupo, their duke,† commences on the northern side of the Pyrenees, at the town of St. Jean Pied-de-Port, crosses the mountains by narrow defiles, which could be successfully defended by a mere handful of men against a large army,‡ and finally expands when near the city of Pampeluna. This pass was not only well known to the Gascon lords, but also to Sir John

* Froissart, liv. i. part ii. pp. 510, 512.

† "When Charlemain and all his peerage fell
By Fontarabia."
—Milton, "Paradise Lost," book i. v. 586.

Mr. James, who seems to have consulted all the authorities, has settled the disputed point, that the Gascons, and not the Spaniards and Moors, attacked the army of Charlemagne. James's "History of Charlemagne," p. 191, note (§), and p. 193, note (†).

‡ Or as Froissart describes it—"there are a hundred places along the pass where thirty men could keep the whole world from passing."—Liv. i. part ii. p. 523.

Chandos, who advised the prince to invite Charles the Bad to a conference at Bayonne, in order to treat with him for the passage of his army through Navarre into Castille. Charles, although he had just concluded a treaty with Henry at Santa-Cruz de Campezco, and had taken an oath, in the most solemn form, not only to prevent the Prince of Wales and Peter the Cruel from using the pass of Roncesvalles through his kingdom, but to aid Henry in person with all his forces against his enemies, yet did not hesitate to attend the conferences at Bayonne, in the expectation of making better terms with a stronger side. In this conference, although, as Froissart said of him, "he was not easy to lead where he saw one had need of him," yet he at length promised, for the same stipulated reward, with the addition of the town of Victoria to the town of Logroño, which Henry had offered him, to open the pass, and join the prince and Peter with all his forces. To Henry, he violated his solemn covenant by leaving the pass open; and, to avoid appearing at the head of his troops, as he had promised both parties, he sent a force of three hundred lances, under Don Martin Enriquez de la Carra, to the aid of Edward and Peter; and, by an agreement with Sir Oliver de Manny, who held the town and castle of Borja, in Aragon, for his kinsman Sir Bertrand du Guesclin, he contrived to have himself taken prisoner, and detained until the battle between Henry and Peter was fought.*

The Black Prince was tempted to undertake the expedition into Spain by the novelty of the enterprise, as well as by the glory which would attend it; and it seemed at first an easy matter to restore the dethroned monarch again to power; but a little reflection served to convince him that,

* Froissart, liv. i. part ii. pp. 512, 526; Ayala, *Cronica del Rey Don Pedro*, pp. 434, 436; and see the treaty of Libourne, between Peter, Charles, and Edward Prince of Wales, in Rymer, vol. iii. par. ii. p. 800.

in order to reinstate a prince who had been driven from his kingdom amidst the almost universal execration of his people, in opposition to one who had many claims to popularity, a great number of men, as well as a large expenditure of money, would be necessary. Not seeing his way so clearly as it appeared at first, he had recourse again to his trusted counsellors, Chandos and Felton, who appear not to have under-estimated either the difficulties or the expense of the expedition; and, to the inquiries of the prince what they thought of it, they replied, that it was a great and lofty enterprise; without comparison more difficult than it was to drive Peter out of his kingdom: for he was hated by all his subjects, and abandoned by every one at the moment of his greatest need; that the reigning monarch was in possession of the entire realm, and enjoyed the love of prelates, nobles, and people, who had made him their king, and who would adhere to him in any event; and that it would be necessary to have a great number of men-at-arms and archers: for a sturdy resistance would assuredly be met with on entering Spain. They therefore advised the prince to break up the greater portion of his plate and convert it into money for the pay of Free Companies, whose service he would need, who would go on account of their love for him, whilst they would do nothing for Peter. They further advised him to ask his father to grant him the instalment of five hundred thousand francs, which was then due on account of the ransom of the late King John of France; and they concluded by telling him to get money wherever he could find it—for he would have abundant need of it—without taxing his people, as he would be thereby better loved and served by all. This judicious advice of his counsellors the prince implicitly followed. He first broke up two-thirds of all his gold and silver plate, and converted it into coin for the pay of his troops; and he obtained from his father, who well knew his necessities, the sum of five hundred thousand francs, which was promptly paid on demand by the king of France.*

The Prince of Wales having made, as he hoped, ample provision of money, next turned his attention to the number and kind of troops necessary for an expedition on which he had now set his whole heart. He first engaged the services of his great vassals; but they better understood the character of Peter the Cruel than their master; and, as they would trust nothing to the word of the king, the prince had to become responsible for their pay, as he had promised. His next object was to secure the services of the Free Companies who had accompanied Bertrand du Guesclin into Spain: for, as they were all hardy veterans, and constituted the most efficient troops then in Europe, Edward well knew that his success would mainly depend on his ability to get a large number of them into his ranks. As many of their leaders were English and Gascons, who acknowledged him as their liege-lord, he sent messengers into Spain to inform them of his wish to employ them himself, and that they must abandon the service of Henry, and return from that country as speedily as possible.

This order was promptly obeyed by Sir Eustace d'Aubrecicourt, Sir Walter Huet, Sir Matthew Gournay, Sir John Devereux, and others, with their companies; and Henry, "who was liberal, courteous, and honourable," made no effort to keep them; but, in parting, thanked them for the services which they had rendered him, and sent them away with many evidences of his bounty. He would willingly have detained Sir Hugh Calverly, with his troop of four hundred lances, and nothing was easier than to have carried his wish into effect; but the king would

* Froissart, liv. i. part ii. p. 515.

oppose no obstacle to his return, "holding that the knight was only doing his duty by going to serve his lord the prince."*

The other companies, previously discharged by Henry, under Sir Robert Briquet, Jean Carsuelle, Nandon de Bagerant, and many other leaders, were dispersed about the country when they received the message of the Black Prince. They soon collected their scattered bands, and attempted to cross the frontiers of Spain; but the passes were closed against them, and they were forced to separate into three divisions, in order to traverse the mountains at different points. This they at length effected, after various successes and reverses; but they all showed evident marks of their long and perilous march: for, before reaching their own frontiers, they were all "oppressed, wearied, ill-armed, badly-mounted, and worse shod."

The two first divisions reached the principality of Aquitaine † without any signal adventure; but the one under Perducas d'Albret was attacked at the town of Montalban by the Count de Narbonne and the Seneschal of Toulouse, with a force outnumbering the Free Companies three to one; where, after a well-fought field, the French were totally defeated, and their leaders, with more than one hundred knights, taken prisoners.‡

By the arrival of the Free Companies the prince received an accession of seven thousand combatants, composed chiefly of English and Gascon men-at-arms. He could have

* Ayala, *Cronica del Rey Don Pedro*, p. 437.

† The duchy of Guienne was erected into a principality, under the name of the Principality of Aquitaine, by Edward III., in the year 1362, as a mark of favour to Edward the Black Prince.—Pub. Acts., vi. p. 384, cited by Rapin, "Hist. of England," vol. i. p. 437. Edward was created Prince of Aquitaine, July 19, 1362.—Rymer, vol. iii. par. ii. pp. 667, 668.

‡ Froissart, liv. i. part ii. pp. 513, 518.

increased his forces by a number of German, Flemish, and Brabançon mercenaries; but he rejected the offers of many foreign soldiers, as he preferred to make up his army from his own vassals.

Besides these, and the contributions of his barons and feudal retainers, Edward III. promised to send him from England four hundred men-at-arms, and as many archers, under the command of his fourth son, John of Gaunt, Duke of Lancaster. The timely arrival of the Free Companies relieved the Black Prince of all anxiety about filling up the ranks of his army: for, before they came, he had retained all sorts of men-at-arms, wherever he could find them; and, in one instance, he engaged a greater number than he was afterwards willing to pay. The incident happened at Angoulême, when the prince was in one of his happiest moods, and was conversing in a bantering manner with certain knights of Gascony, Poitou, and England, about the expedition into Spain. Turning round to Lord d'Albret, he asked:—

"Sire d'Albret, what number of men-at-arms will you follow me with in this expedition?"

"My lord," replied the Gascon knight, without hesitation, "if I were to ask all my friends—that is to say, my vassals—I could bring fully a thousand lances, and still have my lands sufficiently guarded."

"Sire d'Albret, that is a fine thing," said the prince; and then, turning to Lord Felton and some knights of England, he said to them in English:—"By my faith! one should well love the land where we can find a baron who is able to follow his lord with a thousand lances." Then, turning again to Lord d'Albret, he said:—"With great pleasure, Sire d'Albret, I retain them all."

But, after the arrival of the Free Companies, when the prince became annoyed at the heavy expense of maintaining his troops, and at the reiterated complaints of their daily excesses and depredations, which no discipline could restrain, and when he had no longer any difficulty in finding men, but the means for their support, he wrote to the Lord d'Albret countermanding the levy of a thousand lances, and informing him of an order of his council, in which he was set down for the expedition at two hundred only, and that he might disband the rest. Lord d'Albret was extremely irritated, upon the reception of the letter, at this conduct of the prince, which he regarded as trifling with him; and, while under the influence of very excited feelings, he called a clerk and dictated a reply, written with the utmost freedom and asperity.

After alluding to his surprise at the purport of the prince's letter, and his own embarrassment, and that of his council, in what manner he should answer it, he stated very forcibly the displeasure and loss both for himself and men at this change of purpose in the prince, and he concluded with words that were barely respectful:—"Dear Sire, you will please understand that I cannot separate a part from the whole. I am the worst and least of all; but, if some go, all shall go: this I know." The prince regarded this letter as a very haughty response to his own, and, to some knights of England who were by, he said in English, "The Lord d'Albret is a great master in my country, when he wishes to violate an order of my council. By God! it shall not go as he thinks. Now, let him stay, if he chooses: for we can well undertake the expedition without his thousand lances."

The matter did not end here, as Edward could not easily forgive such an affront: "for the prince was high-spirited and cruel in his anger, and wished, right or wrong, that all the lords whom he commanded should yield to him;" but the Count d'Armagnac, who was the uncle of Lord d'Albret, with the aid of Sir John Chandos and Sir Thomas Felton, managed the difficulty so well, that the Lord d'Albret was forced to yield the point which he had made, and the prince was silent and satisfied.*

* Froissart, liv. i. part ii. pp. 515, 519, 521.

CHAPTER III.

Henry prepares to resist the invasion of Castille. Bertrand du Guesclin returns to France for additional troops. The Prince of Wales commences his march across the Pyrenees. The Count de Foix.

WHILE Edward the Black Prince was preparing on a grand scale to invade Spain in favour of Peter the Cruel, Henry, on his part, was not idle or negligent of any prudent measures of defence. He suddenly left Galicia, as has been mentioned, as soon as he heard that the Prince of Wales was collecting troops to invade his kingdom, and assembled the Cortes at Burgos. The liberal aid granted by that body enabled Henry to support a large army; and he immediately set about collecting troops from all quarters. When he ascertained with certainty that Edward had sent for the leaders of the Free Companies, who had been employed by himself in the conquest of the kingdom, he permitted them to go away without any effort to detain them; and, feeling entirely secure in the affections of his subjects, he made rather light of the dangers of the invasion. To Bertrand du Guesclin, who was still with him, he said :—

"Lord Bertrand, it has been told us that the Prince of Wales is preparing to make war upon us, and restore, by force of arms, to our kingdom that Jew who calls himself king of Spain. What say you about it?"

"My lord," replied Du Guesclin, "the prince is so valiant a knight that, since he has undertaken it, he will do all in his power to accomplish his purpose : I advise you, therefore, to guard all the straits and passes of your kingdom, so that no one can go out or come in without your sanction, and take care to preserve the love of your people. I am well assured that you can obtain ample aid from the knights and squires of France, who will cheerfully serve you ; and, by your leave, I will return to that country, and procure for you all the friends in my power."

"By my faith !" exclaimed Henry, "you speak well ; and, moreover, I will be governed by your counsel and advice."

Bertrand du Guesclin thereupon set out for France without delay, and passed through Aragon, where he was kindly received by the king. After remaining fifteen days in that kingdom, he crossed the Pyrenees and had an interview with the Duke of Anjou at Montpelier. After a short time spent with the prince, he went to visit the king of France at Paris, "who received him with great joy."*

The Prince of Wales, having completed all his preparations, was anxious to commence his march towards the frontiers of Spain ; but, as the season was now far advanced, he was advised to wait until after Christmas, "that he might have the winter at his back." To this advice he was the more willing to yield, as the princess was approaching her confinement, and he was reluctant to leave her before that event took place. But Edward was becoming very impatient at the delay, as he was anxious to give active employment to his troops : for he was unable to restrain the Free Companies from committing the greatest excesses, wherever they went, both upon men and women ; and he found, besides, the expense of maintaining them very heavy,

* Froissart, liv. i. part ii. p. 513.

as he had now been charged with their subsistence, as well as the payment of their wages, since the latter part of August. He was soon, however, relieved of all anxiety on account of the Princess of Wales, by her safe delivery of a son;* and he was enabled to leave Bordeaux on the following Sunday, with the part of the army which he had with him, and join the greater portion of it, then encamped near the town of Dax, in Gascony. After waiting here a short time for the arrival of his brother, the Duke of Lancaster, with the men-at-arms and archers from England, he commenced his march across the Pyrenees, leaving his principality under the guardianship of the Count de Foix until his return.†

Gaston Phœbus, Count de Foix and Béarn, was one of the ablest and most notable men of his time. In returning from an expedition into Prussia, as already mentioned, with the Captal de Buch, in the year 1358, he heard, while at Châlons, in Champagne, that the Duchess of Normandy, wife of the Dauphin Charles, and three hundred other ladies, with the Duke and Duchess of Orleans, were besieged in the town of Mieux, in Brie, by the *Jacquerie;* and, without waiting to find out their numbers or fill up his own ranks, he gallantly went to the rescue of the ladies, threw himself into the town with forty lances, and dispersed the infamous rabble with great slaughter.

Thirty years after that event, Froissart went to visit him at his usual residence at Orthez, in Béarn, with letters of introduction from Guy de Chastillon, Count de Foix; and the chronicler has devoted many of the most interesting pages of his great work to what he heard from others or witnessed himself at the court of the Count de Foix.

* He was called Richard, and surnamed *of Bordeaux*, from the place of his birth. He succeeded his grandfather as Richard II.

† Froissart, liv. i. part ii. pp. 519, 521.

Though he found him possessed of only the feudal county of Foix, and the free or allodial territory of Béarn, which were small in extent when compared with the wide domains of the great princes around him, the Count de Foix, by his extraordinary skill, prudence, and resources, had not only kept himself free from any entangling alliances with them, but he had taken no part in their quarrels ; and neither he nor his people had armed themselves in their wars. With some of his less powerful neighbours he had had more than one difficulty ; yet, in every trial of strength, they invariably got the worst of it. In the year 1362 he was attacked by the Count d'Armagnac and the Lord d'Albret, with other nobles of their party ; but they were signally defeated, and all of them taken prisoners. Their ransoms yielded the Count de Foix a million of francs before they recovered their liberty.*

He amassed great treasures from no mere love of money : for no prince of his time lived at greater expense, or gave such frequent and magnificent presents to all strangers who visited him, and, especially, to all heralds and minstrels ; but his wealth was a powerful element of strength in a ruler of such limited dominions, when surrounded by such turbulent neighbours as the kings of France and England. By his ample means, and his readiness to avenge a wrong as soon as it was inflicted, he inspired so much respect in both of these monarchs, that his people were not only exempt from the incursions of the French and English soldiers, but even the dreaded Free Companies, who had little respect for anything else, "dared not touch a hen, without paying for it, that belonged to a subject of the Count de Foix."

He always kept his towns and castles so well garrisoned

* *Chroniques Béarnaises*, par Miguel del Vermes, pp. 582, 583. Edition of Buchon. Froissart, liv. iii. p. 380.

and supplied, that no one ventured to enter his territories without his consent; and so prompt was his preparation, that, on one occasion, when he apprehended an invasion, he suddenly threw into his different fortresses a force of twenty thousand men. He was always strong enough to reject what he thought prejudicial to his best interests: for, as he refused the tempting offer of the county of Bigorre, on the sole condition of doing homage for it to the king of France, so he rejected the demand of Edward the Black Prince to do like homage for the territory of Béarn; and a rupture was only prevented by the expedition into Spain, and the pacific counsels of Sir John Chandos.

To maintain such a state, and to make such costly presents—for he annually spent, in gratuities alone, sixty thousand francs—his ordinary revenues were wholly insufficient; and, as he commonly kept in his treasury at Orthez a sum amounting to three millions of francs, he was necessarily obliged to tax his people heavily, by the imposition of two francs on each fire. This tax, though onerous, was paid without a murmur, as his people knew how greatly superior their condition was to that of their neighbours; that they were not only protected from all injury without, but they found good order, peace, and justice within their borders; and, although the judgments of their master were sometimes terribly severe, yet they were always impartial.

At the time of Froissart's visit, the Count de Foix was in his fifty-ninth year; and he is described as a man of great personal beauty: with a fine figure and commanding person, blue eyes, a ruddy complexion, and a cheerful countenance. He spoke French correctly, and even wrote in that language.* He was regular in all the offices of devotion, and

* Of his literary efforts there remain a chanson in Béarnaise, and a treatise on the Pleasures of the Chase, in French, with the following title: "*Le Miroir de Phébus des Desduits de la Chasse des Bestes Sauvaiges*

daily distributed alms with a liberal hand. He was kind and condescending in his manners, easy of access, courteous and communicative, though brief in his inquiries and answers. He loved dogs above all animals ; and he was fond of hunting, both winter and summer.* He delighted, above all things, in feats of arms and tales of love. He was very fond of music, in which he was somewhat skilled himself; and he took great pleasure in making his clerks sing chansons, rondeaux, and virelays before him. His hall was constantly filled with knights and squires ; and there were always a number of tables set for those who would take supper, which was invariably served at midnight. The count was rather abstemious in his habits ; he seldom ate other meat than poultry, and of these only the wings and thighs, and he drank sparingly. He was prudent, far-sighted, and circumspect in his conduct ; and he would have no jester, fool, or favourite about him. He was distinguished above all the princes of his time for his liberality, and he gave very costly presents ; but he avoided all excess or extravagance, and no one knew better where to bestow his gifts, or what became of his own.

In the collection of his revenue he employed twelve trusted receivers, whom he changed for others every two months, who were required to pay over their receipts and account to a comptroller, who in turn had to account strictly with his master, " by rolls or written books," and leave the

et des Oyseaux de Proie, par Gaston Phébus de Foix, Seigneur de Béarn." See St. Palaye, *Mémoires sur l'Ancienne Chevalerie*, tom. ii. p. 277, and p. 290, note (12) ; and Buchon's note to Froissart, liv. iii. p. 119.

* " The Count de Foix then enjoyed the reputation of being a very skilful hunter. He kept a pack composed of from fourteen hundred to sixteen hundred dogs. He procured them from all countries. Froissart carried him four greyhounds from England, of which he has given us the names : *Tristan*, *Hector*, *Brun*, and *Rolland*."—St. Palaye, tom. ii. p. 277.

accounts with him for inspection. He kept certain coffers in his chamber, where sometimes, but not always, he took the sums which he wished to give to a lord, knight, squire, minstrel, or herald, who came to visit him: for no one ever left him without a present. "In short," observes Froissart, "and everything considered, before I came to his court, I had been in many courts of kings, dukes, princes, counts, and noble dames; but I never was in any that pleased me better, or which was more delighted with feats of arms, than that of the Count de Foix. One could there see, in the hall, the chambers, and the court, knights and squires of honour come and go, and hear them talk of arms and love. All honour was found there; news from every kingdom and country could be heard there: for thither people came from all parts, on account of the valour of the lord."*

It was not, however, in the nature of human things that a life so prosperous should be without its sorrows; and the Count de Foix was destined, like all his fellows of high or low degree, to pass over the "Bridge of Sighs" to the tomb. As his virtues were the result of a noble nature, engaged on great questions, and struggling successfully with the confused elements of society then existing around him, so his vices proceeded from the demoralizing influences of unchecked and long-continued prosperity. With all his wisdom, and prudence, and knowledge of men, he was imperious in his temper and uncontrollable in his anger. When his suspicions were excited and his passions aroused, he could not be persuaded that any opinion could be right but his own; and he carried out the promptings of a savage spirit to the end. Summoning into his presence his cousin, Pierre Arnault de Berne, he required him, in order to oblige the Duke of Anjou, to surrender the castle of Lourdes, which he held under an

* Froissart, liv. iii. p. 400, and liv. iii. *passim.*

oath to Edward III. of England; and, when the castellan refused, on the ground that he held it of the king of England, and he could not give it up without his order, the count, black with rage, on finding one about him who had any other will than his own, hastily drew his dagger and stabbed him to death.

That, however, was not the bloody deed which desolated his hearth, embittered the remainder of his life, sent the heir, for whom he had so painfully toiled, to an early grave, and gave his great treasures and broad lands to one whom he hated. This act was seldom spoken of at Orthez. The cautious knight, from whom Froissart obtained the greater part of his information of the life and court of the Count de Foix, on this subject was silent. After much fruitless inquiry, the indefatigable chronicler wrung out of an old and well-known squire at Orthez that the Count de Foix and his countess, who was the sister of Charles the Bad, king of Navarre, had been for a long time totally estranged from each other. This alienation, he was informed, arose from an offer of Charles the Bad to become the surety of the Lord d'Albret, whom the count then held in prison, for the sum of fifty thousand francs; but, as the Count de Foix well knew the faithless character of his brother-in-law, he would not trust him for the amount, which so provoked the countess, that, on one occasion, she said to her husband:—

"My lord, you do little honour to my brother, when you refuse to trust him for fifty thousand francs; and you know that you ought to have assigned that sum for my dower, and put it into his hands: so that you cannot lose anything."

"Lady, you speak truly," replied the count; "and, if I thought the king of Navarre would divert that sum, the Lord d'Albret should never leave Orthez until I had received the last farthing; but, since you desire it, so it shall be: not for the love of you, but for the love of my son."

Upon this the Count de Foix took the obligation of Charles the Bad, and discharged the Lord d'Albret, who paid the debt at his leisure to the king of Navarre ; but the latter never sent any portion of the money to the count. This conduct of the king of Navarre gave such offence to the Count de Foix, that he said to his wife :—

" Lady, you must go into Navarre to the king, your brother, and tell him that I am greatly dissatisfied with him for not sending me that which he has received of mine."

The countess willingly undertook the journey to Pampeluna, and delivered the message of her husband, to which the king of Navarre replied :—

" My fair sister, this money is yours : for the Count de Foix ought to endow you with it ; but it shall never leave the kingdom of Navarre while I have control of it."

" Ah ! my lord," replied the countess, " you will cause great hatred between my lord and me ; and, if you adhere to your purpose, I will not dare to return home : for my lord will slay me, saying that I have deceived him."

" I do not know," said the king, coolly, " what you will do, or whether you will go or stay. I now hold this money, which belongs to me for you ; but it shall never leave Navarre."

This was the only answer that the countess could ever get from her brother ; and, through fear of her husband, she never returned to Orthez.

Things remained in this state between husband and wife up to the time that Gaston, their son, grew to the age of fifteen or sixteen years, when he was affianced to Beatrice, daughter of the Count d'Armagnac, called *The Gay Armagnaçoise*, on account of her great beauty.* Gaston himself

* Froissart says they were *married*, liv. iii. p. 401 ; but it may be inferred from the immature age of the bridegroom, as well as from the plain import of the words of the Béarnaise chronicler, who was probably

was a gallant young squire, and bore a strong resemblance to his father. In an evil hour he went to Navarre to visit his mother; and, after remaining some time with her, he returned by Pampeluna, to take leave of his uncle, who kept him for ten days, then sent him away with many presents, and among them was a beautiful purse filled with powder. Before taking leave of him, the king took the boy aside, and said to him :—

"Gaston, you must do what I am about to tell you : as you well know that the count, your father, hates your mother, which greatly displeases me, and it should likewise be so to you. Now, to restore all things to a proper footing between them, whenever you get the opportunity, put a little of this powder into the food of your father; but take care that no one sees you : for, as soon as he has tasted it, he will never rest until he has seen your mother, and they will love each other so devotedly for ever after, that they will never again be separated. And take care that you do not disclose it to any one whomsoever who may tell it to your father : for you will then lose all your trouble."

The boy readily promised to do what his uncle bade him. He then left Pampeluna and returned to Orthez, where he was kindly received by his father, who asked about the news from Navarre, and what presents he had received; all of which the boy exposed, except the purse of powder.

It happened at that time that Gaston and his natural brother Evan, who were about the same age and size, often slept together and wore each other's garments. On one occasion, while playing on their beds, they interchanged

better informed of a national event than Froissart, that the parties were only betrothed. *Et fot jurat lo matrimoni de Gaston et la filha d'Armanhac, son nom Madona Beatriz, vulgarment appelada La gaya Armanhaguesa.* —Miguel del Vermes, p. 587.

coats, and Gaston's coat, with the purse, fell upon Evan's bed. The latter, who was somewhat malicious, asked :—

"Gaston, what is that you wear every day in your bosom?"

"Give me back my coat," replied Gaston, petulantly; "it is no business of yours."

Three days afterwards, while the boys were playing at tennis, Gaston got angry with Evan, and gave him a slap on the face, which put a stop to the game; and Evan entered weeping into the chamber of his father, who asked him what was the matter. The boy replied that Gaston had beaten him; but that he deserved a beating worse than himself.

"Wherefore?" asked the count, quickly.

"By my faith!" said the boy, "since his return from Navarre, he carries a purse full of powder in his bosom; but I do not know what it is, or what he intends to do with it, except that he told me once or twice that his mother would soon be more in your favour than ever."

"Ah!" exclaimed the count, deeply moved. "Do you keep silent, and take care that you do not divulge to any one what you have told me."

The mind of the Count de Foix was filled at once with the darkest suspicions. He kept himself concealed until the hour of dinner, and then took his seat at the table as usual. It was the habit of Gaston to serve the meats for his father, and taste his food. As soon as he had placed the first dishes before him, the count looked at him; and, seeing the strings of the purse hanging from his coat, he ordered the boy to come nearer; when, taking a knife, he cut the strings and took the purse into his hand.

"What is in this purse?" he asked.

The poor boy, who was taken completely by surprise, said not a word, but became pale with fear, and began to tremble, for he felt that he was lost. The count opened the bag, put some of the powder on a bit of bread, and, whistling up a greyhound lying near, threw it to the dog. As soon as the hound had tasted the first morsel it fell, and instantly died.

In a moment, when the count saw the effect of the powder on the dog, he hastily rose from the table, seized a knife, and was in the act of throwing it at his son, when several knights and squires sprang before him, and entreated him to inform himself of the whole matter before doing violence to the boy. Arrested for an instant by the interposition of his knights, he exclaimed, in his own Gascon tongue :—

"Oh, Gaston, thou traitor! For you, and to increase the inheritance that soon would have been yours, have I waged wars and incurred the hatred of the kings of France, England, Spain, Navarre, and Aragon, and I have strenuously borne myself against them; and now you would poison me. This comes of your perverse nature. Know that you shall die by this blow."

Then, springing over the table, with his knife in his hand, he attempted to kill the unresisting boy; but the knights and squires fell on their knees before him, and, in tears, begged him, for God's sake, not to slay Gaston, for he was his only child; that, after full investigation, it might appear that he did not know what the purse contained, and he might be innocent. This entreaty changed the purpose of the count, who ordered Gaston to be imprisoned in the tower, and strictly guarded; but his terrible wrath, turned away for an instant from his son, fell with frightful severity on the attendants of the youth. Many of them fled; but fifteen handsome and gallant young men of his court were put to death in the cruellest manner, and for no better reason than that "it could not be otherwise but they must have been acquainted with his secrets, and they ought to have made them known."

The count was not satisfied with the doom of imprisonment he had imposed on his son; he therefore called an assembly at Orthez of the prelates, nobles, and other "notable men" of Foix and Béarn, informed them of the offence committed by his son, and expressed the opinion that he deserved death; but the assembly responded with one voice to this declaration, that Gaston must not be put to death.

The unanimous opinion of his people somewhat restrained the count; so he decided to condemn his son to an imprisonment of two or three months, and then send him to travel in foreign countries for several years, until his crime should be forgotten. He then dismissed the assembly; but those of the county of Foix were unwilling to leave Orthez until the count gave them full assurance that Gaston should not die. The unhappy boy was, however, subjected to a very rigorous imprisonment in the tower of Orthez, where he had little light, and no one near to counsel or console him. He wore, without change, for ten days, the same garments which he had on when he entered the gloomy chamber of the prison, and he left untouched the food that was daily set before him. The servant who waited on him, seeing his melancholy condition, informed the count that Gaston was starving himself: for he had eaten nothing since he entered the prison.

This report of the sad state of his son, which the stern father construed into mere stubbornness, and an additional act of resistance to his authority, excited him into a fury of passion; and, without saying a word, he left his chamber, holding in his hand a long knife, which he commonly used for paring and cleaning his nails, and went to the prison. He opened the door and approached the terrified boy, holding the blade of his knife by the point, and so near it, that the length beyond it was not greater than the thickness of a farthing; but, unhappily, in thrusting this point against the throat of his son, he struck a vein in the neck of the boy, exclaiming at the same time:—

"Ha, traitor! why do you not eat?"

The count, upon this, left the prison without saying or doing anything further; but it was enough: for the poor boy, affrighted at the coming of his father, and weakened with fasting, feeling the knife at his throat, turned over, and immediately expired.

The count had scarcely re-entered his chamber, when he was informed by the servant who waited on Gaston that his son was dead.

"Dead!" exclaimed the count.

"May God help me, my lord," affirmed the servant, "it is true."

The now wretched father still would not believe the report, and he sent one of his knights, who was present, to ascertain the truth of it. The knight soon returned, and confirmed the fact. The count then, saddened beyond measure, bitterly bewailed his death.

"Ah, Gaston!" he exclaimed, "what a poor adventure is this. It was an evil hour for you and me when you went to visit your mother in Navarre. Never shall I have again such perfect joy as I had before."

He then sent for his barber to shave him; and he clothed himself and all his household in black. "Thus took place," concludes the narrator of this sad event to Froissart, "what I have told you of the death of Gaston de Foix. His father certainly slew him; but the king of Navarre gave the deathblow." *

* Froissart, liv. iii. pp. 400, 404.

The Count de Foix continued to be connected with many important affairs during the remainder of his life, and he was still governed by the same maxims of cautious prudence which influenced his conduct in the earlier part of his career. He continued to amass great treasures, but he expended them liberally; though it may be inferred that avarice was added to his other vices, from an incident that occurred towards the conclusion of his days; and, although it was in conformity with the practice of the times, it presents his character in no amiable light. It happened that Jeanne de Boulogne, the daughter of his cousin Aliénor de Comminges and John, Count de Boulogne, had been left with him by her mother, when a child of three years. From this time he had carefully watched over and nurtured her until her twelfth year, when she was sought in marriage by the Duke de Berry, uncle of the king of France.* The old duke, who had lost his first wife, a sister of the Count d'Armagnac, after a failure to obtain the hand of a daughter of the Duke of Lancaster, turned his attention to the ward of the Count de Foix; and he pursued his object with a degree of avidity that was in just proportion to the apparent indifference of the count.

To aid him in attaining his wish, the duke implored the assistance of the king and his brother the Duke of Burgundy. The king laughed heartily at the project, as the Duke of Berry was then quite old, and said to him:—

"Good uncle, what will you do with such a little girl? She is not more than twelve years old, while you are sixty. By my faith! it is a great folly for you to think of such a thing. Try and get her for your son John, who is young, and growing up. The match is much more suitable for him than for you."

* This incident took place early in the reign of Charles VI.

"My lord," replied the duke, "that has been spoken of; but the Count de Foix will not listen to it; and, I believe, because my son comes from the Armagnacs, and they and the count have no love for each other. But, as the daughter of Boulogne is young, I will spare her for three or four years until she is a woman, and grown up."

"But, perhaps," said the king, "she may not spare you;" and he continued, still laughing, "Fair uncle, since you have set your heart so much on this marriage, we will cheerfully do our best to promote it."

The Count de Foix, who perceived the ardent desire of the Duke of Berry, treated vaguely and coldly about the marriage, and only replied by letters, which drew out the negotiations to great length; not that he was really opposed to the match, but he desired to make the best bargain out of the amorous old duke. So, at length, by the intercession of the king of France and the Duke of Burgundy, the count agreed to give up the girl for thirty thousand francs—a recompense, as he alleged, for his wardship of nine years.*

Such was the man, with his virtues and defects, to whom Edward the Black Prince entrusted the principality of Aquitaine during his absence in Spain; and he could not well have left it to a stronger hand.

* Froissart, liv. iii. p. 396, and pp. 757, 758. The Count de Foix died suddenly in the year 1391, while on a boar-hunt in the woods near Orthez.—Ibid., liv. iv. p. 119.

CHAPTER IV.

The Black Prince crosses the Pyrenees into Spain. Henry resolves, against the advice of Bertrand du Guesclin, to give battle to the invaders. First successes gained by the Castilians. Battle of Navarrete, or Najaro. Defeat of Henry. Bertrand du Guesclin is taken prisoner.

THE Prince of Wales, having made all his preparations, commenced his march across the Pyrenees about the middle of February, 1367. He divided his army, which amounted to ten thousand men-at-arms and as many archers, besides the foot-soldiers, into three parts. The division nominally under the Duke of Lancaster, but commanded by Sir John Chandos, first entered the Pass of Roncesvalles; the second, led by the prince in person and Peter the Cruel, followed the next day; while the rear-division, under James, titular king of Majorca,* and the Gascon leaders, started on the third day. Although the army encountered much wind and snow on its passage, especially the division under the Prince of Wales, it reached in safety the neighbourhood of Pampeluna. Meanwhile Henry, by his own activity, aided by the fear

* James II., king of Majorca, father of the James mentioned in the text, had been dethroned by Pedro IV., king of Aragon, who united his estates to Aragon by an act dated the 29th of March, 1344.—Raynaldus, *Annal. Eccles.*, 1343, §§ 26, 31. Buchon's note to Froissart, liv. i. part ii. p. 519.

which the return of Peter inspired among his subjects, had collected a large body of men, both horse and foot, besides the reinforcement of four thousand efficient troops, which he daily expected, under Sir Bertrand du Guesclin; and he looked for these auxiliaries the more anxiously, as he would not have ventured an engagement without them. Learning that Edward had left Navarre, and entered the province of Alava, on the road towards Burgos, Henry passed the Ebro, and pitched his camp in a hamlet near the town of Trevino. Here he learnt that six hundred Castilian horse and genetours,* which he had sent to take the town of Agreda, had deserted his standards, and joined the army of the Prince of Wales; but he was much more than compensated for that defection by the arrival of Sir Bertrand du Guesclin, the Maréchal d'Audeneham, the Begue de Villaines, and upwards of three thousand French and Aragonese soldiers. While here, Henry received a letter from Charles V., king of France, who wrote to advise him to avoid a conflict of arms with the Prince of Wales: for Charles had so little confidence in the event of a battle, from his own experience of the fatal day of Poitiers, that he would never afterwards give his consent to any engagement, if an advantage could be gained in some other way. He therefore urged Henry to decline every trial of strength with the Black Prince: "for he had with him the flower of the chivalry of the whole world;" and advised him to carry on the war in some other manner, as the prince and the Free

* Llaguno, the editor of Ayala, makes the following distinction between these troops:—"The *Castilian horse* were men-at-arms, armed at all points, who used long stirrups; while the *genetours* (ginetes mounted on genets) were Andalusian cavalry, lighter armed, but very efficient, who rode with short stirrups, and were armed with a lance and an oval leather shield."—*Cronica del Rey Don Pedro*, p. 337, note (3).

Companies could not remain long inactive in Castille. To this judicious advice of the king of France, Bertrand du Guesclin, the Maréchal d'Audeneham, and the other French leaders, added all the weight of their influence; but Henry replied to all their arguments, that the members of his special council, and they who most loved his service, were all of opinion that, if he indicated any fear of the result of a battle with Edward, he would be abandoned by all the nobles of the kingdom, whose example would be followed by the cities and towns: for they all entertained the greatest dread of the return of Peter to power; but, if they saw that he was willing to risk a battle, they would trust to the chances of victory. This opinion of his council coincided with his own; and Henry said to the French knights that it would be very dangerous for him to exhibit even the appearance of shunning a battle, or refuse to defend the cities, towns, and lordships which belonged to his adherents; but that, since it was so, he would leave the event in the hands of God.

The conclusion of Henry and his council was doubtless founded on the recent example of Peter, who had lost his kingdom from the want of courage to defend it, without making, on their part, sufficient allowance for the different estimate in which the rival monarchs were regarded by their subjects: for, while Henry was popular with all classes, Peter was hated as much as he was feared. Having resolved, therefore, not to avoid a battle, Henry seemed disposed to use every precaution that prudence dictated; and, upon learning that the town of Salvatierra, in Alava, near the borders of Navarre, had submitted to Peter, he changed the position of his army, and pitched his camp on an elevated ridge near the castle of Zaldiaran, where he could not be attacked without every advantage on his side.*

* Ayala, *Cronica del Rey Don Pedro*, pp. 438, 455; Froissart, liv. i. part ii. pp. 525, 528.

Edward, on leaving Navarre, passed the town of Salvatierra, and took a position before Vittoria, on the road to Burgos, where he encamped for six days, in the hope that Henry would attack him: for the country behind him was so poor and wasted, that the greatest scarcity prevailed in his camp, and it increased to such a degree that, before he left that position, "a small piece of bread was sold among his troops for a florin;" or, in the language of one of Chandos's men, which expressed at once his large means and his great need, "Would to God I only had a cup of wine and three mouthfuls of good wheat bread, even were I to pay twenty silver marks for it."* Henry, however, kept his position at Zaldiaran, and sent out a strong force under his brother, Don Tello, the Count de Denia, and other Spanish nobles, to harass the prince, and prevent his foraging parties from collecting supplies. These Spanish nobles, with a body of six thousand horse, first attacked and cut to pieces a detachment under Sir Hugh Calverly, and chased their leader into the English camp. Flushed with this success, they beat up the quarters of the Duke of Lancaster, aroused the whole camp of the Prince of Wales, and, after some feats of arms between the English and Gascon knights on one side, and the Spaniards on the other, the latter withdrew in good order towards their own army. On their return they encountered Sir Thomas Felton, his brother William,† and other knights, with a force of two hundred men-at-arms, and as many archers, who had been sent to reconnoitre and report the position of Henry's camp. The English knights, when they saw that the Spaniards were preparing to attack them, took advantage of an adjoining eminence, and drew up their

* Froissart, liv. i. part ii. p. 531; Cuvelier, v. 11,540.

† Sir William Felton will be remembered as the opponent of Sir Bertrand du Guesclin, in the trial on the wager of battle before the parliament of Paris.

forces upon it, so as to make the best possible defence. Whilst the Spaniards were arranging the order of their attack, Sir William Felton, seeing no chance of escape from so large a body, boldly descended the hill, with lance in rest, and, putting spurs to his horse, dashed into the very midst of his enemies, struck a Castilian with such force that the lance, piercing his armour, passed through the body, and laid him dead on the spot. The brave knight was, however, soon surrounded; and, after a gallant but ineffectual struggle, he was overpowered and slain. Don Tello then ordered an attack on the English drawn up on the hill, who made a spirited defence; but they were overwhelmed by the numbers of their opponents, and all of them were either slain or taken prisoners.*

Henry was greatly elated at these first successes of his troops; and, while expressing his satisfaction to his brother Don Tello for his good fortune, in the presence of Bertrand du Guesclin and other French leaders, the king seemed to augur a like result in the main battle with his enemies; but the Maréchal d'Audeneham, an old and experienced soldier, who did not participate in his hopes, came forward and said:—

"Sire, under your favour, I do not wish to find fault with your words, but only to amend them a little: for I tell you, whenever you join battle with the prince, you will find with him men-at-arms composed of the flower of the chivalry of the whole world—a body of resolute, wise, and skilful combatants, who would sooner die on the field than fly; but, if you will believe me, you can vanquish them without striking a blow: for you only have to guard your straits and passes, by which they get provisions, and you can starve them out

* Ayala, *Cronica del Rey Don Pedro*, pp. 445, 446; Froissart, liv. i. part ii. pp. 528, 530.

and discomfit them in this way, so that they will retreat in disorder towards their own country, when you can attack them at your pleasure."

"Maréchal," quickly replied Henry to this judicious counsel, "by the soul of my father! I desire so much to see the prince, and prove my power against his, that we cannot part without a battle; and, through God's mercy, I shall have men enough: for, in the first place, I have seven thousand men-at-arms, each mounted on a good war-horse and covered with iron, who fear neither arrow nor archer; then I have fully twenty thousand other men-at-arms, mounted on genets and armed from head to foot, besides sixty thousand men of the communities, armed with lances, darts, and bucklers, who can perform great feats, and who have sworn not to fail me. So, Lord Maréchal, I should not fear the result, but take great comfort under the protection of God and my own people."*

Edward, from the hostile demonstrations made by his opponents while encamped before Vittoria, was in daily expectation of a battle. Here Peter the Cruel received at his hands the order of knighthood, which the prince also conferred on Thomas Holland, his step-son, and several others. At the same time the Duke of Lancaster, Sir John Chandos, and some of the other leaders, created a number of knights, amounting in the whole to upwards of three hundred.† As Henry seemed determined neither to abandon his strong position nor to offer him battle, and as the distress from the want of provisions daily increased in his army, Edward,

* Froissart, liv. i. part ii. pp. 530, 531.

† On the creation of knights before and after a battle, see St. Palaye, *Mémoires sur l'Ancienne Chevalerie*, p. 210, note (15). Four hundred and sixty-seven French knights, he says, were created before the battle of Rosbeck, in 1382; and five hundred before Azincourt, in 1415.

upon the advice of a council of war, resolved to break up his camp, and attempt an entrance into Castille at some other point. He therefore dislodged his army, and, re-entering Navarre, passed along the frontiers until he reached the bridge across the Ebro, opposite Logroño, which he crossed, and took a position not far from that town, near the village of Navarrete. At the same time, Henry, who had been closely watching the movements of the prince, quickly abandoned his position at Zaldiaran, re-crossed the Ebro, and pitched his camp near the town of Najara, on the Najarilla, a small but deep tributary of the Ebro, with high banks, and just opposite the position taken by Edward, with the distance of not more than four or five leagues interposed between the two armies. While the hostile forces were thus encamped on opposite sides of the Najarilla, letters passed between Edward and Henry, in which each attempted to justify the course pursued by himself; but the correspondence led to no other result than, possibly, to create in the mind of Henry an impression that Edward's letter was a defiance: for, as soon as it was received, Henry rashly resolved to cross the narrow river which had served him as a natural entrenchment, and, against the advice of many of his ablest leaders, to offer battle to his antagonist in the plain before Navarrete.*

This inconsiderate determination of Henry to give up every advantage of position on his side was made against the positive admonition of Bertrand du Guesclin, who advised him to strengthen himself by ditches, and the waggons of the army placed in front: for, so great was the distress from famine in the prince's camp, that in three days, he asserted, the enemy would be forced to retreat, and they would fly

* Froissart, liv. i. part ii. p. 538; Rymer, vol. iii. par. ii. pp. 823, 824; Ayala, *Cronica del Rey Don Pedro*, pp. 447, 454.

from him like a stag from a dog, when the king could pursue and take them at his will. This advice of Bertrand du Guesclin was violently opposed by the Count de Denia, the commander of the Aragonese auxiliaries, who attributed such counsel to fear or indifference to the best interests of the king. To this imputation Du Guesclin firmly replied :—

"By the Omnipotent God! if we fight to-morrow, I tell you plainly, we shall be entirely routed, and either slain or taken captive, and great mischief will ensue to both prince and people; but, since you have thus spoken and vilely reproached me, to-morrow let us try the event of battle, and you will then see whether I am a traitor or coward."*

The Black Prince was too good a general not to be delighted at seeing his antagonist give up every advantage of position: for, straitened as he was himself, from the want of provisions for his army, and with a body of the best fighting men in the world, he had everything to gain by an immediate contest in an open field. When, therefore, he was informed that Henry was approaching, he exclaimed :—

"By St. George! this bastard is a valiant knight: for he seems to be desirous of finding us to offer us battle."

On the next day, which was Saturday, the 3rd of April, 1367, both armies appeared on the plain before Navarrete. The forces of the Prince of Wales comprised about forty thousand men; ten thousand of whom were men-at-arms, ten thousand were archers, and the rest foot-soldiers. They were separated into four divisions. The first was commanded by the Duke of Lancaster, under the control of Sir John Chandos; the second by the Count d'Armagnac and the Gascon leaders; the third by the Captal de Buch; and the

* Cuvelier, vv. 11,370, 11,411.

fourth by Edward and Peter the Cruel. On the other side, the army of Henry was composed of four thousand men-at-arms, sixteen thousand genetours, and a body of irregular infantry, amounting to from forty to sixty thousand men, armed with lances, pikes, darts, swords, and boar-spears. This army was also separated into four divisions: of which the first was commanded by Sir Bertrand du Guesclin; the second by Don Tello; the third by the Count de Denia; and the fourth by Henry in person. When his men were all drawn up in order of battle, Henry, mounted on a strong and fleet mule, after the usage of the country, rode through the ranks to each of the leaders, and begged them to strive on that day to save his honour.*

Just before the battle commenced, Sir John Chandos, on the other side, rode up to the Prince of Wales, with his banner, still folded, in his hands, and thus addressed him:—

"My lord, this is my banner; I offer it to you to be displayed in whatever manner it may please you: for to-day I am able to display it, as I have, thank God, lands and sufficient estate to maintain the rank that belongs to it."

The prince then received the banner, "which was a sharp stake gules, blazoned on a field argent," unfolded it, and afterwards returned it by the haft, with these words:—

"Sir John, receive your banner. May God enable you to show your valour under it!"

Sir John Chandos, thus created a knight-banneret, then took the banner, and carried it among his followers, saying:—

"Lords, behold my banner and yours; now guard it as your own."†

* Ayala, *Cronica del Rey Don Pedro*, pp. 440, 443; Froissart, liv. i. part ii. pp. 524, 533, 536.

† Froissart, liv. i. part ii. p. 534. This ceremony was intended to

The two armies commenced their movements early in the morning; and, as it was a rare sight, it was described as a beautiful one, to see such bodies of men, comprising together about one hundred and fifty thousand soldiers, "with their banners floating in the wind, and the sun shining on their armour."* The troops of the Black Prince were distinguished by the red cross of St. George on their shields and banners, while those of Henry had scarves on their banners alone. Before issuing the order to commence the battle, Edward uttered a short but fervent prayer for success on his arms that day; and then, offering his hand to Peter the Cruel, he said:—

"Sir king, you will know to-day if you are ever to possess anything in the kingdom of Castille."

The prince then gave the order: "Forward! forward! in the name of God and St. George!"

confer on Sir John Chandos the rank of knight-banneret. St. Palaye observes:—"If the knight was rich and powerful enough to furnish to the state a certain number of men-at-arms, and maintain them at his own expense, the permission was granted him to add to the simple designation of knight, or knight-bachelor, the higher and more noble title of knight-banneret. The distinction of these bannerets consisted in bearing a square banner on the end of a lance, while those of simple knights were lengthened out to two points, like the streamers used in the ceremonies of the church."—*Mémoires sur l'Ancienne Chevalerie*, pp. 259, 260. Du Cange makes the following distinction between them:—"Knights of the first order are barons and bannerets, who have the right of bearing standards in battle; while a knight of the second order, a knight-bachelor, or a simple knight, was *a knight of one shield:* because, in going on military expeditions, he had no vassal-knight under him."—Glossarium, voc. *Miles.*

* Froissart, liv. i. part ii. p. 534. Cuvelier thus describes the spectacle:—

> "La peussiez véoir moult noble establiçon,
> Banières ventelans et maint doré pennon;
> Les lances en lor poing et au col le blason,
> Les heaumes au chief plus luisant que laiton."
>
> —Ver. 11,484.

As soon as the two armies approached each other, the Spanish slingers came forward, and at first wounded many of the English with the stones, thrown with great force, from their slings; but as soon as they felt the arrows of the English archers, they gave way at once, and they never could be brought into the action again. But neither slingers nor archers were of much avail in deciding the event of this battle. The whole brunt of it was borne by the men-at-arms on both sides, who dismounted and formed in close order under their separate leaders, and then advanced to the attack. It was the fortune of Bertrand du Guesclin, who commanded a body of four thousand men-at-arms, equal in valour and discipline to any in the army of the prince, to be opposed to the division under the Duke of Lancaster, "who was counselled and governed by Sir John Chandos in the same manner as his brother the Prince of Wales formerly was at the battle of Poitiers." These divisions first advanced to the attack, the men-at-arms holding their lances with both hands, and shouting respectively their war-cries: "Guienne, St. George!" and "Castille, Sant Jago!" So rude was this shock, that the men dropped their lances on both sides, when a fierce hand-to-hand conflict ensued with short swords, daggers, and battle-axes. The onset of the division under Bertrand du Guesclin was so irresistible, that their opponents at first were forced to give way. Sir John Chandos, the leader of the opposite division, who entered with his usual ardour and impetuosity into the conflict, was assailed and beaten down by a huge Castilian named Martin Fernandez, renowned among his countrymen for his courage and strength. In the struggle the Castilian fell upon the English knight, bore him to the earth, and used every effort to slay him. Sir John Chandos, though in great peril while lying beneath his huge antagonist, exhibited his usual coolness, and bethought himself of a knife commonly worn in his bosom, which he drew, and applied with such effect on the side and back of his assailant that he wounded him mortally, and at length succeeded in throwing him off. He arose unwounded from the perilous conflict, in time to be joined by his men, who had just been able to break the press around him.

On the other side, Bertrand du Guesclin, the Maréchal d'Audeneham, the Begue de Villaines, and the French knights and squires, when they perceived their opponents give way, pressed on with increased vigour; but they were unable to preserve the temporary advantage which they had gained: for at that moment Don Tello, who commanded the left wing of Henry's army, consisting of a thousand men-at-arms, and ten thousand foot-soldiers,* either through treachery or cowardice, as soon as he saw the division under the Count d'Armagnac approaching, basely left the field, followed by his own command, without striking a blow. The Count d'Armagnac, having no other enemy to contend with, fell upon the flank and rear of Bertrand's division, while, at the same time, the Captal de Buch, finding no opposition, as he expected, from the division under the Count de Denia, attacked Bertrand on the other flank; so that the Breton knight was encompassed on all sides by his enemies. Henry, who commanded the irregular forces of his army, did all that prayers, expostulation, and a brilliant example of courage and constancy could avail, to prevent the loss of the day, and three times he brought back his flying troops. With a large body of genetours, he several times restored order among his dismayed forces, and repaired his broken ranks; but he was forced to yield to the more efficient and better disciplined troops commanded by the Prince of Wales, who behaved everywhere like a good

* Note from Zurita, in Ayala, p. 578.

knight; while Peter the Cruel joined actively in the conflict, and sought his brother over the field, exclaiming, "Where is this son of a whore who calls himself king of Castille!" Henry was at length forced to leave the field; and, passing through the town of Najara, he exchanged his wearied war-horse * for a fresh genet, and escaped in safety into Aragon. His flight was followed by a dreadful slaughter of his troops, and a very large number were drowned in attempting to cross the river.†

In the meantime, Bertrand du Guesclin and the men-at-arms of his division, though assailed on all sides, maintained the contest with great obstinacy; and, when their leader received the summons of Sir John Chandos to surrender, he made no reply in words, but, re-adjusting his helmet, he struck down an English man-at-arms to the earth before him.

At length, seeing nearly all his men either slain or taken around him, Bertrand threw down his arms at the second summons from the Prince of Wales, and was made a prisoner under the banner of Sir John Chandos.‡ Peter the Cruel,

* In a curious memorandum of the times, preserved by Rymer, it is stated that a valet of the Black Prince, named Franskyn Forsset, received 16*l.* 13*s.* 4*d.* for carrying to the king of England a war-horse (*dextrarium*) belonging to Henry, which was taken at the battle of Nazerr (Najara) in Spain.—*Fœdera*, vol. iii. par. ii. p. 825.

† Ayala, *Cronica del Rey Don Pedro*, pp. 454, 456; Froissart, liv. i. part ii. pp. 534, 538. The different accounts of Ayala and Froissart of this sanguinary battle, though they vary considerably as to details, seldom materially conflict, and often essentially aid each other in the comprehension of its various incidents. Ayala has been followed when the facts are differently narrated, as he was an eye-witness of most of the events which he records, and was present in this battle, where "he carried the banner of the scarf."—*Cronica del Rey Don Pedro*, p. 441.

‡ The ancient knight was unwilling, if he could avoid it, to surrender to one of inferior rank to himself; and it is said of the Earl of Suffolk, that, when he was defeated at the town of Jargeau, he was pursued by a

who was present at this act, which ended the battle, was greatly pleased at the surrender of the French leaders, and asked Edward to deliver up to him Bertrand du Guesclin and the Maréchal d'Audeneham, offering for Bertrand his weight in silver, which he promised to find, "even if there should not be a chalice left on an altar in Spain while he lived." But Edward knew too well the sanguinary disposition of Peter to entrust a gallant enemy for a moment to his keeping; he therefore positively refused to give up either of the French knights, and turned over Bertrand du Guesclin to the care of the Captal de Buch, who simply took his prisoner's parole that he would not attempt to escape, and kindly granted him the permission to make up a bed in his own chamber.*

After the surrender of the division under Bertrand du Guesclin, Edward placed his standard on a high bush upon an elevated spot, to serve as a rallying point to his scattered troops; which was also done by the Duke of Lancaster, the Count d'Armagnac, the Captal de Buch, and the other leaders. To the standard of the Black Prince came Peter the Cruel, much heated from the conflict, mounted on a black courser, with his banner, ornamented with the arms of Castille, before him. As soon as he perceived the prince he dismounted, and was about to fall on his knees to thank him for his great services; but Edward, taking him by the hand, would by no means suffer it, when Peter said to him :—

French man-at-arms, named Guillaume Renault, of whom the earl asked :—

"Are you a gentleman?"

"Yes," replied Renault.

"Are you a knight?" again asked the earl.

"No," answered the other.

The earl then created him a knight, and surrendered to him.—*Chronique de la Pucelle*, Edition of Buchon, p. 439.

* Cuvelier, vv. 12,074, 12,192.

"Dear and fair cousin, I should render you much praise and many thanks for the great success of this day, which I have had through you."

"Give thanks to God," quickly replied the prince, "and all the praise: for the victory comes through Him, and not from me."

Edward then sent four knights and four heralds, with orders to search the field of battle, and report the number of the dead and wounded, and particularly to find out whether Henry was among them. After this the prince and his people took possession of the lodges of Henry and the Spaniards, where they found an abundance of everything which they stood in need of; and the victors passed the evening in a great revel. After supper, the knights and heralds who had been sent to examine the field of battle returned, of whom Edward anxiously inquired, in Gascon: "The bastard, is he dead or taken?" and, when the knights answered no, he said prophetically, "Nothing has been done!"* They then reported that they had counted among the slain five hundred and sixty men-at-arms and seven thousand five hundred common soldiers, on the part of the Spaniards, besides those who were drowned; while there were only four knights, about twenty archers, and forty other men slain on the part of the English—a frightful mortality on one side, and, as usual in the battles of that period, a very great disproportion between the contending parties, which proves that such slaughter could not have taken place during the conflict on the field, but after flight in the pursuit of the vanquished. Besides the slain, there was a very great

* "E el Principe de Gales pregunto á los que avian buscado, diciendo en su lengua: '*Lo Bort, es mort ó pres?*' E dixeroule que non, e el respondio é dixo: '*Non ay res fait.*'"—Note copied by Zurita in his *Enmiendas*, and cited by the editor of Ayala, in *Adiciones á las Notas. Cronica del Rey Don Pedro*, p. 578.

number of prisoners, comprising all the French knights and squires under Bertrand du Guesclin, with a large number of Castilian nobles and knights.*

* Froissart, liv. i. part ii. p. 538; Ayala, *Cronica del Rey Don Pedro*, pp. 456, 457. Among the Castilian prisoners was the historian Pero Lopez de Ayala, p. 457.

CHAPTER V

Trial of the Maréchal d'Audeneham, for the breach of a military oath, before a jury of knights. Cruelty and bad faith of Peter after the battle of Navarrete. Quarrel between him and the Black Prince. Edward leaves Spain in disgust. Henry escapes into France, obtains aid from Charles V., and returns to Castille.

AMONG the French prisoners taken at the battle of Navarrete was the Maréchal d'Audeneham; and when he was brought into the presence of Edward and Peter, the interview between the knight and the prince gave rise to a pleasing incident somewhat illustrative of the manners of the times. As soon as the prince observed the maréchal among the prisoners, he denounced him as a traitor and liar, and told him that he deserved death. To this imputation, so offensive to a knight, the maréchal respectfully, but firmly, replied :—

"My lord, you are the son of a king, and I am unable to answer such a charge as I ought; but I am neither a traitor nor liar."

The prince then said to him that, if he would abide the decision of a jury of knights, he could prove the truth of the charge. To this proposition the maréchal promptly assented; whereupon the prince appointed, on the spot, twelve knights— four English, four Gascons, and four Bretons—as judges; and, when the maréchal appeared before them, the prince said:—

"Maréchal d'Audeneham, you will remember that I was victorious at the battle of Poitiers, when John king of France was taken, when you also were a prisoner, and that I had you in my power, and put you at a sufficiently low ransom, for which you gave me your pledge, under oath, on pain of being declared a traitor and liar, that, if you were not in company with your lord the king of France, or some one of the lineage of the Fleur-de-Lis, you would not bear arms against me, nor against the king of England, my father, until your ransom was paid, which up to the present moment is still due: yet, to-day, neither the king of France nor any one of his family was present in the battle, and I saw you clothed in full armour against me. Wherefore I declare that you have violated the oath that you made me, by which you have fallen into a bad case. Besides, you have broken your faith, and therefore lied, since you have not performed the promise you made upon your word in this matter, as I have said."

This serious charge gave much concern to the knights appointed to decide the question, as the maréchal was highly esteemed by them, for he had always been regarded as a good and loyal knight; and he was then seventy years old or upwards, and they did not well see how he could answer it. The maréchal first asked:—

"My lord, I inquire, with humble reverence, if it pleases you to add anything to what you have said to the knights whom you have appointed to decide this case?"

When the prince answered that he had nothing further to add, the maréchal proceeded:—

"My lord, I beg that you will not be offended at me for defending my rights, since this charge touches my reputation and character for truth."

The prince promptly responded by telling him to speak out with perfect security, "as this was an action between knights, done in war, and there was good reason that he should defend his fame and truth." The maréchal then, turning to the prince, said:—

"My lord, it is true that I was taken at the battle of Poitiers, with my lord the king of France. It is also true that I gave you my pledge, under oath, that I would not bear arms against you or the king of England until all my ransom was paid—which, as yet, I have not done—saving that I might arm myself with the king of France or with any of the lineage of the Fleur-de-Lis. And, my lord, I well know that the king of France is not here, nor any of his family; yet, for all that, I am not in a bad case, nor am I a liar, since I have not armed myself against you, as you are not the head of this army: for the captain and head of it is the king, Don Pedro; and you have come here yourself, employed by him, and paid with his wages, and not as the chief of the army, but retained and paid for your services. I did no wrong in bearing arms, as I did not arm myself against you, but against the king, Don Pedro, who is the captain in chief of your party."

This ingenious subterfuge of the worthy maréchal was held good logic by the knights appointed to decide the cause, and they gave it as their opinion that the maréchal had answered well and rightly; whereupon they declared him acquitted of the charge which the prince had made against him. This decision gave much satisfaction to all the knights present at the trial; and Edward, far from exhibiting any ill-temper at the failure to make good his accusation, or any displeasure at being degraded from the position of chief of the expedition, which he unquestionably was, into a mercenary soldier, generously entered into the congratulations of the other knights, and rejoiced with them that the old maréchal had found such good reasons to explain his conduct.*

The Maréchal d'Audeneham, thus exonerated from all censure under the grave charges made by the Black Prince, was not long detained as a prisoner : for he, with the Begue de Villaines and many other knights of France and Brittany, was exchanged for Sir Thomas Felton and the knights who had been taken in the skirmish near the English camp before Vittoria. Bertrand du Guesclin was not so fortunate. He was too important a prisoner to be thus easily disposed of. Besides, Edward was advised by his council not to release him : for, they said, as soon as he recovered his liberty, he would give Henry more effectual aid than before ; and they insisted the more strenuously in urging his detention, when it was afterwards reported that Henry had entered the county of Bigorre, taken the town of Bagnères, and laid waste the whole country around it.†

While the Prince of Wales was exhibiting among the leaders of his army the humanizing influences of the institution of chivalry on a generous spirit, in accepting so readily a specious excuse, which sustained the reputation of a worthy old knight,—his ally, Peter, was displaying before the eyes of all, the worst vices of his character. Abject, cringing, and humble, when begging for aid at the court of the Black Prince, he was haughty, self-willed, and bloodthirsty in the first exercise of restored authority ; and he lost no time in showing that nothing could be more oppressive to so base a nature than the sense of a great obligation conferred. It was therefore scarcely possible that two persons so widely different in their dispositions and character as the Prince of Wales and Peter the Cruel could long agree after circum-

* Ayala, *Cronica del Rey Don Pedro*, pp. 458, 460.

† Froissart, liv. i. part ii. p. 543.

stances had restored them to a footing of equality: for, though Edward was sometimes stern and imperious in his temper, he much preferred to govern by love than by fear; while Peter never practised any means of controlling the actions of men but by blood alone. He had learned no wisdom from the bitter experience of the past; and his first exercise of power on a field of battle, after the victory of Navarrete, was a deed of violence that led to a spirited remonstrance from the Black Prince, which deepened into an estrangement, and ended in a total separation between them. The incident is thus narrated by Ayala.

On the day after the battle, a Spanish cavalier, Inigo Lopez de Orozco, a former adherent of Peter, but who abandoned him the year before while flying from his brother Henry and Bertrand du Guesclin between Burgos and Toledo, was taken prisoner by a Gascon knight; and, while under the protection of his captor, Peter rode up to the prisoner, and slaughtered him in cold blood. The Gascon, indignant at the act, immediately made complaint to Edward of the outrage committed by Peter; and he not only complained of the loss of the ransom which he had sustained by the death of his prisoner, but declared that he felt himself dishonoured by having a knight slain while in his power and entitled to his protection. Upon this, the prince told Peter that he had done a very great wrong: for he well knew that, among other matters agreed on and sworn to between them, it was one of the principal articles that Peter should not put to death a Castilian knight, or any one of condition, while he, the prince, was with him, unless by due course of law—except such as had been condemned by a previous sentence, and that Inigo Lopez was not one of these; that it seemed to him Peter was not disposed to perform the promises which he had made; and he apprehended that he would violate in like manner the other stipulations which had been agreed on between them. Peter attempted to make the best excuse in his power; but he deeply felt the severity of the reproof, and he never forgave the affront.*

Not satisfied with the murder of Orozco, and the punishment of Gomez Carillo and two other nobles, who were probably put to death by a judicial sentence,† Peter the next day asked the prince to give up to him all the knights and squires of note who had been taken in the battle, offering to pay any reasonable price to their captors that the prisoners should be appraised at; and, if the prince would become his surety to the knights and men-at-arms who were entitled to their ransoms, he would give his obligation to the prince for the whole amount—threatening to regard the knights as his enemies if they refused to accept his terms. To this request the prince replied that, "saving his royal majesty," he had asked what was most unreasonable: for the lords, knights, and men-at-arms in his service had fought for fame, and whatever prisoners they had taken were their own; that he knew the knights who held them would not deliver them up to him for any amount in the world, even if it were a thousand times as much as the prisoners were worth, when they suspected that he only wished to get possession of them to put them to death. The prince said, moreover, that he would have nothing to do with the matter, as he had no power to control the action of his people; but, if among the captive knights there were any against whom judgment had been pronounced before the battle, he would order them to be delivered up. To this manly and honourable declaration Peter petulantly replied that, if such was the case, he held his kingdom more lost to him now

* Ayala, *Cronica del Rey Don Pedro*, p. 471.

† *Ibid*, p. 458. Froissart says Gomes Garils, as he names him, was expressly mentioned by Edward in the list of the proscribed.—Liv. i. part ii. p. 539.

than it was before; that all the prisoners were those who had caused him the loss of his kingdom; and, if they should escape, he would regard the aid he had received of the prince as of no value, but that he had spent his treasures in vain. Edward, though highly irritated at this reply, answered Peter with good temper:—

"My lord kinsman, it appears to me that you have more efficacious means to gain the affections of your subjects than you had when you first held your kingdom in possession; and you now govern it in such a manner that you are about to lose it again. I therefore counsel you to acquire the good will of your nobles, lords, and knights, the burgesses of the cities, and the people of your kingdom: for, if you govern them in the same manner that you did before, you will incur great danger of losing both your kingdom and your life; and you will come to such a pass, that neither my father the king of England nor I could assist you, even if we had the will."*

After this well-intended, but severe reproof, which only served to alienate still further an ungenerous nature like that of Peter, the two princes proceeded towards the city of Burgos, which opened its gates to them without delay. Peter took possession of the castle in the city, while Edward was quartered outside, at the monastery of Las Huelgas, with his troops, in the suburbs, around him. Here an additional affront was offered to Edward by Peter, who, as soon as he entered Burgos, seized Jean de Cardalhac, Archbishop of Braga, a relative of the Count d'Armagnac, one of the most powerful adherents of the prince, and sent him to the castle of Alcala de Guadayra, where he was imprisoned in a subterranean dungeon, until he was released by Henry after the battle of Monteil.†

* Ayala, *Cronica del Rey Don Pedro*, pp. 471, 473.
† *Ibid*, pp. 473, 474.

Edward, having now fully performed the promise which he had made to restore the fugitive monarch to his throne, and found out the true character of Peter, was anxious to return to his own country. As soon, therefore, as he perceived that Peter was in no haste to comply with the stipulations which he had agreed to on his part, the prince sent three of his knights to remind him of his promises, and particularly of the obligation incurred to the nobles, knights, men-at-arms, and other soldiers, for the pay of the expedition, besides the sums advanced to the troops before setting out; all of which were now due, and which Peter had undertaken to pay. To these demands Peter replied, by some of his counsellors—for the princes had ceased to have any personal intercourse, and treated by commissioners—that it was true he had undertaken to pay the troops and discharge the prince from all obligation towards his leaders and their men; but he meanly attempted to lessen the several amounts, by alleging that the money given to the knights and archers while at Bayonne had been taken at a great depreciation, and the jewellery and precious stones which he had distributed among them they had received at half their real worth; he therefore insisted that he was entitled to the difference between the real and assumed values of what he had already paid. To the second demand of Edward, that Peter should put him in possession of the province of Biscay, and the cities and towns which he had granted him, Peter replied that it was true he had given him the province of Biscay, and the town of Castro de Urdiales, and he was ready to give him the investiture; but, when the prince sent the Lord de Poyane and the Judge of Bordeaux to receive possession, their application was refused by the inhabitants of the province and town, on the ground that they had positive orders from Peter not to give them possession. The prince next instructed his commissioners to say that, as Peter was now established in his kingdom, and had no longer need for such large bodies of men, he desired to return to his own country, inasmuch as he had received information that the French were preparing to invade his territories. To this Peter only replied that he was pleased to learn that the prince was willing to return ; and coolly requested him to leave behind a thousand lances for his defence.

To the demand of Sir John Chandos, to whom Peter had given the city of Soria, and who asked that it might be delivered up to him, the king gave his assent, and even ordered titles to be made out preparatory to his obtaining the investiture ; but the king's chancellor, Mattheos Ferrandez, charged such exorbitant office fees for them,* that Sir John Chandos refused to take out the papers. After much delay and many conferences, Peter at length agreed to pay half the amount due to Edward for the wages of his troops within four months, in Castille, and the balance in one year, at Bayonne ; but this agreement, although solemnly sworn to by Peter on the high altar of the church of St. Mary at Burgos, was intended, like his other promises, only to amuse Edward, who remained until the expiration of the time fixed for the first payment ; when, disgusted with the baseness and bad faith of Peter, weary with waiting, oppressed with debt, and broken down by sickness, he turned his back on a country where, to gain a fruitless victory and restore an unworthy monarch to his throne, he had lost his health, sacrificed the lives of his people, and involved himself in pecuniary embarrassments, which led to results fatal to his peace, to his possessions, and, eventually, to his life.†

* Ayala says 10,000 doblas.—*Cronica del Rey Don Pedro*, p. 481. The *dobla* was an ancient Spanish coin of uncertain value. The *double* was a silver coin of Algiers and Tunis, worth about two francs, ninety-five centimes of French money.—Bescherelle.

† Ayala, *Cronica del Rey Don Pedro*, pp. 474, 483, 495, and 506;

There has seldom been a more indisputable victory than that gained by the Prince of Wales at Navarrete, or one where the ultimate consequences were so unimportant to the victors. It is true a throne was lost by one party and gained by another, and the rival monarchs, for a season, exchanged places in exile; but the recovered throne was only supported by fear, and it fell as soon as this prop was removed. Henry, following the dictates of an inconsiderate valour, against the advice of his ablest officers, had perilled his whole fortune upon the issue of that one conflict; and he lost everything but his life and liberty, his reputation as a knight, and the suppressed good wishes of his adherents throughout the kingdom. Leaving the town of Najara alone after the battle, he endeavoured, by the shortest route, to reach the frontiers of Aragon; and, while passing through the province of Soria, he was joined by a few fugitives of his party, who had escaped, like himself, from the battle. On the next day, while passing near the hamlet of Borovia, he was discovered by a party of horsemen, who threw themselves in his way, with the apparent design of arresting his progress. Henry, as soon as he discovered their purpose, did not hesitate to attack them; and he slew with his own hand one of the horsemen, who attempted to lay hands on his person. The rest of the party were put to flight by his followers; and he then crossed the borders of Aragon, and reached a lodge belonging to Don Juan Martinez de Luna, near Calatayud, without any further adventure. Here Henry met Don Pedro de Luna,* who acted as his guide, and

Rymer, vol. iii. par. ii. p. 825; Froissart, liv. i. part ii. pp. 543, 544.

* Ayala says he was afterwards Pope Benedict, p. 462; yet he mentions, at page 533, an Aragonese *ricohombre*, of the same name, who was killed the following year on the island of Sardinia, in a battle with Hugh IV., judge of Arborea; of whom a very curious historical

accompanied him until he reached the farther confines of Aragon, where he crossed the Pyrenees at the pass of Jaca, and went to claim the protection and ask the aid of the Count de Foix.

The count greatly regretted the arrival of Henry at his court, as he was unwilling to incur the displeasure of the Prince of Wales—who had left him in charge of his principality during his absence—by giving shelter to his enemy; but the count was too good a knight to refuse the rights of hospitality, even to an enemy in distress; and he not only received Henry kindly, but gave him money and horses, and sent an escort of his own men to attend him as far as Toulouse, where he was again on friendly soil. After remaining here a few days, Henry went to Villeneuve, near Avignon, to visit the Duke of Anjou, who treated him with distinguished kindness. Pope Urban V., who was still at Avignon, favoured the cause of Henry; and, by his counsel, the Duke of Anjou extended to him his protection and aid. But Henry did not visit the pope: for the Prince of Wales was then at the height of his reputation and influence, and there were few men so powerful as not to dread his displeasure.*

The Duke of Anjou soon became apprehensive that he had

monument has been preserved, which has been published of late years by Buchon, in his *Panthéon Littéraire*, with the title, "Relation de l'Ambassade de Louis Ier., Duc d'Anjou, à Hugues IV., Juge d'Arborée, en l'anneé 1378. Par Guillaume Gaian et Migon de Rochéfort, Seigneur de Pomarède."

* Ayala, *Cronica del Rey Don Pedro*, pp. 461, 463. Froissart was evidently mistaken in his account of the flight of Henry, and his interview with the king of Aragon at Valencia, liv. i. part ii. pp. 541, 542. The statement of Ayala has been followed, as his narrative is confirmed by Miguel del Vermes, who says:—"*Et lo princep de Gala vencet al dit Comte de Tarastamera (Henry) lo qual s'enfugit en Bearn al Comte Febus, et d'aqui en fora al rey de Fransa, am qui estet tot l'estieu.*"—*Chroniques Béarnaises*, p. 585.

been too hasty in offering his assistance to Henry, and that the kind reception which he had given him might offend his cautious brother, the king of France, when he remembered the treaties that still existed between Charles V. and Edward III.; and the duke did not then know that his brother was only waiting for a favourable opportunity to renew the quarrel which had been pacified by the hard terms of the treaty of Brétigny. The Duke of Anjou, therefore, drew off from Henry, and attempted to put an end to all intercourse between them; but, when he perceived that he could not well excuse such conduct to a former ally, he visited him in secret, and advised him to send and inform the king of France of his acts and necessities, and ask his aid and counsel as to his future course. This advice of the duke was promptly carried out; and, as soon as Charles was informed of the situation and wants of Henry, he entered warmly into his interests, and not only instructed the Duke of Anjou to advance him, at once, fifty thousand francs of gold, but the king gave him the strong fortress of Pierre-Pertuse, near the borders of Languedoc and Roussillon, in addition to the county of Cessenon, in the diocese of Bézières. After meeting with such a kind reception, and receiving such liberal aid from the king of France, Henry fixed his residence at Pierre-Pertuse, where he was soon after joined by his wife, Donna Juana, and their children, who left the city of Burgos upon hearing the result of the battle of Navarrete, and, after encountering many perils, passed safely through Aragon into France. Here Henry collected a large quantity of arms and equipments to enable him to recover his lost kingdom, and he gave a gracious reception to the knights, squires, and other soldiers, who daily repaired to his standard.*

* Ayala, *Cronica del Rey Don Pedro*, pp. 503, 505, and see note (2), by the editor. Froissart says that Henry was forced to leave France by

During his residence at Pierre-Pertuse, Henry received the most gratifying intelligence from every part of Castille. He learnt that Peter, after renewing his covenants with the Prince of Wales, under the most solemn sanctions, at Burgos, had gone to Seville, without performing any of them; and that Edward, after waiting four months for the first instalment of the amount due for the pay of his troops, and the promised investiture of the province of Biscay for himself, and of Soria for Sir John Chandos, had left Castille, and returned to his principality in the worst temper towards Peter; that many of the knights, lately in the army of the Black Prince, who had formerly served under Henry, were ready to return again to his standard; that all the Castilian knights and squires of his own party who had been taken at the battle of Navarrete had been ransomed; that they had taken possession of the towns, castles, and fortresses which belonged to them, and they were now in open arms against Peter; that a number of important cities, towns, and castles, which had opened their gates under the first impressions of fear caused by the return of Peter to power, had now turned against him; and that the Black Prince would probably find sufficient employment at home, with his discontented vassals, and his ever-vigilant enemy the king of France, to prevent him from returning to Castille.*

Before setting out on his expedition, Henry had an interview with the Duke of Anjou and Guy, Cardinal de Boulogne, at the town of Aigues-Mortes, where he ratified the treaty he had made with the king of France. From Aigues-Mortes he returned about the middle of August to Pierre-Pertuse, where

order of Charles V., upon the complaint of the Prince of Wales; and that he went into the county of Bigorre, in Gascony, took the town of Bagnères, and laid waste the whole country around.—Liv. i. part ii. p. 542.

* Ayala, *Cronica del Rey Don Pedro*, pp. 506, 507.

he had left his wife and children, and the troops which he had collected for the invasion of Castille. While making his preparations to re-enter Spain, he was by no means sure that the king of Aragon would allow him a safe passage through his territories, as he had been informed that Don Pedro IV had changed sides immediately after the battle of Navarrete, and had formed, through the intervention of Sir Hugh Calverly, an alliance with the Prince of Wales, on the ground that Henry had not performed the promises which he had made him, after he had gained the kingdom of Castille. Moreover, Don Pedro had taken away from Donna Juana, on her passage through Aragon, his daughter Leonora, who had been affianced to Don Juan, the son of Henry, declaring that the marriage was no longer desirable.*

As no one knew better than Henry himself that it was the invariable policy of the king of Aragon only to assist those who did not need his help, he had requested the king of France to send a member of his council to Don Pedro, to inform him that he was about to return to his kingdom as powerful as before his late defeat. By the same messenger Henry also wrote to the king of Aragon to request his aid, and remind him, not only of the injuries which Peter the Cruel had done him, but also of the important services which had been rendered to the kingdom of Aragon by himself the year before; adding that, besides the aid he expected from the king of France and the Duke of Anjou, he would take with him three thousand efficient lances into Spain.†

The king of Aragon made no reply either to the message

* Ayala, *Cronica del Rey Don Pedro*, pp. 508, 509, and pp. 463, 465.

† *Ibid*, p. 505, and note (3). Froissart—who appears to have been ignorant of the treaty between the Prince of Wales and the king of Aragon, and says that Henry took leave of the latter at Valencia—estimates the army of Henry at three thousand horse and six thousand foot, with some Genoese.—Liv. i. part ii. pp. 548, 549.

of the king of France or to the letter of Henry; but, when he found that the latter was preparing to cross the frontiers of Aragon on his way to Castille, he sent him word by the governor of Roussillon that Henry must not pass through his kingdom; and, if the attempt was made, it would be resisted. Henry replied to the governor that he was greatly surprised at such a message from the king of Aragon, who well knew that in all his wars he had never failed to support him; and that, on his entrance into Castille the year before, he had delivered up to him one hundred and twenty towns and castles, which Peter the Cruel had taken away from him. But he added, with firmness, that he had to go to Castille, and he could not avoid passing through the kingdom of Aragon; and, if Don Pedro chose to impede his progress, and tried to hinder him, he could do as he pleased; but that he could not prevent his passage, and any attempt to molest him would be resisted with all his power. Don Pedro did make some show of opposition to the passage of Henry; but the latter had a strong party at the court of the king of Aragon, and among his friends was the Infante Don Pedro, uncle of the king, and father of the Count de Denia, who commanded the Aragonese auxiliaries at the battle of Navarrete. This nobleman sent a guide to conduct Henry through his lands of Ribagorza, and until he reached the town of Balbastro. The king of Aragon, hearing of Henry's march through his territories, ordered a body of his troops to assemble at Saragossa and intercept his progress; but the troops refused to obey the order, and Henry was suffered to pursue his way without interruption towards the frontiers of Navarre by the town of Huesca, where he crossed the Ebro into Castille.*

* Ayala, *Cronica del Rey Don Pedro*, pp. 510, 513. Henry was at Huesca on the 24th of September, 1367, from a letter of that date, written near the town.—Note (3) to page 513.

When Henry had passed the river which separated the kingdoms of Castille and Navarre, he was again on his native soil. Here he dismounted, and, falling on his knees to the earth, he drew the figure of a cross upon the sandy bank of the stream, and, devoutly kissing it, exclaimed :—" I swear, by the sign of the cross, that never during my life, for any cause, will I leave again the kingdom of Castille ; but there will I await death, or whatever fortune may befall me." He then knighted Bernal de Béarn, a natural son of the Count de Foix, and a squire named Dolet, who had accompanied him from Orthez. After this ceremony Henry entered the town of Calahorra, where he had first been proclaimed king of Castille, upon his entrance into Spain the year before, and where he was again received, on his return, with prompt submission. Here he was joined by many Castilian knights and men-at-arms, amounting to about six hundred lances, besides a number of other knights and squires of Castille and Brittany, who had been with him at the battle of Navarrete.

Henry was much encouraged by his first successes upon re-entering the kingdom ; he therefore pushed forward with great diligence, and improved every advantage that was offered to him, either by the zeal of his own partisans, or by the oversight of his enemies. The important city of Burgos opened its gates as soon as he appeared before it ; and, although the Jewish quarter and the castle held out for a short time against him, they successively surrendered after a feeble defence. The towns of Duennas, Leon, Madrid, Oterdehurnos, Medina de Rioseco, Buitrago, and other places of note, yielded in like manner to his arms, and he laid siege to the strong city of Toledo ; so that, before the close of the year 1368, the kingdom of Castille was nearly equally divided between the hostile monarchs—Henry holding the northern portion, with the exception of Galicia, a port of the Asturias, and certain isolated fortresses near the northern frontier; while Peter possessed Estramadura, Murcia, and Andalucia, except the city of Cordova, which he besieged with a considerable force of his own, aided by a very large body of Grenadine Moors, under their king, Mohammed; but the city was gallantly and successfully defended by the grand-masters of Sant Jago and Calatrava and Don Juan Alfonso de Guzman, with many other nobles and knights, and a large body of men-at-arms.*

* Ayala, *Cronica del Rey Don Pedro*, pp. 512, note (2), 514, 516, 524, and 526.

CHAPTER VI.

Bertrand du Guesclin is released from captivity on payment of a large ransom. He collects troops, and assists the Duke of Anjou in taking the town of Tarascon, in Provence. He crosses the Pyrenees with five hundred lances, and joins Henry at his camp near Toledo.

WHILE such events were passing in Spain, Bertrand du Guesclin, who had been carried into Aquitaine by the Black Prince, on his return from Castille, was sighing for his liberty in the prisons of Bordeaux. All the other prisoners of any note had long been exchanged, or released on paying their ransoms; but it was not until towards the conclusion of the year 1367 that a favourable change in the humours of the prince, brought about by the intervention of some of the admirers of the prisoner at the court of Edward, led to his release from a wearisome captivity of eight months.* Before this time, no one dared to advise the release of Bertrand; but, on a certain day, when the prince had just risen from dinner and retired to a withdrawing room, and while he was eating comfits with Sir John Chandos, the Lords d'Albret, de

* The battle of Navarrete was fought on the 3rd of April, 1367; and Bertrand's promise to Charles V., to pay him thirty thousand gold doubles, loaned him by the king, to discharge a part of his ransom, is dated the 27th December of that year.—Du Tillet, *Recueil des Traictez, &c.*, and *Inventaire*, p. 94, *verso*.

Clisson, and de Pommiers, Sir Hugh Calverly, and some other knights, and was in one of his most joyous moods, talking of love and arms, of the death of knights, and the ransom of prisoners, it happened that the captivity of St. Louis, and the ransom paid for his release, became the subject of conversation; when the prince remarked that a good knight, whenever taken in arms, and put on his oath by the law of chivalry, should not attempt to make his escape, or leave his prison without his captor's permission; and that the ransom should not be fixed so high as to prevent the knight from arming himself again. Upon this the Lord d'Albret, interposing, said :—

"Noble Sire, be not angry if I mention what I have heard said of you behind your back."

"By my faith!" said the prince, quickly, "I should little love the knight who eats my dinner, and neglects to tell me instantly what he hears that might dishonour me."

"It is said," then spoke out the Lord d'Albret, "that you hold and keep closely confined in your prison a knight whom I can readily name, and whom you do not dare to release, for fear of his great prowess and the injury that he may do you."

"I have myself heard such words many times," added Lord de Clisson; "but, in truth, I did not dare to repeat them."

"I swear to you," said the prince, with much heat, "that I know of no knight, on land or sea, whom I dread so much as to keep confined in my prisons, or that I would not allow to get his discharge."

"What makes you forget Bertrand du Guesclin," said quickly the Lord d'Albret, "who cannot get his discharge?"

At these words the prince coloured deeply, with pride, ire, and disdain struggling for the mastery; and he angrily replied :—

" Bring hither Bertrand, whom you have threatened me with; if he desires his release, he shall have it without delay."

Several knights were at once despatched to the prison of Bertrand, whom they found engaged in a game of chess with Ivon, his chamberlain. As soon as the knights entered the apartment Bertrand arose, and received them with a cheerful welcome; then, turning to his servant, he ordered him to bring some wine; when one of the knights said:—

" A light and joyous heart will accord well with the good news which we bring you."

" My lord," added the oldest of the knights, " come to my lord, the prince: for you are sent for by him. You are not without friends at court, and I believe you will be speedily ransomed."

" Ransomed!" exclaimed Bertrand, " when I have neither denier nor maille, and I owe at least ten thousand livres to the people of this city, which I have spent since I have been here."

" How," asked one of the knights, " have you spent so much?"

" I have eaten and drunk," replied Bertrand, " given it away, and played at dice: for such small sums of money are soon wasted; but I will quickly repay all after I am released."

Bertrand then speedily prepared himself to wait on the prince, and he seemed to have paid but little attention to his toilet, if he had the means: for, when he entered the hall where the prince and his barons were expecting him, clothed in a grey tunic, his appearance was so little imposing, that Edward, smiling, said aside to his lords:—

" By the Virgin Mary! he is not so well habited that, if he had a fair mistress, his embrace would be very agreeable to her."

Bertrand bowed slightly on approaching the prince, who bade him come forward, and inquired of his welfare.

"Sire," replied Bertrand, "I shall be better whenever it shall please you: for a long time I have only heard the rats and mice, until I have had enough of them; and I now await your pleasure to hear again the song of the birds."

"Bertrand," said the prince, smiling at this sally of the Breton knight, "fair sir, this will be as soon as you wish: for it depends only on yourself; but you must take an oath not to arm yourself against me, or my father the king of England, or aid Henry in Spain against Peter. As soon as you have taken this oath, I will not only release you, but I will pay all the debts which you have contracted; and, moreover, I will give you ten thousand florins to provide yourself with arms and horses when you go away. You must take the oath, and then you may leave Bordeaux as soon as that is done; otherwise you shall not go."

Bertrand indignantly refused to take any such oath, declaring that he would sooner die in prison: for he would ever continue to serve those whom he was bound to obey, and especially the king of France.

"Let me go," he added, "as you have already long held me a prisoner against all right and reason: for I had left France, with Sir Hugh Calverly and all my forces, to make war upon the infidels, and thus save our souls."

"And why did you not do it?" asked Edward.

"Because," replied Bertrand, "we found in our way Don Pedro, who had cruelly caused the death of his wife, your cousin, and the daughter of your kinsman the Duke de Bourbon; and we tarried there, not only to avenge her wrongs, but to aid Henry: for I firmly believed him to be the rightful king of Castille. I also remained to put to death the Moors and Jews, whom we found in great numbers throughout that country; but you came with your army for hire, and to obtain the succession to the throne of Castille on the death of Peter, and turned me away from my purpose. And you have lost your own health, famished your people, and sacrificed their lives; while you have been completely deceived by Peter's broken promises and violated covenants."

"There is much truth in what you say," answered the prince; "but you shall not escape me without ransom; and, as it is said that I have kept you in prison through fear of your prowess, to end all such reports, I will discharge you on payment of a just sum."

Bertrand then earnestly entreated the prince at once to fix the amount of his ransom, telling him that he was a poor knight, and not of such a family that he could command large means; that his lands were already mortgaged to pay the expenses of his expeditions; and that he owed, besides, ten thousand livres to the citizens of Bordeaux. The prince then told Bertrand to fix his own ransom, declaring that he should pay no greater sum than that named by himself; whereupon Bertrand, not to be behind the prince in liberality, offered to pay him one hundred thousand gold doubles.*

* There is much diversity of statement among the chronicles as to the amount of the ransom fixed by Du Guesclin. Froissart, who passes hastily over the incidents relating to the liberation of the Breton knight, agrees with Ayala, who is more extended in his account, in stating the sum at one hundred thousand francs. Cuvelier and the anonymous author of the *Chronique de Du Guesclin* make the sum sixty thousand *doubles d'or*. In the chanson, *A Doña Clamenca*, in the Limousin tongue, the amount of the ransom is fixed at *soixanto millia doublous d'or;* while in the obligation given by Bertrand du Guesclin to Charles V., Du Guesclin states that he had undertaken to pay the Prince of Wales for the deliverance of his person "one hundred thousand gold doubles, of the coinage, weight, and alloy of the money current in Castille."—*Pièces Justificatives*, No. XIV., published by Charrière, in his edition of Cuvelier, tom. ii. p. 402. If the double was a coin of Algiers and

At the mention of this sum, Edward and the knights present were greatly astonished. The prince declared that he could not find such an amount of gold, and generously offered to abate one-half of it; but Bertrand persisted in adhering to the sum he had named, not doubting that he would be able to obtain it by the aid of his friends: for he said Henry of Castille would pay one-half of it, and he could borrow the remainder from the king of France; and he confidently added:—

"I dare boast that, if I can get no aid from these two, there is not a spinster in France who can twist a thread that will not thus aid me to procure my ransom, sooner than see me lie any longer in your fetters."

As soon as the amount of the ransom was fixed, Bertrand sent a message to some of his friends in Brittany to inform them of the sum he had to pay for his release, and request them to become his sureties to the Prince of Wales for the payment of the money; adding, that he trusted, through God and the kindness of the king of France, as soon as he was released, to be able to discharge them from the obligation they would thus incur on his account. Immediately on the receipt of this message, the lords, barons, and knights to whom it was sent replied that they were all ready to bind themselves for the amount of his ransom; and, in order to give greater validity to the transaction, each of them sent his squire, with the seal of his master, with power to bind

Tunis, and worth two francs, ninety-five centimes of French money, as stated by some authorities, Froissart and Ayala were evidently mistaken in writing francs instead of doubles: for, apart from the higher evidence of the deed itself, when the amount of the ransom was stated by Bertrand, it was regarded both by Edward and his courtiers as an enormous sum; while Du Guesclin, even before he had acquired any European reputation, had already paid to Sir John Chandos, after the battle of Auray, one hundred thousand francs for his ransom; which, though large for his means, did not occasion at that time any special surprise.

him in any amount that should be necessary. When the squires came to Bordeaux, they saluted Bertrand on the part of their masters, who, they said, had sent him their seals that he might bind them in whatever sums of money he needed, and for any time that was required. Bertrand then arranged his bond with the prince, affixing the seals of the knights to the several sums which each had undertaken to pay.*

Sir John Chandos, to his other good qualities of an able commander and a gallant knight, added the virtue of generosity, even to an enemy. As soon, therefore, as he heard the enormous sum fixed by Bertrand du Guesclin himself as the price of his ransom, he was as much astonished as the other knights, and kindly inquired of him where he would be able to find such an amount. When Bertrand stated that he had many friends, and he had no doubt the money could be easily obtained, Sir John Chandos frankly replied :—

"By my faith ! I shall be rejoiced at it ; but, if you have any need of me, you have only to say so : for I can lend you ten thousand of the amount, as I have that much by me."

"Many thanks, sir," said Bertrand in reply ; "but, before I accept your aid, I desire to test the friendship of my own countrymen."

The surprise of Edward and his knights at the amount of Bertrand's ransom was not confined to the palace of the prince : for, when it became known in the city of Bordeaux, not only the tradesmen, but the better class of citizens, went in crowds to the palace to see a knight who had fixed the

* Ayala, *Cronica del Rey Don Pedro*, p. 499. "In France and England," says the Spanish chronicler, in giving an account of this transaction, "the highest obligation that a knight or man of rank can incur, is in the use of his seal ; as they say it is enough for a man to sign his name, but in the seal are contained the name and arms, as well as the honour of the knight."

amount of his own ransom at one hundred thousand gold doubles. The curiosity of the citizens only served to amuse Du Guesclin, though he probably did not hear the various opinions freely expressed by them as to his appearance, the propriety of his discharge, the means he would employ to procure his ransom, or the spirited defence of him made by one of his admirers among the crowd, who regarded him as one of the best knights in the world, the most skilful in the conduct of a campaign, the most successful in the storming of a castle; and who concluded by declaring that there was not a poor man or woman in France who would not willingly submit to be taxed, or a vine-dresser who would not give a quarter of his wine, sooner than he should longer remain a prisoner.

The Princess of Wales likewise participated in the general curiosity, and she came from Angoulême to Bordeaux, expressly to see Bertrand du Guesclin, whom she sumptuously entertained at dinner; and afterwards, when she had withdrawn to her chamber and ordered wine and comfits, she offered them to him before all the knights present. The princess, who was a great admirer of all gallant and honourable deeds, on taking leave of Bertrand, said to him:—

"My friend, you have been the arbiter of your own ransom, and you have fixed it at a very high price, to which you have been moved by a lofty spirit; but I desire to lessen it, on account of the great virtues which you have shown. Know, therefore, that I will abate ten thousand of your ransom, or pay it out of my own means."

Bertrand, at these words, dropped on his knee before the princess, and profoundly thanked her for her kindness; then said, playfully:—

"Madame, I always thought that I was the most homely knight in the world; but now I see I am handsome, since by the ladies I am loved."

The princess laughed at this repartee, and then dismissed Du Guesclin, who went to make his acknowledgments to the prince before taking leave of him, and whom he found much pleased at the honour done to him by the princess.

After taking the customary oath, that he would not arm himself against the Prince of Wales until his ransom was paid, Bertrand du Guesclin was about leaving the city of Bordeaux, when he was accosted by his old companion in arms, Sir Hugh Calverly, who reminded him of their long service together, how often they had shared equally the booty they had acquired in war and from the ransom of their prisoners, and earnestly pressed on his acceptance ten thousand francs, which he urged belonged not to himself, but to Bertrand, with more besides, which he held at his service. Du Guesclin kindly thanked the English knight for his offer, which he then refused to accept, saying that he did not know how the affair would turn out; but, if he needed his aid, he would not spare him.*

Bertrand du Guesclin, having now gained his liberty, lost no time in putting to the test the faith which he had so confidently expressed in the good offices of his friends, by seeking their aid to enable him to pay his ransom. On his way from Bordeaux he first met the Duke of Anjou, who advanced him thirty thousand francs of the amount he needed; and the king of France, whom he next went to see, loaned him thirty thousand Spanish doubles,† for which he exacted a promise

* Cuvelier, vv. 13,656, 13,765; *Chronique* (Anonyme) *de Du Guesclin*, ch. ciii. civ. cv.

† All the chroniclers who mention the fact assert that it was a *gift* of Charles to Du Guesclin; but Du Tillet shows that it was only a *loan*, which was paid back the following year, by "six bits of paper attached together, serving as receipts for the thirty thousand *doubles of Spain*," which Bertrand, by an obligation dated the 27th of December, 1367, had promised to pay king Charles, as a part of his ransom due to the Prince of Wales.—*Recueil des Traictez, &c.*, and *Inventaire*, p. 94, *verso*;

from Bertrand that he should always hold himself in readiness to come at a moment's warning, whenever his services were required, unless at the time he was a prisoner. With this liberal aid, Du Guesclin then went to visit his friends in Brittany, where the remainder of his ransom was soon made up by Raoul de Treal, Bishop of Rennes, the Viscount de Rohan, the Lords de Laval and de Beaumanoir, Charles de Dinan, and other barons and knights of that duchy. Having thus secured the amount necessary for his own ransom, Bertrand then went to his castle of Roche-Darrien, where "Madame Tiphaine, his wife, was greatly rejoiced to see him."*

Before setting out on his expedition into Spain with the Free Companies, the year before, Bertrand du Guesclin had deposited, for safe-keeping, in the ancient abbey of Mont Saint-Michel, one hundred thousand francs; and, being now in need of all his pecuniary resources, he sent to withdraw the treasure; but he was informed that his wife had taken out and expended the whole of it during his absence; whereupon, when he inquired of her what she had done with the money, she ingenuously answered:—

"My lord, I have distributed it among the knights and squires who have served you, and who came to me to pay their ransoms and provide them with horses, whereby they can again serve you; and all this you may find out from them."

Bertrand was greatly pleased upon learning to what good purposes his treasures had been applied; and he highly applauded the generous conduct of his wife.†

Actes de Bretagne, tom. ii. col. 60; and see *Obligation de Du Guesclin envers Charles V.*, published by Charrière, editor of Cuvelier, tom. ii. p. 402.

* *Chronique* (Anonyme) *de Du Guesclin*, ch. cviii. cix.; Cuvelier, v. 14,302.

† *Chronique* (Anonyme) *de Du Guesclin*, ch. cix.

Having now procured the means of paying his ransom, Bertrand du Guesclin was anxious to obtain his discharge. He therefore completed his preparations for his departure from Brittany without any unnecessary delay, and set out for Bordeaux. While on his way thither, he chanced to alight at an inn by the roadside, where ten knights and squires, who had served under him in Spain, had just stopped for refreshment. They had been taken prisoners at the battle of Navarrete, and released on parole, in order to procure their ransoms. They were all in a wretched condition: some were on foot, the others poorly mounted, while all were meanly dressed, and their clothes worn and broken. After discussing for some time the low state to which they were reduced by their capture and imprisonment, they called the host and ordered some wine.

"And who is to pay for it?" he inquired.

"What are you afraid of?" asked, in turn, one of the squires. "Here are knights and squires enough."

"Knights!" repeated the host, with a sneer; and, with that sharp-sightedness which has always belonged to persons of his occupation, he asked:—"And where have you left your gilded spurs? I could have put up your horses: for I have stable room enough, and oats and hay to feed fifty horses for ten months."

"Ah! good host, do not mock us," said a squire from Nantes. "We come from Bordeaux, and we have had ills enough. Bertrand du Guesclin was our leader, and he was released the other day for sixty thousand gold doubles. Everybody was amazed at the sum, for how can he get such an amount of gold?"

"He will get it easily enough," replied the host: "for I have now ten horses, five hundred head of sheep and fat hogs, and thirty tuns of wine in my cellar, which I will sell for him, besides the furred robes bought by my wife when we were married; and, if he needs them, by God, he shall have all before one can wash a pestle!"

The worthy host then showed that his enthusiasm in the cause of Bertrand du Guesclin was not confined to words alone: for he called his servants, and ordered them to supply his guests with roast meat and pasties, with the best wines of his cellar, and prepare comfortable chambers for them while they remained.

In the midst of their repast Bertrand du Guesclin entered the apartment, where they were seated at table; and, when the knights and squires rose at his approach, he recognised them immediately as his own countrymen, who had formed a part of his command at the battle of Navarrete, although he was much surprised at their altered appearance, and greatly annoyed on seeing their miserable plight. They soon answered his inquiries about their capture, imprisonment, and release; and they informed him of their reception at the inn, and of the good cheer set before them by their host, solely in honour of him. Bertrand then took his seat amongst them, in spite of their protestations that it did not become one so noble as he to sit among such poor knights and squires as they were, and learned from them the sum of their joint ransoms, which amounted to four thousand livres. Calling Ivon, his chamberlain, he ordered him to pay the knights and squires the sum which they had named as the amount of their ransoms, two thousand livres to provide them with horses, and one thousand more for their expenses in going to and returning from Bordeaux, besides one thousand to the host, for an act of generous hospitality towards them on his account. The knights and squires fell on their knees to thank him for such a deed of unexpected liberality from one whom they supposed overwhelmed by the amount of his own ransom, and the innkeeper, with many thanks, begged him to keep his gold and silver, as he had greater need for it than himself; but Bertrand would not listen to the request, declaring that he would not take back a single cross of it.*

Such acts of almost princely liberality, on the part of a knight of ordinary means like Bertrand du Guesclin, might appear simply as an exhibition of unusual and excessive profusion, or as the extravagant statements of a partisan chronicler; but the surprise will be diminished, when it is remembered that no virtue was more extolled among the ancient knights than liberality, and that, on the field or in the hall, it was the constant subject of eulogy with the herald, the minstrel, and the romance writer, who usually made and perpetuated the fame of the knight; although their great exaltation of that virtue did not always merit the praise of disinterestedness, as they were the most common recipients of his bounty.†

The generous conduct of Bertrand du Guesclin towards his destitute soldiers created not a little surprise at Bordeaux, where it was well known how large a sum he had undertaken to pay: for, when the ten knights and squires returned, with the amount of their ransoms, much sooner than they were expected, and announced the fact that Bertrand had not only paid the money for them, but distributed amongst them two thousand livres to equip them again, the seneschal, who heard it, declared that, "in no history since Christ was crucified was such an act spoken of;" and the Princess of Wales, who was informed of it while at dinner with her husband, greatly marvelled at it, and said that she did not regret the assistance she had given him: for she never could employ her means so well.‡

Bertrand du Guesclin continued his journey to Bordeaux,

* Cuvelier, vv. 14,090, 14,239.

† See St. Palaye, *Mémoires sur l'Ancienne Chevalerie*, tom. i. p. 82, and note (73).

‡ Cuvelier, v. 14,273.

where, soon after his arrival, he paid his ransom and obtained his discharge, to the entire satisfaction of the Prince of Wales, who first abated the sum of ten thousand doubles, which the princess had undertaken to pay for him. On leaving Bordeaux, Bertrand went to Montpelier, where he arrived on the 7th of January, 1368, in company with his old companion in arms, the Maréchal d'Audeneham. During their sojourn in this town, Bertrand engaged the services of many leaders of the Free Companies: for he did not intend to abandon the cause of Henry of Castille on account of the loss of a single battle, as he declared to the Duke of Anjou that he would never cease his efforts while he lived, until he had restored King Henry to the place where he was before.

After assembling about two thousand men-at-arms, Bertrand du Guesclin and the Maréchal d'Audeneham commenced their march on the 26th of February, and joined, at Nismes, the Duke of Anjou, who was then making preparations for a military expedition into Provence. It is not known what were the real claims or designs of the duke on that country; but it is supposed that Charles IV., emperor of Germany, having given up to him his rights to the kingdom of Arles,* in the year 1365, the duke had now resolved to profit by the absence of Jeanne, queen of Naples and Countess of Provence, and assert his claims to its possession. As soon, therefore, as he received the very efficient aid brought him by Bertrand du Guesclin and the Maréchal d'Audeneham, the duke crossed the Rhône, and laid siege to Tarascon on the 4th of March. The inhabitants of the town, after enduring many hardships and resisting frequent attacks, both by land and water, for nearly a month, sur-

* The ancient kingdom of Arles comprehended Provence, Savoy, Dauphiné, and Franche-Comté.

rendered to the Duke of Anjou, and acknowledged him as their lord. Encouraged by this success, he then laid siege to Arles, on the 11th of April; but he soon left the conduct of it to Bertrand du Guesclin, and took up his residence at Beaucaire, on the opposite side of the river. During the siege, the pope interposed his good offices between the Duke of Anjou and the queen of Naples; and, while the negotiation was pending, Bertrand raised the siege, and joined the duke at Beaucaire.*

It was not the destiny of Bertrand du Guesclin to be idle for a moment, when so many important events were transacting around him; and, although Charles V. was on the eve of the great struggle with Edward III. for the possession of one-third of his kingdom, yet he regarded the contest then going on in Spain, for the succession to the throne of the Castilles, of sufficient importance to yield up for a time, to his ally Henry, the services of one of his ablest captains. The king of France therefore sent ambassadors into Castille, to renew and extend the treaty of Aigues-Mortes, and inform Henry that he would send immediately to his aid Bertrand du Guesclin, with five hundred lances.†

In consequence of this proceeding of his sovereign, and in accordance with his own expressed determination to restore Henry to his throne, Bertrand du Guesclin, in the beginning of the year 1369, crossed the Pyrenees, and appeared before the camp near the city of Toledo, which had been kept in a state of continued blockade since the

* Cuvelier, vv. 14,329, 14,373, and 14,051; *Chronique* (Anonyme) *de Du Guesclin*, ch. cix.; Froissart, liv. i. part ii. p. 546; Morice, *Hist. de Bretagne*, tom. i. p. 327; Christine de Pisan, *Le Livre des Fais du Sage Roy Charles*, partie ii. ch. x.

† This treaty is dated at the camp, near Toledo, November 20th, 1368.—Ayala, *Cronica del Rey Don Pedro*, p. 536, note (1). Rymer, vol. iii. par. ii. pp. 852, 854.

30th of April of the year before; and, although Henry had many friends in the city, yet all his efforts, by force or address, had proved unavailing, for ten months and a half, against the strength of the fortifications, and the valour and constancy of the garrison.*

* Ayala, *Cronica del Rey Don Pedro*, pp. 534, 535, and 545; Froissart, liv. i. part ii. p. 550.

CHAPTER VII.

Battle of Monteil. Defeat and death of Peter the Cruel.

PETER THE CRUEL, after his unsuccessful attempt on the city of Cordova, returned to Seville, where so many individual deeds of blood had been enacted under his own eyes and by his own hand, to witness the wholesale destruction of his revolted subjects, by his Grenadine auxiliaries. The cities of Jaen and Ubeda were utterly destroyed, the towns of Marchena and Utrera were sacked, and eleven thousand captives—men, women, and children—are computed to have been carried away by the Moors from the latter place alone. With all his irreverence for religion, and contempt for its ministers, Peter was influenced by the gloomiest superstitions; and, acting on the predictions of an astrologer, that he would be forced to stand a siege somewhere, he employed the greater part of his time, after his return from Cordova, in strengthening the fortifications of Carmona, a town about six leagues from Seville, which he supplied abundantly with provisions of all kinds, and where he placed his children and his treasures.*

Unable any longer to resist the importunities of the

* Ayala, *Cronica del Rey Don Pedro*, pp. 527, 529, 536; and *Cronica del Rey Don Enrique Segundo*, p. 15, note (2).

beleagured inhabitants of Toledo, Peter, with a force of three thousand lances, fifteen hundred Moorish horse, and a body of infantry from the towns of Seville, Carmona, Ecija, and Xerez, set out from Seville, with the design of raising the siege of Toledo, or giving battle to Henry. The information of Peter's purpose in leaving Seville was soon brought to Henry, who ordered a council of the leaders of his army to be called; and among them, "in especial, was Sir Bertrand du Guesclin, by whose advice they wished to do everything." In this assembly Bertrand advised Henry to march against Peter without delay, with the greater part of his troops: as their approach would not be expected by him, and much might be gained by taking him by surprise. This advice was followed; and Henry left six hundred men-at-arms, and a portion of his archers and foot-soldiers, under the Archbishop of Toledo, assisted by many nobles and knights, to keep up the blockade of the city. At Orgaz, a town about five leagues from Toledo, Henry was joined by the grand-masters of Sant Jago and Calatrava, Don Juan Alfonso de Guzman, and the other knights and squires, amounting to about fifteen hundred men, who had made the gallant and successful defence of Cordova, against Peter and the Moors of Granada, the year before. These troops, with six hundred lances, under Bertrand du Guesclin, made the forces of Henry amount to about three thousand lances, with some foot-soldiers, who, however, only acted as attendants on the nobles and knights.*

Henry left Orgaz with the intention of giving battle to Peter; and immediately thereafter learnt, through his scouts, who kept him well informed of all the movements of his rival, that Peter had passed Calatrava, and taken a position

* Ayala, *Cronica del Rey Don Pedro*, pp. 546, 547. Froissart, liv. i. part ii. pp. 550, 551, computes the forces on both sides as much greater in number than the Spanish chronicler.

at the castle of Monteil, near the confines of La Mancha. Henry used every means to hasten his march, so as to take Peter by surprise; and in this design he fully succeeded: for Peter, who had no suspicion that his own approach was known, and no fear that he would be attacked by Henry, had taken up his quarters in the castle, and suffered his troops to become scattered about among the hamlets near Monteil. When, therefore, the commandant of the castle saw a number of torches, which were carried by the troops of Henry to guide them through the obscurity of a very dark night, he immediately informed Peter that many large fires could be seen about two leagues from Monteil, and that he would send to ascertain the cause. But Peter had so little apprehension of an attack from Henry, that he told the castellan not to give himself any trouble about the matter, as he supposed the fires proceeded from the troops which had left Cordova, under the grand-masters Mexia and Moñiz, to join Henry at the siege before Toledo; notwithstanding, Peter sent orders to his men to assemble near the castle at daybreak the next morning.

Very early the next day, Henry, who had been on the march with his army since midnight, appeared in sight of Monteil, when he was discovered, and his approach made known by the scouts of Peter, who ranged all his troops, which had then come up, in order of battle. Henry at the same time prepared his men for the attack, and advanced, with the division under his command, against Peter, who was completely surprised by the movement, or, as Froissart expressed it, *taken on one foot;* while Bertrand du Guesclin, with the division composed of the French men-at-arms and the nobles and knights from Cordova, got entangled in an impassable ravine, and, before he could turn the valley and bring his troops into the action, the battle had been already decided against Peter, who took refuge in the castle of

Monteil; and little more was left to be done than the pursuit and slaughter of the vanquished.*

The battle of Monteil was fought on the 14th day of March, 1369, and it seemed likely to decide the hostile claims to the throne of Castille: for Peter had sought temporary safety in a fortress, which, however strong, was not prepared for a siege;† and Henry, with a numerous and well-appointed army, soon showed that he would neglect no means to prevent the escape of a prisoner of such importtance: for he not only threw up a wall of stones around the fortress, but every avenue was strictly guarded; and "it was so closely watched, both night and day, that a bird could not leave the castle without being discovered."‡

As it was soon apparent to every one within the castle that the siege could not endure much longer, and that escape was impossible, but by obtaining the aid of some one of influence in the hostile camp, this expedient was resorted to by Men Rodriguez de Senambria, a liege-man of Bertrand du Guesclin, as Count of Trastamara, but then an adherent of Peter. This knight had been taken prisoner at the siege of Briviesca, in the year 1366, upon Henry's first invasion of Castille; and, as he was a native of the county of Trastamara, his ransom

* Ayala, *Cronica del Rey Don Pedro*, pp. 548, 549. Froissart, liv. i. part ii. p. 551, describes this battle as much more hotly contested than may be inferred from the meagre account of the Spanish chronicler, who is always reluctant to bestow commendation on any but his own countrymen.

† It is said, when Peter entered the castle of Monteil, his superstitious mind at once realized the prediction of the astrologers, who had foretold that he would die in a tower of the star: for "he saw written in gothic letters, on a stone in the tower of homage, these words: *This is the tower of the star.* As soon, therefore, as he read these fatal words, he gave himself up for lost."—Passage copied by Zurita from *El Compendio*, in his *Enmiendas*, and cited by Llaguno, editor of Ayala, in *Addiciones á las Notas. Cronica del Rey Don Pedro*, p. 579.

‡ Froissart, liv. i. part ii. p. 553.

of five thousand florins was paid to his captor, Sir Bernard de la Salle, by Du Guesclin, upon his receiving that county as a gift from Henry. Men Rodriguez, who therefore personally knew Bertrand, requested a private interview with him, which was granted; and, accordingly, one night when the latter was on duty, Men Rodriguez left the castle and came to his post. He opened the conversation by saying :—

"Sir Bertrand, King Pedro, my lord, has commanded me to have a conference with you, and say that you are a very noble knight, and you have always gloried in the performance of heroic actions and good deeds; that you see in what a condition he is; and, if you will deliver him from it, place him in safety, and join his side, he will give you the towns of Soria, Almazan, Atienza, Montagudo, Deza, and Seron, in fee; and he will give you, besides, two hundred thousand doubloons of Castilian gold. And I beg that you will do so: for you will acquire great honour in succouring so powerful a king as he; and all the world will know that by your aid he saved his life and recovered his kingdom."

"My friend," replied Bertrand, "you should well know that I am a knight, a vassal of the king of France and his subject, and that I came to this country at his command to serve King Henry—inasmuch as the King Don Pedro belongs to the English party, and is allied with them, especially against my lord the king of France; that I serve King Henry for pay, and I can do nothing against his interests and honour. Nor should you counsel me to do so; and I beg, if you have ever received any kindness or courtesy from me, that you will never mention this subject to me again."

"My lord Bertrand," rejoined Men Rodriguez, "I well believe that what I tell you may be done without any impropriety; and I entreat, for mercy's sake, that you will take counsel upon it."

Bertrand du Guesclin, upon this, told Men Rodriguez that he would consider the matter, and determine what he would do in such a case; whereupon the Castilian returned to the fortress; and Bertrand the next day related to his friends and kinsmen in the camp, and especially to his cousin Sir Oliver de Manny, what had taken place between Men Rodriguez de Senambria and himself, and asked their advice in the matter: declaring beforehand, that for no inducement in the world would he do such a thing, as King Peter was the enemy of the king of France, his lord, and of King Henry, in whose service he was then engaged; but he desired to know of them whether he should mention to King Henry what Men Rodriguez had offered him, or if he should do anything further about it.

Upon this point all his friends thought that it was his duty to inform Henry of the attempt on his fidelity. Bertrand, acting on their advice, immediately made known to the king the overtures of Peter, through Men Rodriguez; and Henry was so much gratified at the information, that he promised to give Bertrand the same towns and the sum of money which Peter had offered him; but he asked him to assure Men Rodriguez of Peter's safety on coming to his lodge, and that he should be informed of it as soon as Peter came there.

Bertrand du Guesclin gravely doubted the propriety of this step; but his virtue seemed incapable of resisting the manners of his times, the wishes of a king whom he was anxious to oblige, and the importunities of his friends, who urgently pressed him to the measure. He probably felt himself justified in keeping no covenants with a prince whom he regarded as a monster of impiety, lust, and cruelty; and that no faith ought to be observed with one who had attempted to seduce him from his allegiance to his natural sovereign, and his duty to a king whom he was bound to serve. It is not known what assurances were actually given, as the Spanish chronicler goes no further than to assert that "*some persons said*, when Bertrand returned an answer to Men Rodriguez, he assured him of Peter's safety; and that some of his friends promised on oath that he should be put in a place of security." Whatever may have been the promises made, Peter, when he found that he could no longer remain in the castle—trusting to the assurances solemnly given by those with whom Men Rodriguez treated—ventured one night, with Don Fernando de Castro, Diego Gonzalez de Oviedo, Men Rodriguez de Senambria, and others, to go to the lodge of Bertrand du Guesclin, and put himself in the power of the Breton knight. Peter dismounted on reaching the quarters of Bertrand, and, on entering the lodge, thus addressed him:—"Cavalier, it is time for us to go." When Peter received no answer to this remark, he began to doubt the safety of the step that he had taken, and he attempted to remount his horse; when one of the attendants of Bertrand, laying his hand on his shoulder, said quietly:—"Wait a little." Immediately after this Henry entered the lodge, fully armed, with his bacinet on his head.*

* Ayala, *Cronica del Rey Don Pedro*, pp. 551, 555. Such is the account given by Ayala of this transaction; while Froissart makes no allusion to the attempt of Peter to gain over Bertrand du Guesclin to his interests, and only mentions an offer of that prince to the Begue de Villaines, who arrested him in attempting to escape from the castle by night, and promised to provide for his safety; but took him to his own lodge. Cuvelier and the anonymous author of the *Chronique de Du Guesclin* give an account of the affair, in which Bertrand acts no part whatever; and they entirely agree in the following details. One night during the siege, Peter left the castle of Monteil with five attendants; and, in order to descend more secretly, they led their horses by the bridle. The Begue de Villaines was on guard that night; and, when he was informed that some persons were leaving the castle, he took his position, with a body of men, on the causey. When Peter reached that point, and was about to mount his horse, he was arrested by the begue,

Henry, as soon as he came into the apartment where Peter was standing, asked:—"Where is this bastard Jew who calls himself king of Castille?" Peter, who was a brave and haughty man, on hearing this, came forward and said:—"But thou art the bastard; and I am the son of the good King Alfonso." At these words he took Henry by the arms, drew him up, and, in the struggle, threw him—for he was the stronger of the two—and they both fell upon the coverlet of a silken mattress. Peter, who was uppermost, attempted to get at his dagger; when the Viscount de Rocaberti took Peter by the feet and threw him over, which gave the advantage to Henry, who drew a long Castilian knife which he wore under his scarf, and plunged it many times in the body of his brother.*

Thus perished Peter of Castille, on the 23rd day of March, 1369, in the thirty-fifth year of his age. He is represented as possessing many manly qualities. In person

with all his followers. Peter, as soon as he found himself a prisoner, offered his captor every inducement to favour his escape: promising him great riches in gold and jewels, with six cities and twelve castles. The begue rejected all his offers, took him to the tent of Sir Alain de la Houssaie, and sent to inform Henry of the capture. Henry immediately left his lodge, and came where Peter was; and, as soon as he saw him, he called him "Traitor, bastard!"—*Chronique* (Anonyme) *de Du Guesclin*, ch. cxx. cxxi.; Cuvelier, vv. 16,535, 16,761.

* Froissart, liv. i. part ii. p. 534. The personal conflict between the brothers, as told by Froissart, while it does not materially differ from the account of it given by Ayala, is more full and spirited; besides, it is confirmed by an anonymous contemporary Catalan author (Carbonell, it is probable), cited by Llaguno, the editor of Ayala, p. 555, note (8). Cuvelier and the *Chronique de Du Guesclin* give much the same version of the fight as in the text; except that, instead of the Viscount de Rocaberti, the Bastard d'Asnières, at the instance of Bertrand du Guesclin, drew Peter off from Henry; while, in a Spanish ballad of that period, published by Buchon in the appendix to the *Chronique* (Anonyme), p. 97, commencing, *Los fieros cuerpos revueltos*, it is stated that Henry was aided by his own page.

he was of good size, with a ruddy complexion, and he lisped slightly in speaking. He always enjoyed high health: for he was temperate in eating and drinking, and he slept little. He was capable of undergoing great fatigue; and, in some of his journeys, he travelled from twenty to twenty-five leagues in one day. He was excessively addicted to hawking; and it is said that his field sports in that amusement cost him thirty thousand doubles a year. He had a passion for collecting treasures and jewellery; and he carried it to such an extent that, at his death, the jewels of his exchequer, in precious stones, pearls, gold and silver plate, and cloth of gold, were worth thirty millions; while his treasures in gold and silver money, amassed at Seville and other places of security, amounted to one hundred and sixty millions. He was lewd in his habits, irritable in his temper, suspicious in his disposition, and implacable in his anger. Peter fully merited the epithet of *Cruel*, which has been inseparably connected with his name; but, after time had somewhat effaced the memory of his crimes and vices, it came to be remembered by some that "he was a great lover of justice; that his entire kingdom was secure from sedition, theft, and robbery; that he was greatly dreaded by all the kings of Spain, and especially by his ricohombres and knights, who, in their fear of his power, conspired successfully against his throne and his life." *

* Ayala, *Cronica del Rey Don Pedro*, p. 557, and note (8) on page 556.

CHAPTER VIII.

Charles V. is anxious to provoke a quarrel with the English. He entertains an appeal of the nobles of Gascony, who refuse to pay a tax imposed on them by the Black Prince.

BY the death of Peter the Cruel, Henry was now left in undisputed possession of the kingdom of Castille, which he had been effectually aided in gaining through the counsel and arms of Bertrand du Guesclin; but, while he was endeavouring, by the further assistance of the Breton knight, to render the foundations of his throne sufficiently secure to transmit it without question to his posterity, events were rapidly preparing in France which were destined to give full employment to Du Guesclin for the remainder of his life. Charles V of France, who acquired the appellation of *The Wise* by accomplishing the most important results with apparently very inadequate means, was an anxious and well-informed observer of every passing event. Pale, feeble, and sickly; withdrawn from the public gaze in the recesses of his palace; personally little known to his contemporaries, and scarcely known to posterity but by the pedantic and inflated panegyric of Christine de Pisan;—while he took ostensibly no active part in public affairs, suffered no incident to escape him which could be turned to profitable account in accomplishing the great object of his life—the expulsion of the English from

France. The unpopularity of his administration, and the rude treatment which he received while regent, made him distrustful of every one whom he had occasion to employ; while the invasions of his authority by the States-General, and the outbreaks of the people, induced him to entrust no power to the hands of a subject that was not derived immediately from himself, and early determined him to govern alone. Selecting the ministers of his secret and profound policy for their abilities and readiness to serve him, without reference to name or family, he successfully worked out his mysterious plans—leaving scarcely a trace of the means which he employed to execute his designs—without being thwarted by the ambition of his nobles, or defeated by the incompetence of mere rank and power.

Charles, having carefully examined his own situation and resources, gained accurate information of the imprudence and weakness of his adversaries, and fully considered the results of the expedition into Spain, was soon enabled to find a pretext, or, perhaps, a justification, for a rupture with England. He was well persuaded that the English rule was acceptable to very few of the former vassals of the French crown, who had been forced to change their allegiance by the fortune of war, and that nothing would be more agreeable to them than a return to their former masters. He was not unmindful of the ill-feeling between the Black Prince and the Lord d'Albret, occasioned by the peremptory refusal of the prince to retain the men-at-arms whom he had engaged of that nobleman for the Spanish expedition; and he well knew that the career of the Prince of Wales was likely to be cut short by the effects of his exposure to the uncongenial climate of Spain. Charles was therefore prepared to listen to every complaint of his subjects against the Free Companies, who, since their return from the expedition into Spain, had commenced afresh their ravages in the kingdom of France, against the express stipulations of the charters which followed the conclusion of the peace of Bretigny.

It is true that Edward III., by an ordinance dated the 16th of November, 1367, immediately after the return of the Free Companies from Spain, prohibited them from entering France in a hostile manner, under the penalties of banishment from the realm, confiscation of goods, and prosecution as traitors and rebels;* but it probably aggravated the offence in the estimation of the French monarch, that the Black Prince, to whom a special mandate had been sent, enclosing the above-mentioned ordinance, to keep the peace and alliances between the two kingdoms,† when he found himself annoyed by the robberies of the Free Companies, to the number of six thousand, who came to claim the wages that he had promised, but which he was then unable to pay, coolly ordered them out of his principality, telling them that they must live upon some one else, for he would support them no longer. Driven out of Aquitaine, the Companies entered France early in the year 1368, crossed the river Loire, and spread themselves over Champagne and around the neighbourhood of Rheims, Noyon, and Soissons; and, when some of them were taken prisoners, they invariably replied, upon being questioned on the subject, that the Prince of Wales had sent them there.‡

Charles made no formal complaint at that time of the ravages of the Free Companies; but, when the subsequent events, which soon followed, gave him the occasion to use them against the English, he did not hesitate to make them fully available for the important object he had in view. In order to carry out his purposes more fully, he first turned his attention in a different direction; and he not only suc-

* Rymer, vol. iii. par. ii. p. 834.

† *Ibid*, p. 835.

‡ Froissart, liv. i. part ii. p. 546.

ceeded in detaching from Edward a distinguished Breton noble, Sir Oliver de Clisson—who had been a constant adherent of the family of De Montfort and the English, ever since the decapitation of his father, Lord de Clisson, by order of Philippe de Valois, in the year 1343—but he promoted the marriage of Lord d'Albret with Margaret de Bourbon, his sister-in-law; "which marriage," says Froissart, "the Prince of Wales was by no means rejoiced at; but he much preferred that the Lord d'Albret had married somewhere else."*

The Black Prince then lived in great state at Bordeaux, and at greater expense than any monarch of his time: for he and his princess always kept about them a numerous retinue of knights and squires, of dames and damsels.† A large revenue was therefore necessary to maintain such an establishment. Besides, the prince was deeply in debt to the leaders of the Free Companies, for wages due to their troops on account of the expedition into Spain; but he declared that he would pay and satisfy all, wherever the money was to come from, or at whatever cost: for he was resolved to fulfil his own promises, although Peter of Castille had not kept the engagements made with him. The prince was therefore advised by his council, and especially by his chancellor, the Bishop of Bath, to raise a revenue by the imposition of a tax on every fire, throughout the principality of Aquitaine, in order to supply his necessities. Acting on this advice, the prince caused to be summoned the barons of Gascony,

* Froissart, liv. i. part ii. p. 547.

† Cuvelier says of him, verse 10,619, that he would be served only by knights :—

> " Car li princes estoit de telle auctorité
> Que nuls ne le servoit de vin ne de claré,
> Ne d'espices ausi, ne de biens à plenté,
> S'il n'estoit chevalier à esperon doré."

Poitou, and Saintonge, and many influential citizens from the cities and towns of Aquitaine, to a parliament to be assembled at Niort.

When the parliament met, the chancellor, in the presence of the Prince of Wales, explained to the assembly for what purpose the tax was to be raised; and that it was not the design of the prince to make it permanent, but to continue it only for five years, until the money due for the Spanish expedition should be paid. To this imposition the barons and other deputies of Poitou, Saintonge, Limousin, Rouergue, and Rochelle consented, on the condition that the prince would not debase the coin for seven years; but the Count d'Armagnac, the Lord d'Albret, the Counts de Périgord and de Comminges, the Viscount de Carmaing, the Lords de Barde, de Terride, and de Pincornet, and many great barons and knights of the high marches of Gascony, and the deputies of the cities and towns under their jurisdiction, would not consent to the imposition of this tax on their lands, on the ground that, in times past, while they were under subjection to the king of France, they had never been aggrieved or oppressed by any subsidy, imposition, or tax on fire or salt,* nor should any be put on them if they could prevent it: for their lands and lordships were free and exempt from all rents, and the prince himself had sworn to maintain them in that state. They added, notwithstanding, that they would advise about the matter; and, when they returned home, they would assemble the prelates, bishops, abbots, barons, and knights, to whom it appertained to consult with greater deliberation than they had been able to do. This conclusion of the Gascon barons and deputies, however, was only an expedient to get away from Niort without offending the

* Tax on fire or salt: *fouage ou gabelle.* The *fouage* was an annual tax levied on each fire; in the time of Charles V., it was four livres tournois. The *gabelle* was a tax on salt.

prince; but it was all the answer that he could get from them; whereupon the parliament was adjourned, and the members were ordered to reassemble on a day named. But the Gascon lords would not return; and they declared that they would make war on the prince, sooner than this *fouage* should be levied on their lands.*

This bold declaration of the Gascon nobles, however unpalatable to a prince of such will and temper as Edward, was nothing more than what might have been looked for from their situation and his previous course towards them. As tenants *in capite*, they were required to yield him military service, with its attendant incidents, and grant such *aids* as the rigid rules under which they held their lands exacted; but that was all. For the purposes of foreign conquest, or to aid an ally of the prince, with whom they had no sympathy, it was not expected that they were to impose burdens on their people; and, therefore, it was only a reasonable demand, when, distrusting the extravagant offers of Peter the Cruel, they required security for their own pay and that of their troops before setting out on the Spanish expedition; and this the Black Prince at once acknowledged, by promising to become responsible for any failure on the part of the fugitive king of Castille to meet his engagements with them. Taxation was a measure wholly opposed to the genius of the feudal system; and, consequently, it was felt by the Gascon nobles to be an intolerable grievance, and a precedent dangerous in principle, to be forced not only to lose their own stipulated wages, but submit to a tax for the purpose of defraying the expenses of a foreign expedition, which they neither advised nor approved.

Having taken a step so important, which was nothing less than an act of defiance, offered to so haughty a prince as

* Froissart, liv. i. part ii. p. 548.

Edward, the Gascon barons immediately repaired to Paris, brought their complaint before the Chamber of Peers, and claimed the right of appeal to the king of France, as the sovereign to whom they should resort. Charles V well knew how deeply his interference, in a matter of so much delicacy as a contest between a lord and his barons, would be resented by the Prince of Wales. He was, therefore, unwilling to appear as the first to provoke the quarrel; and he answered, warily, that he would assuredly always keep and augment the jurisdiction of his inheritance and of the crown of France; but that he had sworn, with his father, to many parts and articles of a treaty of peace, all of which he did not then remember. He promised at once to examine into it, and aid them to maintain fully everything he found therein favourable to the Gascon lords; adding, moreover, that he would endeavour to bring about a reconciliation with the Prince of Wales, "who, perhaps, was not well advised." The Gascons were so fully satisfied with this reply of Charles, that they did not then return to their own country, but remained near a year in Paris with the king, who paid their expenses, gave them handsome presents in money and jewels, and every day he secretly inquired of the Gascon nobles, if the peace was broken between him and the English, whether they would sustain him.*

Besides such presents to the Gascon lords, Charles V., by a secret treaty with three of their principal leaders, bound these to his interests by large donations in land and money. To the Count d'Armagnac he gave the counties of Bigorre and Gaure, Montreal, Mevin, and a number of other towns, the homage of Casaubon and of many other places, with an annual revenue on the receipts of Languedoc of one hundred thousand francs during the war, for the purpose of

* Froissart, liv. i. part ii. p. 559.

carrying on hostilities against the Prince of Wales, guarding his own fortified places, and attracting adherents to the cause of the king of France. To the Lord d'Albret, besides the dowry of thirty thousand francs, given in consequence of his marriage with Margaret de Bourbon, and other large pensions, he allowed an annual pay of sixty thousand francs for the expenses of the war; and to the Count de Périgord he gave forty thousand francs a year for the same purpose. With all the Gascon lords he made a public treaty on the 28th of December, 1368, in which he promised to entertain their appeal against the Prince of Wales, aid them if either Edward III. or his son made war upon them, and confirm the privileges, franchises, usages, customs, and liberties of all who came under his subjection.*

The opposition of the Gascon nobles only served to make the Prince of Wales more determined than before to persist in the imposition of the *fouage;* and he continued to press the matter the more urgently on the attention of his council. The policy of the measure, however, was not advocated by all the members of that body; and well it might have been for Edward if he had followed on this occasion, as he did whenever he was successful, the advice of the ablest, the wisest, and the most fortunate of his counsellors. It is difficult now to say how much of the reputation accorded to the Black Prince is not really due to Sir John Chandos, who was, without question, one of the most prudent advisers, one of the bravest knights, and one of the most skilful generals of his time. Not to speak of the battle of Crécy, where Edward, when he "won his spurs," was only a boy of sixteen, but ten years later, at Poitiers, Sir John Chandos certainly had the control of every movement of the English army: for, in Froissart's language:—"With the prince, to

* Du Tillet, *Recueil des Traictez, &c.*, pp. 88, *verso*, and 89, *recto*.

guard and counsel him, was Sir John Chandos, who never left him during the day, for anything that happened;" and, ten years after that event, at the battle of Navarrete, the brunt of the contest was borne by the same able leader, who "that day counselled and governed the Duke of Lancaster in the same manner as he formerly did his brother, at the battle of Poitiers." *

Sir John Chandos, on the occasion when the question of the imposition of the *fouage* on the principality of Aquitaine was before the council of the Black Prince, strenuously opposed the project, and urged Edward to abandon the tax; but, when he perceived that his advice was unheeded, and desiring not to be involved in the consequences of a measure which he foresaw would be disastrous to all concerned in enforcing it, he obtained leave of absence from the court of the prince, under a pretext that he desired to go into Normandy to visit his estate of Saint-Sauveur, where he remained about a year.†

The Prince of Wales was extremely irritated on hearing that Charles V had entertained the appeal of the Gascon lords against an ordinance of his council, and he regarded it as an impertinent interference in the government of his principality: for he asserted that, when the king of France gave up the lands in question, under the terms of the treaty of Bretigny, he expressly surrendered all sovereignty and jurisdiction over them, with every claim or right of appeal, and no such right had been reserved by those who formed the treaty on the part of the king of France.‡ To this it was replied, by the Gascon lords, that it was not in the power of the king of France, as a sovereign, to surrender his

* Froissart, liv. i. part ii. pp. 346 and 537.

† *Ibid*, p. 548.

‡ Rymer, *Littera Regis Franciæ de terris liberandis et renuncionibus faciendis*, vol. iii. par. i. p. 522.

jurisdiction over his vassals; and that the prelates and barons and the cities and towns of Gascony would not permit it, even though the kingdoms of France and England should remain always at war.*

The Gascons, having now resolved to throw off the English yoke, continued to press their demands for aid on the French monarch; but Charles, who well knew that the matter would only end in war between the two countries, and being unwilling to declare his intentions until he was ready to act, with his usual prudence and reserve, exhibited the appearance at least of hesitation and doubt concerning the questions at issue between the Prince of Wales and his refractory subjects; when, the barons becoming impatient under the delays of the king of France, threatened that, if he would not do them justice, they would go elsewhere, and resort to the court of some other lord, who would maintain their rights—whereby, they concluded, he would lose his seigniory. To the entreaties of the Gascon lords, the Count de St. Pol, a distinguished French nobleman, who had been one of the hostages in England, until the ransom of King John was paid, added all the weight of his influence. He had broken his parole, and lately left England without leave. Conscious of the grievous wrong he had committed,† he now hated the English; and, as he was anxious to see the two countries involved in war, he counselled Charles to grant the prayer of the Gascon nobles. In this advice, many of the French prelates, counts, barons, and knights joined; and they contended that neither the king of England nor the Prince of Wales had in any manner kept the peace, according to the tenor of the treaty concluded at Bretigny, and afterwards confirmed at Calais: for they had covertly and subtilely made

* Froissart, liv. i. part ii. p. 555.

† See, in Rymer, *Littera Obsidum Regis Franciæ Obligatoria*, vol. iii. par. i. p. 537.

war upon the kingdom of France to a greater degree since than before the peace.

Charles, to preserve still the appearance of deliberation, ordered the charters signed at Calais to be brought before him, and had them examined in the presence of the prelates and barons of France, who, after a mature consideration of their contents, declared that neither Edward III. nor his son had observed the treaty, but that they had taken fortresses, castles, and towns, and held possession of them, to the great damage of the kingdom; that they pillaged the people and put them to ransom, whereby the payment of the redemption of the late king was still in part due; and, therefore, that the king of France and his people had good right and just cause to break the peace, make war on the English, and take from them the possessions which they held in France.*

To this public declaration a secret exhortation was added to the king, to prosecute the war with all vigour, for he had a just cause; that, as soon as it was commenced, three-fourths of Aquitaine would declare for him; that the inhabitants of Poitou, Saintonge, Quercy,† Limousin, Rouergue,‡ and Rochelle, could never love the English, whatever appearances they might put on: for the English were unsociable and disdainful, and held the people in contempt; and, more-

* Froissart, liv. i. part ii. p. 557. The charters signed at Calais, October, 24th, 1360, are found in Rymer, vol. iii. par. i., from page 514 to page 542. Charles V. could have used with more effect the charters entitled *Littera super liberatione fortalitiorum*, p. 535, and *De rebellibus contra pacem reprimendis*, p. 537, than the one recited in full by Froissart, liv. i. part ii. p. 556, which is not in Rymer.

† Quercy was an ancient division of France, forming a part of Guienne. Cahors was the capital. It now comprehends very nearly the present departments of Lot, Tarn, and Garonne.

‡ Rouergue, an ancient province of Guienne. It now forms the department of Aveyron.

over, the gentlemen of the country could never obtain any offices, for the English and the knights of the prince always appropriated everything.

Before acting on this advice, Charles desired to see his course still more clearly; and, although pretty well assured of the favourable inclinations of many of the English vassals in the southern provinces, he was anxious to know how those of Abbeville and Ponthieu, in the north, were disposed towards him. Proceeding secretly, but adroitly, to sound them, he was gratified to find that they desired nothing so much as to become French, so greatly they hated the English. "Thus," adds Froissart, "the king of France gained friends on all sides: for, otherwise, he would not have dared to do what he did." *

* Froissart, liv. i. part ii. pp. 557, 559.

CHAPTER IX.

Charles V. cites the Black Prince to appear before the Chamber of Peers at Paris, on the appeal of the Gascon nobles. Irritation of the prince on receiving the summons. Charles declares war against England.

CHARLES V., having now determined to adopt a recommendation of his council, in citing the Prince of Wales to appear before the Chamber of Peers at Paris, on the appeal of the Gascon lords, had a paper prepared to that effect, which was sent by the hands of Bernard Palot, criminal judge of Toulouse, and Jean de Chaponval. The envoys found the prince at Bordeaux, in the abbey of Saint André, where he lodged and kept his court. They were courteously received by him, who first examined their credentials, and then bade them speak out what they had to say. Bernard Palot produced the paper, which he said he had been ordered by the king of France to read in the presence of the Prince of Wales. At seeing this, the prince coloured up with surprise; however, he restrained himself, and told the messengers to speak out, for he was willing to hear all good news. Palot then read the paper, which was in the form of an ordinary summons, commanding the Prince of Wales to appear in the city of Paris, and present himself, without delay, before the king of France, in his Chamber of Peers, upon a complaint of the Gascon lords, who claimed the right of appeal to his court.*

The prince was mute with astonishment on hearing the purport of this paper. He shook his head from side to side, looking by turns at the two Frenchmen; and, after some reflection, said:—"We will go willingly, since we have been so commanded by the king of France, on our own appointed day; but it will be with a bacinet on our head, and sixty thousand men in our company." The two envoys, frightened beyond measure at the manner of the prince, fell on their knees, and entreated him not to be so angry, or take the matter so much to heart; and reminded him that they were only servants, who were bound to do the bidding of their master. "No," said the prince, "I have no ill-will against you, but against those who sent you here. And your king," he continued, "is not well advised, who bands with my people, and wishes to constitute himself a judge of what in no wise concerns him: for it can easily be shown that, in putting my father in possession of the whole duchy of Aquitaine, he abandoned all sovereignty over it; they who have sent their appeal against me have no other resort than in the court of my father in England; and, before it shall be otherwise, it will cost a hundred thousand lives."

The Prince of Wales then withdrew into another chamber, and the French envoys, upon leave being granted, returned to their hotel in the city, which they soon after left, without hinderance; but they had not proceeded far, when the prince, who was still greatly irritated at the appeal of the Gascon lords, was advised by some of his attendants to order the Frenchmen to be put to death for the insult which they had

* Froissart, liv. i. part ii. pp. 559, 560; Du Tillet, *Recueil des Traictez, &c.*, p. 89, *recto et verso.*

offered him. That he refused to do; but, upon hearing that they had left Bordeaux precipitately, he ordered them to be apprehended and thrown into prison, on the ground that they were the messengers of his subjects, rather than of the king of France.*

Edward was justly irritated at an insult which was as unexpected as it seemed gratuitous and offensive; and he fully designed, as he had said in his reply to the summons, when read by the envoys, to obey it, and appear in Paris the ensuing summer, at the fair of Landi.† He sent, therefore, without delay, to inform the English and Gascon leaders of the Free Companies, who were under his allegiance, that they must not wander off too far, but hold themselves in readiness, as he would soon again require their services. But Edward was no longer the vigorous and enterprising prince who, two years before, entered Spain in high health and spirits, captivated with the reputation which he expected to acquire, by eclipsing the fame of the most distinguished of the French leaders, and restoring a fugitive monarch to his throne.

The climate of that country and the incidents of the campaign had been most unfavourable to both his health and spirits, and he was attacked by a malady which grew worse from day to day; and at this time, to the deep grief of his attendants, by whom he was greatly beloved, it was perceived that he could no longer ride. To no one was the state of his health better known than to his ever-vigilant enemy, the king of France, who was kept accurately informed of every event that passed at Bordeaux; and he was now advised by

* Froissart, liv. i. part ii. pp. 559, 561.

† *La fête du Lendit.* The fair of Landi opened in the month of June. See Du Tillet, *Recueil des Roys de France*, p. 235; Menage, *Dic. Etymol.*, voc. *Landi;* and Buchon's note to Froissart, liv. i. part ii. p. 563.

his physicians that the Black Prince was prostrated by a fatal and incurable dropsy.*

As soon as the Count de Périgord and the other Gascon leaders, who were then on their estates, heard of the imprisonment of the envoys sent to Bordeaux, they resolved to take revenge for the injury; whereupon they laid an ambush for Sir Thomas Wakefaire, the seneschal of Rouergue, and attacked him about two leagues from the town of Montalban. As the Gascons were greatly superior in numbers, the English were soon put to flight, and many of them slain and taken prisoners. Their leader owed his safety to the swiftness of his horse, and took refuge in the friendly town of Montalban. The Prince of Wales was forced to bear, for a time, this additional affront from his rebellious subjects; only threatening them to take speedy and ample satisfaction on the persons and estates of those who had committed the offence. He thereupon sent immediately for his trusted counsellor, Sir John Chandos, who was still in the Cotentin, to come to him without delay.†

Charles V., while covertly using every means to prepare for a rupture between France and England—by tempting the vassals of Edward to revolt, and by retaining all the leaders of the Free Companies whom he could secretly entice from the service of the English—still remained tranquil in Paris, keeping his own subjects quiet, and especially his brother, the Duke of Anjou, who was impatient for the commencement of hostilities between the two countries. Before taking any decisive step that would lead to war, Charles was also anxious to see how the Gascon lords would sustain themselves in their first trial of strength with the Prince of Wales. During this time, while completing his preparations, he endeavoured to amuse Edward III., who was far from seeking

* Froissart, liv. i. part ii. p. 563.

† *Ibid.*

any difficulty with France, by sending him a present of fifty tuns of wine; which, however, the English monarch, now probably aware of the real designs of Charles, coldly returned to the donor.*

Edward III., being informed that Charles V had entertained the appeal of the Gascon lords, sent to require him, by letter, to dismiss their appeal, and declare himself openly against them. To these demands the king of France replied by his ambassadors, the Count de Saarbruck and Sir Guillaume de Dormans; and in turn complained of the ravages of the Free Companies through the remissness of Edward and his son, as well as of the non-performance of certain renunciations that the king of England had promised to make under the treaty of Bretigny. To these complaints of the king of France, Edward responded by an order of his council, "called a bull," to the effect that, if Charles would remedy the wrong which he had committed, in attempting to undermine the authority of the Prince of Wales by entertaining the appeal of the Gascon lords, bring back the appellants into strict obedience to the king of England, make renunciation of all sovereignty and jurisdiction in the question between the prince and his Gascon subjects, and send letters to that effect to Calais—that then the king of England would make the renunciation required to be done on his part. This unsatisfactory paper led to the call of a representative assembly at Paris, on the 9th of May, 1369, which body, after a short deliberation, recommended a declaration of war against England.†

* See Rymer, *Pro pincerna prædicto, de vino, ex parte Regis Franciæ, ad Regem misso, remittendo*, vol. iii. par. ii. p. 864.

† Du Tillet, *Recueil des Traictez, &c.*, pp. 89, *verso*, and 90, *recto.* Froissart, liv. i. part ii. p. 564. Some doubt exists whether the body referred to in the text was an assembly of the States-General or the parliament of Paris. See Du Tillet, *Recueil des Traictez, &c.*, p. 89,

Charles V., having made all his preparations for war, was too impatient even to await the return of his ambassadors, the Count de Saarbruck and Sir Guillaume de Dormans; and, being now ready to strike an effective blow, on an undefended point, he resolved to close every avenue to peace, by a needless and provoking insult. Accordingly, he departed from the usual practice of declaring war through the agency of some one of rank or reputation—as a bishop, a baron, or a knight—and on this occasion, in order to exasperate the English to the utmost, sent a defiance to Edward III. by a common kitchen-boy.

As the success of the blow meditated by Charles against the power of the English depended on expedition, the Count de St. Pol and Sir Hugh de Chatillon, who were lying in wait for the purpose, marched into the county of Ponthieu, as soon as it was believed that the letter of defiance had been delivered to the king of England. With a force of one hundred and twenty lances, they appeared before the town of Abbeville, on the river Somme, which opened its gates without resistance; and, in the space of a few days, the English were driven out of the whole county of Ponthieu, which had cost Edward III., in repairing the castles, towns, and houses, one hundred thousand francs above the ordinary revenues.*

This speedy commencement of hostilities, following so quickly the insult offered to the English monarch, by a defiance sent through a scullion, aroused the English nation

verso; Recueil des Roys de France, p. 177; *Recueil des Rangs des Grands de France*, p. 387; *Histoire des Français*, par M. de Simondi, tom. xi. p. 106; and "Lectures on the History of France," by Sir J. Stephen, p. 275.

* Froissart, liv. i. part ii. pp. 566, 567. The county of Ponthieu was acquired by Edward I. through his wife, Eleanor of Castille, on the death of her mother, the queen of Castille, in 1279.—Rapin, "History of England," vol. i. p. 359.

to very active efforts to maintain what they had acquired in France, at the expense of so much blood and treasure. Besides fitting out a strong naval force, designed to meet a similar armament of the French at sea,* the English parliament, by an act of the 3rd of June, 1369, recommended the king to resume the title of king of France; whereupon Edward wrote to his son, the Black Prince, on the 19th of the same month, that he had not only determined to take again the title of king, but that he had resolved to do everything in his power to recover possession of the realm and crown of France. In order to induce his great vassals and others to aid him more effectually in maintaining his claims and securing his conquests, the king of England granted to them, by Act of Parliament, the right to hold, in fee, whatever duchies, counties, cities, towns, lands, or possessions they might acquire in the kingdom of France.†

While Charles V. was receiving the willing submission of some of the English towns in the north of France, and seizing upon the whole county of Ponthieu, his brothers, the Dukes of Anjou and Berry, in the southern and middle provinces, were prepared with their levies, which were ordered to assemble, the one at Toulouse, and the other in Auvergne, to attack the Prince of Wales along the whole intermediate frontiers of Aquitaine. The Duke of Anjou, then governor of Languedoc, sent ten thousand men to invade the territories of the prince, under the Counts de Com-

* This apprehended invasion of the French must have been regarded as quite formidable by Edward, from an order of his council, dated July 6, 1369, and directed to the Archbishop of Canterbury, in which he requires all abbots, priors, monks, and other ecclesiastical persons, to arm themselves with suitable armour, and hold themselves in readiness to oppose the great fleet of ships which the French had assembled to invade the kingdom.—Rymer, vol. iii. par. ii. p. 876.

† Froissart, liv. i. part ii. p. 567; Rymer, vol. iii. par. ii. pp. 868 and 874.

minges, de Périgord, and de Lille; and, though many feats of arms were performed between the hostile parties, in their various attacks, defences, rescues, and skirmishes, the campaign resulted in nothing more important than the capture of certain fortified places of no great consequence. The Duke de Berry, on his part, assembled the barons of Auvergne, Lyonnais, and the bishopric of Macon, and entered Poitou in a hostile manner; but he found the province so well defended by a competent force of men-at-arms, that he could obtain no advantage over them. Another party of French, at the same time, composed of the nobles of Maine and Anjou, under Lord Amauri de Clisson, attacked the frontiers of Poitou at another point, and pursued an English detachment as far as Saint-Sauveur, in Lower Normandy.*

It was not, however, wholly by arms or open hostility that Charles V. designed to overthrow the English dominion in France. His secret and successful negotiations with nearly all the leaders of the Free Companies who were not English, and whom he seduced from the service of the Black Prince, was a stroke of policy that was especially irritating to Edward, as their defection not only deprived him of a material part of his best troops, but it was probably more keenly felt by him as an indication of his declining credit: for these mercenary soldiers, only intent on pay or plunder, thought that they were now likely to receive higher or more assured wages from the king of France than from the Prince of Wales, who was yet largely indebted to them on arrearages due for their services in Spain.†

With so many motives for hostility towards Charles V.,

* Froissart, liv. i. part ii. pp. 564, 567; *Actes de Bretagne*, tom. i. col. 1632.

† Froissart, liv. i. part ii. pp. 564, 568; Du Tillet, *Recueil des Traictez, &c.*, p. 90, *recto.*

although somewhat surprised at the rapidity with which his blow followed his defiance, Edward III. and the Black Prince were equally diligent in their preparations; and they used every means in their power to avenge the insult offered to the English monarch, as well as to retain their possessions in the kingdom of France. Sir John Chandos promptly obeyed the mandate of the prince, entered into the campaign with his usual ardour, and proceeded, with the Captal de Buch* and a large body of men-at-arms, to invade the territories of the Count d'Armagnac and the other great Gascon barons, who had revolted from their allegiance to his master. Sir Hugh Calverly also returned from Aragon with a considerable force of mercenaries, which, added to some other bands belonging to the Free Companies from Normandy, made his command amount to two thousand fighting men. The Earls of Cambridge and Pembroke were sent from England with a well-appointed army; and their array, when marched to the invasion of the county of Périgord, amounted to fully three thousand effective men. The Duke of Lancaster followed these with a large naval armament; and Sir Robert Knolles, the most powerful leader of the Free Companies, as soon as he heard that the French had declared war against England, left Brittany, where he possessed "a large and fair heritage," and went to serve the Prince of Wales, with a force of sixty men-at-arms and as many archers, at his own expense. Such a leader was, of course, well received by the Black Prince, who immediately created him commander of all the knights of his household, and sent him into Quercy, with a force of five hundred men-at-arms, five hundred archers, and as many foot-soldiers. But all this

* In a grant, at this period, of the county of Bigorre to the Captal de Buch, by the Prince of Wales, Edward styles himself *Prince of Wales, Lord of Biscay and of Castro de Ordiales.*—Rymer, vol. iii. par. ii. p. 874.

preparation was followed by no corresponding result. A few towns changed hands, a few fortresses were taken—sometimes one party gained, and sometimes another; and the campaign is, perhaps, only worthy of note for the excessive severity of the conquerors to the conquered, in the indiscriminate butchery of the inhabitants of certain towns, and, what was far more common, in the predatory incursions of that period, "in laying waste and destroying the whole open country, and reducing the poor people to great misery." *

* Froissart, liv. i. part ii. pp. 563, 581.

CHAPTER X.

A change in the fortunes of Edward III. The death of Sir John Chandos. Bertrand du Guesclin is recalled from Spain. His first exploits after his return to France.

THE life of Edward III. of England had been, up to this period, one of uninterrupted prosperity. He had safely passed through all the dangers of a minority of six years, acquired the respect of his subjects, and extended the English dominion over a third of France. But, as the evils as well as the good of life commonly come in clusters, the latter part of Edward's career was clouded by sorrows; and the success of a prosperous reign of forty-two years was forgotten in the public and private calamities which attended the closing seven years of his administration. The death of his third son, Lionel, Duke of Clarence, recently married to a daughter of the Duke of Milan, before the festivities which followed the wedding were well over, and so sudden that it was not without suspicions of foul play, was the first incident to interrupt the course of his prosperity. This was followed by the revolt of his Gascon subjects and the interference of the king of France in the government of Aquitaine, which incidents were greatly aggravated to Edward by the declining health of the Black Prince. Close upon these events was the death of Philippa, his queen: a woman of sense and character, with whom he had lived in harmony for forty years. To the now certain intelligence of the incurable nature of the malady of the Prince of Wales, was not long afterwards added the saddening news of the death of Edward, the eldest son of the prince,* leaving to the king the gloomy prospect, from his own premature decay, of his grandson exposed, during a long minority, to the ambition of his sons and the turbulence of his nobles.

The incident of this period which closed the year of calamities to the king of England, and which more, perhaps, than any other affected the dominion of himself and the Prince of Wales in France, was the death of the ablest general in the English service, and the only one, except the two Edwards, competent to cope with that leader who was about to be recalled from Spain, and placed at the head of the French armies, with the universal assent of the nation. Sir John Chandos, after the end of the campaign of 1369, having recently been created seneschal of Poitou, upon the death of Sir James Audley, while retaining his other appointments, was returning to the city of Poitiers, after an unsuccessful attempt on the fortress of St. Salvin, when he overtook, about daybreak of the 31st of December, a considerable body of men-at-arms and archers, composed of French and Bretons, at the bridge of Lussac, over the river Vienne; and, although inferior in numbers, he did not hesitate to offer them battle.†

After some threatening language, directed towards the two leaders of the opposite party, Sir Louis de Saint-Julien and the Breton Kerauloet, in which Sir John Chandos charged

* This event did not occur until the beginning of January, 1371.

† Froissart, liv. i. part ii. p. 600, sets down the number of Sir John Chandos's men at forty lances, and mentions the forces of the French as *une grosse route*—a large body, without numbering them. Cuvelier, v. 18,917, and the author of the *Chronique* (Anonyme) *de Du Guesclin*, ch. cxxxix., estimates them at fifty lances and eighteen archers.

them with making frequent inroads into his province, putting the people to ransom, and treating the country as their own, he added, that he had heard that they oftentimes desired to meet him. "So you have found me," he continued, sneeringly: "I am John Chandos; look at me well; and we will test, if God pleases, your great feats of arms, which are now so renowned."

These words provoked a Breton man-at-arms, who struck a squire of Sir John Chandos with his lance, and unhorsed him by the blow. Chandos, seeing this, exclaimed to his troops:—"How! will you suffer this man to be slain? Dismount! dismount!" Immediately he and his men dismounted, and the squire was rescued. In this manner the battle commenced.

Sir John Chandos was a model of knighthood. He was tall in person, and possessed of every manly grace and accomplishment. On this occasion, with his banner displayed before him, and supported by his men, with one foot advanced, and lance in rest, he fell upon the enemy. He had on at the time, thrown over his armour, a large silken robe,* which trailed on the ground. The robe was blazoned in two places with his arms, "which were argent, a sharp stake gules," one in front and the other on the back. The ground was still moist from the dew, and he became somewhat entangled in his robe, which was rather long, so that he tripped and nearly fell. At this moment he received a thrust from a lance, aimed by a squire named Jacques de St. Martin, a strong and expert man-at-arms; and the point entering the

* *D'une blanc samit*, says Froissart. "*Samy*, a kind of half-silk cloth, which resembles satin; but it is narrower, and more lasting."—Menage, *Dic. Etymol.*; and see Du Cange, Gloss. voc. *Exametum.* According to Bescherelle, the name was formerly given to a very rich stuff which came from Venice. It was woven with threads of gold and silver.—Voc. *Samis.*

socket of the eye, which he had lost some five years before, in a stag-hunt near Bordeaux, pierced the brain. Sir John Chandos, upon receiving the thrust, immediately fell upon the ground, and never spoke afterwards. His followers, notwithstanding the mortal wound received by their chief, whom they greatly loved for his knightly qualities, continued the fight until they were overpowered by the superior numbers and endurance of the French; but a body of two hundred English lances coming up, under Lord Guiscard d'Angle, the lately victorious French, seeing no chance of escape, as their horses had been carried off by their servants, yielded themselves as prisoners to those whom they had just defeated, instead of to the new comers, under Lord d'Angle. "The gentle knight," says Froissart, in his warm tribute to the worth of Sir John Chandos, "lived after this wound but a day and night, and then died. God has the soul of him for his gentleness: for never, during a hundred years, was one more courteous, or full of all good and noble virtues and conditions among the English, than he."*

Edward III., deserted by fortune, and though not old, yet feeling the pressure of age, was no longer the haughty and confident prince who, under a mere shadow of right, had, during three successive reigns, inflicted unnumbered woes on France. He therefore endeavoured to bring back his Gascon vassals to their allegiance by gentler methods than those which he first employed; and, accordingly, he addressed letters patent to all their leaders in Aquitaine, and sent copies, secretly, to those who were in Paris, prepared in the most conciliatory spirit, in which he promised that the Prince of Wales should thereafter desist from all attempts to levy impositions on them; that all grievances should be redressed; and that full pardon should be granted to all who had taken

* Froissart, liv. i. part ii. pp. 598, 602.

sides with his enemy the king of France. But the stern and inflexible administration of the Black Prince in Aquitaine, the wasteful extravagance of his court, and the supercilious manners of his English subjects, had so far alienated the affections of his Gascon vassals, that the letters of Edward produced not the slightest effect upon them. The king of England, now finding that he had humbled himself in vain, sent the Duke of Lancaster into Aquitaine, to the aid of the Black Prince, with a body of four hundred men-at-arms and as many archers, besides a large number of the same description of troops, under Sir Robert Knolles, to invade France on the side of Picardy.*

The king of France, having now involved himself in a war with England, in which he would be required to put forth his whole strength, sent for his brothers, the Dukes of Anjou, Berry, and Burgundy, to come to Paris, and confer with him on the state of the kingdom and the best means of driving the English out of France. Charles, having determined that he would be satisfied with nothing less than the expulsion of the English from the kingdom, obtained a decree of the Court of Peers, on the 14th of May, 1370, declaring that the duchy of Guienne, and all the fiefs possessed by Edward III. and the Prince of Wales, were confiscated to the crown of France. To carry out this decree, it was then decided to assemble two large armies, to invade the territories of the Prince of Wales: one, under the Duke of Anjou, to enter Guienne on the side of La Réole and Bergerac; and the other, under the Duke of Berry, on the side of Limousin and Quercy, where it was designed they should unite their forces and besiege Angoulême, one of the usual residences of the Black Prince. At the same time, after further deliberation, it was also decided to recall Bertrand du Guesclin

* Froissart, liv. i. part ii. pp. 604, 609.

from Spain, where he was still employed in the service of Henry.*

The king of Spain, ever since the death of Peter the Cruel, had been engaged in settling the affairs of his kingdom, and, with the assistance of Bertrand du Guesclin, in reducing to subjection the towns and fortified places which, for a time, resisted his authority. He had just abandoned the siege of Ciudad Rodrigo, on account of the height of the waters, and called a cortez at Medina del Campo, when he was forced to yield up the services of Du Guesclin to the higher claims of his sovereign the king of France. Before parting with a leader from whom he had received such inestimable services, he rewarded him by the grant of the towns of Soria, Almazan, Alienza, Deza, Monteagudo, and Seron, with the title of Duke of Molina; and he paid him one hundred and twenty thousand doblas, partly in money, and partly by the ransom of the king of Majorca, which was fixed at seventy thousand.†

* Froissart, liv. i. part ii. p. 608; Du Tillet, *Recueil des Traictez, &c.*, p. 90, *verso.*

† Ayala, *Cronica del Rey Don Enrique Segundo*, pp. 12, 13; *Actes de Bretagne*, tom. i. col. 1628, by which it appears that the grant was made the 4th day of May, 1369. The towns mentioned in the text will be remembered as those which Ayala says Peter the Cruel promised to give Bertrand du Guesclin, if he would aid him to escape from the castle of Monteil—and Henry afterwards agreed to confirm the grant, if Du Guesclin would connive at the deception to be practised on Peter, in order to get him into his hands; but, as the complicity of Bertrand in this transaction may well be doubted, from his established character for chivalric honour, as well as from the silence or disagreement of the other chroniclers, the whole charge was most probably an afterthought, suggested by the gift of Henry, which was not an unreasonable reward for the invaluable services rendered by Du Guesclin. Ayala, who was a mere chronicler, seems not to have had much love for the Breton general, or any of the foreign leaders who were the recipients of Henry's bounty; and, therefore, he was not likely to take any special pains to suppress a scandal, however slightly sustained, to the prejudice of any of them.

Froissart says that Bertrand du Guesclin was created Constable of

Henry did not confine the manifestations of his gratitude to the material offerings made to Bertrand du Guesclin; but he had the manliness, at the moment of leave-taking, to say openly:—"Ha! Lord Bertrand, how can I recompense you for the services you have rendered me?—for, if I have a kingdom, seigniory, or other goods, it is through you. And I can well affirm, before the chivalry here assembled, that, but for you, I should be the poorest knight in the world."*

Bertrand du Guesclin, upon taking leave of Henry, did not immediately quit Spain, as it was necessary for him to get possession of the towns which he had received from the king; and among these was Soria, which obstinately refused to receive him within its walls. This town had already stood a siege of a month against his lieutenant, Jean de Beaumont, and a large body of men-at-arms; but it yielded to a violent assault made by Du Guesclin in person. While here, he received the fifth message from King Charles of France, urging his immediate return;† to which he replied by promising a speedy compliance, quaintly adding, by way of an excuse, the necessity of arranging his own affairs in Spain before waiting on his master—that his shirt was certainly nearer to him than his coat.‡

Castille, liv. i. part ii. p. 554; but Ayala makes no mention of it, nor is it mentioned in the grant, dated at Seville, May 4, 1369, of the six towns and the duchy of Molina, in which Du Guesclin takes the title of Count de Longueville. Froissart sometimes uses the word constable as synonymous with commander, as in liv. i. part ii. p. 610.

* *Chronique* (Anonyme) *de Du Guesclin*, ch. cxxv.

† Ayala says:—"The king of France sent every day to ask the king Don Enrique to send him."—*Cronica del Rey Don Enrique Segundo*, p. 12, note (4).

‡ Cuvelier, vv. 17,200, 17,230. Charrière, the learned editor of Cuvelier, conjectures that "the politic delays, which the chronicler attributes to Du Guesclin, may have been caused by the propositions he received at that time from the king of Aragon. Sardinia had just been wrested from his dominion, under the conduct of a lord of the house of

On leaving Soria, Bertrand du Guesclin crossed the Pyrenees into the territories of the Count de Foix, by whom he was cordially welcomed, and treated with every demonstration of respect and honour. During his stay, the count complained of the conduct of his brother, Oliver du Guesclin, who had taken service under the Count d'Armagnac, and who was then doing him all the injury in his power. To this complaint Bertrand replied that his brother was a soldier of fortune; and he did nothing more than his duty in serving his employer for his pay to the best of his ability, as he would do himself under like circumstances. The Count de Foix then proposed to Du Guesclin an offensive and defensive alliance, against all persons, which the latter accepted, against every one but the king of France and his family. Bertrand then offered to make peace between the two counts; and, if he could not induce the Count d'Armagnac to listen to the terms proposed, he promised the Count de Foix that he would withdraw Oliver du Guesclin from the service of his opponent.*

On leaving the territories of the Count de Foix, Bertrand du Guesclin went immediately to Toulouse, where he arrived about the middle of July, 1370; and where he found the Duke of Anjou, at the head of a large and well-appointed army, anxiously awaiting him. The duke had under his command the Count d'Armagnac, Lord d'Albret, the Count de Périgord, the seneschals of Toulouse, Carcassonne, and Beaucaire, and the principal Gascon nobles, with two thousand lances of knights and squires, besides six thousand foot-soldiers armed with pikes and bucklers. Du Guesclin

Arborée. He offered to Du Guesclin the command of this expedition; and he was on the point of concluding an arrangement with this prince, when he received the orders of Charles V."—Cuvelier, tom. ii. p. 376, note (62).

* Cuvelier, vv. 17,274, 17,315.

was placed in command of all the men-at-arms; and the extraordinary success of the campaign fully justified the propriety of the appointment. Setting out from Toulouse, the Duke of Anjou marched into Agénois, and took, with little resistance, the towns of Moissac, Agen, St. Marie, Tonneins, and Montpelier;* and even the strong castle of Aiguillon, which had stood a successful siege of many weeks against a force of one hundred thousand men, during the reign of Philippe de Valois, surrendered after a feeble resistance of four days; though Froissart adds:—"At that time there were not in the town and castle of Aiguillon such valiant men as when Sir Walter Manny and his companions had the command of them.†"

After the surrender of Aiguillon, the Duke of Anjou marched towards Bergerac, on the Dordogne, and laid siege to the strong town of Linde, situated on the same river, about a league from Bergerac. After some parleys between the French leaders and the governor, Sir Thomas de Batefol, the latter was induced, by the offer of a sum of florins, as well as the anxious desire of the citizens to throw off the English yoke, to surrender the town. This treacherous purpose of the governor was discovered before its consummation by the Captal de Buch and Sir Thomas Felton, who were then quartered at Bergerac. The intelligence greatly surprised them; but, as they were determined not to give up a strong town thus lightly, which they had recently supplied with provisions for a siege, they declared that they would be present at the delivery of the place. Accordingly, they set out from Bergerac, after midnight, on the morning when the

* Froissart was evidently mistaken in the name of the town here mentioned, as none of that name lay in the route of the army of the Duke of Anjou. See Buchon's note to Froissart, liv. i. part ii. p. 611.

† Froissart, liv. i. part ii. pp. 610, 611; and liv. i. part i. pp. 213, 215.

French were to take possession of Linde, accompanied by two hundred lances, and reached the town about daybreak. They ordered the gate on the side towards Bergerac to be opened, and rode through the town to the opposite gate, where the French were ready to receive possession from the governor. The Captal de Buch dismounted on reaching the gate; and, drawing his sword, he said, on approaching Sir Thomas de Batefol:—"Ha! vile traitor, you shall die at this moment. Never shall you commit treason again." With these words he gave him a thrust with his sword, and with such force, that the blade, entering the body of the knight, passed more than a foot beyond it on the opposite side. The knight fell dead, and the French, who came to take possession of the town, fled in affright from the gate.*

The army of the Duke of Anjou, after this failure to get possession of Linde, laid waste the neighbourhood around Bergerac, and extended its incursions to within five leagues of Bordeaux. In six weeks the leaders had received the submission of more than forty cities, towns, castles, and fortresses belonging to the English; and, hearing that the Prince of Wales was assembling an army at Cognac, and that the Duke of Lancaster had arrived in Aquitaine with a large body of men, the Duke of Anjou called a council of war, to decide upon the further operations of the campaign. Bertrand du Guesclin was specially invited to be present at this council, at which, after full consideration, it was decided to disband the army, and distribute the troops among the garrisons throughout the country recently conquered, as they had already done enough for one season.†

Bertrand du Guesclin, after leaving the army of the Duke of Anjou, took his way towards Limoges, which was then be-

* Froissart, liv. i. part ii. p. 612. † *Ibid*, p. 616.

sieged by the Duke of Berry, who had entered Limousin with twelve hundred lances and three thousand foot-soldiers, taken a number of towns and castles, and burnt and laid waste the country wherever he went. In passing through the county of Périgord, Du Guesclin was hospitably entertained at Périgneux by Taillerand de Périgord, a brother of the count; and, while enjoying the fresh air after dinner, on the donjon of the castle, Bertrand, observing the figure of a leopard on a banner which floated from the steeple of a neighbouring monastery, asked with surprise :—"What do I see there? Have you English neighbours as near as that?" And, when he was informed that the English had held possession of the abbey for more than a year, he swore by St. Ives that he would not go away until he had supped within the abbey, and restored the abbot and monks to their cloisters.

Bertrand du Guesclin thereupon descended immediately from the tower, sent for his herald, and ordered him to summon his men, who were scattered among the neighbouring villages, and inform them of his design to attack the abbey, and drive the English out of it without delay. His troops assembled at the sound of the trumpet, and providing themselves in the town with doors, window-shutters, and about one hundred ladders, they proceeded at once to the assault. Taillerand de Périgord proposed to have three engines hauled up on waggons to the abbey, to aid in the attack; but Bertrand rejected the offer, saying, "We shall not want them; before they can be erected, we shall be drinking plentifully of the wine in the abbey."

Delaying the attack for a moment, Bertrand du Guesclin advanced to the gate of the abbey, and, in a parley with the commander, advised him to surrender the place to the abbot and monks, as he was living in great sin, and under excommunication. To this admonition the captain replied, with a supreme contempt for all ecclesiastical restraints, common to the lawless men of that period:—"We count that nothing: for we can be well enough absolved whenever we desire it. He can greatly transgress who is able to pay well for it; and that man is a good clerk who has plenty of money."

Du Guesclin then made a peremptory demand of surrender, which was as positively rejected; when the captain was plainly informed that, if the abbey were carried by storm, he would certainly be hanged. Without further delay the trumpets were sounded, when the besiegers commenced the attack by a discharge of arrows and darts, while at the same time a portion of them began to fill up the moats with earth and fascines; others, protected by targets and window-shutters, planted scaling-ladders against the walls. Among the first who mounted them was Bertrand du Guesclin himself, followed by Oliver de Manny, John and Alain de Beaumont, and other gallant knights. The English resisted the attack by all the usual modes of defence known at that time, and threw down upon their assailants red-hot bars of iron, quick-lime, and huge cross-beams of timber; but the defence availed nothing against the determined ardour of the French. Bertrand, closely followed by his men, entered the place, encountered the captain, and cut him down to the teeth by one blow from his formidable battle-axe. The garrison, after this, made no further resistance; and the abbey was restored to its owners by Du Guesclin, who supped there that night, as he had sworn to do, and then returned to Périgueux, where he remained a few days to refresh himself and his men.*

Upon leaving Périgueux, Bertrand du Guesclin went to

* Cuvelier, vv. 17,372, 17,504; *Chronique* (Anonyme) *de Du Guesclin*, ch. cxxviii. cxxix.

join the Duke of Berry in his camp before Limoges, which place the duke was then besieging. The city at this time was under the command of the Bishop of Limoges, with whom Du Guesclin successfully negotiated a treaty, in a few days after his arrival, for the surrender of the place. Here, after a short stay, the Duke of Berry was advised to imitate the conduct of his brother, the Duke of Anjou, and end the campaign by distributing his troops among the different towns and fortresses under his command; as it was thought they had done enough for one season, in taking so important a city as Limoges. The duke, at the request of the bishop, left a hundred men-at-arms, under the command of Lord John de Villemur, Sir Hugh de la Roche, and Roger de Beaufort, to aid in the defence of the city.*

* Froissart, liv. i. part ii. pp. 616, 617.

CHAPTER XI.

The sack of Limoges by the Black Prince. Bertrand du Guesclin is created Constable of France.

THE Black Prince was greatly irritated on hearing of the surrender of Limoges, and the more especially as the Bishop of Limoges had been his friend and confidant, who had been present at all his treaties, and who had often assisted in drawing them up; so that this conduct, on the part of one in whom he had placed so much confidence, "greatly diminished the respect which the prince had hitherto entertained for all churchmen." On being informed of the surrender of the city, Edward swore, by the soul of his father, that he would listen to nothing, until he could get the place back again, and make the traitors pay dearly for their offence. He thereupon immediately collected his troops, and set out from Cognac, with an army composed of twelve hundred men-at-arms, one thousand archers, and three thousand foot-soldiers. As he could not ride, he had himself carried in a litter, until he came before Limoges, where he quartered his troops near the walls. After a careful examination of the circuit of the city, the strength of the fortifications, and its other means of defence, in the number of effective men composing the garrison, it was decided not to attempt to carry the place by storm, but by the slower process of a mine. The prince had in his army a large number of miners, whom he set to work immediately; and, in about a month, he was informed by them that, whenever he desired it, they could throw down a part of the wall. During this time there was neither assault nor sally: for, while the prince was pushing his mine, the besieged were attempting a countermine; but they failed in piercing the mine, and, when his preparations were complete, Edward ordered his miners to finish their work. Early the next day they threw down a large extent of the wall, which filled up the moats, and gave the besiegers an easy entrance into the city.

As the besieged were taken completely by surprise, the prince passed without resistance over the broken wall a portion of his troops, who immediately ran to the gate, cut the iron fastenings, and broke down all the barriers. Swollen with dropsy, but deaf to every sentiment of pity towards the inhabitants of the doomed city, Edward caused himself to be conveyed through the gates, accompanied by the Duke of Lancaster, the Earls of Cambridge and Pembroke, the Lord d'Angle, and the great body of his army, who were instructed to spare neither property nor life within the walls of Limoges. This brutal order was carried out to all its fearful consequences before the eyes of the prince, who looked, unmoved by pity or remorse, on the awful spectacle of men, women, and children butchered in cold blood by his stern followers; and, when the wretched victims, in their agony, threw themselves at his feet, crying out to him, "Mercy, gentle Sire!" he turned a deaf ear to their prayers, and suffered the horrid butchery to go on unchecked. "I do not know," says Froissart, "how they could not have had pity on the poor people, who were guilty of no treason; but they paid more dearly for it than the great masters, who had committed the offence. There is no one so hard-hearted," he continues, with a just indignation, "who, if he had been in the city of Limoges, and been mindful of God, would not have wept tenderly at the great mischief which was done there: for more than three thousand persons—men, women, and children—were seized and put to death that day. God has their souls, for they were true martyrs."

On entering the city, a body of English soldiers proceeded to the palace of the Bishop of Limoges, whom they took prisoner, and carried before the Prince of Wales, with little reverence for the sacredness of his office; and the best word that the bishop could get out of the prince was an oath, by God and St. George, that he would have his head cut off, with a peremptory dismissal from his presence.

When Lord John de Villemur, Sir Hugh de la Roche, and Roger de Beaufort, who had been left by the Duke de Berry to aid in the defence of the city, witnessed the indiscriminate massacre of the citizens, they determined to sell their lives as dearly as possible; and, accordingly, they drew up their followers, to the number of eighty men-at-arms, and, forming them in good order, with their banners displayed, and with their backs against an old wall, they awaited the onset of the English. When they were drawn up in this state, the Lord de Villemur said to Roger de Beaufort, a son of the Count de Beaufort:—

"Roger, you must be created a knight."

"Sire," replied the young squire, modestly, "I am not yet so valiant that I deserve to be made a knight, although I am greatly indebted to you for proposing it to me."

Nothing further was then said or done, for the Duke of Lancaster and the Earls of Cambridge and Pembroke, with a body of men, came up at that moment, and, dismounting from their horses, proceeded to attack them.

The contest began by a personal encounter between the leaders, in which the Duke of Lancaster was opposed to the Lord de Villemur, the Earl of Cambridge to Sir Hugh de la

Roche, and the Earl of Pembroke to Roger de Beaufort. As they were all valiant and skilful combatants on both sides, many gallant feats of arms were performed by them, while their followers looked on. The Black Prince had himself conveyed to the scene of the combat; and he whom no entreaty nor tears from the innocent but undistinguished rabble could move, was so softened by witnessing a knightly conflict of arms, in which he could no longer participate, that he looked from his litter with stern pleasure on the varying changes of the fight, and even recovered something of his good-temper again. After a well-sustained encounter the French leaders surrendered, asking to be treated as prisoners under the law of arms, which was promptly acceded to by the English knights. The city of Limoges was sacked and burnt; and the bishop was only saved by the intervention of the pope, with the aid of the Duke of Lancaster. The Black Prince, whose health grew worse from day to day, ended the campaign with the sack of Limoges, and returned to Cognac, where he disbanded his army for the season.*

While the Black Prince was before Limoges, Bertrand du Guesclin, who had left the city at the time when the Duke of Berry adopted the counsel to disband his forces, went into the viscounty of Limoges, and, with a force of about two hundred lances, overran the county, as an adherent of Jeanne, Countess of Penthiévre, the widow of Charles de Blois; and although daily complaints were brought to the Black Prince of the success of the Breton knight, in taking towns and fortified places, Edward was too intent on the punishment of his traitorous vassals to be diverted from his revenge by any other object. Bertrand du Guesclin was, therefore, permitted to prosecute, without interruption, the

* Froissart, liv. i. part ii. pp. 617, 620.

siege of St. Yriex, in Limousin, a town on the river Isle, which yielded to his arms after a feeble defence: for the inhabitants were so frightened at his approach, and by the impetuosity of his assault, that, though the town was well fortified, it made little more than a show of resistance. After the surrender of St. Yriex, he took the town of Brantome, in Périgord, on the river Drôme; and while here he received a peremptory order from the king of France to come to Paris without further delay: for, although unusual successes had attended the French arms during the campaign in the southern and middle provinces, it was necessary to adopt some decided measures to oppose the progress of Sir Robert Knolles in the north, where he had extended his predatory incursions, without opposition, from Artois to the very gates of Paris.*

Setting out from Calais towards the end of July, 1370, Sir Robert Knolles,† with a large force of men-at-arms and archers, laid waste along his route the whole open country of Artois, Picardy, the Isle of France, and Champagne. Leaving behind him the fortified places, which required time and labour to take, he went along at easy marches of three or four leagues a-day, and destroyed with fire and sword everything in his route, except the property of such persons as were able or willing to pay for his forbearance: for Sir Robert Knolles, though the commander-in-chief of a well-appointed army, could not forget his old practices as the mercenary leader of a Free Company; and, whenever he came before a fortified town or castle, he inquired of the owner how much he would pay to have his lands exempt

* Froissart, liv. i. part ii. pp. 614, 619, 621.

† The commission, dated July 1, 1370, is directed to Robert Knolles, Aleyn Buxhill, Thomas Granson, and John Boucher, *together, three or two of them, of whom Robert Knolles shall be one and the principal.*—Rymer, vol. iii. par. ii. p. 894.

from pillage. From many he received large compositions; and he amassed in this manner, on his march, a sum of money which amounted to about one hundred thousand francs; but his avarice had well-nigh brought him into some danger with Edward III., before whom he was charged with greater care for his own interests than those of his master. Sir Robert Knolles, however, was able to render so satisfactory an excuse for his conduct, or possibly Edward III., in the decline of his fortunes, was too weak to punish so powerful a subject, that the charge was only prejudicial to the accuser, who was publicly hanged for his pains.*

Charles V., who could see from his residence in the Hôtel de St. Pol, in the city of Paris, the smoke towards the Gâtinois, made by the army of Sir Robert Knolles from the burning houses of his unprotected subjects, still adhered to the policy he had first adopted, of placing strong garrisons in the cities, towns, and fortified places liable to attack, with a stern injunction that no sally, under any pretext whatever, should be made against the invaders. With a large body of high-spirited nobles and knights around him, this order was obeyed with much impatience and dissatisfaction; and it provoked from Lord de Clisson, then one of the most trusted of his counsellors, a remonstrance, which contained a sneer at the over-cautious policy of the king:—"Sire, you have nothing to do but to employ your people against these madmen; let them go out, and tread them under foot: for they cannot take away your inheritance, nor drive you out by smoke."† But Charles had little reason, from his past experience, to trust to the military skill of those about him; and he consequently now urged the speedy return of Bertrand du Guesclin, to take command of his armies.

On receiving the last summons of the king, Bertrand du

* Froissart, liv. i. part ii. pp. 609, 614. † *Ibid*, p. 618.

Guesclin distributed his troops among the towns he had conquered; and, placing his nephew Oliver de Manny in command of all his conquests, he left Périgord in disguise, and set out for Paris, in a simple grey coat, and accompanied by only six attendants. He was met near the city by the favourite minister of Charles, Bureau de la Rivière, by whom he was conducted to the king. Before his arrival it had been decided, by the advice and counsel of the prelates and nobles, and by the united voice of the whole kingdom, that it was necessary to have a constable appointed to command the armies of France, as Sir Moreau de Fiennes, through age and infirmities, was no longer competent to discharge the duties of constable, and he was anxious himself to resign the office; and, "by common consent, it had been resolved to call Bertrand du Guesclin to assume the office, as the most valiant and best suited to do so; as the most virtuous and fortunate in his enterprises of all who at that time were in arms for the crown of France."*

Charles V., when Bertrand du Guesclin was ushered into his presence, was attended by the lords of his household and a number of the members of his council, by whom the Breton knight was received with a cordial greeting, and treated with every demonstration of respect. The king then informed him of his election as constable of France; but Du Guesclin was far from being satisfied with the appointment, as he well knew the duties and responsibilities of the office, and as he probably fully understood the character of Charles—his suspicious nature, his extreme caution in every matter of war,

* Froissart, liv. i. part ii. p. 621; Cuvelier, vv. 17,503, 17,751.

> "La n'i ot chevalier, prince, conte, ne per,
> Escuier et bourjois, qui ne soit escriez:
> 'A Bertran! A Bertran! l'espée li livrez!
> Voir, s'il est connestable, Englois seront grevez.'"
>
> —v. 17,862.

and his closeness in all money transactions; he therefore earnestly entreated the king to permit him to decline the office, modestly declaring that he was not worthy of it; that he was a poor knight and simple bachelor, in comparison with the great lords and valiant men of France, although fortune had a little advanced him. The king replied that he excused himself in vain, and that he must assume the office, as it had been thus ordered by the whole council of France, which he was unwilling to oppose. Du Guesclin then attempted in another way to decline the proffered honour, by saying:—

"Dear Sire and noble king, I neither will, nor can, nor dare oppose your good pleasure; but it is too true that I am a poor man, and one of humble birth, and the office of constable is so grand and noble, that it is necessary for him who would discharge it properly to exercise higher command over the great than the small; besides, there are your brothers, nephews, and cousins, who will have charge of soldiers in the army and on expeditions, and how can I command them? Surely, Sire, the envious are so powerful that I may well fear them: therefore, I sincerely beg that you will permit me to decline this office; that you will give it to one more willing to assume it, and who will know better how to discharge its duties than I."

"Sir Bertrand," replied the king, "you cannot get off in this way: for I have no brother, cousin, nor nephew in my kingdom, who will not obey you, and, if one of them should do otherwise, he would so anger me that he would soon perceive it; now take the office cheerfully, I beg you."*

Bertrand du Guesclin, finding that such excuses availed nothing against the fixed resolution of the king, before yielding his consent, said:—

* Froissart, liv. i. part ii. p. 621.

"But one request I entreat you to grant me—it will not lessen your honour or your treasury to do so; but, if it is refused, I cannot accept the office."

"Bertrand," replied the king, "tell what boon you require; I will not refuse it, provided you do not ask for my bright crown or my noble wife."

"No," said Du Guesclin, playfully, "I have one wife enough already, and too much by half; but, Sire," he continued, "I will undertake the office, if you will promise not to believe anything said to my prejudice, behind my back, until the same is repeated to you in my presence."

The king readily promised to grant the request; whereupon Bertrand du Guesclin was invested with the office of Constable of France, upon taking the oath, and receiving the naked sword as the badge of his office; and, to do him greater honour, the king seated him by his side at his own table.*

* Cuvelier, v. 17,890; *Chronique* (Anonyme) *de Du Guesclin*, ch. cxxxi.; Froissart, liv. i. part ii. p. 622. Christine de Pisan says Bertrand du Guesclin was appointed Constable of France, October 2, 1370.—*Le Livre des Fais et Bonnes Meurs du Sage Roy Charles*, partie ii. ch. xviii. p. 256.

CHAPTER XII.

Bertrand du Guesclin, upon assuming the office of Constable, collects troops and marches against the English. The battle of Pontvalain.

BERTRAND DU GUESCLIN, upon assuming the office of Constable of France, determined at once to follow Sir Robert Knolles into the provinces of Maine and Anjou, as soon as he could collect a sufficient number of troops to oppose the English general; but in carrying out this design, his fears of the parsimonious and timid policy of Charles V. were speedily realized, as Du Guesclin only received fifteen hundred men-at-arms, with pay for four months. To the respectful but firm representation of the constable, how totally inadequate so small a body of men would be to make head against his enemies, the king coolly replied that he did not desire him to engage the English in a pitched battle; but he only wished him to pursue, harass, and keep them in check, and he had already given him men enough for that mode of warfare. Such timid counsels did not suit the temper of Du Guesclin, who said, in reply, that it would be a great reproach to him if he, the commander of the armies of France, should meet the enemies of the king and turn his back without attacking them. He hinted at the ill-effects of too great parsimony in matters of war; that low wages paid to troops often led them to acts of pillage; and he plainly declared his determination, if he met with the enemies of his country, to fall upon them "like a wolf in a sheepfold," and that he intended to give full pay to all who would come to serve him.*

Setting out with this resolution from Paris, the constable first went to Pontorson, in Normandy, where he formed an alliance with his distinguished countryman, Oliver Lord de Clisson, "against all persons who could live and die," except the king of France and his brother, the Viscount de Rohan, and other lords of whom they held lands.†

From Pontorson the constable went to Caen, where he established his head-quarters for the time, and where all were ordered to come who desired to serve him. He was soon enabled to fill up his ranks: for no leader of his time was more popular among all classes of soldiers, on account of his acknowledged reputation as an officer, his well-known liberality, and his personal prowess, that led him to share every danger to which he exposed his troops. As soon, therefore, as his summons was known, there repaired immediately to his standard a large body of knights and squires, until his levies amounted to upwards of three thousand men-at-arms. The constable retained them all, and paid them, as they came, in ready money as long as he had any left; and, when he had exhausted all his means at hand, he sent for his wife to come without delay to Caen, and to bring with her all his plate and her own jewels, as he wished to hold a plenary court in that town. Lady Tiphaine, although she

* Cuvelier, vv. 17,917, 17,949; *Chronique* (Anonyme) *de Du Guesclin*, ch. cxxxi.

† Froissart, liv. i. part ii. p. 622, says the constable, immediately after his appointment, followed Sir Robert Knolles into Anjou and Maine; but the deed of alliance between Du Guesclin and De Clisson shows that he was at Pontorson October 23rd, 1370.—*Actes de Bretagne*, tom. i. col. 1642.

did not know the design of her husband in this request, did not hesitate to comply with it; and, on her arrival at Caen, she was received by him with a warm embrace.

The constable had made preparations on an ample scale for the entertainment of the noble and gallant visitors whom he had requested to join his standard; and, immediately after the arrival of his wife, he invited the barons and knights to a sumptuous dinner in a large hall, where he made a dazzling display of the plate which he had acquired in his last expedition into Spain. Among his most distinguished guests were the Counts d'Alençon and du Perche, the Viscount de Rohan, the old Maréchal d'Audeneham, the Lords de Clisson and de Rais, Sir John de Vienne, Alain and Jean de Beaumont, Oliver du Guesclin, and Pierre d'Estrée. The dinner was well ordered and served, and the number of foreign dishes was the subject of admiration to the guests, as well as the weight and beauty of the plate, which was richly carved, while all did full honour to the grace and accomplishments of the noble hostess. During the dinner, when the conversation happened to turn on the incidents of the campaign, Lord de Clisson said:—

"Lord Bertrand, I think there are more than three thousand men now here who have come to serve you, while the king has only given you pay for fifteen hundred; and I fear, if their application for service is rejected, that they will go back and join the English."

"Sir," replied the constable, "by the honoured Virgin! all of them have been retained already at full pay; and, if they were twice as many, I have gold and silver enough to pay them. Do you not see the plate with which this hall is filled? By my faith! I have not pawned it, nor am I wedded to it; I can, therefore, spend it at my pleasure. I will lend it to the king, until a day when the English shall pay it back, which will be before a year is past."

The dinner-party passed off to the satisfaction and wonder of all: for probably none of the guests had ever witnessed an entertainment on a scale of greater magnificence. On the third day thereafter the constable pawned and sold his plate for ready money, and distributed portions of it among the knights and squires, until he had retained in his service above three thousand combatants, whom he also provided with arms and equipments. Having also collected sufficient provision for the support of his army, he ordered that every one should hold himself in readiness to march at a moment's warning. This order was promptly obeyed by all; and everywhere could be seen the preparations, as if for immediate conflict, of the men-at-arms getting ready their coats of mail, furbishing their bacinets, polishing their swords, sharpening the points of their lances, and getting their horses shod; and, while at their work, they said one to another:—"Long live this Bertrand! who will not wait for the English to seek him, but who will boldly march on them."

Before breaking up his quarters at Caen, the constable took an affectionate leave of his wife; and, on parting, said to her:—

"Lady, you can remain here if you desire to do so, or return to Roche-Derrien, at your pleasure; but pray to God that I may be brought back safely from this expedition: for I will never come here again until I shall have met in battle the commander of the English forces or his lieutenant."

"My lord," replied the wife, "I do pray to the Most Wise to guard you safely from death and imprisonment; and I beg that you will be mindful of the perilous days that you have to encounter. Before the battle of Nadres (Navarrete) you rejected my counsel: for, if you had believed me, the battle would not have been lost."

"Lady," rejoined Bertrand, "I know full well that he who will not listen to his wife will repent of it in the end." *

From Caen the constable marched to Vire, which was the rendezvous of his army; and, while there, he received from Sir Thomas Granson, the commander of a detachment of the English forces, then quartered at Pontvalain, near Mans, a formal challenge, sent in a letter, by a herald, to appoint a day and place for a battle between their respective forces. Du Guesclin gave the letter to his secretary, Hélie, to read; and, as soon as he was informed of the purport of it, he said that the English would find him sooner than they expected. He then ordered his treasurer to give the herald thirteen silver marks, and, in dismissing him, said:—"Tell your masters that they will soon hear news of me: for, if they wish to meet me in the field, I have still greater desire to find them."

The constable then consigned the English herald to the charge of his own heralds and minstrels, who took such good care of him, that, by the aid of some drugged and other wine, with which they bountifully supplied him, he got very drunk, and, falling asleep, he remained in their tents during the whole night. When Du Guesclin was informed of the condition of the herald, he ordered his troops to get themselves in readiness for an immediate march; as he said he wished to carry a response himself for the English herald, whom St. Martin's sickness still detained in his camp.†

The order for an instant march was reluctantly obeyed by

* Cuvelier, vv. 17,963, 18,110; *Chronique* (Anonyme) *de Du Guesclin*, ch. cxxxii.

† Cuvelier, v. 18,220. "St. Martin's sickness"—*Le mal de Saint Martin*—was an allusion of the chronicler to the drunken condition of the herald. *Faire la Saint Martin* was a local proverb, which meant *to make good cheer*.

the greater part of the army: for the night was not only very dark, but a cold and high wind was then blowing, and a heavy rain falling, which increased every instant. Some of the soldiers entreated the constable to delay the time for setting out until daylight, as they said no horse or rider could endure such weather; but Du Guesclin was not to be diverted, by such obstacles as wind, rain, or darkness, from an important enterprise, conceived with the design of showing that there was a new leader at the head of the armies of France. When ready to commence his march, he said, aloud:—"At dawn we must be upon our enemies. I vow to God! that I will not undress, taste bread, drink wine, or dismount of my own will from my horse, until I have encountered the English. Come with me, without hesitation, who will."

Having given the order for the march, the constable did not wait to see it executed; but, putting spurs to his horse, he took the road, followed at first by only five hundred of his more immediate retainers, among whom were Oliver de Manny, Jean and Alain de Beaumont, and his brother, Oliver du Guesclin. The other leaders set out as soon as they could get their men ready for the march; but they could only follow their impetuous commander at ever-increasing distances: for not only many of his own more immediate followers were overcome by fatigue and the failure of their horses, but the constable himself, on that night's march, "broke down a war-horse and a good steed of Aragon." To the complaints of several of his chiefs, that they had lost their horses and some of their men, who had strayed off in the darkness, he replied that it would soon be day, when they could surprise and defeat the English, and when all who were in want of them would be able to get horses enough.

When the constable reached the English camp near Pontvalain, early the next morning, and looked round upon his followers, wearied and travel-stained by a night's march of twenty leagues, he could only number about two hundred horsemen who had been able to keep up with him. The rest of his own troop came up dispersedly; and, as they reached him, they were ordered to dismount, regirth their saddles, and wring the water out of their garments, which were thoroughly soaked by the rain. At this time the rain ceased and the sun came out, which moderated the weather to the chilled, drenched, and wearied Frenchmen. The constable then informed his men that he designed to attack the English camp with such forces as had then arrived, and, although they were few in numbers, yet he knew that he should soon be aided by Lord de Clisson, the Viscount de Rohan, and the other leaders who were near at hand; and he exhorted his followers to be of good cheer, "for the man who is frightened is already half dead."

The constable then ordered his men to refresh themselves with such supplies of bread and wine as they had brought with them. Some of the soldiers took the bread reverently, as in the communion, and confessed their sins one to another; while others repeated many prayers, and besought the Almighty to guard them from all evil and danger. They then remounted their horses and rode forward until they could plainly see the English encamped on the field before them.

The constable approached the English camp without sound of trumpets or display of banners; and he instructed his men to cover their bacinets with cloth, so as to conceal the brightness of their armour. When he came within a half bow-shot of the English camp, he ordered his men to dismount; and, ranging them in order of battle, with banners displayed, he gave the command to charge. The order was obeyed with great alacrity by the troops, who shouted, as they approached, their various war-cries: "Montjoy!" "Our

Lady!" "The king of St. Denis!" "Guesclin the bravest!" "Death to the English!"

Nothing could have been more unexpected by the English than such an attack at that moment. Sir Thomas Granson, who had in his camp a force of seven or eight hundred men, while the rest of his troops were lodged in the neighbouring villages, was then awaiting the return of the herald sent to the constable with his defiance; and he did not conceive it possible that his opponent could have answered it already, in person, from such a distance, and in such a tempestuous night. The surprise, therefore, was complete. The constable and his men-at-arms dashed in among the tents and lodges, overturned them, slew at the first onset a large number of the English, and put many of them to flight. But the English general, although surprised, did not lose either his courage or his presence of mind. He soon rallied his troops, and, aided by David Holgrave and Geoffrey Worsley, he opposed an obstinate resistance to the French, and bore himself bravely in the conflict. The combat lasted for some time, when it was decided in favour of the French by the arrival of Lord de Clisson and the other leaders. Sir Thomas Granson continued the fight, notwithstanding the discomfiture of his men, and at length surrendered to the constable, who called upon him to yield instantly, or he would be slain.*

Having enriched his men by the number of prisoners and the amount of booty acquired by the defeat of the English,

* Cuvelier, v. 18,233; *Chronique de Du Guesclin*, ch. cxxxiii. Froissart, liv. i. part ii. pp. 622, 623, in giving an account of this battle, estimates the number on both sides as much smaller than the other authorities. Barnes puts the number under Sir Thomas Granson at "200 spears and 6000 others," and says, on the authority of Du Cheyne, "about 1200 English were slain on the spot."—"Hist. Edward III.," p. 811.

the constable followed his enemies, who no longer offered him any resistance in the field, and besieged a part of them in the town of Vas, whither they had taken refuge. The governor refused to surrender the town at the summons of Du Guesclin, who threatened him that, if the fortress was carried by assault, he should be hanged. To this threat the governor coolly replied that he had no doubt of it; when the constable swore, by our Lady and the body of St. Benedict, that he would sup that night in the chief donjon of the castle. Fully supported by the ardour of his men, he was enabled to accomplish his vow, as well as execute his threats to the governor: for few of the garrison escaped with their lives.

In like manner the constable took the towns of St. Maur on the Loire, Rulli, and Neroux, which were carried by assault, and abandoned to the pillage of the soldiers. Sir Robert Knolles did not await the approach of the constable; but he avoided an attack by disbanding his troops and taking refuge in his strong fortress of Derval, in Brittany. Lord de Clisson, hearing of the departure of the English, obtained permission of the constable to pursue a body of them under Sir Robert Neufville, whom he overtook as they were about to embark for England. The action which ensued was spirited and well contested; but the French were victorious, and a large number of the English were slain on the field. The rest, with their leader, surrendered as prisoners of war. The constable heard this welcome intelligence on the 1st of December, 1370, at Caen, whither he had gone to attend a levy of troops; but the season was too far advanced to attempt any new enterprises, and he went immediately thereafter to attend the king at Paris.*

* Cuvelier, vv. 18,492, 18,730; *Chronique* (Anonyme) *de Du Guesclin*, ch. cxxxvi.; *Actes de Bretagne*, tom. i. col. 1644.

CHAPTER XIII.

Results to the French of their success at Pontvalain. The Black Prince leaves France and goes to England. The siege of Montpaon. Successes of Bertrand du Guesclin in Poitou and Auvergne. Death of Tiphaine Ravenel, wife of the constable.

IT may well be conceived that Bertrand du Guesclin met with a cordial reception at the court of Charles, on his return to Paris at the end of the campaign. It is true the surprise at Pontvalain was in itself an achievement of no great moment, as the number of men engaged was inconsiderable; but it was the first time since the coronation of Charles V that the French had dared to attack the English in the open field. There is no reason to believe that the individual French knight was inferior in courage or skill to a knight of any other nation; but such had been the impression produced by the disastrous days of Crécy and Poitiers, that, since the success of Du Guesclin at the battle of Cocherel, just before the coronation of Charles, no superiority of numbers seemed sufficient to induce the French to meet any considerable body of English in a pitched battle.*

In the preceding year the king of France had provided a number of ships at Harfleur, and collected a large army

* The battle of Auray, in Brittany, was a civil conflict, in which the Bretons were chiefly engaged on both sides.

at Rouen, under the command of his brother, Philippe Duke of Burgundy, "as if to destroy everything in England;" but, on learning that Edward III. had sent a considerable force to invade France, under the Duke of Lancaster, the Duke of Burgundy abandoned the design of invading England, and went to oppose the Duke of Lancaster, who had now landed his army at Calais, and drawn out his men near that town. The French did not dare to attack them. They broke up their camp at midnight, and turned their backs upon an enemy whom they outnumbered as seven to one.*

Influenced by the same counsels, the Duke de Bourbon, with the strongest personal motives to govern him, and with a superiority of forces of at least three to one, declined a contest with the Earl of Cambridge, who had not only challenged him to select a field for a combat between them, but had marched out in battle array before him, with banners displayed and music playing, and with Madame de Bourbon—the mother of the duke and of the queen of France, whom the earl had detained a prisoner at her fortress of Belle-Perche—mounted on a palfrey, in the midst of the English ranks.†

In like manner Sir Robert Knolles, with a force only numbering fifteen hundred lances and four thousand archers, laid waste the country with fire and sword from Calais to the gates of Paris, and from Paris to Maine, without meeting with even a show of resistance, until he encountered Bertrand du Guesclin, who cut to pieces a portion of his command at Pontvalain, and drove the rest out of the kingdom.‡

* Froissart, liv. i. part ii. pp. 584, 587, 595.

† *Ibid*, pp. 607, 608.

‡ *Ibid*, p. 612. The number here given probably only included the more effective troops, as Froissart seldom mentions foot-soldiers in his report of the numbers of an army. Other authorities estimate the

The constable, who bore his new honours with dignity and grace, accompanied by Lord de Clisson, took his prisoners to Paris, where they were suffered to go at large, without other restraint than their parole. "They did not put them in prison, or irons, or bonds," says Froissart, "as the Germans do their prisoners, in order to augment their ransoms. Cursed be they! Such people are destitute of pity or honour, and they should not be received to mercy. The French, on the contrary, treat their prisoners kindly, and ransom them courteously, without pressing or burdening them too much."*

The unusual success which had attended his arms during the last campaign gave new hopes to the French monarch, and induced him to make greater efforts than before to prosecute the war against the English; he therefore permitted the constable, during the month of January, 1371, in person and by his lieutenants, the Lords de Rais and de Hunandie and Sir William Boitel, to make new levies of knights and squires at Paris and Blois.†

During the early part of the year 1371, Charles V was for ever freed from his ever-vigilant and successful enemy, the Black Prince, whose increasing infirmities, leaving no prospect of amelioration in France, induced his physicians to recommend a change to his native air. Acting on this advice, Edward went over to England with his family, and left his principality under the command of his brother, John of Gaunt, Duke of Lancaster.‡

The duke was not permitted to remain long idle in his new government: for, while he was attending to the obsequies

forces of Sir Robert Knolles from 12,000 to 30,000 men.—Barnes's "Hist. Edward III.," p. 800, and note.

* Froissart, liv. i. part ii. p. 623.

† *Actes de Bretagne*, tom. i. col. 1646, 1647.

‡ Froissart, liv. i. part ii. p. 625.

of his nephew Edward, the eldest son of the Black Prince—who had died at the age of six years, just before the departure of his parents from Aquitaine—he was informed that four daring French knights, Guillaume de Longval, Alain de la Houssaye, Louis de Mailly, and Lord d'Acy, had issued from the town of Périgueux with a force of two hundred Breton lances, and, with the connivance of the governor, "whose courage was more French than English," had taken the strong castle of Montpaon, within a few leagues of Bordeaux.

The Duke of Lancaster could not permit such an act of daring, committed almost within his eyesight, to remain unpunished; he therefore speedily got together a force of seven hundred lances and five hundred archers, and marched without delay towards the castle of Montpaon. He commenced the siege at once, and invested the place on all sides. He employed the peasants of the neighbourhood in cutting and bringing near the walls a great quantity of wood, plank, and other materials, with which he filled up the fosses, and then covered the whole with straw; and for twenty days nothing else was attended to. When the ditches were sufficiently filled with the materials to enable the besiegers to skirmish with the garrison on the walls, the attack was commenced; and every day there were five or six assaults against the castle. "And there took place," says Froissart, whose enthusiasm is always excited by the conflict of arms, "the most beautiful combats in the world: for the four Breton knights who had undertaken to keep the castle were men-at-arms of the proper sort, who defended themselves so well, and combated so valiantly, that they deserved great praise; neither were they frightened, although the English and Gascons approached them as near as I tell you, nor did their enemies gain any advantage over them."

Near the castle of Montpaon was the fortress of St.

Macaire, which was commanded by two Breton squires, Jean de Malestroit and Silvester Budes. These two squires, who heard every day of the gallant feats of arms performed by their friends in the castle of Montpaon, had a great desire to participate in them; but, as both could not leave their fortress at the same time, a contest ensued between them which should go. As neither was disposed to give way to the other, Budes said to his comrade:—

"By God! Jean, either you or I must go: now see who it shall be."

"Silvester," replied Malestroit, quickly, "you must stay, and I will go."

After further contention they proposed to draw straws, in the presence of their companions; and they bound themselves by an oath, that whoever got the longest straw should go. The trial was accordingly made, and Silvester Budes drew the longest straw, to the great amusement of the spectators. The gallant squire soon prepared himself for the expedition, and set out, accompanied by twelve men-at-arms, for Montpaon, where he arrived at evening; and he was admitted, with his followers, into the castle, to the great joy of the garrison.

The assaults on the castle had been kept up, for several days after the entrance of Silvester Budes, with equal advantage on either side, when the English prepared some machines to put their men under cover. The besiegers, protected by their bucklers, made their approaches to the castle, and with pick-axes broke through the wall, and in a short time threw down more than forty feet of it. At this opening the English stationed a strong force of archers, who discharged their arrows on the besieged, with such effect, that no one dared to approach the breach.

When the Breton knights saw that they could no longer hold the castle, they sent a herald to the Duke of Lancaster to propose terms of surrender; but the duke at first would listen to nothing less than an unconditional submission. The Bretons then appealed to Lord Guiscard d'Angle, who had been sent to treat with them, that they were soldiers of fortune, earning their bread by the profession of arms, like his own men, and that it would be hard for them to surrender as he had demanded; they thereupon entreated him to ask the duke to admit them to ransom, as he would desire to be done to his own soldiers in a like case—threatening, otherwise, to sell their lives so dearly, that it would be spoken of for a hundred years to come. The duke, on hearing this appeal, listened to the gentler measures proposed by the Lord d'Angle and the Captal de Buch, and accepted the surrender of the Breton knights and Silvester Budes as prisoners of war.*

Bertrand du Guesclin was informed at the time of the siege of Montpaon, and he would willingly have aided its gallant defenders, but he was otherwise fully employed: for, after completing his levies of troops, he left Paris early in February, 1371, and marched into Auvergne, where he laid siege to the strong town of Usson.† He was accompanied by the Dukes de Berry and de Bourbon, the Counts d'Alençon, du Perche, de St. Paul, and many other nobles and knights, with a large body of men. Failing in his attempt to take Usson, from the want of adequate means to carry it by storm, he marched into Poitou, and took the towns of Bressuire, Chauvigny, Moncontour, and Montmorillon.

After these successes he returned to the siege of Usson, taking with him several large military engines, which he

* Froissart, liv. i. part ii. pp. 626, 628.

† See the testimony of Sir Geoffroi Budes, taken in the *Enquête faite à Angers pour la Canonisation de Charles de Blois.—Actes de Bretagne*, tom. ii. col. 26.

had hauled on waggons from Rion and Clermont, and which he erected, without loss of time, before the fortress. These preparations for an immediate assault so alarmed the garrison, that they soon entered into terms of surrender with the constable; and they were permitted to leave the town with whatever property they could carry before them. The constable, after these conquests, returned to Paris, where his services were required in terminating a protracted negotiation for peace between his master and Charles the Bad, king of Navarre.*

The alliance of Charles the Bad, on account of the ports which he possessed in Normandy, as Count of Evreux, was equally advantageous to the kings of France and England; and, therefore, soon after the breaking out of hostilities between the two kingdoms, the king of Navarre received propositions from both Charles V. and Edward III., which he held in suspense for months, uncertain which to choose, only determining to sell his alliance to the highest bidder. To the king of England he was inclined by feeling, as he hated his brother-in-law, Charles V., with intense animosity; but his interests led him to make peace with the king of France.

Acting with his usual duplicity and bad faith, the king of Navarre concluded a treaty with Charles V., on the 29th of March, 1370, of which he deferred the execution under various pretences; and, on the 2nd of December of the same year, he signed one with Edward III., which was defeated by the refusal of the Black Prince to agree to one of the clauses of the treaty, whereby the prince was dispossessed of the viscounty of Limoges.†

* Froissart, liv. i. part ii. p. 630; Morice, *Hist. de Bretagne*, tom. i. p. 335.

† Secousse, *Hist. de Charles le Mauvais*, part ii. pp. 116, 124; Rymer, vol. iii. par. ii. p. 907.

Charles the Bad, finding the treaty with Edward III. thus broken off, renewed his negotiations with Charles V; and at length he was forced to accept the same conditions which he had at first rejected. The hostages which he required for his safety were conducted to him by Bertrand du Guesclin, on the 25th of March, 1371; and on the same day the king of Navarre left Evreux, under the escort of the constable, accompanied by three hundred men-at-arms, and reached Vernon, where he was cordially received by the king of France.

On the 30th of the same month, the king of Navarre rendered liege-homage to Charles V. for the lands which he held in France—an act which gave great satisfaction to the people of that kingdom, as it was feared that Charles the Bad might yet declare for the English, and it could still be remembered what evils he had brought on the country, by his counsels and conduct, during the regency of the reigning monarch.*

The constable could enjoy but little repose while he had so many enemies around him; and, therefore, as soon as the negotiations for peace were concluded at Vernon, he took the field again, and in a short time recovered a number of towns and castles belonging to the English in Rouergue, Poitou, and on the frontiers of Limousin. It was, however, in the province of Poitou that the horrors of war and the disorders of the times pressed most heavily. Towns, castles, and fortified places were taken and re-taken; the Free Companies were permitted by the Duke of Lancaster, who was afraid to offend them, to pillage both friend and foe; "and both men and things were in such confusion, that the strong oppressed the feeble, and there was no one to impart justice, or law, or reason, to any: for the towns

* Secousse, *Hist. de Charles le Mauvais*, part ii. p. 132.

and castles were completely intermixed—some belonging to the English and others to the French, who overran, pillaged, and ransomed each other without cessation."* After a short but successful military expedition, the constable returned to Pontorson, where he ordered a muster of new levies, on the 1st of May, 1371.†

During this season a deliberate inquiry was made at Angers, with a view to the canonization of Charles de Blois, slain at the battle of Auray in a contest with Jean, Count de Montfort, for the duchy of Brittany. The commission, which was obtained from Urban V at the request of Charles V of France, of the Countess of Penthiévre, widow of Charles de Blois, and of her two sons Jean and Guy, was permitted to be opened out of the duchy of Brittany, on account of the opposition of the duke, and the commissioners assembled at the Convent of the Cordeliers in the town of Angers. Here more than two hundred witnessess were examined by them, on the life, merits, and miracles of Charles de Blois. The Duke of Brittany bore very impatiently a procedure which would place among the number of the saints his late rival, who could not be regarded as such, "without having his pretensions to the duchy canonized at the same time;" without renewing the long-buried quarrels of twenty years, and taking away from himself the affections of his subjects. He therefore strenuously opposed the proceeding, and appealed to the pope to revoke the commission granted to the Bishop of Bayeux and his assistants; but the appeal was disregarded, and the commissioners were ordered to prosecute the inquiry in spite of the opposition of the duke, although no use was afterwards made of their report, as the new pope, Gregory XI., who in the meantime had succeeded Urban V.,

* Froissart, liv. i. part ii. pp. 629, 630.

† *Actes de Bretagne*, tom. i. col. 1650.

feared thereby to offend not only the Duke of Brittany, but his ally and father-in-law, the king of England.*

Edward III., who saw his affairs everywhere declining in his French possessions, especially since the elevation of Bertrand du Guesclin to the office of constable, endeavoured to form new alliances with the continental princes. He therefore proposed a treaty, dated the 4th of November, 1371, with the Duke of Brittany, by which the latter should bind himself to aid the king of England in his wars, and especially against the king of France; to do liege-homage for the duchy of Brittany to Edward, as king of France; and to give free access to all the ports of the duchy to the English troops during the war.†

The duke was unwilling to disoblige the king of England in any matter, yet he was afraid at the same time to offend the king of France; so, after much deliberation, he replied somewhat evasively to the propositions of Edward III., that he desired to form a strict alliance with him, and that he would ratify no treaty with his adversary without including him.‡

These negotiations were not unknown to the king of France, who was kept duly informed of the affairs of Brittany by Lord de Clisson, now become a deadly enemy to the duke. De Clisson had been raised up among the English, and he had acquired a very high military reputation in their service. He greatly distinguished himself at the battle of Auray; and Jean de Montfort was much indebted to him for the victory, which secured to him the possession of the duchy of Brittany. But De Clisson quarrelled with the duke for refusing him the grant of the lordship of Gavre, which had been already given to Sir John Chandos. De Clisson

* Morice, *Hist. de Bretagne*, tom. i. pp. 336, 337, and *Actes de Bretagne*, tom. ii. col. 1, *et. seq.*

† Rymer, vol. iii. par. ii. p. 927.

‡ *Ibid*, p. 935.

greatly coveted the possession of that property, as it was situated near his castle of Blein; and, failing to obtain it by entreaty, he swore that he would give himself to the devil, sooner than have an Englishman for his neighbour, and thereupon he set fire to the house. Not content with that deed, he carried off the stones of the building to Blein, and used them to fortify his castle. This step induced him to embrace the cause of the Countess of Penthiévre against the Duke of Brittany; and soon after he entered the service of the king of France, who treated him with marked distinction, admitted him into his counsels, restored the lands belonging to his father, which had been confiscated after his decapitation, and created him lieutenant-general of Touraine, Maine, and Anjou. These offices permitted him to maintain correspondence in Brittany and the adjoining provinces; and thus he was enabled to inform Charles V of the secret negotiations between the Duke of Brittany and Edward III.*

Following closely on these transactions between the king of England and the Duke of Brittany, took place the double marriage of the Duke of Lancaster and the Earl of Cambridge with Constance and Isabel, daughters of Peter the Cruel, by Maria de Padilla. These poor girls, who had been left as hostages by their father, since the year 1366, for the performance of his extravagant but broken promises to the Black Prince, were still at Bayonne; and the Duke of

* *Actes de Bretagne*, tom. iii. col. 837; Morice, *Hist. de Bretagne*, tom. i. p. 338. M. Secousse gives a very different reason for the animosity of the Duke of Brittany towards De Clisson, taken from the depositions of De Rue, chamberlain of Charles the Bad, who stated that he had heard it said, and that it was a common report while the king of Navarre was at Nantes, that he said to the duke, "he would sooner die than endure such vile treatment as he had received from De Clisson: for he was in love with his wife, and he had seen him kiss her behind a curtain."—*Histoire de Charles le Mauvais*, part ii. pp. 148, 149.

Lancaster was advised by Lord Guiscard d'Angle and some of the Gascon barons, as he was then a widower, to marry the eldest daughter of Peter, which would give him the legal title to the throne of Castille. The duke was easily persuaded to this step by the prospect of a crown; and he immediately sent for the ladies, who came at his bidding. He set out himself with great preparation to meet them; and he espoused Constance, the eldest, at the village of Rochefort, not far from Bordeaux. The younger sister was soon after married to the Earl of Cambridge; but these matrimonial alliances of his two sons were productive of no beneficial result to Edward III., as they only served to bind the kings of France and Castille in a closer union, which soon brought new disasters to the English arms.*

While such events were passing around him, and he was in the full career of his conquests, Bertrand du Guesclin was forced to turn aside and indulge his own bitter private griefs, amidst the general rejoicings of his countrymen for the success of his arms. Tiphaine Ravenel, whom he had first known as "the fair maid of Dinan," and whom he had wooed and won whilst he was an humble adventurer—she who had so long participated in all his joys and sorrows, who had sympathized in his misfortunes and enjoyed his triumphs, who had seen him rise, step by step, from a low estate to the highest position under the king in the realm, was now no more. She is represented, by all the authorities that allude to her, as a woman of rare beauty and accomplishments, of good sense and eminent virtues, and well worthy of being the wife of the greatest subject in the kingdom. She died during the year 1371, and was buried in the church of the ancient monastery of Mont St. Michel, near Pontorson.†

* Froissart, liv. i. part ii. pp. 633, 634.

† Morice, *Hist. de Bretagne*, tom. i. p. 374.

CHAPTER XIV.

Sea-fight off Rochelle. The English are unsuccessful both on sea and land. The king of France orders new levies of troops. The constable marches into Poitou, and takes the strong castle of Montcontour. St. Sevère is carried by storm.

DURING the winter of 1371, Edward III. designed to make preparations, on a very extended scale, to invade France, through Picardy and Guienne at the same time; but he found that an offensive war was no longer at his option, and that all his efforts would be required to maintain his former conquests. He accordingly fitted out an expedition during the early part of the year 1372, designed for the defence of his possessions in Aquitaine, under the Earl of Pembroke, who set sail from Southampton, and made for the port of Rochelle. Here the English were met by a strong fleet of Spanish vessels, sent by the king of Castille, at the request of the king of France, under the command of Admiral Bocanegra, who was duly advised of the approach of the Earl of Pembroke. The Spaniards were drawn up ready to receive the English, and, taking advantage of the wind, they commenced the attack. The English did not decline the engagement, although the Spaniards were superior in the number of vessels and men, and the contest was kept up until night terminated the combat, in which the English lost two transport vessels.

The engagement took place in sight of Rochelle, and the seneschal, John Harpedan, made great efforts to induce the Rochellois to aid the Earl of Pembroke; but the sympathies of the citizens were on the side of the French, and they excused themselves on the ground that they were soldiers, not seamen; that they did not know how to fight on water, and against the Spaniards. Both fleets remained at anchor during the night. As the seneschal of Rochelle could get no other answer from the citizens, he set out in four barges from the port, accompanied by the lord of Tounai-Bouton and two other knights, with a few men-at-arms; and about daylight he reached the English fleet without challenge. Early in the morning the combat was renewed, and it was kept up until mid-day; when, at length, the Castilians were victorious, and the English were all slain or taken prisoners, with the loss of the vessel containing the treasure designed by Edward III. for the payment of three thousand troops during the approaching campaign.*

About the time of the sea-fight off Rochelle, Evan of Wales, who claimed to be descended from the ancient princes of that country, set out from the port of Harfleur, with a number of vessels and a body of three thousand combatants, entrusted to him by the king of France, and made a descent on the island of Guernsey. He was not permitted to land without strenuous opposition from the governor, Edmund Ros,† who speedily collected a body of eight hundred men, and offered him battle. After an obstinate combat, the English were defeated, and above four hundred men slain

* Froissart, liv. i. part ii. pp. 635, 639; Ayala, *Cronica del Rey Don Enrique Segundo*, pp. 31, 32. The Spanish chronicler differs from Froissart as to the number of ships engaged and the vessel containing the lost treasure.

† That is the name given him by Barnes, "Hist. Edward III.," p. 833. Froissart calls him Aymon Rose.

on the field. Ros took refuge in Cornet Castle, which was strongly fortified, and well provided for a siege, whither he was soon followed by Evan of Wales. The French first attempted to carry the castle by storm; but they found it so well fortified, that all their assaults were unsuccessful; and they invested it on all sides, determined to take it by the slower process of a siege. While thus engaged, Evan received a message from the king of France, who had been informed of the naval victory off Rochelle, ordering him to raise the siege of Cornet Castle, send back his troops to Harfleur, go himself to the court of Henry of Castille, and ask the king to send him a force of ships and men to blockade Rochelle by sea.*

These disasters to his arms, both by sea and land, were as humbling to the pride of Edward III. as they were gratifying to Charles V., who had already been so fully impressed with the successful results of the last campaign, that he determined to prosecute the war against the English with all vigour. He had observed the last festival of Christmas with great solemnity at Paris, and he had invited all the higher officers of his army to be present at it. On that occasion the constable, Bertrand du Guesclin, served the king at table, uncovered, with his baton in his hand; and he was assisted by the two maréchals and the leader of the cross-bows. On the day after the festival the king assigned the troops to the different leaders of his army, who were ordered to hold themselves in readiness for service by the end of March. The constable took under his immediate command fifteen hundred men-at-arms; among whom was one of the maréchals and the leader of the cross-bows, with six hundred cross-bowmen. To the Duke de Bourbon was assigned eight hundred men-at-arms and two hundred cross-bowmen, and to Sir Louis de Sancerre five hundred men-at-arms. The Lord de

* Froissart, liv. i. part ii. p. 640.

Sempy was ordered to guard the frontiers around Calais, with five hundred men.

These troops, with the exception of those under Lord de Sempy, were designed for service in Guienne; and King Charles instructed the leaders to march into Poitou, and lay siege to the important city of Poitiers; but the Duke de Bourbon replied that it would be best to attack St. Sevère first, as it lay in their way towards Poitiers. This opinion of the duke was sustained by the constable, who said:—"My Lord de Bourbon is right: for no good captain will leave anything to conquer behind his back; and, in going towards Poitiers, we shall see what the people of St. Sevère mean to do." On the day fixed, the constable assembled his troops near the frontiers of Berry, to the number of three thousand men-at-arms, and eight hundred Genoese cross-bowmen.*

The constable set out from Blois with a splendid retinue of French nobles, and many distinguished knights, among whom, besides the Duke de Bourbon and Sir Louis de Sancerre, with their commands, were the Duke de Berry, the Count d'Alençon, the Dauphin d'Auvergne, the Viscount de Rohan, the Lords de Clisson, de Laval, and de Beaumanoir, with many of the other great barons of France. He marched into Poitou, and retook, with little resistance, Montmorillon and Chauvigny, which he had taken the year before; but they had been afterwards recovered by the English. The town and castle of Lussac surrendered at the first summons.†

While engaged in taking these places, the constable sent Lord de Clisson, with seven hundred lances, to make an examination of the defences of Montcontour, one of the

* *Vie de Louis de Bourbon*, par Jean Cabaret D'Orronville, ch. xi. xii. pp. 111, 112, Buchon's edition; Froissart, liv. i. part ii. p. 642.

† Cuvelier, v. 19,661; Froissart, liv. i. part ii. p. 642.

castles which had been taken by the French, and retaken by the English the preceding year, and which was then under the command of John Creswell and David Holegrave. After six days of unsuccessful assaults on the castle, De Clisson sent to inform the constable of his want of success; and requested him to come himself, as a gross insult had been offered to him by an English officer, who had hung up a painted representation of his arms, in a reversed position, near the gate of the castle, and proclaimed him false and perjured. This indignity was offered him on the ground that the constable had failed to discharge an obligation given to the Englishman, after the battle of Navarrete, to pay him a sum of money on a day fixed.*

The constable was a knight of too high spirit to suffer such an insult to remain long unavenged; and, accordingly, he set out immediately for Montcontour with his whole army, threatening to inflict the severest punishment on the Englishman for an outrage so gross and unprovoked. He admitted that the debt which he had incurred for the ransom of one of his soldiers was still due, and that he had bound himself, his lands and goods, by a sealed instrument, for the payment of the money; but he justly contended that, if the day named had passed, and the money was not paid, the claimant had a remedy against his property; and the insult, therefore, was wholly gratuitous. "Never," he swore, "will I taste meat, sleep in a bed, or undress, until I shall have taken the castle of Montcontour, and hung up the Englishman who has treated me so vilely on the very spot where he has suspended my painted shield."

The constable did not delay a moment after receiving the message of De Clisson; and he ordered his trumpets to be

* D'Orronville says the Englishman was a captain, and he calls him Jannequin Lovet.—*Vie de Louis de Bourbon*, ch. xxx. p. 181; Cuvelier, vv. 19,666, 19,688.

sounded for an instant march. In his impatience to reach Montcontour he suffered no obstacle to impede his progress, and, while on the way, gave no heed to the murmurs of some of his soldiers, who complained that they had marched all night without stopping to take a morsel of bread or a cup of wine, and added, that no Frenchman would ever have repose while Bertrand lived.

When the constable reached Montcontour, he said to Lord de Clisson, in a tone of half displeasure, half raillery :—

"Olivier de Clisson, why did you not storm and take this castle ?—and how have you suffered such an indignity to be offered to my arms ? This fellow would willingly have served me, if in his power, as he has done my shield ; but—I will not conceal it—I tell you plainly, you, who have so many and such efficient troops, ought to have taken the place, and hung up the Englishman who has done me such dishonour."

"Ah, Sire !" replied De Clisson, "trouble not yourself about it. To you belongs the honour of assailing these people, who, as soon as they find that you are with us, will be already half-conquered." *

As soon as his troops reached Montcontour, the constable began his preparations to carry it by storm. As the castle was surrounded by deep and wide ditches, he ordered the peasants of the neighbourhood to cut and bring a quantity of wood and trees, with which he filled up the fosses, and then covered the whole with straw and earth. This work was completed in four days, so that the besiegers could approach the walls without difficulty. On the fifth day the constable ordered the trumpets to be sounded for the assault ; when his troops, well armed with pikes, and provided with scaling-ladders, covered by their shields and protected by the

* Cuvelier, vv. 19,691, 19,720, and "MS. of the Arsenal," tom. ii. pp. 218, 219.

archers and cross-bowmen, marched up to the walls, under the lead of the constable in person, and commenced a vigorous attack. The garrison, under their leaders, John Creswell and David Holegrave, made a sturdy resistance with darts and arrows, and threw down from the walls on their assailants hot-water, quick-lime, boiling pitch, barrels filled with stones, and large beams of timber. The assault lasted the entire day, but with evident disadvantage to the garrison at the close. On the sixth day the besiegers renewed the assault with increased ardour, and, with pick-axes and mattocks, made openings at many places in the walls. The commanders of the garrison, seeing that they could not hold out much longer, proposed terms of surrender. Upon the delivery of Jannequin Lovet, who had so wantonly insulted him, the constable granted the lives of the garrison; but he would not suffer them to carry off any other property than the gold and silver which they possessed. Lovet was given up to De Clisson, who hanged him with his own hands on the very spot where he had suspended the arms of the constable.*

The news of the recovery by the French of the castle of Montcontour soon reached Sir John Devereaux, then governor of Rochelle, who was also informed at the same time that the constable had inspected the defences of Poitiers, and that the citizens apprehended an immediate siege, in the absence of Sir Thomas Percy, the seneschal of Poitou. Thereupon Sir John Devereaux, placing his command, during his absence, in charge of a squire named Philippe Mansel, left Rochelle with fifty lances, and threw himself into the city of Poitiers.

Sir Thomas Percy was also informed of the danger which

* Froissart, liv. i. part ii. pp. 642, 643; Cuvelier, vv. 19,725, 19,775; *Chronique de Du Guesclin*, ch. cxliv.

threatened the chief city of his province while on an expedition with the Captal de Buch, then left in charge of the principality of Aquitaine, during the absence of the Duke of Lancaster, who had gone over to England, early in the spring of 1372, with his Spanish bride. The captal, although urgently solicited by the seneschal to march to the relief of Poitiers, was unwilling to abandon the enterprise on which he was then engaged; but he permitted Sir Thomas Percy to go himself, accompanied by fifty lances.*

The constable, on learning that the garrison of Poitiers had been strengthened by the addition of the troops under Sir John Devereaux and the seneschal of Poitou, abandoned the design of laying siege to the city at that time; and, leaving a strong garrison in the castle of Montcontour, he proceeded with his army towards the province of Berry, and on his way to St. Sevère took a number of towns, castles, and fortified churches from the English. He found the Dukes of Berry and Bourbon engaged in the siege of St. Sevère, a strongly fortified town belonging to Sir John Devereaux, and situated near the southern border of Berry, on the river Indre.†

After joining his forces to those under the Dukes of Berry and Bourbon, the constable found himself at the head of four thousand men-at-arms; and his first act, on setting down before St. Sevère, was to make a careful examination of the defences of the town, in company with Lord de Clisson and the warlike Abbot of Malepaye. The experienced eye of the constable soon discovered that both the town and castle were strongly fortified by high and thick walls, strengthened by towers, and the whole surrounded by a deep moat; and so well defended by a large body of skilful men-at-arms, under experienced leaders, that he said to his attendants:—

* Froissart, liv. i. part ii. p. 643.

† "Saincte-Sevère sied deçà Poictiers dixhuict lieues," says D'Orronville, *Vie de Louis de Bourbon*, ch. xii.

"It will cost him dear, whoever will attempt to carry it by storm."*

Before the constable had completed his preparations for the attack, an incident took place which brought it on sooner than was expected or desired by either side. While he, with the other leaders of his army, was at dinner, a man-at-arms, named Geoffrey Payen, accompanied by several others, was examining the strength of the walls and fortifications; and, while standing near the exterior slope of the ditch, the earth gave way under his battle-axe, on which he was leaning, and the axe fell into the moat. Geoffrey was unwilling thus to lose a favourite weapon, which he had used in many a conflict; and he swore that he would sacrifice his life, sooner than return without it. He therefore first called to the sentinels on the walls, and begged them not to discharge their arrows or darts at him whilst he was attempting to recover his axe, as he had not come with his companions to commence the assault, but only to take a little fresh air. The sentinels would listen to no entreaties; and they ordered him off peremptorily, telling him that he should never get his axe again.

"By God the Just!" swore Geoffrey, "without my axe I can neither eat nor drink, sleep nor watch; and have it I will, cost what it may."

"You must love your axe, then," replied an Englishman on the walls, "better than a woman her husband or a man his wife."

Geoffrey Payen had not made his vow lightly; and he immediately procured the aid of some of his comrades to enable him to recover his battle-axe. With ten of them he made a chain, by holding to each others' hands, in order to reach the weapon; but the accumulated weight broke the

* Cuvelier, v. 19,820; Froissart, liv. i. part ii. p. 644.

hold of the upper man, and all the others tumbled confusedly into the moat.

The adventure was witnessed by the sentinels on the walls, who immediately began to discharge their arrows at Payen and his companions; but they were armed in proof, and the missiles had no other effect than to irritate the men-at-arms, who resolved not to return without making some display of their valour against the English. Calculating on the aid they were likely to receive from their friends in camp, Payen and his companions clambered up the scarp to the foot of the wall, and commenced an attack with such weapons as they had with them. As they had anticipated, their perilous situation was soon discovered by their comrades, who immediately came to their assistance, to the number of four hundred men, with such arms as could be hastily procured.

The constable was still at dinner, when he received the information that his men had commenced the assault on the town. Taken completely by surprise at the news, he suddenly sprang up, overturning the table, with everything upon it, and, calling to the leaders to prepare for the assault, he assigned to each his position as he came up—to one an attack on one of the towers, to another a certain extent of the wall. The order was promptly obeyed by the leaders and well seconded by the men, who carried with them, besides their other arms, scaling-ladders, with pickaxes and mattocks, to perforate the walls. At the same time he ordered the archers and cross-bowmen to advance, so as to protect the men-at-arms engaged at their work.

Although the assault was unexpected, the garrison was well prepared to resist it; and they met the assailants at every point of attack with equal skill and courage. Well provided with the means of repelling an assault, the besieged not only kept up a steady discharge of arrows and darts, but they threw down on the besiegers below casks filled with flint stones, and immense beams of timber.

The constable discharged the duties of a good general in applying every resource at his command where it could be used with the greatest effect, and in directing the efforts of both leaders and men where they could be employed to the most advantage. When he observed the Duke de Bourbon labouring with the miners at the foot of the wall, he called out to him:—"Ah! Sire, it is very foolish in you to remain where a villain may slay you as easily as the bravest knight engaged in this siege. It does not become you to work in that manner; but you should hold yourself in readiness for the shock of battle: for a prince or duke has little honour in being put to death by a varlet or army-boy. Get aid to erect a ladder against the walls, and you will find on the top an enemy worthy to contend with. Cursed be he of God who first invented darts and arrows: for no brave man would ever have thought of them."

The duke followed the advice of the constable, and, with the aid of his people, erected a ladder against the wall; when the impetuous Abbot of Malepaye* anticipated his attempt to mount it, and ascended before him; but the warlike priest had no sooner reached the top, and begun to use his arms, when a beam of timber, thrown from above, broke the ladder in the middle, and the abbot was precipitated from the top of the wall to the bottom of the moat. He was not seriously hurt, however, but only stunned by the fall; and, in a short time, he returned to the assault.

After the contest had continued for some time, the constable called upon the garrison, through their leaders, to surrender, offering to grant them a full pardon for all

* He is called "Alain de Taillecol, Esquire, otherwise named Abbot of Malepaye," in *Preuves de Du Guesclin*, par Du Chastelet, pp. 340, 341.

their misdeeds; but, in case they were taken by force of arms, he added, all the gold in the world could not save them from being hanged. Upon the refusal of the garrison to listen to his proposals, he renewed the attack with greater impetuosity than before; and he ordered every one, who could throw a stone or help to raise a ladder, to march up to the walls.

The constable, who suffered nothing to escape his attention, overheard a brave man-at-arms say to one of the army-women, who served the troops with water during the heat of the conflict:—"One should, in such an enterprise as this, drink the best wine that can be found: for good wine begets hardihood." On receiving this hint, the constable said aloud:—"Forward, my good friends! I will make you all rich; before sunset you shall be served with the best wines." He then ordered his butler to cause a number of tuns of wine to be brought up, and their heads knocked out, for the refreshment of the men. This order was promptly obeyed; and, after drinking, the French returned to the assault, "braver than lions or wild boars."

The assailants at length began to make an impression on the walls with their pickaxes and mattocks; when the besieged, no longer able to show their heads above the parapet, on account of the precision with which the French archers and cross-bowmen discharged their arrows, protected themselves by counterpanes, cushions, and carpets, while throwing large stones and other projectiles on the besiegers below; but the constable ordered the archers to approach near the walls, so as to discharge their arrows under the coverings, and the besieged were again driven back. The miners were thus enabled to work with less danger at the foot of the walls, and they made breaches in several places; but the garrison resisted the entrance of the besiegers by setting on fire bundles of hay, slightly moistened, at the inner openings of the breaches, which drove the besiegers back by the density of the smoke.

The Abbot of Malepaye, however, effected an entrance through the smoke at one of the breaches, and he used his lance with such skill as to drive the English before him; but, in the conflict, he received a blow from a battle-axe which stunned him, and beat down his bacinet on his head. As soon as he fell, the English took hold of him by the legs and attempted to drag him off; but his comrades, coming to his assistance, seized him by the head and arms; and so protracted was the struggle, that he was in some danger of being dismembered, before he was rescued by his friends. The abbot soon recovered from the blow; and, after drinking a cup of wine, returned to the assault, which was now conducted on one side with the greatest ardour and impetuosity, and still sustained on the other with manly courage and endurance. The French, at length, effected a large breach in the wall; but the garrison assembled at that point in such strength that the besiegers were kept in check. At other places the French mounted the walls on scaling-ladders; but they were stoutly resisted, hand to hand, by the English on the ramparts, so that large numbers were slain on both sides without deciding the conflict.

As the garrison at length perceived that they could not hold out much longer against such determined assailants, the governor* obtained from the constable a suspension of the assault, in order to submit proposals of surrender; but, as he not only asked that the English and their allies should be permitted to leave the town with all their goods, and demanded, besides, thirty thousand francs for the delivery of

* Cuvelier and the anonymous author of the *Chronique de Du Guesclin*, ch. cxlvi., call him Richard Gilles. Froissart says Sir William Percy, Richard Gille, and Richard Holme were the captains.—Liv. i. part ii. p. 644.

the town and castle, the constable unhesitatingly rejected his propositions; declaring that he would not pay a single parisis for the surrender of the town; that the English would be admitted to ransom; but the French, who had renounced their allegiance to the Duke of Berry, should be hanged without respite.

" Surrender, if you please," continued the constable, in an indifferent tone; " but the longer you hold out against us, the less you will find us friends at your need: for you will be recompensed according to your deserts."

The governor, in turn, rejected as promptly the hard conditions offered by the constable, and swore that he would not surrender the town as long as there was a rock or stone left in it; although, in that particular, he had nearly exhausted his resources: for the pavements had been taken up, and, in many places, the walls had been half torn down, to afford projectiles for throwing down on the besiegers.

After a brief suspension of arms the assault was renewed, and the indefatigable Abbot of Malepaye made a breach in the wall, "large enough to admit the head of a whale;" and through it he entered into the town, when he observed a barn, near the entrance, filled with hay. This barn he set on fire, and, the flames soon spreading, the strength of the besieged was weakened by being withdrawn from the walls, in order to extinguish the fire; when the assailants entered by escalade, and through the breaches already made in the walls, and the town was gained.*

The conquest of St. Sevère was a great triumph to the French arms, as it was brought on without any preparation of military engines or towers, or even without the common expedient of filling up the moats with fascines and earth;

* Cuvelier, vv. 19,776, 20,372; *Chronique* (Anonyme) *de Du Guesclin*, ch. cxlv. cxlvi.

and it was gained by mere force of arms and impetuous courage on the part of the assailants. D'Orronville, while giving full credit to the Duke de Bourbon for the part which he took in the attack, says :—"One of the most beautiful assaults that has been seen in this kingdom or elsewhere for a long time was the conquest of St. Sevère—the best assailed and the best defended."* Froissart, without entering into much detail, describes it as an assault in which marvellous feats of arms were performed by the besiegers: "for the greater part of them," he continues, "passed through the ditches filled with water, marched up to the walls with their shields above their heads, and never recoiled from anything that was thrown upon them from above, but continually pressed forward. Near the ditches were the Dukes de Berry and de Bourbon, the Count d'Alençon, the Dauphin d'Auvergne, and other great lords, who urged on their respective troops to the assault; and the men, thus encouraged by the presence of their leaders, went forward the more willingly, fearing neither danger nor death." †

The first step taken by the victors, after the surrender of the town, was to extinguish the fire; when they proceeded to collect together an immense booty—the fruit of many years of plunder by the Free Companies—in corn and good wine, in bacon and bolted flour, in jewels, gold and silver money, in helmets, coats of mail and swords, with many piles of cloth, both of wool and linen.‡

Besides the booty thus acquired, the leaders obtained

* *Vie de Louis de Bourbon*, ch. xii.

† Froissart, liv. i. part ii. p. 645.

‡ *Et de lange et de linge*, Cuvelier, v. 20,399. Jean Marot, speaking of the dyer, Paul de Nove, whom the people of Genoa had created duke, says:—"*Bon taincturier tant en lange qu'en linge:* that is as well *in wool as in linen.*"—Le Duchat, in *Dic. Etymol.*, par Menage, voc. *Langes.*

large sums from the English prisoners, all of whom were admitted to ransom; but their allies of the French nation were seized and coupled together, by the constable's order, to await the punishments which their various acts of pillage and disloyalty, as members of the Free Companies, so fully merited. After these dispositions were made, the Duke de Berry called together all the knights of the army, to thank them, in the name of his brother the king of France, for their gallantry in the conquest of the important town of St. Sevère. Wine was brought, and the duke first offered it to the constable, who declined to take any; when the duke, though somewhat displeased, said kindly:—

"Friend Bertrand, why do you not take wine? Are you afraid that we design to poison you?"

"I am ready to obey all your commands," replied the constable, bowing low to the duke; "but I have made a vow which I am unwilling to violate. It is this. My lord, you know that the people of all others who have done the greatest injury to France are those belonging to this kingdom, who have joined the enemies of the king and yourself. You well know, my lord, that many Frenchmen have been taken in this town, who have aided in sustaining the siege so long, and by whom many a good man has lost his life. For this reason I have vowed and promised that I would neither eat nor drink as long as any of them are alive."

The Duke de Berry, pleased to find that the constable had no other cause for anger, said:—

"Friend Bertrand, every loyal subject has great reason to sustain his lord; and no brave man would dissuade you from such counsel. Now I desire you to know, that the same oath that you have taken I take: and I vow to God that I will neither eat nor drink while a single Frenchman is alive who has been taken with the English in St. Sevère."

The constable thanked the Duke de Berry for seconding

his design so warmly; and he ordered all the French prisoners to be brought out and hanged, by the servants of the army, on the trees nearest to the town. The English prisoners of any note were discharged on arranging the amounts of their ransoms, while the constable permitted a number of small householders to go away without charge. The Duke de Berry then took possession of the town, which he furnished with a sufficient garrison of men-at-arms.*

* *Chronique* (Anonyme) *de Du Guesclin*, ch. cxlvii.; Cuvelier, vv. 20,405, 20,450.

CHAPTER XV

Voluntary surrender of the city of Poitiers to the French. Capture and imprisonment of the Captal de Buch. Important conquests of the French in Poitou, Saintonge, and Angoumois. Surrender of Rochelle.

IT was a fortunate circumstance for the success of the French arms at St. Sevère, that the accidental fall of Geoffrey Payen's battle-axe precipitated the assault: for Sir John Devereaux had been informed of the design of the constable in going to assist the Duke de Berry in the siege of that town, and the English knight had lost no time in obtaining the effectual aid of Sir Thomas Percy and the Captal de Buch in procuring a body of men to raise the siege. The captal, who was then at St. Jean d'Angely, soon collected from the provinces of Saintonge and Poitou a force of nine hundred lances and five hundred archers, and marched to the relief of St. Sevère; but he was too late: for, while on his way, he met the broken, wounded, half-naked, and disarmed remains of the late garrison of that town. This unlooked for spectacle was so irritating to the English leaders, that the captal, Sir Thomas Percy, and Sir John Devereaux took an oath that they would not enter a fortress in Poitou until they had given battle to the French.*

* Froissart, liv. i. part ii. pp. 644, 645; Cuvelier, v. 20,473.

During the absence of Sir Thomas Percy and Sir John Devereaux from Poitiers, much dissension had arisen in the city between the great body of citizens, who wished to return to their former allegiance to the French crown, and the mayor, Jean Regnault, who, with the officers of the prince and some of the more influential men of the city, preferred the English government. The dissension increased at length to such a degree, that the parties nearly came to blows. As the citizens attached to the French interests foresaw, from the ill-success of the English arms in Aquitaine, what was eventually to be the fate of their own city, they contrived to send a secret message to the constable, to the effect that, if he came with a sufficient force to hold the city, they would deliver it up to him.

The constable, who was then in Limousin, did not hesitate to act on this invitation; and, leaving the great body of his army in command of the Dukes de Berry and de Bourbon, he set out with three hundred chosen lances, all well mounted: for he designed to make the journey of thirty leagues in a day and night. As it was important to the success of the enterprise that his design should not be known, he was forced to avoid the direct and open road, and to travel through woods and heaths, along by-paths and uninhabited tracts; and, if a horse broke down on the march, both horse and rider were left behind.

The mayor of Poitiers, who suspected what had been done by the disaffected portion of the citizens, sent word to Sir Thomas Percy, the seneschal of Poitou, to hasten his return to the city: for there was great strife among the citizens; that five parts of them desired to turn French; and that he, the mayor, was in great peril of his life. He urged the seneschal to come with all speed, as he feared that it would then be too late to save the city. Sir Thomas Percy was in the company of the Captal de Buch when he received the message from the mayor of Poitiers; and, when the captal was informed of the purport of the communication, he told Sir Thomas Percy that he could not then spare him, as he was one of the most trusted of his officers, and one in whose counsel he put the greatest confidence; but that he would send Sir John d'Angle, with one hundred lances, to the assistance of the loyal party in the city. Immediately after his appointment, Sir John d'Angle set out, with his followers, for Poitiers; but he was anticipated by the constable, who had presented himself before the gates, which were thrown open to him, with many demonstrations of joy, just before the arrival of the English knight. Sir John d'Angle, when within a league of the city, found out that he was too late; he therefore instantly turned back: for he perceived very soon that he would have enough to do if he could save himself and his followers from being captured.

The voluntary surrender by its citizens of the important city of Poitiers to the constable of France, was a disastrous blow to the English interests in Aquitaine; and the news, when communicated in the camp of the Captal de Buch, was received with the utmost consternation: for it led at once to suspicion and distrust among the leaders; and, although no special charge or crimination was then made, their mutual want of confidence broke up the army of the captal, by the Gascons withdrawing to St. Jean d'Angely, the Poitevins to Thouars, and the English to Niort.*

The constable did not fail to profit by this feeling of impatience on the part of the French population under the English yoke; therefore, soon after he took possession of the city of Poitiers, he sent the Lord de Pons, with three hundred lances, against the strong castle of Soubise, situated on the river Charente. The castle was under the command of a

* Froissart, liv. i. part ii. pp. 645, 647.

woman, called the Lady of Soubise, who, as soon as she was informed that her castle was about to be besieged by the Lord de Pons, sent to the Captal de Buch, then at St. Jean d'Angely, and begged him to aid her in the defence of the castle. The captal, who, "like a courteous and valiant knight, was always inclined to give every aid and comfort to both dames and damsels, in whatever situation they might be, as every noble and man of gentle blood should do," said to the messenger who brought the request:—"Return to the Lady of Soubise, and tell her from me to console herself: for I will listen to nothing until I shall have aided her, and raised the siege; and commend me to her more than a hundred times." *

The Captal de Buch soon assembled a body of four hundred lances to make good his promise to the Lady of Soubise; but his design was found out by Evan of Wales, who was then lying off the port of Rochelle with a fleet of vessels, which he had procured from Henry of Castille, at the solicitation of the king of France. Evan manned thirteen barges, and, with a body of four hundred chosen men, rowed up the Charente until he reached the castle of Soubise; when he placed his troops in ambush, without his approach being known, either to the Captal de Buch or the Lord de Pons.

In the meantime the Captal de Buch, who had been misinformed as to the number of men under Lord de Pons—for he had been told that they did not exceed one hundred men-at-arms—left one-half of the force which he had collected for the expedition, and set out from St. Jean d'Angely with two hundred lances only. With these he rode all day, and, towards night, came near the camp of the French. He then entered an adjoining wood and made his men dismount, in order to tighten their armour and re-girth their saddles.

* Froissart, liv. i. part ii. pp. 647, 648.

When all his preparations were completed, he marched up, without noise, to the tents of the Lord de Pons, whom he completely surprised, and succeeded in slaying or capturing the whole force of the French.

Evan of Wales, who was on the watch, being apprised of what had taken place, came out from his cover, and marched up behind the lodges of the English, with his men-at-arms, bearing a number of lanterns and lighted torches; when, shouting their war-cries, they attacked the English in their tents, sword in hand, and in a short time the Captal de Buch and his whole command were defeated and made prisoners.

This was a fortunate turn of affairs to the French, and especially to the Lord de Pons, who was the first Poitevin nobleman to desert the English standards the year before; and, by changing situations in captivity with the Captal de Buch, he probably escaped the same severe punishment—the loss of liberty, and, eventually, of life—which was the hard fate of the latter, as the result of this gallant but unfortunate enterprise. The captal was taken prisoner by a squire named Pierre Longvillers, under the pennon of Evan of Wales; and he soon afterwards came into the hands of the king of France.

The English were fully conscious of the loss which they had sustained by the capture of the Captal de Buch; and Edward III. and his council forthwith offered in exchange for him, not only the Count de St. Pol, but three or four good prisoners besides, whom they would not have ransomed for a hundred thousand francs. To this exchange the king of France would in no wise consent, although he had only allowed his captor the very moderate sum of twelve hundred francs for his prisoner. The captal justly complained that he was detained in prison against the law of arms, and insisted that he ought to be admitted to ransom; but his remonstrances were unheeded by the king of France. The

French knights, however, sympathizing with the captal, frequently urged their master to release him from imprisonment; but Charles, if he had had the generosity to pardon an indignity offered him by the captal seven years before, in renouncing his homage and sending back his gifts, was too politic a prince to release an enemy whom he so greatly feared. The king of France would never listen to any proposals made for his enlargement—rejecting, without hesitation, the offer of his prisoner to pay five or six times the amount of his annual revenues for his ransom; and the captal was conducted to the castle of the Louvre at Paris, and afterwards confined in the tower of the Temple until his death, after a weary imprisonment of five years.*

The imprisonment of the Captal de Buch was a fatal blow to the English cause in Aquitaine, as he was the only leader then in France capable of opposing any effectual resistance to the progress of the French arms, under the impulse recently given to them by the uninterrupted successes of Bertrand du Guesclin. Profiting by the depressing effects

* Froissart, liv. i. part ii. pp. 647, 649, and 654. The incidents relating to the termination of the captal's imprisonment are told in Buchon's edition of Froissart, p. 713, very differently from many of the other editions, as follows:—"The Lord de Coucy, when pressed by Charles V. to declare what grace he ought to accord to the prisoner, replied:—

"'Sire, if you make him swear that he will never arm himself against the kingdom of France, you may well deliver him, and the act will do you honour.'

"'We desire it to be so,' said the king; 'but let him do it.'

"The captal was then asked if he would bind himself by such an agreement. He replied that he would take time to consider the proposition; but, during the time that he took to advise about it, he was so overwhelmed by trouble and melancholy, that he fell into a sort of frenzy, when he would neither eat nor drink, and he became so enfeebled, that he settled down into a languor which lasted till his death. Thus died the Captal de Buch, a prisoner, after a close imprisonment of five years."

of the recent reverses on the English and their allies, the constable sent the Lords de Clisson, de Pons, de Laval, de Beaumanoir, the Viscount de Rohan, with other leaders, and a force of Bretons and Poitevins, amounting to five hundred men-at-arms, against some of the most important strongholds which the English still possessed in Saintonge and Angoumois. The French troops first marched boldly into the former province, and made their dispositions to attack St. Jean d'Angely, lately commanded by the Captal de Buch; but the garrison was so frightened at the approach of a hostile force—as they had no one of rank or authority within their walls to advise them, and as they could look to no quarter for aid—that they surrendered at the first summons, and took the oaths of fealty and obedience to the king of France.

After this important conquest, the French marched to the city of Angoulême, which, like St. Jean d'Angely, had lost its seneschal, Sir Henry Haye, who, with Sir Thomas Percy, was taken, together with the Captal de Buch, at Soubise; and the city surrendered in like manner, and took the same oaths. Taillebourg, on the Charente, was gained in the same way; but Saintes offered greater resistance: for Sir William Fermiton, the seneschal of Saintonge, who was then in the town with a force of sixty men-at-arms, declared that he would not surrender so easily; and ordered all the gates to be closed, and all the citizens to man the defences of the town, whether willingly or otherwise. Thereupon the French attacked the town with great spirit, and kept up the assault all day without any advantage; but, in withdrawing at night, they threatened to renew the assault the next day; and declared that, if the town was taken by storm, it should be pillaged and burnt, and the inhabitants put to the sword. This threat immediately produced its intended effect on the great body of citizens, and especially on the bishop, Bernard de Sault, who advised the people to seize the seneschal and his principal officers, and threaten them with instant death, if they would not consent to surrender the town. The counsel of the bishop was followed; and, at night, Sir William Fermiton was seized in his house, with eight of his squires, who promised, when threatened with the consequences of their refusal, to let the citizens have their own way.

The next morning, when Lord de Clisson and the other leaders ordered the trumpets to be sounded for the assault, they were equally surprised and pleased to find that they had brought under the obedience of their king, by the unconditional surrender of the inhabitants, so important a city as Saintes, without any effusion of blood. The French troops next marched to Pons, which still resolutely adhered to the English, although its lord had joined the French the year before; but, when the inhabitants saw their town encompassed by their enemies; when they found out that Poitiers, St. Jean d'Angely, Saintes, and Angoulême—the most important towns in Poitou, Saintonge, and Angoumois—were in the possession of the French; that the Captal de Buch was a prisoner; and that the English were losing some material advantage every day,—they offered to surrender, upon permission being granted to all who still adhered to the English cause to leave the town without loss or injury, and go in safety to Bordeaux.*

While his troops were making these important conquests, the constable was not idle at Poitiers; and both he and Evan of Wales, who still kept up the blockade of Rochelle, were entertaining secret negotiations for the surrender of the town; but the citizens were restrained by Philippe Mansel, who had been left in command of the castle by Sir John

* Froissart, liv. i. part ii. pp. 649, 651.

Devereaux, with a garrison of sixty men-at-arms. The constable, in one of his interviews with a deputation of citizens from Rochelle, endeavoured to persuade them to return to their allegiance to the king of France, who, he said, was well able to protect them from all danger from the king of England; threatening, in case of their refusal, to burn their town, and leave standing in it neither fortress nor wall, nor habitable house.

"Sire," said one of the deputation, named Tholomer, "will you be able so easily to rase such a town?"

"Yes," replied the constable; "you cannot hold out against us: for, just as you can see the bright sunlight pass through a glass, so you will see the French pass through your walls; and, if the sun of heaven can enter your town, I doubt not that I can enter it."

"Sire," rejoined the citizen, "we should not doubt your words; but there will be no need for us to resist you, if you will grant us a boon, which will neither impoverish the king nor injure you."

"Ha!" exclaimed the constable, "I can already guess what you would demand. You wish to hold your town without paying tax or service to any one."

"That is true," said the citizen; "and will you grant it?"

"We will advise about it," answered the constable.

While these secret conferences were taking place at Poitiers, events were rapidly preparing at Rochelle, which soon transferred all further negotiations to that place. Sir Jean Caudorier was at that time mayor of the city—a man of much adroitness and subtlety, and thoroughly French at heart. He made known his wishes and plans to a number of the citizens of Rochelle, whom he found entirely willing to support him in all his designs. He well knew the character of the governor of the castle, who, though an expert man-at-arms, was careless and unsuspecting. When his plans were sufficiently matured, the mayor invited Mansel one day to dinner, with some of the citizens of the town. The governor, suspecting nothing, came readily. Before setting down to dinner, the mayor, who had taken every precaution to play off successfully the deception which he designed, said to the governor :—

" I received a piece of news yesterday from our dear lord the king of England, which touches you nearly."

" What is it?" eagerly asked Mansel.

" I will show it to you," replied the mayor, " and have it read in your presence : for it is but proper that you should hear it."

He then went to a desk, and took from it an open letter, to which was appended the great seal of England, and showed it to the credulous governor, who at once recognised the seal as genuine, although he was unable to read a word of the letter. The mayor then called a clerk, whom he had instructed beforehand as to the part he had to play, and ordered him to read the paper. The clerk read, as if out of the letter, that the king of England commanded the mayor to order a muster of all the men-at-arms in Rochelle, so as to report, by the bearer of the letter, the number of effective men in the city, and also those of the castle : for he hoped soon to be amongst them. When the clerk finished reading, the mayor said :—

" Castellan, you hear what the king our lord commands me to do ; so that from him I order you to muster your men in the square before the castle ; and, immediately after you are done, I will make mine, so that we can both certify to the truth of the report to our very dear lord the king of England. Besides, if your men want money, I think I can advance you some when the review is over, that you may pay their wages : for our lord the king of England so ordered it, in a sealed letter, in which he commands me to pay them by virtue of my office."

The governor, who believed every word uttered by the mayor, exclaimed :—

"Mayor, by God ! since it is to-morrow that I am to have my parade, I will do it willingly ; and my men will also be greatly rejoiced on account of the pay, as they all want money."

After dinner the governor returned to the castle, and informed his men of the parade to take place the next morning, and that they were to receive their pay immediately thereafter. The soldiers, whose wages were some three months or more in arrear, received the information with evident satisfaction; and they began at once to furbish their bacinets, to put in order their coats of mail, to polish their swords and whatever other armour they possessed.

On the same afternoon, the mayor secretly imparted his scheme for obtaining possession of the castle to the greater part of the citizens of Rochelle, who agreed to assist him in carrying it out; and he gave orders in what manner they should act on the morrow. Near the castle, and close to the square where the parade was to take place, were some old and uninhabited houses, wherein the mayor designed to station a body of four hundred men-at-arms, with orders to prevent the return of the garrison to the castle as soon as they issued out the next morning for parade. These dispositions were carefully made during the night, the officers appointed, and all fully armed and instructed as to their duties. After sunrise the next morning, the mayor, attended only by the échevins and others attached to his office,* came

* Froissart uses the words, *Le maieur et les jurés et cils de l'office tant seulement.*—Liv. i. part ii. p. 652. As to the identity of the *jurés*, and

forth on the square without arms, in order to give greater confidence to the garrison of the castle. He and his suite were mounted on strong horses, to enable them to get away whenever the *mêlée* should commence. The governor, as soon as he saw the mayor and his attendants on the ground, hastened the preparations of his men; and, soon after, his whole command appeared on the square, leaving in the castle but a few valets and menials, and even leaving open the castle-gate, as he expected to re-enter it in a short time. As soon as the soldiers of the garrison formed on the parade, the mayor engaged their attention by addressing himself in familiar speech to one, and then to another, in such words as these:—

"You have not yet all your harness on to entitle you to full pay; you must amend that."

To which some of them replied, in the same humour, "Willingly."

The mayor kept them in such friendly chit-chat until the men-at-arms whom he had placed in ambush sallied out, threw themselves between the soldiers of the garrison and the castle, and took possession of the gate. As soon as the governor and his men saw this movement, they at once knew that they had been duped and betrayed. At the same moment the mayor and his attendants took to flight, leaving the matter to be settled by his troops with the garrison, who, seeing all resistance vain, suffered themselves to be disarmed and led off to different places of imprisonment in the town. The castle offered no resistance.*

The Dukes of Berry, Burgundy, and Bourbon, who had

the *échevins* or *scabini*, who were municipal officers charged with the administration of the police and the affairs of the commune, see De Savigny, *Histoire du Droit Romain du Moyen Age*, tom. i. ch. iv. §§ 68, 75; and Du Cange, Gloss. voc. *Jurata.*

* Froissart, liv. i. part ii. pp. 651, 652.

kept upon the frontiers of Auvergne and Limousin ever since the surrender of St. Sevère, as soon as they heard that the citizens of Rochelle had taken possession of the castle which had hitherto kept them in check, broke up their quarters, and marched towards Poitiers to join the constable, who was still in that city. On their way they took the towns of St. Maixent, Civray, and Mellé; and they left no town or castle behind them which did not owe obedience to the king of France.

Soon after the princes reached Poitiers, the Duke de Berry held a council, in which it was decided to send messengers to Rochelle to inquire what the Rochellois designed to do; as nothing was known of their intentions or wishes since they had taken the castle. The messengers of the duke and the constable were well received by the citizens of Rochelle, who returned, as their answer, that they desired to make certain demands of the king of France; and, if they were granted, the Rochellois would always thereafter continue good Frenchmen. Upon this they received assurances from the constable and Evan of Wales that no injury should be done to them while prosecuting their demands.

The Rochellois accordingly despatched twelve of the most notable of their citizens to the king of France, at Paris, who was so anxious to have them as friends and subjects, that he received them with marked kindness, and patiently listened to all their demands. The extravagant character of these demands, at a time when the communes obtained their franchises very grudgingly from their lords, shows how highly the Rochellois estimated their own importance in the opinion of Charles V They first asked that the castle of Rochelle should be rased to the ground, and that their town should for ever be held by the king of France and his heirs, as the proper domain of the crown of France, without the power of alienating it by any peace, contract, marriage, or alliance whatsoever, with the king of England or any other power. Besides these articles, they demanded that the king of France, in minting their florins and other money, should make them of the same weight and alloy as the money of Paris; and that neither the king of France, nor any of his heirs or successors, should impose on them any subsidy, fine, imposition, tax on salt or fire, or anything which resembled it, without their consent. They then entreated the king to absolve them from the oaths which they had taken to Edward III., and which they declared weighed heavily on their consciences; and they further begged that he would, at his own expense, obtain absolution from the pope for their sins. Charles took some time, with the aid of his most trusted counsellors, to consider these demands; but, as the Rochellois would abate none of their pretensions, the king at length granted their whole petition: for he regarded Rochelle as the most important city, next to Paris, in the kingdom.

The Rochellois, who were greatly pleased, upon the return of their deputation, to find that all their demands had been granted, sent to inform the Duke de Berry that he might come whenever he pleased; and they would gladly receive him, in the name of the king, into the city, and do everything besides that they ought. Whereupon the constable, who had the authority to take possession of the city for the king, left Poitiers, with one hundred lances, and entered Rochelle, where he was received with many demonstrations of joy by the citizens, on his showing them the procuration of the king, by which he had been appointed the representative of his sovereign in that part of the kingdom. The constable, after taking the usual oaths of homage and fealty from the citizens, "by whom he was treated like a king"—receiving large gifts and handsome presents from the men, and returning equally valuable ones to the ladies and damsels of the city—remained there three days, and then returned to Poitiers.*

* Froissart, liv. i. part ii. pp. 653, 654. Buchon, in his edition of Froissart, in which he is followed by Sismondi, *Hist. des Français*, tom. vi. p. 327, says, on the faith of Cascales, a Spanish authority, that Rochelle surrendered to the French on the 15th of August, 1372; but this date is evidently erroneous: for the brief of Edward III., directed to the Archbishop of Canterbury, to offer up public prayers for the success of the expedition to France, is dated August 11th, 1372; and that expedition was undertaken to relieve Thouars, which was not besieged until some time after the surrender of Rochelle.—Rymer, vol. iii. par. ii. p. 960.

CHAPTER XVI.

The constable takes the castles of Benon, Marant, and Surgières, near Rochelle, and the town of Fontenay-le-Comte. Secret negotiations between the Duke of Brittany and the king of England. The constable lays siege to Thouars. Unsuccessful attempt of Edward III. to relieve it.

SOON after his return from Rochelle, the constable set on foot an expedition against certain castles and towns belonging to the English, which kept the Rochellois in a state of constant perturbation, by the marauding bands daily sent out from the garrisons of those places. After making his preparations, he left Poitiers, accompanied by the Dukes of Berry, Burgundy, and Bourbon, the Dauphin d'Auvergne, the Maréchals of France, and above two thousand lances, and came first before the castle of Benon. This castle belonged to the Captal de Buch, and it was then commanded by a squire of the county of Foix, named Guillaume de Pau, and a Neapolitan knight called Sir Jacques, two very expert men-at-arms, who were supported by a confident garrison, with ample provision of food and military stores. Thus defended, the castle stood several assaults without damage. During the siege, sixty men-at-arms from the neighbouring garrison of Surgières left their fortress about twilight, came towards Benon, which they reached near midnight, and made an attack on the French, then asleep in their tents. They chanced to fall upon the quarter occupied by the constable ; and, in the *mêlée*, a squire whom he greatly valued was slain. As soon as the French soldiers awoke and began to arm themselves, the assailants fled, and gained admittance into the castle. When the constable was informed in what manner his favourite squire had been slain, he was wholly overcome by passion, and swore that he would never leave the castle of Benon until he had taken it, and put to death every one within it. The next day, after the burial of the squire, he ordered all his men to arm themselves for the assault of the castle, and he advanced himself to the attack. After a well-sustained and long-continued defence, the castle was taken by storm ; and the constable carried out his fearful oath by putting to death, without mercy, every one found within the walls of Benon.*

After the surrender of Benon, the constable marched to Marant, a castle about four leagues from Rochelle, commanded by a German named Wissebare, with a German garrison ; but the governor and his command were so frightened at the approach of the constable, after the fate of Benon, that they offered to surrender their fortress and join the French, if the wages which had been promised them by the English were paid. The constable, after taking possession of Marant on the terms proposed, next marched to the castle of Surgières ; but he found the gate open and the castle empty : for the garrison had been so much impressed

* Froissart, liv. i. part ii. p. 655. Cuvelier and the anonymous author of the *Chronique de Du Guesclin*, ch. clvi., both concur in stating that the squire slain was Geoffrey Payen, who had so distinguished himself at the siege of St. Sevère ; and that he belonged to Lord de Clisson, who avenged his death, after the surrender of Benon, by putting the garrison, severally, to death with his battle-axe. Jean Cabaret d'Orronville says there were *four* squires of the constable engaged in playing at dice in his tent, who were slain.—*Vie de Louis de Bourbon*, ch. xxxi.

by the fate of their comrades who had been slaughtered at Benon, that, as soon as they heard of his approach, they abandoned the castle, and took refuge in some of the other English fortresses. The French army next proceeded to attack the town and castle of Fontenay-le-Comte. Both the town and castle were found to be strongly fortified, and well defended by a hardy and numerous garrison, amply provided for a siege. Here were frequent assaults, skirmishes, and gallant feats of arms performed every day, in which many were wounded on both sides. The garrison, if there had been a hope of relief from any quarter, could have held out much longer; but, as they feared that they would at length be taken, they offered to capitulate, upon being permitted to carry away their property under a safe-conduct to Thouars, where the Poitevin lords were assembled.*

While the constable was making these conquests, the Duke of Brittany was attempting to amuse the king of France by protestations of fidelity to his person and attachment to his interests, and, at the same time, was secretly renewing his treasonable alliances with the king of England. To Charles the duke sent the Dean of Nantes and Sir Guy de Rochefort, to apologize for the employment of so many Englishmen about his person, and to assure the king that he was then, and he would always be, a good and loyal subject; and to Edward he sent Sir Thomas Melbourne, who, with Robert, Lord de Neufville, seneschal of England, concluded a treaty on the 19th of July, 1372, in the name of Edward III. and the Duke of Brittany, by which the contracting parties bound themselves to aid each other against their common enemy, and to make no treaty without the consent of each other. By the same paper, the duke bound himself to join the king of England with one thousand men-at-arms, when-

* Froissart, liv. i. part ii. pp. 655, 656.

ever the latter should invade France; and the king of England agreed to send three hundred men-at-arms, and as many archers, to serve the duke at his need.*

As soon as this treaty was concluded, Edward III. sent Lord Neufville into Brittany to obtain confirmation by the duke of all that had been agreed upon at Westminster. The duke, while awaiting the return of his ambassador, Sir Thomas Melbourne, made strenuous efforts to gain over to his interests the great Breton nobles; but he failed utterly in his attempts on the Viscount de Rohan, and the Lords de Clisson and de Laval. These nobles were closely united in policy and principle, and they possessed great influence in the duchy, through their large possessions, the number of their vassals, and their alliances. They could not, as loyal subjects of the king of France, tolerate such close intimacy as existed between the duke and the king of England; and it was still more offensive to them that the duke always kept such a great number of English about his person and in his house. Acting on their suspicions of a secret treaty already concluded between the king of England and the duke, they sent word to the latter that, if he still continued to favour the English as he had been doing, they would not only abandon him, but drive him from his estates. The duke had already taken the precaution to bind over to his interests other nobles and knights of the duchy; and he continued to take his measures with such secrecy, that they were kept for a time from the knowledge of the king of France.†

The constable, after the surrender of Fontenay-le-Comte, returned to Poitiers to refresh his troops for a season; but he was there only four days, when he determined to lay siege to Thouars, where fully one hundred Poitevin lords and knights,

* *Actes de Bretagne*, tom. ii. col. 34; Rymer, vol. iii. par. ii. p. 953.

† *Actes de Bretagne*, tom. ii. col. 33; Morice, *Hist. de Bretagne*, tom. i. p. 342.

who still adhered to the English interests, were assembled with their forces. Setting out from the city of Poitiers with a body of three thousand lances, and four thousand other troops armed with bucklers, including the Genoese cross-bowmen, he marched to Thouars, which he invested so closely on all sides that no one could enter or leave it. As the town was defended by a large body of men-at-arms, commanded by a number of distinguished nobles and knights, the constable resolved not to imperil the lives of his men by attempting to carry the place by assault, but to starve out the besieged.

When the Poitevin lords perceived the intention of the constable, and in what manner he had disposed his troops for a protracted siege, they met in council to determine what they should do. In that assembly, Sir Percevaux de Cologne, "a sage, imaginative, and well-spoken knight," declared that it was well known to all how faithfully they had maintained their loyalty towards the king of England; that they had adventured their bodies and employed their means, without reserve, in his service, and in aiding to defend his inheritance; that it could not be that the king of England was ignorant of the danger they were in, or that every day he was losing some portion of his possessions; that if he was willing to incur the loss, they could not prevent it, for they were not strong enough to resist the power of the king of France, as it could everywhere be seen throughout the land that cities, towns, castles, and fortresses, with prelates, barons, knights, dames, and communities, were every day turning over to the French and making war upon them, which they could not hold out against much longer; and he concluded by advising that they should treat at once with the French leaders, and endeavour to obtain a truce, to last for two or three months, or as long an interval as they could get, in order that they might have full time to inform the king of

England plainly of their situation; and that, if he or one of his sons should come with a force sufficient to raise the siege of their town, they would remain loyal subjects as before; but, if otherwise, that they would then become French from that day forward.

This well-considered opinion gained the assent of the whole assembly, as the best means by which they could escape from their present peril, and preserve their honour and loyalty; and, accordingly, they at once proposed the terms agreed upon among themselves to the constable and the Duke de Berry. The negotiations lasted for many days, as neither the constable nor the duke was willing to accede to the terms proposed without the assent of the king of France. At length it was decided that the besieged should remain secure within the walls of Thouars until the day of St. Michael next—the 29th of September; and if within that time the king of England or one of his sons should come into Poitou, with a sufficient force to hold Thouars against the French, that the Poitevin lords and knights, with their lands, should belong to the English for ever; but, if neither the king of England nor one of his sons could *keep the day*, that then the nobles and knights within Thouars should put themselves and their lands under subjection to the king of France.

The Poitevin lords lost no time in sending to inform the king of England of the condition of the country, and of their own danger; imploring him, for mercy's sake, and in God's name, to provide some remedy, for it concerned him more than all the world beside. When Edward III. heard these unwelcome tidings, he resolved to go in person to keep the day before Thouars, and take with him all his sons, upon the declaration of the Black Prince, who, though still the victim of disease, said that he would go, if he died on the voyage. The king thereupon gave a special command to all his knights and squires, in and out of the kingdom, to prepare for the expedition; and he obtained three hundred lances from the king of Scotland. It so happened at that time that large provision had been made during the season to fit out an expedition against France, to land at Calais, under the Duke of Lancaster; so that it was easy to divert the preparation of men and ships already collected to this more pressing emergency. Edward, therefore, after leaving his infant grandson nominally as the guardian of the kingdom during his absence, in order to strengthen his title to the succession against the pretensions of his uncles, was ready to embark from Sandwich by the 1st of September, 1372, with a fleet of four hundred vessels, and a well-appointed force of four thousand men-at-arms and ten thousand archers.*

All this preparation and expense, however, turned out in the end to be utterly fruitless. Fortune seemed to have for ever deserted Edward. A favourable wind, to waft his fleet towards the coasts of France, was all that he wanted; but that was denied him. He would gladly have landed anywhere—in Poitou, in Saintonge, in the Rochellois, or in any of the neighbouring provinces. He sailed from one quarter to another, and tried every breath of wind that came to aid his progress; "but his fleet was driven as far back in one day as it had advanced in three." Anxious to relieve his loyal subjects, and recover some of the immense losses which he had sustained in his French possessions, Edward bore with extreme impatience the vexatious delays opposed by the unchanging winds; until, at length, he saw with dismay the 29th of September, the last day of the appointed time, expire, without having been able to land a soldier on

* Froissart, liv. i. part ii. pp. 657, 658; Rymer, vol. iii. par. ii. p. 692.

the coasts of France. For four long weeks he had been driven about by adverse winds; and, as he now regarded the province of Poitou as lost for this season, angered at heart, he made for the coast of England, uttering, in bitterness of spirit:—"God and St. George aid us! There never was in France so vile a king as the present one; and yet there never was a king who gave me so much to do." *

The day fixed by the barons and knights of Poitou for the expiration of the truce was well known to Sir Thomas Felton, seneschal of Bordeaux, who also knew that the king of England had been duly informed of the situation of the beleaguered knights. As he feared that his master, Edward III., might not come in time to save Thouars, he collected all the Gascon lords who still adhered to the English cause, and, with their retainers, set out from Bordeaux, and marched to Niort, where the English knights were assembled. After joining the forces which he brought with him to those which he found at Niort, Sir Thomas Felton was able to bring into the field twelve hundred lances; and he then ascertained that the king of England had not arrived in Poitou, although the truce had expired. Notwithstanding, after full consultation with the English and Gascon knights, he sent a message to the Poitevin lords in Thouars, that he and his men would adventure their bodies to save the inheritance of their master, the king of England, if the Poitevin lords would leave Thouars, and appoint a day to give battle to the French.

This proposition was discussed with some warmth by the Poitevin nobles and knights; and one of them, the Lord de Partenay, proposed to accept the offer, on the grounds that it was well known that either the king of England or one of his sons was then at sea, with a sufficient force to relieve

* Froissart, liv. i. part ii. p. 658.

them, but that the expected succour was prevented from landing in Poitou by adverse fortune ; and, moreover, that although they had sealed and sworn to certain terms of a truce with the French, they had no authority to alienate the possessions of the king of England without his consent.

These reasons were, very wisely, deemed insufficient by the Poitevin knights, in view of the irresistible force then under the constable, which they well knew would effectually prevent all escape or relief under any aid which they could expect to receive, even if they had been willing to break their plighted faith with the French leaders. To the number of men with which the constable had originally invested Thouars, the king of France had since added a very large body of men-at-arms and foot-soldiers, as he expected that the king of England or one of his sons would attempt to relieve the town ; and, accordingly, Charles had not only collected the flower of the men-at-arms from Brittany, Normandy, Burgundy, Auvergne, Berry, Touraine, Blois, Anjou, Limousin, and Maine, but he had taken into his pay a large body of foreign mercenaries from Germany, Flanders, and Hainault ; amounting, in the whole, to fifteen thousand men-at-arms, and thirty thousand other troops.

The Poitevin lords, whatever may have been their motive, rejected the proposition of the English and Gascon leaders, and sent word to the constable and the French princes that they were ready to comply with the terms of the truce. Thouars, in consequence, immediately opened its gates to the victors ; and the barons and knights placed themselves, their people and lands, under the protection of the crown of France.

After the surrender of Thouars, besides the town of Niort, the English only possessed, in the whole province of Poitou, but some nine fortresses. To one of these—Mortagne—Lord de Clisson laid siege, upon the return of the constable to Poitiers with his army. The garrison of Mortagne was commanded by an English squire named James Clerk, who defended the castle with great valour against the assaults of De Clisson; but, as he well knew that he could not long hold out against such attacks, and how little he had to expect from the clemency of an antagonist who had earned among his English countrymen the appellation of *The Butcher*, he secretly sent word to the English and Gascon barons and knights, who were still at Niort, to inform them of his own danger, and the position of De Clisson and his men, in camp before Mortagne. The English and Gascon lords were so much pleased at this intelligence, that they declared they would not take forty thousand francs for the news, so greatly they desired to get De Clisson into their hands; accordingly, they set out from Niort, without a moment's unnecessary delay, with a body of five hundred lances, and rode with all secresy and speed for Mortagne. Lord de Clisson was, however, too wary a knight to be easily taken by surprise; and he received timely information from a spy whom he had stationed at Niort, who left that town as soon as he could find out which road the English troops would take; and, as he knew the country well, he outrode them, and startled De Clisson, whom he found at supper with his knights, by the announcement:—"Quick, Lord de Clisson! to horse! Leave this place without delay, and take care of yourself: for more than five hundred English and Gascons will soon be upon you, uttering great threats, and saying that they are glad not to have taken you before, for the pleasure they will have in taking you now." De Clisson did not hesitate a moment to act on this warning; and, rising hastily, he overthrew the table at which he was sitting, and shouted out to his men to mount. The command was promptly obeyed, but with the utmost confusion, as no attempt was made at arrangement or order: for no one waited upon another, and the servants had no time to carry off the tents, or anything in them. They had some difficulty in saving themselves, and following their masters on the way to Poitiers.

Great was the disappointment and chagrin of the English and Gascon knights when they entered, sword in hand, into the lodges of the Lord de Clisson, and found them empty. As the late occupants were gone, the English and Gascons took possession of their quarters during the night, with the provisions left in them; and the next morning they carried off the tents and pavilions to Niort, leaving the provisions of meat, bread, wine, and salt for the garrison of Mortagne.

Soon after the failure of this attempt to seize Lord de Clisson, the Gascon lords returned to Bordeaux, leaving the English knights at Niort, who took command of the few fortresses which yet remained to them in Poitou, and from which the garrisons continued to send out frequent marauding expeditions, taking and ransoming prisoners, and laying waste the whole open country. The constable was still at Poitiers, which he made his head-quarters during the winter; and, when he was informed of these depredations, he replied that the following season he would make the English restore all that they had pillaged from the country.*

* Froissart, liv. i. part ii. p. 661.

CHAPTER XVII.

The constable invades Brittany. Campaign of 1373. Battle of Chizey. Defeat and capture of Sir John Devereaux. The constable takes Niort. Flattering reception of the constable, by both king and people, on his return to Paris.

TOWARDS the close of the campaign of 1372, the Duke of Brittany advanced as far as Brissac, in Anjou, with the design of aiding his English allies in Poitou, as well as to look after his own interests in those parts: for Edward III. had been so much pleased with the recent conduct of his son-in-law, that, besides the earldom of Richmond, he had granted him the *marche* between Brittany and Poitou.* As soon as the king of France was informed of this movement on the part of the duke, he ordered the constable to enter the duchy of Brittany. This order was promptly obeyed by Du Guesclin, as he had no love for the duke. Apart from his inflexible loyalty to the crown of France—a virtue so rare in that age, when the servility of the inferior nobles and knights to some more powerful lord was the surest passport to advancement —the constable had other causes of complaint against the

* Rymer, vol. iii. par. ii. pp. 949, 956. The word *marche*, during the Middle Ages, after Charlemagne, served to designate the frontiers between neighbouring sovereignties, which were usually governed by a military commandant, called a Margrave or Marquis.

Duke of Brittany. The latter had taken possession of Roche-Derrien, a property belonging to the constable, for default of homage, and given it in charge to Pierre de Kerimel, who, without consultation with any one, restored the castle to Du Guesclin, whom he greatly admired and loved; but, upon finding that the duke was much displeased at the act, Kerimel took it back from the people of the constable, and kept it for the duke. The constable, who believed that this conduct of Kerimel was authorized by the duke, received with pleasure the orders of the king to enter Brittany, and make war upon the duke, if he refused to drive the English out of his estates. The constable thereupon entered the duchy with a force of four thousand men-at-arms, passed under the walls of Rennes, and advanced as far as Gael.*

The Duke of Brittany did not await the approach of the constable, but retired before him, leaving a portion of his troops to strengthen some places that were insufficiently garrisoned. When the French army reached Rennes, it was ascertained that the Duchess of Brittany had just left the town, and had taken the road towards Vannes. The constable and the Duke de Bourbon quickly followed in pursuit, with five hundred horse, and soon overtook her. The duchess, when she observed the Duke de Bourbon among her captors, said to him:—

"Fair cousin, am I a prisoner?"

"No, madam," replied the duke; "we do not wage war against women; but we have good cause to do so against the duke, your husband, who acts very strangely towards his liege-lord, in undertaking a foolish enterprise, which he can never bring to a good end."

The constable and the Duke de Bourbon then issued an

* D'Orronville, ch. xiv.; Guil. de St. André, vv. 1787, 1805; and Morice, *Hist. de Bretagne*, tom. i. p. 343.

order that, if anything had been taken from the duchess by the French soldiers, it should be restored without delay, under pain of the gallows. This order was instantly obeyed; and whatever had been taken from her was returned, except certain important papers, which turned out to be the letters of alliance between the Duke of Brittany and the king of England. These were kept to be sent to the king of France; and in the end they were productive of very serious consequences to the duke.

As soon as the constable had sent the duchess, under a safe-conduct, to one of her castles, called Loheac, he dislodged his army and marched to Redon, a town commanded by the Lord de Rieux, to whom he showed the letters of alliance which had been taken from the Duchess of Brittany. Lord de Rieux, who was a loyal and valiant knight, and one of the most distinguished of the Breton barons, was greatly astonished at this conduct of the Duke of Brittany; and he declared openly that he would never serve the duke his lord, as long as he held this course towards the king of France. The exhibition of copies of the letters produced the same effect on the Count de Penthiévre (Henry de Blois) and the Lord de Hunandie. Upon the retreat of the Duke of Brittany the constable withdrew his troops from the province, as the season was now far advanced.*

After the return of the French army, the Duke of Brittany went to St. Mahé to meet Lord Neufville, who had recently arrived at that port from England, with four hundred men-at-arms, and as many archers. On the 22nd of November, 1372, the duke ratified the treaty which Sir Thomas Melbourne had signed in his name the 19th of July previous. The Bretons were greatly displeased upon the arrival of the English troops; and immediately thereafter a number of pre-

* D'Orronville, *Vie de Louis de Bourbon*, ch. xiv.

lates, barons, and knights, and the town councils from many of the cities and towns of the duchy, appeared before the duke, and boldly expostulated with him on the fatal consequences of his continued attachment to the English interests. The duke excused his conduct in such fair words, that the assembly dispersed without any open manifestation of displeasure; but he and his people parted from each other with mutual distrust and ill-will.*

The constable, after withdrawing his troops from the duchy of Brittany, went to the city of Poitiers, where he remained during the winter, in order to make preparation for the approaching campaign, which was destined to prove so eventful to the kingdoms of France and England; but, before engaging in any new enterprise, he was anxious to settle his accounts with Charles V., as the sums were large which had been advanced on both sides, and the constable knew that the king was as exacting as a merchant in his money transactions. On the part of the king, there were two large payments made to Sir John Chandos and the Black Prince, for the ransom of Du Guesclin, at different times; and on the part of the latter, considerable advances had been made to the troops, for their pay, during the preceding campaigns. As the amounts which each owed the other turned out to be nearly equal, the king and the constable passed receipts "of everything that one could demand of the other," on the 19th of January and the 15th of February, 1373.†

As soon as the season was sufficiently advanced for mili-

* Froissart, liv. i. part ii. p. 662; Rymer, vol. iii. par. ii. p. 964; *Actes de Bretagne*, tom. ii. col. 53.

† *Actes de Bretagne*, tom. ii. col. 60; Du Tillet, *Recueil des Traictez, &c.*, and *Inventaire*, p. 94, *verso*. There is a difference of a year between the dates in the *Actes de Bretagne* and Du Tillet. In this transaction Du Guesclin takes the titles of Duke de Molina, Count de Longueville and Borja, and Constable of France.

tary operations, the constable left Poitiers with a body of fifteen hundred men-at-arms, chiefly Bretons, and laid siege to the town and castle of Chizey, about four leagues from Niort, which were commanded by two English knights, Sir Robert Miton and Sir Martin Scott. As he had determined to continue the siege until the town was taken, the constable strengthened his position by a ditch and palisades, to secure his troops from surprise. His first attempts against the walls were unsuccessful, and they served only to excite the sneers of the garrison, who said, in derision, to the French assailants :—" Go, drink your wine at Paris, swallow your soup, and roast your puddings : for you can do nothing in an assault ;" but the leaders, seeing that they could not hold out much longer against the skill and power of the constable, contrived to send a valet with a letter to Sir John Devereaux, at Niort, begging him to come and raise the siege of their town. They also informed him of the position and number of the troops under the constable ; but in this latter respect they misled him, as they stated in their letter that the forces of the French before the town did not exceed five hundred men-at-arms.*

After a short deliberation, Sir John Devereaux decided to go to the relief of Chizey ; and he ordered the neighbouring garrisons of Lusignan and Gensay to join him. Having made these additions to his troops, he set out from Niort with a force of seven hundred and three men-at-arms, and three hundred pillagers from the provinces of Brittany and Poitou.

Before leaving Niort, by the counsel of Jacounelle, captain of Chievray,† each man-at-arms threw over his coat of mail a piece of white cloth with the red cross of St. George

* Froissart, liv. i. part ii. p. 663.

† He is called *Jaquentré, Capitaine de Chivré*, by the anonymous author of the *Chronique de Du Guesclin.*

upon it; and, in great array, with banners displayed, they left the town.

These preparations of Sir John Devereaux did not escape the vigilance of Lord de Clisson, then engaged in the siege of Roche-sur-Yon; and he sent word to the constable to take care of himself, as the English in Niort were preparing for an expedition, designed, as he supposed, to relieve either Chizey or Roche-sur-Yon. The constable rewarded the herald who brought the message from De Clisson by the gift of a good war-horse, and sent him back, with many compliments, to his master. This timely notice of the designs of the English at Niort gave the constable full leisure to prepare for the reception of Sir John Devereaux, who designed, by a rapid march upon Chizey, to take the French by surprise. The English, upon coming near the town, halted behind a neighbouring wood; and, while here, two waggons loaded with wine, intended for the French troops then engaged in the siege of Chizey, attempted to pass them. The English stopped the waggons, took out the tuns of wine, knocked out their heads, and began to drink the wine with their helmets, gauntlets, and such vessels as they had at hand.

"Ye gods!" exclaimed one of the English soldiers, "I never tasted such wine before."

"Nor I," replied another; "and, while there is a drop remaining, I will not leave this place."

"I will stay with you," said a third, named Gervay, "as I can fight better when I have drunk enough: for, if I am beaten, I shall not feel the blows; and, if I am slain, I shall die with a light heart."

Heated by the wine, the English soldiers were clamorous to march at once against the French, although a few knights, more prudent or less drunk than the rest, advised their comrades to remain in their present position during the day, and attempt to surprise the French by a night-attack. Sir John Devereaux, who was still under misapprehension as to the number of men under the constable, by the letter of the commandants of Chizey, was in favour of an open attack in daylight; and, as his opinion prevailed, a herald was sent to the constable to offer him battle. The constable at that moment was reposing in his tent; and, as soon as he received the challenge, he called a council of his principal officers, consisting of the Count de Perche, the Viscount de Chatelherault, Sir Jean de Vienne, Sir Oliver de Manny, Sir Alain de Beaumont, and many other knights and squires, to whom, when assembled, he said:—

"My lords, here before us are our enemies, who offer us battle; and, just now, a horseman has arrived, by whom the king has written to me, that, if the English in any force should offer us battle, we must not dare to meet them; so that, in this business, there is nothing but dishonour to me, unless you can give me some other counsel."

The knights, after some deliberation, replied that there was no other course of safety but to obey the king's command; and that it was best for him to remain within his entrenchments. This opinion of his advisers was very distasteful to the constable, who was extremely anxious to march out against the English; and it brought from him a very earnest expression of his own views upon the subject. This was responded to on the part of the knights by a reluctant acquiescence in his opinion. To the more timid policy recommended by them, the constable firmly replied:—

"My lords, I am the representative of King Charles, my sovereign, to defend his rights; and I firmly believe that the duchy of Guienne of right belongs to him; so that I would not fully discharge my duty if I did not defend his property. And, since I know these things to be true, and that he is a true Catholic, God, in whom I put my trust, will aid me to maintain his right. And so, if you please, we will fight the English."

The constable then drew up his men in order of battle within his entrenchments, while the English were ranged in the plain without. After making his dispositions for an immediate engagement, he left Sir Jean de Beaumont behind, with eighty men concealed in the tents, with orders to attack the garrison if they sallied out of the castle.

Sir John Devereaux, who was impatient to begin the battle, sent forward the Breton and Poitevin pillagers of his army to skirmish near the entrenchments of the French, in order to draw them out, promising to support them as soon as the action began. The pillagers, though reluctantly, obeyed this order, and approached near the palisades; when they were recognised by some of the Breton troops within, who commenced a parley with them, which soon ended in their desertion of the English and turning over to the French. When the constable was informed by the pillagers that the English had only seven hundred men-at-arms, he changed his order of battle by assigning three hundred men each to Sir Alain de Beaumanoir and Sir Geoffrey de Quaremiel, with orders to attack the English in flank, while he, with the remainder, would oppose them in front. He then ordered the palisades to be cut down; and suddenly, with banners and pennons displayed, marched out into the plain in close order, accompanied by the pillagers who had recently deserted their standards.

The English then discovered that the pillagers had gone over to the French, yet they did not, on that account, give up all for lost; but, with great confidence and bravery, even when they now saw that they were betrayed by their friends and outnumbered by their enemies, they marched up to the combat, and, all on foot, joined battle with the main body of the French under the constable. In this conflict, which was protracted and well-sustained, many gallant feats of arms were performed on both sides.

As soon as the garrison of Chizey perceived that the French had crossed over their entrenchments and joined battle with the English without, they lowered the drawbridge of the castle and sallied out, with the design of aiding their countrymen; but they were met by Sir Jean de Beaumont and his men, who came forth from their tents; and, after a sharp contest, the garrison were defeated, and, with their captains, taken prisoners. This success was known by the French while engaged in battle, and it greatly tended to increase their ardour.

In his instructions to his troops before the engagement took place, Sir John Devereaux ordered his men-at-arms, after the first shock with the lance, to drop that weapon, and endeavour with their battle-axes to cut in pieces the lances of their opponents. At the first onset the French gave way, and recoiled more than twenty paces; until, encouraged by the precept and example of the constable, they not only recovered their lost ground, but when the English, following the order of their commander, threw down their lances and tried to maintain the combat with their axes, and to cut up the lances of the French men-at-arms, the latter forced them back in turn; and, when the English would have retaken their lances, it was too late, as they had been driven beyond the ground where they had dropped them.

At this juncture, the detachments under Sir Alain de Beaumanoir and Sir Geoffrey de Quaremiel attacked the English on the flanks and rear; while the constable in front, shouting his war-cries—"Montjoy, St. Denis!" and "Guesclin!"—mingling in the conflict with his usual impetuosity, struck right and left against the English. In the fight he was assailed by Jacounelle, the English captain, who had vowed to take him alive, and carry him back to Niort, where he had ordered a chamber to be prepared for his intended captive; but the constable, seizing him by the visor, disarmed him, raised him slightly from the ground, and struck him a blow that put out one of his eyes; then, throwing him among his followers, he said to them:—"Slay me this ribald, who is annoying me."

The constable was well sustained by the Lords Ricon and Lacounet, by Thibaut du Pont, Sylvester Budes, Alain de St. Pol, and Aliot de Calais; while, on the part of the English, they who most distinguished themselves were Sir John Devereaux, Lord Angus, Sir Jeffrey d'Argenton, Sir Aymery de Rochechouart, and the squires Creswell, Holmes, and Holegrave. But the valour of the English could not endure against equal valour and superior numbers on the part of the French; and, when they found themselves pressed in front by the constable, and assailed in the flanks and rear by the knights De Beaumanoir and De Quaremiel, the English general, after losing more than three hundred men-at-arms, surrendered with his whole command, among whom the French found above three hundred knights and squires of repute, whose ransoms, with their harness, yielded a large booty. This battle was fought on the 21st day of March, 1373.*

After the battle the town and castle made no resistance: for the garrison had been taken prisoners, and none but servants remained in the castle. The constable, after taking

* Froissart, liv. i. part ii. pp. 662, 665; *Fragment d'une Chronique Françoise*, published by M. Secousse in *Recueil sur Charles le Mauvais*, p. 650; Cuvelier, vv. 21,908, 22,466; *Chronique* (Anonyme) *de Du Guesclin*, ch. clix. Cuvelier and the author of the *Chronique* (Anonyme) amplify many details of the battle of Chizey, far more than Froissart, and there is some discrepancy between them; but Froissart has been followed where there is any material difference of statement.

possession of the town and castle, set out with all expedition for Niort; but, before starting, he ordered his men to mount the captured horses, and throw over their own armour the tunics of white cloth which had been worn by the English in the recent battle. This expedient had the desired effect: for, when a body of the constable's forces presented themselves before Niort, mounted on English horses, and dressed in the same manner as the English soldiers were on leaving the town, they were readily mistaken for the same troops by the citizens, who immediately lowered the drawbridge, when the French entered and took possession of the town.*

After the constable had refreshed his troops for four days in Niort, he set out for the castle of Lusignan; but, on approaching, he found it empty—as the garrison, left there by Lord Robert Grenake, who had been taken prisoner at the battle of Chizey, abandoned it as soon as they learnt the issue of that battle. After leaving there a castellan and a garrison of men-at-arms sufficient to keep it, the constable marched with his army to Castle-Achard, which was held, in her own right, by Lady Plainmartin, wife of Lord Guiscard d'Angle.

As soon as the lady heard that the constable was coming with a large force to make war upon her, she sent a herald to request that she might be permitted to come, under a safe-conduct, and have an interview with him. This the constable unhesitatingly granted, besides her further request, that she might be allowed to go to Poitiers and speak to the Duke de Berry. In the meantime, the constable withdrew his troops from before Castle-Achard, and laid siege to Mortemer.

The lady, upon presenting herself before the Duke de

* Cuvelier, v. 22,479; *Chronique* (Anonyme) *de Du Guesclin*, ch. clxii.

Berry, was received very courteously by him, who prevented her from kneeling while presenting her petition. She commenced by saying:—

"My lord, you know that I am a lone woman, the widow of a live husband, if God pleases: for my Lord Guiscard lies a prisoner in Spain, in the power of the king. So I humbly entreat you to do me the favour, while my lord is a prisoner, that my castle, my lands, and people, my body and goods, may remain undisturbed; and, while we make war on no one, that we may be at peace."

The duke granted the lady's petition, and gave her letters to the constable, who cheerfully performed all that the duke had promised. Mortemer did not hold out long against the French troops; and the Dame de Mortemer, who commanded the fortress, placed herself and her lands, with the castle of Dienne, in subjection to the king of France.*

After such a successful commencement of the campaign, the constable returned to Poitiers, where he was cordially welcomed by the Dukes of Berry, Burgundy, and Bourbon. He there disbanded his army, permitting the leaders, with their men, to go home, or to the different garrisons, until their services were needed. The constable then, in company with the three dukes, went to Paris, where he was received, by both king and people, with every demonstration that gratitude and admiration could prompt. The king, stirred up to liberality beyond his nature, kept open court for three days, and gave away large gifts and handsome jewels; and the people manifested their appreciation of the services of the constable to such a degree, that, as a contemporary chronicler expressed it:—"They could scarcely have done more, if God himself had descended upon the earth." †

* Froissart, liv. i. part ii. pp. 665, 666.

† *Ibid*, p. 667, and *Chronique* (Anonyme) *de Du Guesclin*, ch. clxii.

This exhibition of popular feeling was not a mere outburst of applause to add to the general huzza of a triumphal procession, but it was the sincere homage of an entire people for real services rendered to the country; it was the effusion of deep gratitude to one who had taught the French again how to conquer; and, if the constable was unable to efface the humiliating days of Crécy and Poitiers, he had already, during his short service, done much to obliterate their effects. To the king of France and the French people, the unbroken success of Bertrand du Guesclin was as grateful and inspiriting as it was mortifying to the pride of Edward III. and the English, who had seen not only Saintonge, Angoumois, and Aunis, with the city of Rochelle, change masters, but also the large and important province of Poitou, which had been claimed as a fief of the English crown for more than two hundred years, gradually wrested from them, until nothing was left but a few scattered and unimportant fortresses which they could call their own.

CHAPTER XVIII.

The king of France resolves to drive the Duke of Brittany from his duchy. The constable invades Brittany with a large force, and compels the duke to take refuge in England. The sieges of Brest and Derval.

THE king of France, in pursuance of his cautious policy of opposing but one enemy at a time, thinking that Edward III. would be unable very soon to fit out another expedition against him, after the utter failure of his attempt to relieve Thouars, now determined to keep no measures with the Duke of Brittany, of whose treasonable alliances he had the fullest evidence. The greater barons, and most of the towns of the duchy, were in avowed opposition to the duke, on account of their hatred of the English, whom the duke persisted in employing about his person, and treating with more confidence than his own subjects; and the king of France succeeded in corrupting, by gifts of money or offices, most of the inferior nobles and knights, whose prejudices or patriotism could be influenced by no higher incentives.*

As Charles V. had now resolved upon the destruction of the Duke of Brittany and his expulsion from the duchy, he found sufficient justification for the harsh measures which he

* Guil. de St. André, v. 1942; *Chronicon Briocense, sub anno* 1373; Du Tillet, *Recueil des Traictez, &c.*, and *Inventaire*, p. 100, *verso*.

was about to adopt, in the recent conduct of Edward III. and the duke. The king of England, learning that the French, under Evan of Wales, in conjunction with the Castilians, under Don Ruy Dias de Rojas, had a large fleet at sea, fitted out an expedition from Cornwall, under the Earl of Salisbury, to watch the hostile fleet, as well as to ascertain the present intentions of the Duke of Brittany and the Bretons in reference to English affairs. The English fleet, on reaching the coast of Brittany, entered the port of St. Malo, where they found seven large Spanish merchant vessels at anchor, laden with merchandise. The English burnt the vessels, with their contents, and put to death all the Spanish sailors on board. They then entered the town of St. Malo, and took by force whatever provisions they wanted.

This news soon spread over the whole duchy, and it confirmed the suspicions of the Bretons as to the conduct of the duke, whom they now openly charged with bringing the English into the country; and they declared that, as he showed clearly his attachment to England against his own country, it was but right that he should lose his lands. They thereupon fortified their cities, towns, and castles with sufficient garrisons, and closed their gates against him.

The distrust, complaints, and consequent determination of the Bretons soon reached the ear of Charles V., who was ever on the watch for any advantage that he could avail himself of against his enemies; he therefore eagerly listened to the representations of the Breton barons and knights, who came to Paris to inform him of the means employed by the Duke of Brittany in bringing a large force of English into the duchy, against the declared will of his subjects, who wished to continue good and loyal Frenchmen. To the inquiry of the king, who graciously asked them what they wanted him to do, they replied that he ought to fit out and send into Brittany a large force of men-at-arms to anticipate the designs of the duke and the English on the country; and that he ought to take possession of all the cities, towns, and castles, as they declared the duke had forfeited his lands.

Nothing could have accorded better with the wishes and designs of Charles than this advice of the Breton barons and knights; and, accordingly, he ordered the constable of France to enter Brittany, with such a force that he would be able to take possession of the entire duchy. This order the constable promptly obeyed; and he collected forthwith at Angers a body of four thousand lances and ten thousand other troops, and set out for Brittany, accompanied by the Duke de Bourbon, the Dauphin d'Auvergne, and the Counts d'Alençon, du Perche, and de Boulogne, with all the Breton barons.

The Duke of Brittany was at Vannes when he was informed of the steps taken to dispossess him of his duchy. As he was under constant apprehension of being taken prisoner, he left that town and went to Auray, which he likewise soon abandoned, as he knew of no fortress in Brittany where he dared to shut himself up. At Auray he left his duchess, with a part of his troops, and went to St. Mahé, on the coast; but, on demanding admission, it was refused, and the gates were closed in his face. This treatment confirmed his apprehensions for his safety; and, leaving Sir Robert Knolles governor of the duchy in his absence, he embarked at Concarneau, and sailed for England.*

The constable, who was commissioned by the king of France to take possession of the whole duchy of Brittany, left Angers, and first marched to Rennes. The citizens of

* Froissart, liv. i. part ii. p. 669; *Chronicon Briocense, sub anno* 1373.

the town, on his approach, threw open their gates, as they saw that all resistance would be vain against such a force as the constable had with him; and they took the oaths of obedience to the king of France. The constable next went to Sucinio, a handsome castle, and a frequent residence of the duke, which was defended by a garrison of English soldiers, who closed the gates, and put themselves in a posture of defence. The constable sat down before it; and, while the army servants were preparing lodges for the troops, he ordered an attack with his men-at-arms, although, at this first assault, "he gained nothing but blows." The garrison made an obstinate defence; but, after four days of hard fighting, the castle was forcibly entered, and all within it were put to the sword.*

The constable then dislodged his army, and marched upon Jugon. Before leaving Angers, he said to the Duke de Bourbon:—"There is a castle about fourteen leagues from hence, which is one of the strongest and most beautiful places to be found in the duchy; and, if it can be taken, the duke will have sustained a great loss: for it is a proverb in Brittany, *he who has Brittany without Jugon, has a hat without a cap;*† and I believe that the duke has not been advised to provide for its defence, so that we can take it easily." When, therefore, the constable approached Jugon, he found it without other garrison than the usual inhabitants of the place; and the captain, Robert de Guitry, surrendered the fortress as soon as he saw the letters of alliance between the Duke of Brittany and Edward III.‡

The constable next took, with little or no resistance, Guy-la-Forêt, Roche-Derrien, Ploermel, Château-Josselin,

* Froissart, liv. i. part ii. p. 670.

† *Qui à Bretagne sans Jugon,*
Il à chappel sans chapperon.

‡ D'Orronville, *Vie de Louis de Bourbon*, ch. xv. p. 115.

Faouet, Guinguant, St. Mahé, Quimperlé, and Quimper-corentin.*

The Earl of Salisbury, who was still at St. Malo, fearing for his own safety from the uninterrupted progress of the constable, left that port, and sailed for Brest, where he would be more secure from the French and Castilian fleet, which was still at sea, off the coast of Brittany; and, at the same time, he could avail himself of the fortifications of Brest, then "one of the strongest castles in the world." Here he found Sir Robert Knolles, who had been appointed governor of Brittany during the absence of the duke, and who had lately left his own castle of Derval in charge of his cousin Sir Hugh Brooks, and taken command of Brest. Here also the earl met Lord Neufville, who had been sent into Brittany the year before, with a body of four hundred men-at-arms and as many archers, to conclude the treaty of alliance between Edward III. and the duke. The Earl of Salisbury quitted St. Malo just in time to escape being besieged, as the constable arrived there the day after the English left the place.

After taking possession of St. Malo, the constable marched to Hennebon, then under the command of an English squire named Thomelin Wick, with a garrison of one hundred and twenty men. As the constable knew, from the strength of the fortifications, that he could not take the town if the garrison should be aided by the citizens, he approached the barriers before he proceeded to the assault, and said, in the hearing of the garrison:—"Men of the town, we will have you, whether you are willing or not; and we will enter the town of Hennebon, if the sun can enter it; but know that, if any of you take part in the defence, we will cut off your heads without respite, besides the rest of the citizens—men,

* Froissart, liv. i. part ii. p. 670.

women, and children." This threat so alarmed them, that they refused to take part in the defence of the town; and in a body they informed the English of their resolution. As the captain well knew that he could not long maintain a siege, unaided, against such a body of assailants, he entered into terms with the constable for the surrender of the town, and obtained permission for all who favoured the English cause to leave it, with what property they could carry away.

After the conquest of the town and castle of Hennebon, the constable decided not to make any attempt on Brest, as he well knew that a siege would be fruitless against a place of such strength, aided by the forces within it, under the Earl of Salisbury. He, therefore, after leaving a sufficient garrison in Hennebon, marched towards Nantes, placing the whole country on his route in subjection to the king of France. While on his way to Nantes, he turned aside to attack the castle of Derval; and, in order to convince the garrison that he was resolved to take it, he invested it formally, and built temporary forts on all sides of it.*

The departure of the French army from the neighbourhood of Brest induced the Earl of Salisbury to withdraw his forces from that town, where the provisions were sensibly diminishing, to Guerande. This withdrawal of the English from Brest was discovered by the constable; and he immediately sent a body of one thousand men-at-arms to besiege the town, under Lord de Clisson, who invested it so closely, "that a bird could not leave it without being seen." At the same time the Duke of Anjou was keeping up the siege of Roche-sur-Yon, in Poitou, one of the very few fortresses that yet remained to the English in that province; while some Norman and Breton lords were engaged in the siege of Becherel.†

* Froissart, liv. i. part ii. p. 672.

† *Ibid*, pp. 666, 671, 672.

During the siege of Derval there were many assaults and sallies, and almost every day some gallant feats of arms were performed before the castle; but, the castellan, Sir Hugh Brooks, seeing what dispositions the constable had made for the siege—that he could look for relief to no quarter, and that he could not even make his situation known to Sir Robert Knolles—resolved to offer terms for the surrender of the place; and he proposed to give up the fortress, unless within forty days he was aided by a force strong enough to raise the siege. The constable was unwilling to accept the terms without consulting the Duke of Anjou; and, accordingly, letters were despatched to the duke, then before Roche-sur-Yon, who advised the constable to accept the proposals of surrender; but on the condition that ample hostages were delivered up, to secure a strict compliance with the stipulations. This suggestion of the duke occasioned some delay in concluding the treaty; but, as the constable was firm in his demands, he not only obtained two knights and two squires as pledges for the faithful performance of the terms agreed on, but also an additional clause, that the garrison of Derval should receive no one into the castle unless accompanied by a force strong enough to raise the siege. After sending the hostages to the Duke of Anjou at Roche-sur-Yon, the constable left four thousand combatants to keep up the siege of Derval; and, with five hundred lances, he marched to the city of Nantes.

On approaching the city, he found the gates closed against him; but, after several conferences with the citizens, upon showing the commission by which he was authorized to take possession of the duchy in the name of the king, they consented to admit him into their city, on the conditions that, if the Duke of Brittany returned and desired to continue a good Frenchman, they would acknowledge him as their lord, and that the revenues of the duchy should remain in their hands until, as they added, "we have other news, which will please us better, perhaps, than these." The constable, who saw in this conduct of the citizens of Nantes only a proper sentiment of loyalty towards the duke, replied that he did not wish them to do otherwise than they had proposed. He then entered the city, where he remained eight days; when he took up his quarters at a beautiful manor-house belonging to the Duke of Brittany, on the river Loire, where he could get the earliest information from the sieges which he was then carrying on in Brittany and Poitou, and also from the king of France, "who greatly loved him, because he understood his business so perfectly."*

The constable had not long been settled in his pleasant quarters near Nantes, when he heard the agreeable intelligence that Roche-sur-Yon, after a protracted siege, had surrendered to the Duke of Anjou; and, shortly afterwards, he was almost as agreeably surprised to hear from Lord de Clisson and the Breton barons engaged in the siege of Brest that the garrison of that almost impregnable fortress had proposed terms of surrender, and that they had granted a safe-conduct to a knight and two squires sent to him by Sir Robert Knolles, with the articles of capitulation.

Sir Robert Knolles, who was anxious to save his castle of Derval, as well as the town of Brest, and expected by this expedient to obtain the aid of the Earl of Salisbury and his forces, agreed to surrender Brest, upon conditions similar to those which were accepted for Derval, if within a month he was not aided by a force sufficient to raise the siege. Hostages were demanded by the constable, and given by Sir Robert Knolles; and the French troops were withdrawn to the neighbourhood of Nantes, to await the expira-

* Froissart, liv. i. part ii. p. 673.

tion of the time agreed upon for the surrender of Derval and Brest.

Sir Robert Knolles, taking advantage of the withdrawal of the French army from Brest, left his command in that fortress, and threw himself into his castle of Derval, in violation of one of the articles agreed to by his cousin, Sir Hugh Brooks. Before leaving Brest, he wrote to inform the Earl of Salisbury, then near Guérande, that a day had been proposed by him, and accepted by the constable, for the surrender of Brest, if not relieved within the time by a sufficient force.

The earl made no delay after receiving the information; and, collecting his troops, which amounted to two thousand men-at-arms and two thousand archers, he set sail, and arrived at the harbour of Brest, disembarked his troops, and selected a suitable field, not far from his fleet, where he drew up his forces in order of battle. At night he returned to his ships. This he did for six successive days; but, when he saw that no one came to accept his challenge, he sent a herald to the constable, still at his quarters near Nantes, to say that he had come to keep the appointment made by Sir Robert Knolles, and that he was ready to give him battle or to raise the siege of the town of Brest and take back the hostages. He therefore required the constable to come forward and give him battle, or, if he were otherwise advised, to send back the hostages.

The constable seemed unwilling to risk a battle with the English under the walls of Brest; he therefore replied evasively, and told the herald to inform his masters that he had as great desire to fight as they; but that they were not in the place where the treaty was first proposed and agreed to; and that, if they would come to him, he would fight them without fail.

This reply of the constable took the English by surprise,

and the Earl of Salisbury called a council of his principal officers to advise with him on the subject. After some deliberation, it was decided to send the herald back, to say for them that they were seamen, who had brought no horses with them, and it was not reasonable to expect them to go so far on foot; but, if the constable would send them horses, they would meet him willingly; and, if he would do neither one thing nor the other, he ought to send back the hostages, for he was bound to do so.

This message the herald reported to the constable, who replied:—

"Herald, we have use for all our horses; and, therefore, it is not a reasonable request on their part. So tell your masters, good friend, that we will not give our enemies such an advantage as to send them our horses; and, if we were advised to do so, we should require sufficient pledges for their safe return."

"That is true," said the herald; "but I was not charged with anything on that subject."

"Then," added the constable, "since they are unwilling to come out, and they excuse themselves on the ground that they are seamen, neither we nor they are in the place where the meeting was agreed on; so say on your return, that we will give them so much advantage as to go to the proper place, and let them come there if they please, and we will offer them battle."

With this reply the herald returned to the Earl of Salisbury. Immediately thereafter the constable marched, with his army of four thousand men-at-arms and fifteen thousand other troops,* to within a day's journey of Brest, and there halted

* This is Froissart's estimate. Du Tillet assigns as the reason why the constable was unwilling to meet the English, "that he was the most feeble; having, since the treaty, disbanded the greater part of his

and encamped his forces in a strong position. He then sent word to the English that he had come to the place where the treaty with the garrison of Brest had been ratified, and, if they would come there, he would give them battle; but, if not, they would lose their hostages.

When the Earl of Salisbury and his council received this proposition of the constable, they regarded it as an evasion, and as an indication that he had no design to meet them; they thereupon sent back word that, if the constable would come two-thirds of the way, they would, on foot, endeavour to go the other third; and, if he would not do that much, but come one-half of the way, they would go the other; but, if he would do neither, he was bound to send back the hostages, as he had no right to retain them: for the English had done their duty by the law of arms, and they were still willing to do it.

As neither party seemed willing to forego the advantages of their position, the armies approached no nearer. The English thereupon strengthened the garrison of Brest with a sufficient body of men-at-arms, and supplied the castle with provision and arms; then, entering their ships, they sailed for St. Mahé. They made no attempt to relieve Derval—as, apart from the difficulty of doing so without horses, Sir Robert Knolles had written to the English not to give themselves any concern about him, as he would contend single-handed against the French.

After the departure of the English from Brest, the constable immediately decamped, and proceeded first to Rennes. While at this town, the necessity of paying the troops then engaged in the sieges of Derval and Becherel compelled him to raise money for the purpose; and, accordingly, on

troops."—*Recueil des Traictez, &c.*, p. 90, *verso*, and Morice, *Hist. de Bretagne*, tom. i. p. 347.

the 20th of August, 1373, he imposed a tax of a franc, or twenty sols, on each fire in the bishoprics of Rennes, Dol, St. Mahé, St. Brieux, and Vannes.* He then marched to Derval, to keep the day appointed by the treaty; but Sir Robert Knolles told him that it was a loss of time for him to stay there, as he would on no account give up his castle under any treaty or composition that had been made, as he contended his people had no right to make any treaty for the surrender of his property without his knowledge, and that which they had made was of no avail. This declaration of the English knight greatly astonished the constable, Lord de Clisson, and the French and Breton barons; "and the wisest of them, and those most inured to arms, said that the affair could not be nor remain thus, as the treaty which Sir Hugh Brooks and his brother had made was a good one."

This determination of Sir Robert Knolles was forthwith communicated to the Duke of Anjou, who, as soon as he received the message, left Angers with a large body of men-at-arms, and marched to Derval. The duke, who was harsh and imperious in his nature, and of a temper little capable of enduring opposition, attempted, on his arrival, to alarm the fears of Sir Robert Knolles, by threatening to put the hostages to death, if the castle was not surrendered according to the terms of the treaty; but the stern freebooter, inured by long years of lawlessness to every form of violence, was not to be diverted from his purpose by menaces, or even by blood; and he replied with fearful composure to the threats of the Duke of Anjou, that it was at the pleasure of the duke to make good his words; but he was equally determined, if the hostages were put to death, to treat in the same manner four good French knights, whom he held as

* *Actes de Bretagne*, tom. ii. col. 77.

prisoners within the castle, and for whom he could get large ransoms.

This defiant reply so irritated the Duke of Anjou, that, without giving a moment to reflection, he ordered the four hostages, two knights and two squires, to be led out as near the castle as it was safe to take them; and there, against the earnest entreaties and prayers of many leaders of the French army, they were all decapitated, in full view of the garrison of Derval.

This revolting scene was witnessed by Sir Robert Knolles from the windows of his castle, and he immediately ordered a platform to be erected on the outside of the same windows, and three knights and one squire, for whose ransoms he had refused ten thousand francs, to be led out. On this scaffold he made them mount, one after the other, and their heads were struck off successively, and thrown, with their bodies, into the castle moat. From this atrocious spectacle all good men turned aside with horror; and it terminated at that time the military operations before Derval, as the constable and the Duke of Anjou, with the whole army, were recalled to Paris to oppose a formidable invasion then threatening the safety of France.*

* Froissart, liv. i. part ii. pp. 674, 677, 682.

CHAPTER XIX.

Invasion of France by the English, under the Dukes of Lancaster and Brittany. The king of France adopts a policy wholly defensive. Fruitless results of the expedition.

IRRITATED by the loss of a great portion of his possessions in France, and mindful of the vexatious failure of his attempt to relieve the Poitevin lords in Thouars in the preceding campaign, Edward III. was resolved on making a great effort to retrieve his losses; but, as he was unwilling to trust his fortunes again to the uncertain winds, he fitted out an expedition, with great preparation, early in June, under the command of the Dukes of Lancaster and Brittany, to march through France, from Calais to Bordeaux, with the triple purpose of humbling the king of France, relieving the fortresses in Brittany then besieged by the French, and establishing the Duke of Lancaster in his new government of Aquitaine, of which he had been created "special lieutenant and captain-general, as well of the kingdom of France and elsewhere beyond sea," on the resignation of that principality by the Black Prince, who had given up with it all hope of life.*

The Duke of Lancaster, having completed his preparations,

* Froissart, liv. i. part ii. p. 674; Rymer, vol. iii. par. ii. pp. 974, 982.

embarked his troops, which amounted to three thousand men-at-arms, six thousand archers, and two thousand other troops,* and reached Calais during the month of July, 1373. After remaining a few days in that town, to load up his waggons and shoe his horses, he set out through Picardy, at easy marches of not more than two or three leagues a day, and encamped each day at noon. The vanguard, or first division of the army, was commanded by the two marshals, the Earls of Warwick and Suffolk; then came the division under the Dukes of Lancaster and Brittany; this was followed by the baggage-waggons and other carriages, while the rear was commanded by the constable of the English army, Lord Edward Spencer. In this order they passed St. Omer, Aire, St. Pol, and Arras, without any adventure worthy of note, until they reached the neighbourhood of St. Quentin.

At Roye, in Vermandois, the Duke of Brittany sent a letter of defiance by a herald to the king of France, abjuring all faith and homage due to the crown of France, declaring himself the enemy of the king, and threatening to avenge himself for the injuries which he had sustained. Charles V. was extremely offended at the tone of the letter, although he affected to laugh at it. He did not think proper to accept the challenge contained in the letter, but he contented himself with providing the cities, towns, and castles, along the route of the English, with sufficient garrisons and supplies of provisions to withstand a siege, and ordering the people of the open country to take whatever property they could carry with them into the fortresses, on pain of being abandoned to the enemy.†

* Other authorities estimate the English army much higher than Froissart. D'Orronville says they had 16,000 combatants.—*Vie de Louis de Bourbon*, ch. xx. In the *Hist. de Bretagne*, par Morice, tom. i. p. 348, and Barnes's "Hist. of Edward III.," p. 857, they are computed at 30,000 men.

† Froissart, liv. i. part ii. pp. 674, 678; *Chronicon Briocense, sub*

Near Ribeumont, and not far from St. Quentin, a detachment of English troops, amounting to about eighty men, belonging to the forces under Sir Hugh Calverly, was roughly treated by a body of French men-at-arms, under Lord de Bousies and Sir Jean de Bueil; and a like fate attended another portion of the same troop, who came to attack Ribeumont and avenge the defeat of their comrades.*

The Duke of Lancaster, in passing through Picardy, the Isle of France, and Champagne, found the country plentifully supplied with provisions, as it was the season of harvest; and he obtained from the peasants of the open country and the inhabitants of the villages large quantities of wine and corn, with numbers of cattle and sheep, which most of the defenceless people readily brought to save their property from fire, and more indiscriminate plunder.

The English desired nothing so much as a battle with the French; but the cautious and impassible Charles would trust nothing to chance, when he thought he could otherwise accomplish the discomfiture of his enemies, even at the sacrifice of his wretched subjects. He therefore refused to entrust a large body of troops to any leader, and gave strict orders to all to attempt nothing more than to watch the movements of the English, cut off their detachments, and restrain their foraging parties from collecting provisions. Lord de Clisson, accompanied by Lord de Laval, the Viscount de Rohan, and other nobles and knights, with about four hundred lances, acting under strict injunctions from the king, followed the route of the invading army; and the hostile parties often rode so near each other that they exchanged greetings or threats, as it suited their humour. On one occasion Sir Henry Percy, "one of the gentle barons of Eng-

anno 1373; *Actes de Bretagne*, tom. i. col. 67; Guil. de St. André, v. 1983.

* Froissart, liv. i. part ii. pp. 679, 680.

land," was riding through the open country with his troop while Sir Guillaume des Bordes and Sir Jean de Bueil were marching with their commands in the same direction, and near enough to distinguish each other, but without meeting. Sir Henry Percy, recognising among the French forces Lord Aymery de Namur, son of the count, said to him :—

"It is now fine weather for flying: why do you not fly, since you have wings ?"

"Sire de Percy," replied Lord Aymery, spurring his horse and riding out a short distance from his troop, "you speak true : flight would be agreeable to us all ; and, if I had my way, we would soon fly over to you."

"By God ! Aymery, I believe you fully. Now stir up your comrades for flight : here you will find good game."

In such an interchange of bantering expressions and courteous chit-chat they often indulged at a distance ; but they approached no nearer to each other. When, however, the English army was in the neighbourhood of Soissons, and near a village called Ouchy, a daring attempt was made to beat up the quarters of the English, notwithstanding the positive prohibition of the king of France. The adventure took place on an occasion when Sir Walter Huet was one night on guard ; and, having retired, near daylight, to get some repose in his tent, and while he was disarming himself, Sir Jean de Vienne, with one hundred and twenty lances, made an attack on that part of the English camp where Sir Walter Huet was on duty. The English knight, as soon as he heard the noise, issued out in such haste that he was only partly armed ; and in that condition, mounting his horse, with his shield at his neck and his lance in rest, he boldly charged the assailants.

As soon as he came out of his tent he was observed by Sir Jean d'Elmant, a bold and valiant French knight, armed at all points and well mounted, who, putting spurs to his horse, attacked him with his lance, and struck him with such true aim, that the imperfect armour of the English knight availed him nothing; and, the weapon entering his body, he was thrown from his horse a dead man. His companions, attempting to avenge his death, were all slain or taken prisoners; and the affair was over in so short a time, that, before the marshals could arouse the camp and come to the support of their comrades, the French had withdrawn with their prisoners into a neighbouring wood, and put themselves beyond the danger of pursuit. This encounter took place on the 21st of September, 1373.*

At this time the constable and the three brothers of the king of France, the Dukes of Anjou, Berry, and Burgundy, were at Paris, under the order of the king. Here they were joined by Lord de Clisson, who had been sent for by Charles to advise with him in a close council, composed of the constable and his three brothers, on the question whether he should give battle to the English or not: for, it was said, "many barons and knights of France, as well as the members of town councils, murmured among themselves, and even said, publicly, that it was a very unbecoming thing and a great shame for the nobles of the kingdom, where there were so many barons, knights, and squires renowned for their valour, to permit the English thus to pass, at their ease, without a battle; and for this they were blamed by every one."

When these special counsellors were assembled, the king opened the conference by a statement of the question before them; and he entreated them to listen with attention to what should be said on the reasons for fighting or not fighting, and to give him the best advice in their power. The constable was first called on to declare his opinion, as he

* Froissart, liv. i. part ii. pp. 681, 682.

had been engaged in the most important affairs against the English; but he begged to be excused from expressing an opinion until the brothers of the king had been heard. Notwithstanding his excuses, he was urged to speak first; and, as he well knew beforehand what counsel would be most acceptable to his master, he commenced by saying:—

"Sire, they who speak of fighting the English do not sufficiently consider the peril of such a course. I do not say that we should not fight them; but I mean that it should be done at our pleasure, as the English themselves know so well how to do when they are concerned, and as they have already done many times at Crécy and Poitiers, in Gascony, Brittany, France, and Normandy. Such victories have greatly endamaged your kingdom and the nobles of France, and so puffed up the English with pride, that they prize no nation but their own, on account of the great ransoms which they have received, whereby they have become enriched and emboldened. But here is my companion in arms, the Lord de Clisson, who can speak of them with greater certainty than I can: for he has been bred up among them since infancy, and he knows their conditions and manners better than any of us; so I beg, if it is your pleasure, dear Sire, that he may aid me to finish my speech."

Lord de Clisson, on being thus called on, and likewise urged by the king, without any hesitation warmly advocated the policy which had been recommended by the constable, and added:—

"If God pleases, my lord, the English are such excellent soldiers, and they have achieved so many successful battles, that they think they cannot be conquered; and in war they are the most confident people in the world, for the more blood they see, whether it is their own or their enemies, the more excited they become, and more eager for fight; and they say that this fortune will never desert them while their king lives. Therefore, everything considered, in my humble judgment I do not advise a battle, unless they are taken at a disadvantage, as one should take his enemy. I regard the affairs of France now in good condition, and that which the English once held in the kingdom they have now lost by cautious warfare. Then, Sire, you have had good and trustworthy counsel; so trust to it still."

"By my faith," said the king, "Lord de Clisson, I do not design to go out myself, nor put my people or kingdom in danger of being lost, for a little open country; and I give you in charge, together with my constable, the protection of my kingdom, for your opinion coincides with my own. And what say you, my brother of Anjou?"

"By my faith," replied the duke, "he is no loyal subject who would counsel you otherwise. Let us make war on the English as we have hitherto done. When they think to find us in one part of the kingdom, we will be in another, and we will take from them at our leisure the little that they now have. I hope to succeed so well, with the aid of these two companions in arms, here present, that, within a brief space, the English will be able to count on very little that they now hold within the boundaries of Aquitaine and Gascony."

The king was greatly pleased to find his cautious policy sustained by the concurrent advice of his most trusted counsellors, and he consoled himself for the pillage and ruin of his wretched peasantry with the declaration of his council, concerning this invasion of the English:—"Let them go; by smoke they cannot come at your heritage. They will wear themselves out and come to nothing: for, though a tempest sometimes appears in a country, it passes off and wastes itself. Thus it will become of these English."*

Acting on this advice, the king entrusted the constable

* Froissart, liv. i. part ii. p. 682.

and Lord de Clisson with a force of only five hundred lances, and ordered them to watch the motions of the English, and carry out the mode of warfare which they had recommended. The constable found that the English, after leaving the neighbourhood of Soissons, had passed by the towns of Vertus and Epernay to Châlons in Champagne, crossing and recrossing the river Marne, as they were well provided with engineers and carpenters for constructing bridges whenever they found them broken down. From Châlons they marched to Troyes, levying contributions on the defenceless people, and burning and laying waste wherever their demands were not complied with. The constable had reached Troyes before them, where he found the Dukes of Burgundy and Bourbon with a force of twelve hundred lances.*

From Troyes the English marched to Sens, on the river Yonne, where a detachment of their army fell into an ambuscade laid for them by Lord de Clisson. At the distance of a league from Sens, De Clisson had placed two hundred men-at-arms, with orders to retreat, as soon as the English approached, on his main body of one thousand lances, which he concealed on the roadside a league further on. The English, seeing the first body fly, followed in pursuit, until they came suddenly on De Clisson, who issued from his covert in good order, attacked the English scattered along the road, slew above six hundred of their number, and took many prisoners.†

While the summer season lasted, and while the English were marching through the more plentiful portions of France, they had few difficulties to contend with, on a fruitless marauding expedition, in which not a fortress was gained or a

* Froissart, liv. i. part ii. p. 684.

† D'Orronville, *Vie de Louis de Bourbon*, ch. xx.

successful skirmish achieved; but, when, on the approach of winter, they had to pass the bleak mountain regions of Auvergne, and to traverse the wasted provinces of Limousin, Rouergue, and Agen, which had been devastated by previous wars, they had to encounter the two great scourges of an army—cold and hunger. To add to their distress, they were followed by an active, vigilant, and exasperated enemy of more than three thousand lances, who hung on their flanks and rear, cutting off every detachment that left the main body; so that the English were compelled to forage with their whole army. Provisions of all kinds, in consequence, became so scarce that, for five and six days at a time, some of the highest rank in the army were without bread, and their horses died in such numbers that they lost more than two-thirds of them before they reached Bordeaux. Many knights and squires died of sickness, resulting from cold and starvation; and Lord Edward Spencer, the constable of England, and other knights, died afterwards of diseases contracted by want and exposure on this disastrous march.*

With the loss of his men and horses, and the utter failure of the expedition, the Duke of Lancaster also lost his temper: for, without apparent reason, he became embroiled in a bitter quarrel with his brother-in-law and colleague, the Duke of

* Froissart, liv. i. part ii. p. 687; Guil. de St. Andrè, v. 2011; *Vie de Louis de Bourbon*, ch. xx. p. 120. D'Orronville, who probably gives an exaggerated account of the loss of the English, says:—"Of 16,000 combatants, which left Calais, not 8000 reached Brives, in Limousin." Of this expedition old Fabian quaintly remarks:—"So that the French book sayth, for so moche as for lacke of mete for their horses, and other paynfull thynges, that in that journay to theym happenyd, that though that journay were unto the Englyssemen honorable to ryde so ferre in the Frenshe kynge's land unfoughten with, yet it was to theym very paynfull, consyderynge the manyfolde chaunces fallynge to theym, as losse of horses and other thynges durynge that passage."—"Chronicles of England and France," p. 484.

Brittany, which ended in their separation. It is probable that the troops, whose wages were only paid for six months, were now clamorous for their wages, and the Duke of Lancaster called upon the Duke of Brittany to pay his proportion of what was due to the men-at-arms. Upon this demand, the Duke of Brittany told the Duke of Lancaster that he knew before leaving England that all his available means had been exhausted in paying his troops their wages then due; and that he had not, at that time, a denier to apply to that object; but he was willing to fulfil all his obligations; and, if the Duke of Lancaster would lend him the money, he would punctually repay it.

To this the Duke of Lancaster replied, disdainfully:—

"I prize too little what you say. If you have wasted your means, that is no concern of mine; but, if you desire to remain in my army, you must not expect to be the master of it. Wherefore, it would be best for you to withdraw: for with me you can no longer stay."

The Duke of Brittany was extremely hurt at the irritating language of the Duke of Lancaster; whereupon he left his presence and sought out his own people, whom he found reduced to sixty men. He immediately set out from the camp of the Duke of Lancaster with these—some on foot and some on sumpter-horses; and, after various fortunes, he reached Bergerac in safety. From Bergerac he marched to Bordeaux, where the opportune arrival of a cargo of salt from the port of Guérande, in Brittany, which he claimed as his own, enabled him to discharge his debts, and keep up his state during the winter. Here also the Duke of Lancaster arrived about Christmas, with the broken remains of his army.*

During this year the constable, Bertrand du Guesclin,

* Guil. de St. André, vv. 2025, 2379.

married, in second nuptials, Jeanne de Laval, the only daughter of Jean de Laval, Lord de Chatillon, and Isabella de Tinteniac.*

* Morice, *Hist. de Bretagne*, tom. i. p. 374, and Du Chastelet, *Hist. de Bertrand du Guesclin*, p. 250. In an *extract from the account of Jean Flamant, treasurer of the king*, dated the 3rd of May, 1380, the constable takes the titles of Count de Longueville, Sire de Tinteniac, and Constable of France.—*Actes de Bretagne*, tom. ii. col. 419.

CHAPTER XX.

Efforts of the Pope to make peace between the kings of France and England. Success of the French under the constable in Gascony. The Duke of Brittany obtains troops from Edward III., and returns to his duchy. Narrow escape of De Clisson and other Breton lords.

DURING the progress of the marauding expedition under the Duke of Lancaster, and just before the English army reached Troyes, Pope Gregory XI. made an attempt to bring about a peace between France and England; and to that end he sent the Archbishop of Ravenna and the Bishop of Carpentras first to the king of France. Charles received them kindly, and heard their propositions; but referred them to the leaders of a hostile force then in his kingdom, and to his constable, Bertrand du Guesclin, and Lord de Clisson, who were entrusted, on his part, with the entire conduct of a war simply of defence. The legates, upon this, made no delay in Paris; and, mounting their horses, rode to Troyes, where they found the constable, the Dukes of Burgundy and Bourbon, Lord de Clisson, and a number of French nobles, by whom they were cordially welcomed.

To the proposals of peace the constable and De Clisson replied, very briefly, that it did not belong to them to treat of peace, but to the English, who were then invading their country. The envoys of the pope, receiving no satisfaction from the French, turned to the English, and went to the camp of the Dukes of Lancaster and Brittany, then before Troyes, whom they found equally disinclined to entertain any propositions tending to a reconciliation between the two kingdoms; and they could get no further answer from the English leaders, than that it was not in their power to give or accept any truce or respite, nor listen to any terms of peace whatsoever. Thus ended the pacific efforts of the pope during that year.*

Before the opening of the campaign of the year 1374, the Earl of Pembroke and Lord Guiscard d'Angle, who had been taken prisoners in the sea-fight off Rochelle, recovered their liberty, by the intervention of the constable of France. The English prisoners, after their capture in the year 1372, had been taken to Castille, where they were detained by King Henry, who consented to release them at the solicitation of Bertrand du Guesclin, upon the surrender by the latter of the valuable fief of Soria, and the towns of Almazan, Atienza, and other places, which the constable had received in recompense for his services to the Castilian monarch, after the battle of Monteil and the death of Peter the Cruel. This property was estimated at two hundred and forty thousand doblas, and it was returned to the king of Castille, partly in exchange for the person of the Earl of Pembroke, who offered to pay the constable one hundred and twenty thousand francs for his ransom—fifty thousand of which he paid at the time, and gave the burgomasters and échevins of Bruges as sureties for the remainder of the stipulated sum.

It was made a condition, by those who signed the contract on the part of the earl, that he was to be delivered safe and sound in the town of Calais before the payment of

* Froissart, liv. i. part ii. pp. 685, 686.

the balance should be demanded. Upon this being done, the earl left Spain and travelled through France, under the safe-conduct of the constable; but he was attacked by a serious malady on the way, and with difficulty reached Arras, where he died. The constable, regarding the death of the earl as an act of God, which no precaution on his part could prevent, brought an action against the sureties for the payment of the seventy thousand francs still due; but, failing to recover any portion of it by law, he transferred all his interest in the suit to the king of France for fifty thousand francs.*

At the same time Sir Oliver de Manny, the nephew of the constable, surrendered the lordship of Agreda, in Castille, for the ransom of Lord Guiscard d'Angle. Sir Oliver, then deeply enamoured of a rich heiress of Picardy, the only daughter of the Lord de Roye, was advised that the surest means to obtain the hand of the daughter was to procure the deliverance of the father. The Breton knight found out that the king of England was very desirous to bring about the liberation of Lord Guiscard d'Angle, and he conducted the negotiation with such success, that he obtained the person of the English nobleman and his nephew, William d'Angle, for the lands of Agreda, which were valued at four thousand francs a year. The exchange of the English prisoners for Lord de Roye was easily made; and Sir Oliver de Manny espoused the daughter, and soon after obtained all the possessions of the father, who lived but a short time after the recovery of his liberty. Lord d'Angle gave up all his property in Poitou, from whence he removed with his wife and children to England; but, before going away, he

* Froissart, liv. i. part ii. p. 684; Ayala, *Cronica del Rey Don Enrique Segundo*, pp. 31, 32, and 66; Du Tillet, *Recueil des Traictez, &c.*, p. 90, *recto;* and see *Traicté fait touchant le differend avec les Bourgmestres de Bruges*, in *Preuves de Du Guesclin*, par Du Chastelet, p. 454.

did not forget his obligations to the Duke de Berry, whom he profoundly thanked for his gallant forbearance towards his wife, when besieged, during the preceding campaign, in his fortress of Chatel-Achard.*

Early in April of the year 1374, the Duke of Anjou assembled a large army in the city of Périgueux, to carry out his promise to his brother the king of France, that he would drive the English out of Aquitaine and the higher marches of Gascony. Accordingly, he collected a body of ten thousand men-at-arms, fifteen hundred Genoese cross-bowmen, and thirty thousand other troops, under the command of the constable of France, assisted by Lord de Clisson and a number of the great Gascon nobles. Setting out from Périgueux, the French army first came to the abbey of St. Sever, in Upper Gascony, belonging to the English ; but, before the siege was commenced, the abbot discreetly proposed, as he was a churchman, and disinclined to war, that he would pledge himself to abide by whatever the great temporal lords would consent to do. Whereupon his lands were left undisturbed, upon the delivery of hostages for the due performance of the agreement.

From St. Sever the army marched to Lourdes, in Béarn, which was commanded for the Count de Foix by Sir Ernant de Béarn. The constable laid siege to the town, and for fifteen days all his assaults were resisted with great obstinacy ; but, at length, it was taken by storm, the town was pillaged, and a great number of the garrison were put to the sword or made prisoners. The French, after laying waste the lands of the Viscount de Castelbon and the Lord de Chastelneuf, besieged a town and castle called Sault, be-

* Froissart, liv. i. part ii. p. 685. Ayala states that Lord Guiscard d'Angle, and another knight, called the Lord de Poyana, were delivered up to the constable for thirty-four thousand francs.—*Cronica del Rey Don Enrique Segundo*, p. 67.

longing to the Count de Foix. The politic count, during the whole period when his powerful neighbours, the kings of France and England, were more equally matched, had contrived to keep aloof from their quarrels, and maintain his position as an undisturbed spectator of the important events passing around him; but now, since the fortunes of Edward III. had declined, and the power of England was scarcely felt in Aquitaine, he wisely determined to give way to a pressure that he could not resist; and, accordingly, he sent word to propose to the Duke of Anjou that, if his lands were left undisturbed until the middle of the following August, he would render homage and obedience to either the king of France or England, who, at that time, would prove himself the stronger, before the town of Moissac, on the Tarne. To these terms the Duke of Anjou, by the advice of his council, assented; and full information of their import was given to the Duke of Lancaster, who was still at Bordeaux.

The Duke of Lancaster had permitted a portion of his troops to return to England, and he was now much more inclined to listen to the pacific measures which were still urged on both parties by the legates of the pope. He therefore consented to send three knights of his council to the Duke of Anjou and the constable at Périgueux, to treat of peace. With much difficulty a truce was agreed upon, by the agency of the constable, to continue until the last day of August. The English thought that the *day of Moissac* was included in the treaty; but in that they were disappointed, as the French construed it otherwise. The Duke of Lancaster then, after appointing Sir Thomas Felton seneschal of Bordeaux, as his lieutenant in Aquitaine, returned to England with the rest of his army.

When the day approached which had been appointed by the Count de Foix to test the strength of the French and

English power in Aquitaine, the Duke of Anjou led his whole army before Moissac. No one appeared on the part of the English but Sir Thomas Felton, who came under a safe-conduct; and he expressed his surprise at finding what construction had been put on the truce by the leaders of the French army, as he affirmed that the Duke of Lancaster had agreed to the suspension of hostilities under the supposition that the day of Moissac was included in the truce; but it was asserted on the opposite side that it had been overlooked by the English, since no mention was made of it by them. As Sir Thomas Felton was wholly incapable of enforcing his view of the question, the Count de Foix interposed no difficulty on his part, and he rendered homage for all the fiefs which he held dependent on the crown of France. Upon taking possession of the town and castle of Moissac, the Duke of Anjou marched his army to Toulouse.

After a short repose at Toulouse, the duke set out, on the 7th of September, for La Réole, one of the strongest fortresses still held by the English. It was situated on the Garonne, and at no great distance from Bordeaux. The French army was composed of the same troops which marched into Upper Gascony in the earlier part of the campaign, and "the whole country trembled before it." The inhabitants of La Réole desired nothing so much as the supremacy of the French in Aquitaine, so they opened their gates without hesitation, and submitted themselves to the dominion of the crown of France. This example was followed by Langon, St. Maquaire, Condon, St. Bazille, Pertudaire, Mauléon, Dion, Sebillac, and above forty walled towns and strong castles besides. In this campaign nothing withstood the French: for, apart from their ability, with a numerous and well-appointed body of troops, to take whatever place they attacked, they were met everywhere by a voluntary submission of the people to the dominion of France.*

The legates of the pope, not content with the temporary suspension of arms which they had effected between the Dukes of Anjou and Lancaster in the south of France, went to St. Omer, in Picardy, where they could urge with more facility their pacific counsels on the kings of France and England.

Edward III., now broken by age and grief, distrustful of fortune by his late reverses, inclined to ease, and addicted to vicious indulgences since the death of his queen, was extremely disposed to peace, and the more especially as he saw that nearly every day brought information of the loss of some town or fortress, or some new disaster to his arms, and to which he could oppose no effectual remedy. Moreover, he keenly felt the vagabond condition of his son-in-law, the Duke of Brittany, who had lost the affections of his subjects, and who, in consequence, had been driven from his estates on account of his obstinate attachment to English interests. The king of France was not disposed to offer any obstacle to a peace between the two countries; and he accordingly ordered the Duke of Anjou and the constable to disband their army and return to him at Paris. The duke and the constable, with De Clisson and the other leaders, retaining only the Breton men-at-arms, left Rouergue without delay, in obedience to the orders of the king, by whom they were very cordially received at Paris.†

A short time after the return of the constable from the south of France, the term approached which had been agreed on for the surrender of the town of Becherel in Brittany. This strong fortress had been besieged for about fif-

* Froissart, liv. i. part ii. pp. 687, 690.

† *Ibid*, p. 691.

teen months by Lord de Blainville and the Maréchal Louis de Sancerre, when the commanders of the garrison, Sir John Appert and Sir John Cornwall, finding, from the failure of their provisions, that they could not hold out much longer, agreed to surrender by the feast of All Saints—November the 1st—unless relieved before that time by a force sufficient to give battle to the French. As the king of France greatly desired to take this fortress, he wrote to the constable to collect such a body of troops before Becherel, on the day fixed for the surrender, that he would be able to meet the English successfully if they came to raise the siege.

Accordingly, on the day appointed, the constable appeared before Becherel with ten thousand lances; and, as no force came to dispute his right to take possession, he accepted the surrender of the fortress, according to the terms agreed upon, allowing the garrison to leave the place with such property as they could carry with them, and go, under a safe-conduct, to St. Sauveur-le-Vicomte, in Normandy. This last-mentioned town was then closely guarded off the coast by Sir Jean de Vienne, admiral of France, and Evan of Wales, aided by a Castilian fleet under Ruy Dias de Rojas, to prevent succour arriving by sea.*

As soon as the constable had taken possession of Becherel, he went into Normandy, and laid siege to St. Sauveur. Immediately after his arrival, as the town was well fortified, he erected large engines, which threw, night and day, great stones against the towers and ramparts of the town and castle. The fortress was commanded by a brave and skilful man-at-arms, named Quatreton, for Sir Aleyn Buxhill, assisted by Sir Thomas Trivet and other knights, besides the officers and men-at-arms who had lately joined them from the town of Becherel. The garrison of St. Sau-

* Froissart, liv. i. part ii. p. 689, 695.

veur, though greatly annoyed by the stones thrown from the military engines, which shattered the tiles and broke through the roofs of the houses and towers, defended themselves with great bravery, often making sallies, and performing gallant feats of arms at the barriers with the knights and squires of the besieging army. As the fortress was well supplied with provisions, as the commanders expected aid from the Duke of Brittany, and as they hoped at least that the Duke of Lancaster would be able to agree with the French upon some truce or respite, the siege was kept up during the whole winter.*

The Duke of Brittany, upon leaving Bordeaux, early in the season, was anxious to join his duchess, whom he had left at Auray under the charge of Lord John Augustin, as well as to collect a body of troops to raise the siege of Becherel. He accordingly went over to England, and obtained from Edward III. two thousand men-at-arms and four hundred archers, under Edmund, Earl of Cambridge, who was accompanied by many nobles and distinguished knights. As the expedition could not be fitted out in time to relieve Becherel,† the duke hoped to be able to raise the siege of St. Sauveur; and he attempted to coast along the shore of Normandy, with the design of giving battle to the French and Spanish fleet, which was lying off against St. Sauveur; but he was driven by adverse winds on the coast of Brittany, and he landed at St. Mahé. The duke, still feeling deep resentment against the garrison of that town for closing their gates in his face, when he applied for admittance during the year 1373, attacked the castle, which was situated on the outside of the town, carried it by storm, and put to

* Froissart, liv. i. part ii. p. 695.

† By a paper preserved in Rymer, *super passagio comitis Cantabrigiæ*, it is shown that the expedition did not leave England before the 18th of November, 1374.—Vol. iii. par. ii. p. 1017.

the sword all within it. After the conquest of the castle the town made no resistance.*

As soon as the constable was informed of the landing of the Duke of Brittany and the English troops at St. Mahé, he sent four of the most distinguished Breton barons, Lord de Clisson, the Viscount de Rohan, and the Lords de Laval and de Beaumanoir,† with between three and four hundred lances, to watch the movements of the duke. These lords took up their quarters at Lamballe, near St. Brieux.

The duke made no delay at St. Mahé, and, after taking St. Pol-de-Leon, laid siege to the strong town of St. Brieux. As it was too well fortified to be carried by storm, he set his miners to work, who made such progress in fifteen days, that they informed him they were able, whenever he gave the order, to throw down a large expanse of the wall. During the time that he was engaged in this work he received the information that the garrison of St. Sauveur, no longer able to resist the attacks of the French, and hoping to get a respite for a month, had proposed to surrender the town and castle if they were not relieved before the approaching Easter. This news produced much distraction in the councils of war held by the Duke of Brittany and the Earl of Cambridge, as many of the members advised an immediate march to relieve St. Sauveur, while others thought that it was best to continue the siege of St. Brieux, which could not hold out many days longer, when they would still have time to march on St. Sauveur, as proposed.‡

While these events were passing, Sir John Devereaux,

* Froissart, liv. i. part ii. p. 696.

† It is probable that Lord de Rochefort was one of the number, as Froissart mentions them afterwards as *five* Breton barons; and Rochefort is mentioned among the others in a popular song of that period, hereinafter given.

‡ Froissart, liv. i. part ii. p. 698.

after he had been driven with the English out of Poitou, had fortified an eminence about two leagues from Quimperlé, which was called the New Fort, where he had collected a strong garrison; and, by the aid of his troops, he made frequent predatory incursions around his fortress, and became so dangerous as a neighbour, that no one dared to go from one town to another without his consent. The reputation of the New Fort was not confined to the neighbourhood of Quimperlé, as the young people of Brittany had composed a chanson, commencing "Beware of the New Fort," which came to be sung by the boys and girls over a great part of the duchy.*

* As Buchon, in his edition of Froissart, asserts that this chanson has been found in no other manuscript than the one used by him, it is here given entire, as an illustration of the popular ballad poetry of the times:—

CANÇON.

"Gardés vous dou Nouviau Fort,
Vous qui allez ces allues;
Car laiens prent son déport
Messire Jehan d'Evrues.

Il a gens trop bien d'accord,
Car bom tout leur est viés et nues;
Il n'espargnent foible ne fort;
Tantost ils aront plains leurs crues
De la Mote-Marciot
D'autre avoir que de viés oes,
Et puis meneront à bom port
Leurs pillages et leur conques.
Gardés vous dou Nouviau Fort,
Vous qui allez ces allues;
Car laiens prent son déport
Messire Jehan d'Evrues.

Clichon, Rohem, Rochefort,
Biaumanoir, Laval, entrues
Que li dus à Saint Brieu

This chanson happened to be sung in the presence of De Clisson and the Breton barons who were still at Lamballe, and who, on hearing it, exclaimed:—"Please God! these children will teach us how to fight. Truly it does not become us to know that our enemies are so near, who have this whole season pillaged the country without our going to look after them. It behoves us to march against this New Fort, and endeavour to take it with Sir John Devereaux in it. He can by no means escape us; and we will make him render an account of all his robberies."

Upon this the Breton lords left a part of their forces at Lamballe, and, with the rest, numbering about two hundred lances, they rode to the New Fort. As soon as they reached it they environed it on all sides, so that no one could escape them. For several days after the arrival of the Bretons there were frequent assaults, and some were wounded on

Dort, chevauchez les frans allues.
Fleur de Bretaigne, oultre bort
Estre à renommés sues,
Et maintenant outes mort;
Dont c'est pités et grans dues.
Gardés vous dou Nouviau Fort,
Vous qui allez ces allues;
Car laiens prent son déport
Messire Jehan d'Evrues.

Remonstre la ton effort,
Se conquerre tu le pues;
Tu renderas maint sourcot
A nos mères se tu voes.
En ce païs ont à tout
Pris et moutons et cras bues,
Ou paieront il leur escot
A ce cop, se tu t'esmues.
Gardés vous dou Nouviau Fort
Vous qui allez ces allues;
Car laiens prent son déport
Messire Jehan d'Evrues."

both sides. The fort, although well provided with the means of defence, was incapable of withstanding many such attacks.

While the Breton barons were thus pressing the siege of the New Fort to a close, the Duke of Brittany, almost at the same moment, was informed that his miners had lost their course, and it was necessary to start a new mine; that the Duke of Lancaster had made no progress in the treaty of peace; and that the Breton barons were closely besieging Sir John Devereaux in his new fort. As soon as the duke heard this last piece of news, he cried out:—

"Quick, to horse! Let us march hastily this way: for I shall esteem the capture of these five knights of more value than the surrender of any city or town in Brittany; as these barons, with my Lord Bertrand du Guesclin, are they who have done me the greatest injury, and whom I desire most to have in my power. We can never take them more easily than in the place where they are now. They will await us there, I doubt not, provided we make haste: for they are intent on taking the knight, Sir John Devereaux, who well deserves that we should sustain him, and rescue him from this danger."

At these words the duke and the English lords armed themselves, then mounted their horses, and set out, attended by the knights and squires of their respective troops, with their servants, who followed in the best way they could. "So hastily," says Froissart, "was the siege of St. Brieux raised."

The Duke of Brittany and his English allies, who equally hated Lord de Clisson, were so anxious to take the Breton barons by surprise, that they only stopped on the way to take breath, and they reached the neighbourhood of the New Fort with their horses dripping with perspiration; but, with all their despatch and haste, they were unable to take

De Clisson entirely at a disadvantage: for he had such timely notice of their approach as to enable him to mount his men on horses already saddled, which gave him so much the start that, upon looking back, when ready to commence his flight, he could see the dense array of the duke coming down upon him at full gallop. "Then the horses in the troop of Lord de Clisson knew what spurs were worth," as their riders neglected no means to urge them to their utmost speed, while followed all the way by the duke in eager pursuit. De Clisson owed his safety to the freshness of his horses, while those of the duke were wearied and overworked by their rapid march, which enabled the Breton lords to make good their entrance into the friendly town of Quimperlé.

The duke reached the town very soon after the Bretons had entered it, and immediately ordered an assault; but he was advised to encamp his troops and give the men a little repose after their exhausting march, while he would have leisure to examine the fortifications. "They are completely surrounded," it was added, "and they cannot escape you, unless they can fly through the air. Quimperlé is not so strong as to resist your power." Acting on this advice, the duke made formal preparations to lay siege to the town.

The first day the English did nothing but lodge themselves comfortably, and on the next morning they commenced the assault on the town. De Clisson prepared himself for the attack, as he well knew what to expect; and few men of that period understood better how to avail himself of every possible means of defence. This day an impetuous assault was made, which continued without pause till past noon; but it was resisted at every point: for there was not a man or woman in Quimperlé who was not employed at some work, either in unpaving the streets, bringing stones, filling pots with quick-lime, or carrying water for the men engaged in the defence of the fortifications. Next day the assault was renewed, with the same result.

Notwithstanding their success so far, De Clisson and the Breton lords were ill at ease, as they knew that the town could not hold out long against such assaults; and they thought it would be much safer to surrender and pay a ransom than run the risk of being taken in arms: for they well knew the deadly hatred of the duke towards all of them. They accordingly sent a herald to him to signify their wishes; but the duke would not listen to their offers, to which, without hesitation, he sternly replied:—

"Herald, go back and tell them who sent you, from me, that I will receive nothing from them unless they surrender without condition."

"Dear Sire, that would be great severity," replied the herald, who was probably instructed as to his answer, "if for loyally serving their lord they have brought themselves in this danger."

"Their lord!" returned the duke, with disdain. "They have no other lord but me; and, if I take them, as I hope to do, I will show them that I am their lord. So, herald, return; you will take back nothing else from me."

The answer of the duke, as reported by the herald, gave rise to the liveliest apprehensions on the part of the Breton lords: for it confirmed their fears of the unrelenting hostility of the duke; and they were well assured that they could not make good their defence, as they would be unable to continue such resistance as they had made on the two first days of the siege. They therefore sent the herald back to the duke, to propose an unconditional surrender, if they were not relieved within fifteen days. The duke, after some conference with the Earl of Cambridge and the English leaders, agreed to accept the terms proposed; but limited the time specified to eight instead of fifteen days. The Breton barons were forced to content themselves with the short respite allowed them, trusting to some unforeseen accident of fortune to relieve them from their perilous situation, as they could hope for nothing from the duke, "who mortally hated them, and declared that he would take no ransom."*

It happened, fortunately for them, that the king of France was informed of the siege of Quimperlé and the situation of the Breton lords; and, as Charles was extremely anxious to save such important adherents to his cause from the wrath of the Duke of Brittany, he had five or six couriers going night and day between Paris and Brittany, and from Paris to Bruges, "who reported, every day, news from eighty to one hundred leagues distance." As soon, therefore, as he was informed of the imminent danger of the Breton lords in Quimperlé, and as he knew how little they had to expect from the clemency of the Duke of Brittany, the king sent a message to the Duke of Anjou, and charged him, at whatever cost, to conclude a treaty forthwith, so as to include the boundaries of France, giving him, at the same time, the reasons for the step. The Duke of Anjou, "who had the legates of the pope in his hand," set to work, and immediately concluded a truce to last from the 27th day of June, 1375, to the last day of the same month in the year 1376.†

As soon as the treaty was signed, and a copy of it delivered by the Duke of Lancaster to two of his knights to be taken to the Duke of Brittany, the Duke of Anjou, in order to expedite them on their journey, and to show them their way, ordered two sergeants-at-arms belonging to his brother the king of France to attend these knights; and the sergeants

* Froissart, liv. i. part ii. pp. 698, 701.

† *Ibid*, pp. 701, 702; Rymer, vol. iii. par. ii. p. 1031. This treaty was signed by the Duke of Burgundy for France, and by the Duke of Lancaster for England.

were instructed to procure fresh horses all along the route, and stop neither night nor day until they had found the Duke of Brittany. The knights were entreated by the Duke of Anjou and by the legates of the pope, and also charged by the Duke of Lancaster, to lose no time on their journey. Upon this they made such haste that, in five days, they rode from Bruges to Quimperlé, where they found the Duke of Brittany in his tent, playing chess with the Earl of Cambridge.

The knights immediately laid before the duke the paper containing the treaty, with the order of the Duke of Lancaster to raise the siege of any place that he might be engaged in without delay. The Duke of Brittany was extremely angry when he received this order. He shook his head from side to side, and, after remaining silent for some time, the first words that he uttered were :—"Cursed be the hour when I agreed to grant a truce to my enemies."

In this manner was the siege of Quimperlé raised, as much to the chagrin of the Duke of Brittany as it was to the satisfaction of the Breton barons, who, on the morning of the day when they were relieved, would have given two hundred thousand francs to have been safe in Paris.

Thus terminated the expedition into Brittany, so profitless in every way to the duke. The Earl of Cambridge and the English lords returned immediately afterwards to England. The Duke of Brittany, after visiting his duchess, whom he had left at Auray for more than a year, went to Brest, where he remained for some time, in order to settle his affairs.*

As the Duke of Brittany was required by the treaty of Bruges to leave the duchy without delay, his prolonged residence there gave umbrage to the constable and Lord de Clisson, who wrote to remind him that he had violated the

* Froissart, liv. i. part ii. pp. 695, 702.

treaty by remaining himself, and keeping with him a greater number of men-at-arms than he was allowed to retain in the castles which still belonged to him. To this letter the duke replied from Brest, on the 2nd of September, 1375, that he had done nothing contrary to the terms of the treaty; and that, if anything had been done as stated, without his knowledge, he was ready to repair it; but that he would leave Brittany when he pleased. The duke, however, was unable to maintain the defiant attitude assumed in his reply; and he was constrained to leave the duchy soon after, taking his duchess with him to England.* The town and castle of St. Sauveur were delivered up to the constable, in conformity with one of the modifications of the treaty of Bruges, on the payment of forty thousand francs by the king of France.†

* The chronicler of St. Brieux says the Duke of Brittany visited his wife at Auray the year before, and then took her with him to England. *Chronicon Briocense, sub anno* 1374.

† Rymer, vol. iii. par. ii. p. 1033. Froissart asserts, at page 702, in which he has been too carelessly followed by others, that the French maintained that St. Sauveur was not included, like Quimperlé, in the treaty, and that it was given up against the remonstrances of the governor, through fear of the threats of the constable. Whereas Rymer not only gives the terms upon which it was agreed to be surrendered, as referred to, but he publishes the receipt for the 40,000 francs paid by the king of France to Edward III., in proof of compliance with the stipulation.—Vol. iii. par. ii. pp. 1040, 1041, 1048.

CHAPTER XXI.

The legates of the pope prolong the truce between France and England for another year. Death of Edward the Black Prince. Charles V. prepares to invade England by sea. Death of Edward III. Coronation of Richard II. Success of the French arms in Picardy and Aquitaine.

ON the 1st of November, 1375, the conferences were renewed at Bruges, between the Dukes of Anjou and Burgundy on the part of France, and the Duke of Lancaster, the Earl of Cambridge, and others, on the part of England. About that time the commissioners and their attendants were invited by the Duke of Burgundy to a grand festival at Ghent, where a tournament was proclaimed for fifty knights and fifty squires. It was also attended by a large number of distinguished nobles and ladies of high rank, and the jousts and dances were kept up for four days. After the festival was over, the commissioners met at Bruges, where various propositions, tending to peace, were submitted through the intervention of the legates of the pope; but, as each party demanded what the other was unwilling to grant, it was found impossible to reconcile their conflicting claims. Edward III. required that all the conquests which had been made by France should be restored; that the balance of the ransom of King John, due at the breaking out of the war between the two kingdoms, should be paid, and that the Captal de Buch should be liberated. On the part of Charles V., it was demanded that the money already paid for the ransom of the late king of France should be refunded, and that the fortifications of Calais should be demolished. As neither party would concede any of their pretensions, the commissioners found, at length, on the 12th of March, 1376, that they could effect nothing more than to prolong the truce until the 1st of April of the following year.*

By the suspension of hostilities between the two countries many members of the Free Companies, who had found employment for their arms during the wars between France and England, were now thrown out of service; and they speedily resumed their old practices of robbery and pillage. The complaints of his subjects, on account of their outrages, reached the ears of the king of France; and, not knowing how otherwise to rid his kingdom of these pestilent freebooters, he applied to Lord Enguerrand de Coucy, who, he was informed, was anxious to prosecute certain claims which he had on Austria, to lead them out of the country. Lord de Coucy caught readily at the proposition; and, with the aid of the king of France, who advanced a part of the funds required to pay the leaders, he collected the scattered bands, and led them as far as the banks of the Rhine. Here the leaders of the Free Companies found out that the Duke of Austria, hearing of their approach, had burned and laid waste the country for three days' march from the river; and, as these Companies would never take the trouble to make war on a country that was not worth plundering, they refused to march any further. Whereupon Lord de Coucy, fearing lest their leaders might seize his person and deliver him up to the

* Froissart, liv. i. part ii. p. 704; Rymer, vol. iii. par. ii. pp. 1040, 1041, 1048.

Duke of Austria, left his camp by night, in disguise, with only three attendants, and returned in haste to Paris. Upon the sudden disappearance of Lord de Coucy, the Free Companies soon followed him back into France.*

On the 8th of June, 1376, Edward the Black Prince, whose health had been continually failing, died at Westminster, in the forty-sixth year of his age. He was universally lamented by the English nation, as the greatest expectations had been formed of him, from the many brilliant qualities which he had exhibited, and from the invariable success of all his measures up to the termination of his unprofitable expedition into Spain. He was a prince of many virtues and few defects. He was well skilled in all martial exercises, and thoroughly imbued with the chivalric spirit of the age. Fond of display, he lived at great expense, and no monarch of his time kept a more splendid court. His manners were polished by constant intercourse with the refined society which he drew around him by his liberality and his cultivated tastes. He was courteous, condescending, and easily approached; but he was obstinate in his purposes, inflexible under opposition, stern, and even cruel in his anger. He had the judgment to select and the steadiness to retain able ministers about his person; and, both in peace and war, he was always served by the best counsel. Froissart, with whom the prince was a favourite, sums up his good qualities by describing him as the flower of all chivalry of the world in his time, and one who had been most fortunate in great feats of arms and in accomplishing important enterprises.

The king of France had leisure now to contemplate the situation of his affairs; and he could not regard otherwise than with the utmost satisfaction the complete success which had attended his inflexible but cautious policy. The

* Froissart, liv. i. part ii. pp. 703, 706.

English had been driven out of nearly all their possessions in France, and their ally, the Duke of Brittany, had been dispossessed of his entire duchy, except Auray, Brest, and St. Mahé. As much of this success was achieved by the arms and counsel of his constable, Bertrand du Guesclin, the king manifested his appreciation of such services by granting him the viscounty of Pontorson.*

During the winter of 1376, and the following spring, the new commissioners, who had been appointed by France and England to renew the efforts at peace between the two countries, used every means to accomplish the object of their mission; but they approached no nearer in reconciling the conflicting claims before them than their predecessors had done the previous year. It is probable that the design of Charles V., in offering to treat at that time, was only to amuse the English, as he knew that Edward III. was on his bed of death, and, amidst the distractions of a new reign, that every advantage over the child who was to succeed him was likely to be on his own side. While, therefore, his commissioners were receiving propositions of peace and offers of alliance between the two crowns, the king of France was making preparations, on an extensive scale, to invade England by sea, under Sir Jean de Vienne and the Admiral of Castille.†

These preparations were well known in England, and they caused much disquietude to the ministers of the king; but the startling news that his old enemy, whom he had so

* *Actes de Bretagne*, tom. ii. col. 173, and *Preuves de Du Guesclin*, by De Chastelet, p. 455. This grant was dated the 16th of December, 1376. A short time afterwards the constable reconveyed to the king of France, for the sum of 15,000 francs, the county of Montfort l'Amaury, which the king had previously given him.—*Preuves de Du Guesclin*, p. 460.

† Froissart, liv. i. part ii. pp. 708, 709.

often vanquished, was ready to descend on his shores, never reached the English monarch: for Edward was then beyond the reach of this world's business. In his palace of Shene * the worn-out king was then lying, unconscious of the affairs of state, and striving, with what strength he could, to prepare for his final hour. The Duke of Lancaster then received all applications intended for the king; Alice Pierce still ministered at his bedside; but his physicians at length gave him over: and Edward expired on the 21st of June, 1377, in the sixty-fifth year of his age, and the fifty-first of his reign.

The death of Edward III. was deeply deplored by the English nation: for he was a wise and strong man, who really had at heart the good of his people. His domestic government was characterized by many salutary laws, designed for the better regulation of trade and the more efficient administration of justice; and his foreign policy was popular, although it was marked, throughout the greater part of his long reign, by hostility to France, which resulted in a bloody and expensive war, that was wholly unjustifiable in its inception, exhausting in its prosecution, fruitless in its results, and fatal in its consequences; yet it elevated the military character of the English nation, ministered to the vanity of the people, and gave to the king the title of conqueror, which in all ages, though least entitled to the admiration of men, has been found the most coveted by sovereigns, and the most applauded by subjects.

Fortune did not always follow the footsteps of Edward; and there has seldom been presented in the lives of eminent men a more marked contrast than is afforded by the sunshine and success of the early and middle part of his course, and the clouds and disasters which gathered round its close. From the invasion of France, in the year 1345, under the

* Now Richmond.

Earl of Derby, to the battle of Navarrete, in 1366, Edward's military career, personally, or by his lieutenants, was an uninterrupted series of successes, while his domestic life was scarcely disturbed by a single sorrow, and his firm yet equitable administration of the laws did not give rise to an open murmur; but after that period his life, to its close, presented nothing else than a succession of private griefs and public disasters—when he lost his queen, the best and worthiest of his sons,* and fell under the censure of his parliament for an improper attachment to unworthy favourites;† and, of all his old claims and new conquests in France, he held at his death very few places of any consequence in Aquitaine, except Bordeaux and Bayonne, and little besides Calais in Picardy.

Edward III. had taken the precaution, during the year preceding his death, to have his grandson Richard acknowledged by his people, in a solemn act at Westminster, as his successor. By letters patent, dated the 20th of November, 1376, Richard was invested with all the titles of his late father the Black Prince, as Prince of Wales, Duke of Cornwall, and Earl of Chester; and, though a mere child of ten years, he was empowered to assemble parliament by his summons. All these precautions were adopted by the prudent king, lest his eldest son, John of Gaunt, Duke of Lancaster, who had assumed the empty title of king of Castille by virtue of his marriage with Constance, daughter of Peter the Cruel, might aspire to more substantial honours

* Lionel Duke of Clarence and the Black Prince.

† "More over the sayd Commons complayned them upon dyvers offycers, causers of this mysordre; whereof the Lord Latymer was noted for pryncipale, with also dame Alys Pyers, the whiche the kynge had long tyme mysused for his concubine, and one named Syr Richard Scurry, knyght, by whose counsaylles and sinistre means the kynge was mysgyded, and the rule of the land mysorderyd."—"Fabian's Chronicles," p. 486.

at home, at the expense of his infant nephew. The duke was far from being popular, as the great body of the English nation entertained the same suspicions of him as those which influenced the conduct of the late king; but he was too prudent to interfere with the wishes of his father and the English people, as to the succession to the throne. Richard therefore was crowned without question, with great pomp and acclamation, on the 11th day of July, 1377, in the eleventh year of his age.*

While the ceremonies which attended the coronation of Richard II. were taking place at Westminster, a French fleet, under the command of Sir Jean de Vienne, admiral of France, made a descent on the English coast, and took the town of Rye, on the borders of Sussex and Kent. After plundering the town the French set it on fire, and then, entering their ships, made for the Isle of Wight, where they took, plundered, and burnt the town of Yarmouth. Upon leaving the island, they took without opposition the towns of Plymouth, Dartmouth, Winchelsea, and Lewes, on the main land. These towns they also pillaged and set on fire; and they collected a large booty, chiefly in a number of rich prisoners, whom they carried away from the towns and the open country along their route.

After the sack of Lewes, Sir Jean de Vienne, with his fleet, sailed for Dover, where the Earl of Cambridge and his younger brother, Thomas of Woodstock, lately created Earl of Buckingham by his nephew Richard, were awaiting him, with a body of four hundred lances and eight hundred archers. The French admiral, being advised of the preparations made for his reception, did not attempt to land, but sailed directly for Calais. Here he remained at anchor for

* Froissart, liv. i. part ii. pp. 707, 710; Rymer, vol. iii. par. ii. pp. 1065, 1070.

several days, when a violent wind drove him down the coast of Normandy, and he was forced to seek refuge in the port of Harfleur.*

The town of Calais, in the hands of the English, was a source of perpetual annoyance to Charles V., as it gave them an easy entrance at any time into his kingdom; and as it was impregnable by any means known at that period, while it could be approached and supplied by sea, the king of France resolved, since he could not take the town, to deprive the English of certain castles which they held in the neighbourhood of Calais. The garrisons of these fortresses made frequent predatory incursions throughout the adjoining counties, and daily complaints of their outrages were brought to the king. He therefore fitted out an expedition, under his brother, the Duke of Burgundy, who set out immediately, with a force of twenty-five hundred lances, to attack these castles. The duke first approached Ardres, where he encamped a portion of his troops under temporary lodges made of the branches of trees, while the greater number of his men had no other protection than the naked sky. He brought with him large engines (cannons) which discharged heavy triangular arrows of two hundred weight.† The duke, thus provided with ample means for attack, soon reduced the castles of Ardres, Planche, Balinghehen, and Odruick;‡ permitting the garrisons of each to leave the castles with their baggage. These conquests restricted the English possessions in Picardy to the town of Calais.§

* Froissart, liv. i. part ii. pp. 710, 712.

† "Ils firent dresser et appareiller leurs canons, qui portoient carreaux de deux cents pesant."—Froissart, liv. i. part ii. p. 714.

‡ *Vanclingen* and *Arduic*, according to Morice, *Hist. de Bretagne*, tom. i. p. 353.

§ Froissart, liv. i. part ii. pp. 713, 716.

While the king of France was endeavouring to keep the English employed at home and in the neighbourhood of Calais, he fitted out another expedition, under the constable and the Duke of Anjou, at Toulouse, to dispossess them of the few fortresses which they still held in Aquitaine. With a large body of men-at-arms and other troops, commanded by a number of French, Gascon, and Breton nobles, the constable marched to Bergerac, and encamped near the town on the river Dordogne. As the town was strongly fortified, nothing took place during the first eight days of the siege but some unimportant skirmishes at the barriers, between the young knights and squires of the opposite parties. The leaders of the besieging army, therefore, decided in council to send to La Réole for a large military engine capable of throwing huge stones, and which could contain a hundred fighting men within it. On this expedition Sir Pierre de Beuil was sent, with three hundred lances of select men, who passed the river Dordogne, and took the shortest way for La Réole. The siege of Bergerac was not unknown to Sir Thomas Felton, seneschal of Bordeaux, who had been advised of the preparations of the Duke of Anjou, and he had sent to England for reinforcements; but, as the councils of the young king were distracted by the incidents of a new reign and the invasion of the English soil by a French fleet, his demands were unheeded. The only aid that he could get at that time was from four Gascon nobles, the Lords de Mucident, de Rosem, de Duras, and de Langurant, who joined him at Bordeaux with about five hundred lances. After this accession to his forces, Sir Thomas Felton, with the Gascon barons and above three hundred lances, left Bordeaux to watch the movements of the French army, and took a position at Aymet, between La Réole and Bergerac.

The constable of France was speedily advised that a body

of English men-at-arms had left Bordeaux under Sir Thomas Felton; and, fearing for the safety of the detachment under Sir Pierre de Beuil, he sent Sir Pierre de Mornay and Evan of Wales, with a select force of near three hundred lances, to join their comrades. The first detachment reached La Réole without molestation; and, after placing the engine for which they were sent on a number of waggons, they started by another way on their return to Bergerac than the one by which they went, as it required a more open road for the engine to pass. Near Aymet, where Sir Thomas Felton was lying in wait for them, they were joined by the detachment under Sir Pierre de Mornay; and they then marched with greater confidence, as their joint forces now numbered near six hundred men.

As soon as Sir Thomas Felton was informed that a body of French were approaching from La Réole with a large military engine, he ordered his men to arm themselves and mount their horses for an immediate attack. The French were no less anxious for an engagement; and, therefore, as soon as the two parties approached each other, they put spurs to their horses, lowered their lances, and, shouting their respective war-cries, commenced a bloody conflict, first with lances and then with swords, which was maintained with great spirit on both sides, as the combatants were chosen men; until at length the English were forced to give way, after many were slain, and their commander, Sir Thomas Felton, with the four Gascon lords and a number of others of inferior rank, were taken prisoners.

The day after the engagement near Aymet, the French troops reached Bergerac with the engine, which they soon erected before the town; and it so greatly alarmed the inhabitants, who had also been informed of the defeat and capture of Sir Thomas Felton, in whom alone they trusted for succour, that they urgently pressed upon the governor of the fortress the necessity of capitulating at once, as they had no aid to expect from any quarter, and they could not hold out much longer. The governor, Sir Perducas d'Albret, a bold and experienced partisan, was resolved to hold on to the fortress to the last; he therefore attempted to quiet the apprehensions of the citizens, by telling them that they were well supplied with provisions and artillery, and fully able to defend the town against any force likely to assail them; that, such being the case, they ought not to give it up so lightly. These arguments, though strenuously urged, proved insufficient against the admonitions of the constable, who sent to inform the citizens that all their principal leaders had been taken prisoners, so that they must now rely on themselves alone; and he warned them that, if they persisted in their refusal to surrender, and the town should be taken by storm, none of them would be received to mercy. This threat proved effectual; and the inhabitants of the town held a meeting, without the knowledge of the governor, and proposed to capitulate, on the condition that no men-at-arms should be placed as a garrison in the town. Sir Perducas d'Albret, on being informed of the proposition of the citizens, instantly mounted his horse, and, accompanied by his own people, left the town and marched to the fortress of Moncuq. Whereupon Bergerac immediately opened its gates to the French army.

The Gascon barons who had been taken prisoners at Aymet, under Sir Thomas Felton, took the oaths of homage and fealty to the Duke of Anjou; and, as they promised to become loyal Frenchmen for ever after, they were accordingly acquitted of all ransom. Shortly after their discharge, two of them, the Lords de Duras and de Rosem, left the camp of the French army, with the avowed design of returning to their own castles; but, when they found themselves again free, they took other counsels, and they asked each other :—

"How can we serve the Duke of Anjou and the French, when we have always been loyal Englishmen? It would be much better for us to forswear ourselves towards the duke than towards the king of England, our natural lord, from whom we have received so many benefits."

Quieting their consciences by such arguments, the two barons returned to Bordeaux, and reported themselves to the seneschal of Landes and the mayor of Bordeaux, to whose inquiries concerning the manner of their deliverance they replied:—"We assure you that, in taking the oath, we always tacitly reserved our faith towards our natural lord, the king of England; and for nothing that we have said or done will we remain French."

This act of bad faith on the part of the Gascon barons was soon found out by the Duke of Anjou, who swore that he would listen to nothing until he had laid waste the lands of the Lords de Duras and de Rosem.

After the surrender of Bergerac, the other towns and castles belonging to the English besieged by the French army made but a feeble resistance; and, in a short time, Châtillon on the Dordogne, Sauveterre, St. Bazille, Montsegur, Auberoche, and St. Macaire, opened their gates to the French. While engaged before St. Macaire, which held out somewhat longer than the other towns, the constable sent out several strong detachments, under Sir Louis de Sancerre, maréchal of France, Evan of Wales, Lord de Coucy, Sir Percevaulx d'Aineval, and Guillaume de Montcontour, to drive the English out of the country. These companies were out six days, and in that time they received the submission of a number of towns and fortresses.* They met with little opposition anywhere, as but few English

* Morice says more than three hundred places and fortresses are computed to have surrendered to the French in the space of three months.—*Hist. de Bretagne*, tom. i. p. 355.

men-at-arms were left in the country; and they, on the approach of the French, took refuge in Bordeaux.

After the surrender of St. Macaire, the French army marched to Duras, and attempted to carry it at once by an escalade. A number of ladders were placed against the walls, and the assault was maintained for the greater part of the day, during which many daring and gallant feats of arms were performed on both sides; but the besieged made good their defence until evening, when the marshals of the French army ordered the signal for retreat to be sounded, and the army returned to camp.

The next morning, before the assault was recommenced, the Duke of Anjou offered, by a herald, who proclaimed it throughout the camp, a reward of five hundred francs to be given to the one who should first enter Duras. The magnitude of the offer tempted many needy men-at-arms to unwonted acts of valour, while a number of others, stimulated only by the fame of the adventure, attempted to scale the walls. Among the latter was the Lord de Langurant, one of the Gascon barons taken with Sir Thomas Felton at Aymet, who first mounted a scaling-ladder, sword in hand, and attempted to enter the town. He was greatly provoked at the desertion of his late companions in arms, and he was probably influenced by a desire to show his new allies that they had no cause to fear a like act of bad faith from him. In this assault he performed prodigies of valour, and the spectators witnessed his feats with fear and wonder: for he put his life in great peril, as, in the attempt to gain the top of the wall, he lost his bacinet with all his head-armour, and he would have been slain on the spot, if one of his squires, who followed him closely, had not protected his head by a target, and enabled him to descend to the ground. Influenced by motives equally chivalric, Sir Jean de Jumont and Sir Jean de Rosoy performed many gallant feats of arms. At a different point the Lord de Sorel mounted a ladder, and fought hand to hand with the besieged on the ramparts. He maintained the combat with such skill and endurance, that the spectators all thought he was in the fairest way to gain the prize of valour; but he received a thrust from a lance which threw him from the wall, and, tumbling from the top to the bottom of the moat beneath, his neck was broken by the fall. At length Sir Tristan de Roye and Sir Jean de Rosoy made the first entry, and the town was gained. After these conquests the Duke of Anjou ordered Evan of Wales, with a large force of Poitevins, Bretons, and Angevins, to lay siege to Mortagne on the Gironde, commanded at that time by the Souldich de l'Estrade. The duke then disbanded his army and returned to Toulouse, where he gave a magnificent entertainment to the constable and the other lords who had served in this campaign.*

* Froissart, liv. ii. pp. 3, 11.

CHAPTER XXII.

Charles V. resolves to drive the king of Navarre out of his possessions in Normandy. Assassination of Evan of Wales. Unsuccessful attempt of the English to invade France, under the Duke of Lancaster and the Earl of Cambridge. The constable lays siege to Cherbourg.

THE king of France, having driven the English out of most of their possessions in his kingdom, had now to turn his attention to an old and implacable personal enemy, Charles the Bad, king of Navarre. The death of the queen of Navarre, a sister of the king of France, which took place on the 3rd of April, 1373, not without suspicions of poison,* severed the only tie which ever existed between the two kings. Always restless and intriguing, and now fretting under the failure of his schemes and the loss of a portion of his estates, Charles the Bad had not only kept up his intercourse with the English court, since the year 1375, by attempts to contract

* Such was the character of the king of Navarre, that no person of any consequence died within his reach during his reign without exciting suspicions of violence, by poison or otherwise. Du Tertre, however, in his depositions, very positively asserts that there was no ground for the charge in the case of the queen of Navarre, and that she died from disease of the heart.—*Procès Criminel fait à Pierre du Tertre, Secrétaire du Roy de Navarre*, in *Recueil sur Charles le Mauvais*, by Secousse, p. 410.

alliances to the prejudice of the crown of France, and used every means to create disturbances in the interior of the kingdom by fomenting a quarrel between Charles V. and a prince of the blood, Philippe d'Alençon, Archbishop of Rouen, but there is strong evidence that he set on foot a deliberate plan to poison the king of France himself.

This wicked design seems to have been projected soon after the death of the queen of France, which took place on the 6th of February, 1378; as, not long after that event, Charles V was informed by letters, received from several distinguished persons, of the machinations of the king of Navarre, and that his chamberlain, De Rue, was advised of the whole plot. De Rue was shortly afterwards arrested, and subjected to a rigid examination by a commission, at the head of which was the Chancellor of France.

In his depositions—which he acknowledges to have been made without constraint, but this may well be doubted from the nature of the transactions brought out by his confession—De Rue states that he remained with the king of Navarre fifteen days after the departure of his eldest son, Charles, infant of Navarre, for France; and that during the interval the king of Navarre told him that he had long entertained the design of poisoning the king of France, and explained the steps which he had taken to accomplish his purpose. The king of Navarre went on to inform De Rue that he had used a poison made in Navarre by a Jewess, which he had given to his valet-de-chambre and an officer of his pantry, named Drouet. This person the king of Navarre designed to send to his son, under some supposed pretext; and, after conference with De Rue, Drouet was instructed to find one of his cousins who was employed in the kitchen or fruitery of the king of France, and endeavour to corrupt this cousin, and engage him to put the poison into the food to be served on the table of Charles V. De Rue also added that he had been informed afterwards of all this detail by Drouet himself.*

With this information, and much other testimony, as to the criminal designs of Charles the Bad, gathered from the depositions of De Rue, the king of France resolved to keep no measures with such an enemy as the king of Navarre, and to drive him out of all his possessions in the kingdom. Charles V. granted a safe-conduct to Charles, infant of Navarre, then in Normandy, to come to Paris, who readily accepted the invitation, and brought with him a number of the principal commanders of the fortresses held by the king of Navarre in Normandy. The young prince, when informed of the arrest of his father's chamberlain, begged for his release; to which the king of France only responded by charging one of his counsellors to inform the prince of the crimes and treasonable attempts of the king of Navarre against the crown and kingdom of France, and to read to him the replies of De Rue in his recent examination. The prince, then only sixteen years of age, was struck with horror at the crimes charged against his father; and he testified his open disavowal of them by aiding his uncle, the king of France, to obtain possession of the fortresses of the king of Navarre in Normandy.

As it was the policy of the astute king of France to drive an intriguing and unscrupulous enemy out of his kingdom, and deprive him of the means, through his possessions in Normandy, of giving to the English an easy access to his dominions, he was prepared with an army, under the constable and the Duke of Burgundy, to carry out promptly the design which he meditated. These leaders were therefore soon ready to march into Normandy; and one of their first

* Secousse, *Hist. de Charles le Mauvais*, part ii. pp. 154, 156, 172; *Déposition de Jacques de Rue, Chambellan de Charles Roy de Navarre*, in *Recueil sur Charles le Mauvais*, by Secousse, pp. 373, 379.

conquests was the town of Bernay, in the diocese of Lisieux, where they took prisoner Pierre du Tertre, the confidential secretary of the king of Navarre, one who had served him as a pliant tool for twenty-six years, and who, during that period, had been informed of the most secret counsels of his master. Du Tertre surrendered upon the assurance given by the constable and the Duke of Burgundy that they would write to the king of France in his favour; and the constable promised moreover that he would introduce Du Tertre to the king when he came to court.

Charles V. had other designs upon the secretary of the king of Navarre than those suspected by the leaders of his army, as it was his object to give greater colour to his scheme for dispossessing Charles the Bad of his Norman fortresses, by rendering his character odious to all men. The king of France probably expected to get as much available information out of the secretary as he had already gained from the chamberlain of the king of Navarre; and, accordingly, Du Tertre was conducted to the châtelet at Paris, and subjected to the like rigid examination as that which had been resorted to on the trial of De Rue; and a long confession, touching many important transactions of the reign of Charles the Bad, was drawn out of him.

In his depositions, Du Tertre recited, with great clearness and every appearance of truth, many of the negotiations with which he had been charged; he gave, with much detail, the projects of his master, with the key of the cipher which they had used in their correspondence; and, although he admitted that he had participated in many hostile designs against the king of France, he repelled with indignation the charge of complicity in any attempt at administering poison, either to the king of France or to any one else.

Although the confession of Du Tertre did not involve any crimes which a foreign monarch might lawfully punish, yet he was forced to share the fate of De Rue; and they were both condemned by the parliament of Paris on the 16th of June, and sentenced to be decapitated at the market-place, where their heads were to remain, while the four limbs of each of them were to be suspended on eight gibbets to be erected near the four principal gates of Paris. This sentence, with all its revolting details, was fully carried out on the 21st of June, 1378.*

Charles V., in pursuance of his design to deprive the king of Navarre of his possessions in France, sent an order to his brother the Duke of Anjou to seize Montpelier and all the lands which Charles the Bad held in Languedoc. On receiving this order, the duke despatched Jean de Beuil, seneschal of Toulouse, to Montpelier, who reached that town on the 20th of April, 1378, and exhibited at once the order of the king of France to take possession of it in his name. The officials at first showed some hesitation in complying with the requisition; but so great was the indignation among the inhabitants of the town on being informed of the treasonable attempts of Charles the Bad against the king of France, that they immediately consented to all that De Beuil required of them.†

While these events were taking place, the forces of the king of France, under the constable and the Duke of Burgundy, assisted by the Count de Harcourt, Bureau Lord de la Rivière, and other leaders, were not idle in Normandy. One of the first fortresses which they took from the king of

* Secousse, *Hist. de Charles le Mauvais*, part ii. pp. 179, 191; *Procès Criminel fait à Pierre du Tertre, Secrétaire du Roy de Navarre*, in *Recueil sur Charles le Mauvais*, by Secousse, p. 388.

† Froissart relates otherwise the recovery of Montpelier by the king of France, liv. ii. p. 25; but Secousse, who has been followed here, is sustained by Aigrefeuille, in his history of Montpelier, from the archives of that town.—*Histoire de Charles le Mauvais*, part ii. pp. 196, 197.

Navarre, was Breteuil, where Pierre de Navarre, second son of Charles the Bad, was made prisoner, with his sister Bonne. After the capture of Pierre de Navarre, both of the sons of Charles the Bad were induced, by their uncle, the king of France, to co-operate with the leaders of his army in gaining possession of the fortresses of Normandy, the wardship of which he claimed for his nephews on the death of their mother.* The commandants of these fortresses, however, refused to yield obedience to the summons of the infants of Navarre; but few of the garrisons did more than make a show of resistance; and, during the months of April, May, and June, the French obtained possession, by force or capitulation, of Pontdouve, Avranches, Remerville, Beaumont-le-Rogier, Evreux, Mortain, Pontaudemer, Pacy, Nogent-le-Roy, Anet, and Breval.†

The castle of Gavrey,‡ where a large amount of money was deposited, besides the valuable crown jewels belonging to the king of Navarre, made a stout resistance under Fer-

* Froissart, liv. ii. p. 23; but see Secousse, *Hist. de Charles le Mauvais*, part ii. p. 194.

† Froissart's account of the campaign in Normandy is not only incomplete, but contradictory. In the concluding chapters of his first book he only mentions Pontaudemer and Mortain as surrendering to the French, and Pontdouve, Carentan, St. Lo, and St. Sauveur as receiving French garrisons; and in his second book he only adds Avranches, Moulineux, Conches, Pacy, and Evreux. Again, in his first book he assigns the command of the army to the constable, assisted by Lord de la Rivière; and in the second he makes no allusion to the constable as taking part in these operations; while it is very certain that the constable and the Duke of Burgundy, aided by the Count de Harcourt and Bureau Lord de la Rivière, were the chiefs of the army. —*Recueil sur Charles le Mauvais*, by Secousse, pp. 437, 455, and Secousse, *Hist. de Charles le Mauvais*, part ii. pp. 181, 216.

‡ Gavrey is mentioned, with Avranches, Cherbourg, and Coutances, among the principal castles held by Prince Henry, afterwards Henry I. of England, in the Cotentin, in the year 1090.—Ord. Vitalis, liv. viii. ch. xv. It is a burgh of Normandy, four leagues from Coutances.

rando d'Ayens,* who had succeeded in making his escape from the siege of Evreux; but, after he had taken command of Gavrey, while passing near a magazine of cannon-powder contained in one of the towers of the castle, the powder caught from a lighted candle which he carried in his hand, and he, with two attendants, was burnt to death.

The garrison, notwithstanding the dismay occasioned by this accident, still held out; but the troops of the Duke of Bourbon secured a lodgment in the walls near the castle-gate; while the constable pressed them so closely on the other side that, after a few days, they were forced to surrender. The constable secured all the treasures contained in the castle for the king of France, who liberally rewarded him by a gift of the money, amounting to forty-two thousand one hundred and thirty-one francs of gold, besides a present of four thousand francs for the jewels and plate which the constable saved from plunder.† These conquests reduced the possessions of the king of Navarre in Normandy to the strong fortress of Cherbourg.

While the king of France was receiving nearly every day the gratifying intelligence of some town or castle taken by his troops from the king of Navarre in Normandy, he heard, with great regret, of the loss to his service of one of his most trusted officers in a different part of the kingdom. Evan of Wales, who had laid siege the year before to Mortagne-sur-Mer, in Saintonge,‡ on the Gironde, had in-

* This is the surname given him in the depositions of Du Tertre, *Recueil sur Charles le Mauvais*, by Secousse, p. 401. He is the same person mentioned as Ferrandon by Froissart, at the siege of Evreux, as *un fol Navarrois qui là étoit.*—Liv. ii. p. 34.

† D'Orronville, *Vie de Louis de Bourbon*, ch. xxiv. p. 124, and *Preuves de Du Guesclin*, by Du Chastelet, p. 466.

‡ Froissart says, "Mortagne-sur-Mer, in Poitou." There is a Mortagne in Poitou, but it is not on the sea.—Note by Buchon, liv. ii. p. 11.

vested it so closely on all sides, that the garrison, reduced to great want of everything, were not likely to hold out much longer. While thus employed, he received into his service a Welshman by the name of James Lamb, who insinuated himself into his confidence by well-dissembled professions of attachment to his person, and imposed on his credulity by false representations of the national feeling of his countrymen in his favour. By these means Lamb obtained a situation near the person of his master, and he was soon after made his chamberlain.

Evan, while engaged in this siege, was accustomed to walk out early in the morning, if the weather was fair, and to sit on the trunk of a tree in front of the castle. Here he often combed his hair and completed his toilet; and here persons on business came to look for him. One bright morning he rose earlier than usual, as the night was so hot that no one could sleep, and walked out in an undress with a mantle thrown loosely over him. Everything was quiet in the tents; no sentinels had been posted, for the castle was regarded as already conquered. Evan went to his usual seat, accompanied only by his chamberlain Lamb, whom he sent back to his lodge for a comb. With the comb Lamb brought a short Spanish dart; and on his return, without saying a word, he plunged the weapon into the exposed body of his master, who fell dead on the spot.

The assassin immediately fled to the castle of Mortagne, and, making himself known at the barriers, he was admitted into the castle, and brought before the Souldich de l'Estrade.

"Sir," said Lamb to the castellan, "I have delivered you from one of the greatest enemies you have ever had."

"From whom?" inquired the souldich.

"From Evan of Wales," replied Lamb.

"In what manner?" again asked the souldich.

"In this way," replied Lamb; and he went on to tell how he had committed the deed. When the castellan had heard him through, he shook his head from side to side, and, looking sternly at the Welshman, said:—

"You have murdered him; and surely if, everything considered, I did not see our very great advantage in this act, I would cut off your head, and throw you, body and head, into the castle moat. Since, however, it is done, it cannot be undone; but it is a great outrage for a gentleman to be thus put to death, and we are likely to receive more blame than praise for it."

After the death of Evan of Wales, the garrison of Mortagne still held out, although greatly distressed for want of provisions, until they were relieved and the siege was raised by Lord Neufville, who had been recently appointed seneschal of Bordeaux.*

The English were still smarting under the insult offered them by the invasion of their soil during the last season by the French, under Sir Jean de Vienne, and they resolved to take ample satisfaction for it; therefore, as soon as the internal affairs of the kingdom were sufficiently settled, the Duke of Lancaster and the Earl of Cambridge, with a large fleet, a numerous and well-appointed army, and a great retinue of nobles, embarked from England, and sailed first for the coast of Normandy. They expected to encounter the French fleet off that coast; but, on finding that the French were no longer at sea, the English made for the coast of Brittany, and anchored in the port of St. Malo. They soon after landed near the town, and made preparations to besiege it.

The town of St. Malo was then commanded by a Breton

* Froissart, liv. ii. pp. 32, 37.

squire, a very expert man-at-arms, named Morfouace,* who was not at all dismayed at the prospect of a siege; but he made his preparations with equal skill and bravery to defend the town to the last extremity. The approach of the English was speedily made known throughout the country, and the Viscount de Rohan, Lord de Combourg, and Sir Henry de Malestroit threw themselves into the town, with two hundred men-at-arms; and their opportune arrival added greatly to the strength and confidence of the garrison.†

The king of France, who had been informed of the landing of the English, was extremely anxious to prevent the town of St. Malo from falling into their hands, as it would always give them an easy entrance into Brittany on that side. He therefore ordered an extraordinary levy of troops, and soon collected a large body of barons, knights, and men-at-arms, amounting to above ten thousand, under the constable of France, assisted by the maréchals De Sancerre and De Blainville. The French army, when assembled, marched directly to St. Malo, and encamped as near the English as they could get. There was seldom found near each other so great an assemblage of nobles and distinguished knights as was then in Brittany, for both the French and English were there in great force.‡ Between the two armies there was a canal which was filled twice a day by the sea, and even at ebb-tide there was always a small stream of water.§ Here, at the reflux of the sea, was the

* "Gillaume Picaud dit Morfouace," says Morice, in *Hist. de Bretagne*, tom. i. p. 357.

† Froissart, liv. ii. pp. 30, 31.

‡ Froissart, liv. ii. p. 31, says the English had four hundred cannon. This number is supposed to be an error or an exaggeration; and, if otherwise, that the pieces must have been of small calibre; or probably Froissart used the word *cannon* to designate the different military engines in use at that period.

§ Morice, *Hist. de Bretagne*, tom. i. p. 358.

scene of frequent skirmishes between the young knights and squires of the two armies, and many adventurous feats of arms were performed by them. The French were frequently drawn up by their leaders in battle order, and the English thought, at every such formation, that it was designed to give them battle; but they were as often disappointed, "as the king of France had such fear of all perilous adventures, that he would not consent for his people to trust to the hazards of battle unless they had five out of six." *

After several such displays, without result, the Earl of Cambridge swore that, if he saw any further attempts at bravado by the French, he would attack them, let come what would of it. The next day the constable of France, as before, formed his battalions on foot, as near the canal as he could bring them; when the Earl of Cambridge, who commanded the first division of the English army, said to his men:—"Let him follow who loves me: for I am resolved to fight them." He then advanced to the edge of the water. The tide was just then coming in, and his archers began to discharge their arrows against the French. The constable thereupon withdrew his forces into the adjoining plain, as he expected that the English designed to give him battle; and he was anxious for them to come on, as he could attack them while in the water. The Duke of Lancaster, who witnessed these movements, was ready, with a large division of the English army, to support his brother, if there was need; but, when he saw that the French had withdrawn from their first formation near the canal, he said to Girard de Biez, a squire of Hainault, standing near him: "Girard, look at my brother, how he adventures himself; he shows the French that he would willingly give them battle; but they have no desire for it." At this moment the

* Froissart, liv. ii. pp. 35, 36.

flow of the sea drove back the Earl of Cambridge and his troops, and both the English and French returned to their respective camps.

The French guarded so carefully their front on the canal that the English did not dare to pass it; and nothing took place for some time between the two armies but an occasional unimportant skirmish between the foraging parties. The Duke of Lancaster, seeing that he made no progress in the conquest of the town, resolved to resort to a mine; and, accordingly, he set his engineers to work, who laboured diligently night and day at their task. This mode of attack was greatly feared by the governor, Morfouace, who was well assured, from the strength of the fortifications and the abundance of provisions in the town, that he need apprehend danger from no other quarter. He therefore used every means to find out where the miners were at work, that he might defeat the object of the besiegers. It happened one night, when the Earl of Arundel was on duty, that the fact was found out in St. Malo; and as it was known to some in the town that the earl was not very vigilant, Morfouace, on being informed of it, secretly left the town with a select body of men, and went to the place where the miners were at work. As he expected, he found the sentinels all asleep. He thereupon destroyed the mine without resistance, and threw down a portion of it upon the miners then within it. After this exploit, Morfouace and his men boldly determined to awake the sentinels on duty in the camp next to the town; and, accordingly, they fell upon the tents sword in hand, shouting their war-cries; and, after slaying and wounding a number of the English, they returned without loss into the town. The English troops, in great terror, armed themselves and gathered around the tent of the Duke of Lancaster, who was much astonished at the commotion, and curious to find out the cause. When he was informed that not only the night attack on the camp, but the destruction of the mine, was caused by the want of vigilance on the part of the sentinels on duty, the Earl of Arundel was summoned before the Duke of Lancaster and the Earl of Cambridge, and severely reprimanded by them for his negligence. "The Earl of Arundel excused himself in the best way he could; but he was greatly ashamed of it, and he would rather have lost a hundred thousand francs."

The destruction of the mine and the approach of winter induced the English leaders to raise the siege of St. Malo; so that, with all the preparation, expense, and display of this expedition, not a single object was gained from it which the projectors promised themselves. Nor did the leaders escape the murmurs of the people at home, of which a good share fell to the portion of the Earl of Arundel.*

After the departure of the English, the constable supplied the town and castle of St. Malo with provisions, and then determined to lay siege to Cherbourg. He disbanded the greater portion of his army, giving leave to the leaders, among whom were the Dukes of Berry, Burgundy, and Bourbon, the Count de la Marche, and the Dauphin d'Auvergne, to return home with their troops; and he only retained Lord de la Rivière, with about three hundred Breton and Norman men-at-arms.

Cherbourg was then one of the strongest fortresses in the world; and, as it could only be reduced by famine, it was safe from the attacks of the French, since the English were in command of the sea, and it could be easily supplied with provisions from that quarter. The constable, however, invested it closely on the land side, and made use of every resource at his command to gain possession of it; but the

* Froissart, liv. ii. pp. 39, 40.

strength of the fortifications and the resistance of the garrison defeated all his efforts.

During the siege, which was kept up for the remainder of the season, Sir Oliver du Guesclin, the brother of the constable, with about forty lances, set out from Valognes, and approached near the walls of Cherbourg to examine the fortifications. On the same day, Sir John Arundel was riding through the town, in company with a Navarrois squire named Jean Cocq, when the news came to the latter that some French troops could be seen from the ramparts. "Sir!" said Jean Cocq, turning to Sir John Arundel, "I have just learnt that Sir Oliver du Guesclin, a brother of the constable, has passed the woods and come to examine our fortress. For God's sake let him be pursued. I know how to conduct you so that he cannot escape us; and we will divide the booty equally." The English knight gave his immediate consent; and both he and the Navarrois squire quickly armed themselves, mounted their horses, and, with about one hundred chosen lances, left the town and entered the wood where the French had been seen.

When Sir Oliver du Guesclin had sufficiently examined the fortifications to satisfy himself that they were impregnable, he returned towards Valognes by the same way by which he had come. He had not ridden two leagues on his return before he was overtaken by Sir John Arundel and his troops, who instantly charged the French, shouting their war-cry, "Our Lady! Arundel!" The French made no resistance. They scattered in every direction, and fled into the woods, each attempting to save himself; but at length Sir Oliver du Guesclin was captured by Jean Cocq, and ten or twelve of his men were taken prisoners by the English, and carried to Cherbourg.*

* Froissart, liv. ii. pp. 31, 40, 41, and liv. i. part ii. p. 718.

The king of France, having now driven the king of Navarre out of the county of Evreux, and reduced his possessions in Normandy to the single fortress of Cherbourg, was determined to crush him entirely, by inducing his ally the king of Castille to attack him on the side of Navarre. Henry of Castille was reluctant at first to adopt hostile measures against Charles the Bad, as his son and heir, John, had the year before married Leonora, the daughter of the king of Navarre; yet, after being informed of the conduct of Charles the Bad towards the king of France, and calling to mind the insult offered to himself in the treaty made by Navarre with England the year before, he sent his son John with an army to besiege Pampeluna;* but Lord de Neufville, seneschal of Bordeaux, hearing of this projected invasion of Navarre, sent Sir Thomas Trivet, with a force of five hundred men-at-arms and one thousand archers, to the aid of Charles the Bad, whom he found at St. Jean Pied-du-Port. The English knight joined his troops with the Navarrois, and the combined army marched to the relief of Pampeluna. The Castilians, after some deliberation, thought it most prudent not to await the approach of the king of Navarre and his allies; and, accordingly, they raised the siege and returned to Castille.†

The check to the progress of his arms at Cherbourg, and the fruitless invasions of Navarre by his ally, Henry of Castille, were not the only incidents of this campaign which gave annoyance to the king of France. Other occurrences of greater or less magnitude made this year a turning-point to the almost uninterrupted success which had attended the schemes and policy of Charles V. since the return of Bertrand du Guesclin from Spain. Among those of minor im-

* Ayala, *Cronica del Rey Don Enrique Segundo*, pp. 85, 90; Froissart, liv. ii. p. 26.

† Froissart, liv. ii. pp. 43, 45.

portance was the defection of another of the Gascon lords, who had been taken prisoner at Aymet the year before. Of the four barons who were released without ransom, on the condition of taking the oaths of homage and fealty to the king of France, two of them, the Lords de Duras and de Rosem, returned immediately thereafter to their former allegiance to the king of England. Lord de Mucident remained with the Duke of Anjou until the conclusion of the campaign, and then went to Paris, where he resided for more than a year. He was either dissatisfied at his treatment, or, finding the condition of things at the court of Charles V. different from what he had expected, he began to repent of the step taken by him in abandoning the service of the king of England. He therefore, after consultation with his friends, secretly left Paris, and, accompanied by only four attendants, went to Bordeaux, where he was followed by his people, in small parties. Here he reported himself to Sir John Neufville, seneschal of Bordeaux, to whom he declared that he preferred to abjure his allegiance to the king of France than to his natural lord the king of England. This act of bad faith on the part of Lord de Mucident gave especial umbrage to the Duke of Anjou, before whom the oaths had been taken; who swore that, if ever he caught the Lord de Mucident again, he would have his head struck off. The Gascon baron heard this threat of the Duke of Anjou, and he ever afterwards took good care that it should not be put into execution.*

The Lord de Langurant, who was taken prisoner at the same time as the other Gascon lords, not only preserved his loyalty to the French, but made frequent inroads upon the lands of his old companions in arms, the Lords de Duras, de Rosem, and de Mucident, with whom he was extremely

* Froissart, liv. ii. pp. 49, 50.

offended for holding their oaths so lightly. He was a skilful and adventurous knight; and, while riding one day, with about forty lances in his train, he came to the castle of Carvilac, then commanded, for the family of the Captal de Buch, by a squire named Bernard Courant. Concealing his men in a wood near the castle, Lord de Langurant rode up to the barriers and asked of the guard:—"Where is Bernard Courant, your captain? Tell him that the Lord de Langurant demands of him a joust. He is too good a man-at-arms to refuse it, for the love of his lady. If he rejects it, it will turn out greatly to his prejudice: for I will proclaim wherever I go that he has refused, through cowardice, a joust with me at the point of the lance." This challenge was made in the hearing of a valet of Bernard Courant, who went immediately to tell his master what had occurred.

The squire was very angry on hearing the defiant tone of the message, and he called out to his attendants:—"Here! my arms! saddle me a courser; he shall not go off with a refusal." He immediately armed himself, mounted his horse, and, taking his shield and lance, ordered the gate and barriers to be opened, and rode out into the field before the castle.

When the Lord de Langurant saw the squire come out to meet him, he was greatly rejoiced. He lowered his lance, and put himself in preparation for the onset. The same was done by Courant; and, without further delay, they both put spurs to their horses against each other. In the shock the lances were both so well aimed, that they splintered to pieces on the shields. In passing, however, Courant struck the shoulder of Lord de Langurant, which threw him out of his saddle, and he fell to the ground. When the squire saw his antagonist unhorsed, he turned quickly upon him, and, before he could recover himself, Courant, who was a strong and active man-at-arms, seized him by the bacinet with both hands, drew it from his head, and threw it under his horse. At this moment the followers of Lord de Langurant, who were in ambush, seeing the danger of their master, began to advance to his rescue; but Courant, happening to look that way, observed their movements, and, drawing his dagger, he said to Lord Langurant:—"Surrender, Sire de Langurant! rescue or no rescue, or you are a dead man." The Gascon baron, who yet hoped that his followers might come in time to save him, made no reply. When Courant could get no answer, and seeing that he had not a moment to lose, he struck the baron on the naked head with his dagger, which he drove up to the hilt; then, drawing it out, he put spurs to his horse, leaped him over the barriers, entered the castle, and put his garrison in order for defence, if there should be need.

When the followers of Lord de Langurant came up to their master, they found him mortally wounded. They took him up and carried him, in the best manner they could, back to his castle, where he died the next day.*

* Froissart, liv. ii. pp. 50, 51.

CHAPTER XXIII.

The king of France resolves to annex the duchy of Brittany to the domains of the crown. He obtains a decree of the parliament of Paris against the Duke of Brittany. Opposition of the Bretons to the measure.

THE defection of one of the Gascon lords and the death of another, with the loss of certain fortresses in Gascony, which had been recently retaken by the English from some Breton adventurers, were only trivial interruptions to the successful policy of the king of France up to this time; but, in his subsequent conduct towards the Duke of Brittany, by over-estimating his own resources and miscalculating the feelings of the Bretons towards himself, he committed a blunder which he did not live long enough to correct.

Charles V had meditated for some time the design of annexing the province of Brittany to the crown, on account of the facility with which the English could be introduced into the kingdom by any owner of the duchy who might feel himself aggrieved by the king of France. No time appeared more favourable for the execution of this design than that juncture, when the English had lost nearly all their possessions in France except Bordeaux and Calais; when the king of Navarre was driven out of every important place in Normandy but Cherbourg; when the Duke of Brittany, by the loss of Auray,* was reduced to the single fortress of Brest; when the greater part of the Breton nobles, by distinguished favours or open bribes, were in the interests of France; and when the great body of the people were strongly attached to the constable, under whom most of their effective men had done service in war. Influenced by these considerations, the king of France resolved to carry out his purpose without further delay.

It is probable that his resolution was strengthened, and the execution of his design hastened, by an incident that took place during this season, which tended to irritate the king still further against the Duke of Brittany. Charles V., in order to give the English employment at home and divert them from the re-conquest of the castles lately taken from them in Gascony, sent Lord de Bournisel into Scotland to persuade the king of the Scots to make war on England. This Bournisel, who was a vain and frivolous person, got as far as Sluis, in Flanders, where he was forced to wait for some time in expectation of a favourable wind. By his ostentatious displays, and other fooleries, he attracted the attention of the people, and, at length, of the bailiff of the town, who gave information of his conduct to the Count of Flanders. The count, whereupon, ordered his arrest, and Bournisel was taken to Bruges. When he was conducted into the presence of the count, he dropped on one knee before him, and said:—

"My lord, I am your prisoner."

The count was much irritated at the words and manner of Bournisel; and he replied, angrily:—

"How, villain! Say you that you are my prisoner because I sent for you to come and speak to me? The people of my lord may, without offence, come to speak to me, and you

* Froissart, liv. i. part ii. p. 719; *Chronicon Briocense*, col. 49.

have but ill acquitted yourself when you remained near me so long at Sluis, and deigned not to come and see me."

"My lord, save your grace!" was the only reply of Bournisel to the rude speech of the count.

The Duke of Brittany, who was present on this occasion as a guest of the count, then interposing, said :—

"Among you tattlers and tale-bearers at the palace in Paris, and in the chamber of my lord, you put the kingdom at your disposal, do what you please, and whatever good or evil that suits you; so that no high princes of the blood, should they chance to incur your displeasure, can ever be heard. There will yet be hanged so many of such people, that the gibbets will be full of them."

Bournisel made no reply either to the duke or the count; and he withdrew from their presence as soon as he was permitted. He returned to Sluis, where he was diverted from his purpose of going to Scotland, for fear of being taken prisoner by the English, who were said to be on the look out for him; and he thereupon went back to Paris.

As the king of France was greatly surprised at the speedy return of his envoy, Bournisel was summoned to give an account of the failure of his mission, which he attributed to his detention by the Count of Flanders; and he gave a full narrative of his adventure and of the manner in which he had been treated by the count and the Duke of Brittany. This statement was made in the presence of many knights of the bedchamber, among whom was Sir Jean de Ghistilles, of Hainault, a cousin of the Count of Flanders. This knight, with great difficulty, suppressed his anger while Bournisel was speaking; and, as soon as the other concluded, he said to him :—

"I cannot hear, my lord, the Count of Flanders spoken of in this manner; and, chevalier, if you will maintain what you have said, or that the count has prevented your voyage, I challenge you to the field: and here is my gauge."

"Sir Jean," replied Lord de Bournisel, without hesitation, "I do affirm that I was taken by the bailiff of Sluis and carried before the Count of Flanders; and that all the words I have repeated were spoken by the count and the Duke of Brittany; and, if you maintain otherwise, I will take up your gauge."

"I do," answered the knight of Hainault.

"Come, come!" interrupted the king; "we will hear no more of this."

Charles V then withdrew into his own chamber; and he expressed great pleasure to some of his attendants that Lord de Bournisel had replied with so much spirit to Sir Jean de Ghistilles.

"He has answered him bravely," said the king, laughing; "I would not take twenty thousand francs that it should not have happened."

Nothing further came of the altercation between the two knights; but Sir Jean de Ghistilles found himself in so little favour at the court of Charles for so readily espousing the cause of one with whom the king was offended, that he left Paris soon after, and went to Brabant.

Upon the report by Bournisel of his treatment in Flanders, the king of France wrote to the count a menacing letter, charging him, among other things, with giving an asylum to his enemy the Duke of Brittany. The count, in his reply to this letter, endeavoured to excuse his conduct in the best way he could; but the king would not listen to his excuse; and he wrote back to the count a more threatening letter than the first, and plainly informed him that, unless the duke was speedily sent away from his court, he would take satisfaction for the affront.

The count, seeing that the matter was likely to take a

very serious turn, assembled the burgesses of the towns of Flanders, to ask what reply he should make to this threat of the king of France. Upon their assembling at Ghent, the count informed them that he had incurred the displeasure of the king of France for refusing to turn out of his house, and drive from his territories, his friend and kinsman the Duke of Brittany; and he asked them if they would sustain him in the position which he had taken. To this inquiry the burgesses replied, with one voice :—

"My lord, yes; and we know of no sovereign, whoever he may be, if he would make war upon you, who would not find, in your county, two hundred thousand men, fully armed, and well prepared to defend themselves."

This defiant response of the Flemish towns to the threats of the king of France, though greatly displeasing to Charles when he was informed of it, led to nothing further from him than an ill-natured remark that the Count of Flanders was the proudest and most presumptuous prince that he knew; and that he would gladly see his pride humbled. The Duke of Brittany, after remaining a short time in Bruges, without molestation, went over to England.*

Charles V., having now resolved to deprive the Duke of Brittany of his estates, proceeded to take the step under the sanction of certain legal formalities; and, accordingly, on the 4th of September, 1378, he assembled the peers of his realm in a parliament at Paris, and proposed to them that, as "Sir Jean de Montfort, knight, lately Duke of Brittany," had rebelled against him and traversed the kingdom with a great body of armed men; had plundered his subjects and burnt some of the cities and towns of the kingdom; had defied him, his king and liege lord, and denounced him as an usurper of the crown of France: that for these

* Froissart, liv. ii. pp. 52, 53.

and many other offences he ought to be deprived of his duchy and county, and that these possessions should be united to the crown.*

After some deliberation, the parliament decided that the duke should be cited personally to answer these charges at Paris, before the king, on the 9th day of December following; and this citation was proclaimed in the towns of Rennes, Nantes, and Dinan, in the duchy of Brittany. On the day fixed for the appearance of the duke, the king held his *bed of justice*, to decide the important question as to the confiscation of the duchy of Brittany. He was attended by the dauphin, the six ecclesiastical peers, four lay peers, six bishops, four abbots, the Count de Harcourt, a German count, and Sir Jean de Harcourt. After six days' deliberation, it was decided by the parliament, that, since the duke failed to appear before the king, he should be deprived of the duchy of Brittany and the county of Montfort, which should be held as confiscated on account of the offences committed by the duke, and that the duchy and county should be united to the domain of the crown of France. To carry out this sentence the king appointed the Duke de Bourbon, Sir Louis de Sancerre, maréchal, and Sir Jean de Vienne, admiral of France, with other leaders to go into Brittany and take possession of the duchy, in the name of the king.†

This decree of the parliament of Paris was not made without strenuous opposition on the part of the representatives of the Countess de Penthiévre,‡ widow of Charles de Blois, who

* *Chronicon Briocense*, col. 49; Guil. de St. André, v. 2502; *Actes de Bretagne*, tom. ii. col. 201.

† *Chronicon Briocense*, col. 49; *Actes de Bretagne*, tom. ii. col. 201.

‡ The Countess de Penthiévre, who still retained the title of Duchess of Brittany, was informed beforehand of the design of the king; and she sent Gui de Cleder and Raoul de Keradreux, doctors-in-law, with Hue des Fossés, Olivier de la Villeon, Geoffrey de la Motte, and Jean

asserted that the decree was unjust and illegal, for the duke could not thus be deprived of his lands. That, even granting the decree to be legal in respect to the duke, the duchy could not legally be confiscated to the prejudice of the Countess de Penthiévre and her children, who, by the treaty of Guerrande, were the declared heirs of the duke, if he died without male issue. Other arguments, founded on law and fact, were adduced to sustain the claims of the Countess of Penthiévre, but they were disregarded; and, thereupon, her representatives returned into Brittany to report to their mistress the loss of her cause before the parliament of Paris, and to exclaim against the illegality and injustice of the decree.

On the part of the Duke of Brittany the decree was held illegal, because the summons was not properly served on him, for he was only cited once; whereas, by law, he should have been cited three times before he could have been regarded as manifestly contumacious. Besides, it was asserted that the citation was only made in the kingdom of France, in places where the duke had neither domicil nor attorney, when it was well known that he had resided in England for more than a year, and that he knew nothing of the citation until some months after the promulgation of the decree against him. It was contended, morever, that no safe-conduct had been sent to him by the king; and it was scarcely to be expected that he would expose himself to the danger of death among his personal enemies, without some guarantee for his safety.*

The king of France had entirely misapprehended both the cause and extent of the opposition to the Duke of Brittany on the part of the Bretons; and, therefore, he was greatly

le Vayer, to defend her rights to the duchy.—Morice, *Hist. de Bretagne*, tom. i. p. 362.

* *Chronicon Briocense*, col. 50, 51.

deceived when he supposed that their previous conduct had proceeded from love for himself, rather than hatred towards the English, and that the Bretons desired anything further than the punishment of their master for employing foreigners in his service, in place of themselves. Charles was, consequently, taken completely by surprise, when he found the Bretons of all classes nearly unanimous in their opposition to an arbitrary measure of his parliament, adopted without any inquiry as to their wishes, or any consultation with them, and carried out against all the forms of law, by which their liege lord was stripped of his estates, and his duchy confiscated and annexed to the crown.

To provide against this unexpected state of things in Brittany, the king of France sent for four of the most influential Breton nobles, whose fidelity to his person and attachment to his interests he least doubted; and he thought, with the support of the constable, Bertrand du Guesclin, Lord de Clisson, the Viscount de Rohan, and Lord de Laval, that he could have no difficulty in suppressing what he regarded as nothing more than a temporary manifestation of popular discontent. These lords promptly obeyed the summons, and went to Paris; when the king informed them of the steps which he had taken to dispossess the Duke of Brittany of his estates; and he asked them how far they would give him their aid against the duke and his adherents; and, further, if they would deliver up to his troops, whenever required, certain towns and castles belonging to the duke which they then held.

The constable and De Clisson, both of whom hated the Duke of Brittany, promised, without hesitation, to do all that the king demanded of them; the Viscount de Rohan, afraid of the consequences of a refusal, dissembled his real sentiments, and took the oaths which the king required of him; but the Lord de Laval acted with more firmness, and declared that he would keep, himself, the fortresses under his charge; that he could not consent to the ruin of his kinsman the duke, yet he would ever be a loyal subject of the king. Charles professed himself satisfied with all their promises, and took leave of the Breton nobles, who returned to their respective commands, except the constable, who remained longer in Paris. The king soon found, however, that, even with the aid of the greatest of the Breton barons, he had excited a ferment in Brittany which was not so easily quelled.*

The decree of the parliament of Paris being now generally known in Brittany, a number of Breton lords commenced, by secret unions, and afterwards by open associations, to oppose the confiscation of the duchy; and Raoul Lord de Montfort headed a movement at Rennes, by an act, dated the 25th of April, 1379, which was signed by forty knights. In this document the signers pledged themselves to aid each other in defending the *ducal rights* of Brittany against all who should attempt to take possession of the duchy, except those to whom it would belong in the line of succession, and the king of France in sovereignty. In order to pay the troops destined for the defence of the country, they imposed a levy of a franc on each fire throughout the duchy; and they appointed four knights, Amaury de Fontenay, Geoffrey de Kerimel, Etienne Goyon, and Eustache de la Houssoye, maréchals of Brittany. To show that they were in earnest in their proceedings, they declared, moreover, that, if any of their associates took any step contrary to their act of confederation, all the others should declare against him; and, if he should make any terms with the enemies of the country, without the consent of the others, that he should be regarded as false and perjured; that all should implicitly obey the

* *Chronicon Briocense*, col. 52; Guil. de St. André, vv. 2888, 2974.

leaders whom they had appointed for the defence of the country; and that the entire revenue of the duchy should be appropriated under the orders of the Lords de Montfort, de Montafilant, de Beaumanoir, and de la Hunandaie, who were the four principal chiefs of the league.

The confederates were not satisfied with forming this mutual league, they also invited the citizens of Rennes to join them; and, on the same day, all the knights, squires, and burgesses of Rennes signed another document, pledging themselves to maintain the rights of the duchy; and they appointed Sir Amaury de Fontenay, Lord de la Motte au Vicomte, captain of the town and castle of Rennes, with whom they joined twenty-two gentlemen of the association.*

The king of France, now finding that he would meet with a strenuous opposition to the decree of his parliament, sent the Duke de Bourbon into Anjou, who advanced as far as Châteauceaux, with a large army, to take possession of Brittany; and his first object was to gain the town of Nantes, then under the command of Lord de Clisson. The Bretons, hearing of the approach of the Duke de Bourbon, resolved to oppose him with all the means at their command, with the unanimous declaration that they would not thus permit the king of France to usurp the duchy, and dispossess their duke of his inheritance. When, therefore, Lord de Clisson endeavoured to obtain the consent of the citizens of Nantes to deliver up the town to the Duke de Bourbon in the name of the king, they positively refused; but, in a friendly manner, they reminded De Clisson when, on a former occasion, having obtained, with their consent, the command of the town, he had promised them not to surrender it to any one but the Duke of Brittany, their natural lord, if he came to claim it, unaccompanied by the English.

* *Actes de Bretagne*, tom. ii. col. 214, 216.

De Clisson admitted the promise, and declared that he would perform it. Finding now that he was powerless in the town of Nantes, he hastily left it, with everything that he possessed there, and went to join the Duke de Bourbon at Châteauceaux. He informed the duke that the whole province of Brittany was in arms against the king of France, and that the citizens of Nantes had driven him from their town. He said he was at a loss what to advise, and he begged the duke to make his excuses to the king for his inability to deliver up the town of Nantes, as he had promised. The Duke de Bourbon, upon the receipt of this unwelcome news, left Châteauceaux, withdrew his army to Angers, and soon after returned to Paris to get further instructions from the king.*

After the retreat of the Duke de Bourbon, the Bretons were not content to act on the defensive. They entered the province of Anjou with a considerable army, took the fortresses of Pouancé and Rochediré, and laid waste the open country around, without meeting with any resistance from the French.†

These acts of open hostility by the Bretons against the king of France determined the chiefs of the league to send deputies to the Duke of Brittany, then in England, to urge his speedy return to his estates; and Etienne Goyon, Rolland de Kersallion, Berthelet d'Engouelvent, and Jean de Quelen were appointed on this commission. Their letter of credence was dated from Brittany, the 4th of May, 1379.

The duke received with great pleasure from his people this deputation, which, from their past conduct, he had no reason to expect; and he at once endeavoured to form an alliance with the English, to enable him to get possession

* *Chronicon Briocense*, col. 52.

† *Ibid*, col. 53; Guil. de St. André, v. 3257.

of his estates. The council of the young king of England, hearing from the Breton deputies the favourable turn which things had recently taken in Brittany for the duke, were persuaded, without difficulty, to grant his demands, as they were fully assured of the advantages that would result from the measure; and, accordingly, "power was given to Thomas Percy, Hugh Calverly, and others, to treat with the duke and the prelates, barons, nobles, and communities of Brittany." The treaty was concluded on the 13th of July, 1379, by which the duke received a force of two thousand men-at-arms and two thousand archers, with the wages of these troops and his own paid for four months and a half. The chief consideration for this important aid was that, if the king of England should cross the sea in person, the Duke of Brittany would be required, at his own expense, to join him for nine months, with one thousand men-at-arms and as many other combatants. With this force, the Duke of Brittany embarked from Southampton, and entered the river Ranche, near St. Malo, on the 3rd of August, 1379.*

The rumour of the arrival of the Duke of Brittany in his duchy having been spread abroad, the Bretons, who had been in subjection to the crown of France for seven years, and lately in open arms against the king, now felt so much strengthened by the presence of their natural lord, that they were wild with delight. In an assembly of the clergy and people, called in the town of Dinan, the duke was received by all classes of citizens with every demonstration of pleasure and regard. In that assembly—which was composed of nearly all the barons of Brittany, and even the Viscount de Rohan was expected to be present, for the duke had written

* *Actes de Bretagne*, tom. ii. col. 219, 220; *Chronicon Briocense*, col. 54; Guil. de St. André, v. 2780. Froissart, liv. ii. p. 84, only estimates the forces of the duke at two hundred men-at-arms and two hundred archers.

to invite all the Breton nobles, except Bertrand du Guesclin and Lord de Clisson*—they complained how the king of France, by an illegal decree, had attempted to dispossess him of his duchy, and to reduce the Bretons to servitude. The duke heard all these grateful murmurs against the king of France very complacently; and afterwards, in a chamber belonging to the preaching friars of Dinan, with whom he was then a guest, made a formal harangue, in which he declared that he had come, at their request, to defend their common liberties and country against the encroachments of the king of France.†

The Countess of Penthiévre first replied to the duke in a very spirited speech, which was echoed by several of the Breton barons, among whom was the Lord de Malestroit, who declared that he was ready to bring to his support four hundred combatants to carry on the war. The Viscount de Rohan promised three hundred men-at-arms,‡ Jean Lord de Beaumanoir offered to increase the army of the duke by one hundred and twenty men, and many other lords and knights declared that they were ready to die in his service.

The duke, seeing his subjects prepared to obey him with the most unexpected but gratifying unanimity, ordered them to return to their respective homes, get themselves ready for service, and prepare to meet him at the town of Nantes, on a day to be named, in order to march against the Dukes of Anjou and Bourbon and the constable of France, then at Pontorson.§

Charles V. was equally surprised and irritated on hearing

* *Lettre de Bertrand du Guesclin au Duc d'Anjou*, in *Actes de Bretagne*, tom. ii. col. 225.

† *Chronicon Briocense*, col. 54; Guil. de St. André, v. 3062.

‡ According to an original paper, in *Actes de Bretagne*, tom. ii. col. 281, the oath of fealty, made by the Viscount de Rohan to the Duke of Brittany, is dated the following year, April 13, 1380.

§ *Chronicon Briocense*, col. 55.

of the union of the Bretons, and of their audacity in taking the castles of Pouancé and Rochediré, in Anjou; and, fearing lest he might incur greater losses, he ordered all his fortresses bounding on Brittany to be strengthened immediately. Notwithstanding these precautions, Lord de Beaumanoir entered Normandy with two hundred men-at-arms, put a number of the inhabitants to the sword, laid waste the open country, and returned into Brittany in triumph.

No one witnessed these events with more solicitude than Bertrand du Guesclin. Apart from his personal dislike to the Duke of Brittany, whom he never regarded as the rightful possessor of the duchy, the constable was too loyal a Frenchman to esteem otherwise than as a foe one who had ever been in league against his own countrymen. But he was also a Breton; and he watched with deep concern the first exhibitions of the popular discontent, and its rapid increase, until it manifested itself in a general outbreak against the authority of the king, and in the restoration of the duke to the confidence of his subjects. The constable well knew that these dissensions could only lead to civil war, and that he must greatly suffer, whoever might prove the victor.

One of the first effects of the change in the sentiments of the Bretons towards the Duke of Brittany was the loss of influence, by the constable, on the minds of those who had hitherto so implicitly followed his guidance. And, as the popular enthusiasm in the cause of the country increased in intensity, he was not only abandoned by the great body of veterans who had been trained in his service, but even his personal friends and kinsmen were carried away by the patriotic emotion; and they exclaimed against the obstinacy of his resistance to what they regarded the acknowledged rights of his liege lord.*

* Guil. de St. André, v. 3106.

Lord de Clisson, who was as firm in his opposition to the duke as the constable, was equally powerless in Brittany; and, after witnessing the loss of Guerrande, which he was unable to prevent, and the surrender of Baaz, St. Nazaire, the isle of Rancoet, and the neighbouring country, to the Duke of Brittany, he joined the constable in going to meet the Duke of Anjou at Pontorson.*

* Guil. de St. André, v. 3126.

CHAPTER XXIV.

The king of France entertains suspicions of the loyalty of the constable. Indignation of the constable at the imputation that he was an adherent of the Duke of Brittany. He tenders to the king the sword of his office. He is sent to the south of France. His death.

DURING the month of October, 1379, an attempt was made to bring about a reconciliation between the king of France and the Duke of Brittany, and their differences were at length referred to the Duke of Anjou, on the part of the king, and to the Count of Flanders, Lord de Laval, and others, on the part of the duke; but Charles V was so obstinately bent on executing the decree of confiscation, that the negotiations were without result. Some of his courtiers still flattered the king with the assurance that he would yet be successful in his efforts to unite Brittany to the crown, and his first chamberlain, Bureau de la Rivière, attempted to impress him with the belief that the failure of his enterprises in Brittany arose from the remissness of the constable, who had forborne to exert his usual vigour and zeal against his countrymen. Lord de la Rivière had conceived some prejudice against Bertrand du Guesclin, and he endeavoured to excite a suspicion against his fidelity, as he wished to make Lord de Clisson constable.*

* *Actes de Bretagne*, tom. ii. col. 233; Guil. de St. André, v. 3226; D'Orronville, *Vie de Louis de Bourbon*, ch. xxxvii. p. 138.

The constable soon heard that the king had listened to insinuations against his fidelity, and conscious how long and devotedly he had served him, like a high-spirited knight, he could not restrain the feelings of an honest indignation, and he said, with great earnestness, to his friends:—"Since the king, whom I have so loyally served, regards me with suspicion, I will remain no longer in his kingdom. I will go to Spain, where I am yet esteemed; and I will return the king his sword." Charles was speedily informed of this resolution of the constable; and, as he was convinced of his injustice in entertaining for a moment the slightest suspicion against one who had rendered him such signal services, he was solicitous to repair the wrong which he had done; and he sent the Dukes of Anjou and Bourbon to appease the anger of the constable.

These two great nobles willingly undertook the commission: for both of them had always shown the greatest regard for the constable. They found him at Pontorson; and the Duke of Anjou commenced the conversation by stating that the king of France had heard of his dissatisfaction at the imputation that he was an adherent of the Duke of Brittany, and that the king had sent him with the Duke de Bourbon to say that he never believed the report. "Here," the Duke of Anjou concluded, "is the sword of honour of your office: take it back, the king desires it; and return with us."

The constable replied with dignity and firmness, but with the utmost respect, that he thanked the duke for his information, and he thanked the king for not believing the charge against him, notwithstanding all the scandal which had come of it. He repelled, with warmth, the imputation that he could ever serve the Duke of Brittany: for he wished, he said, to preserve the little honour which he had acquired in the world; and he desired the king to be informed that he preferred his reputation to all the rewards which it was in his power to bestow. He concluded by declaring that he could not retake the sword. "Give it," he said, "to another who can please him: for, to remove all suspicion from him and others, I will go to Spain." The Duke of Anjou continued to implore him not to adhere to his resolution; and the Duke de Bourbon added his entreaties, begging him not to abandon the king in that manner; but the constable was inflexible, and the dukes left him, without accomplishing the object of their mission.*

However fixed the resolution of the constable seemed to be, under the first impressions of his anger at an imputation which concerned his honour, the king, by changing the theatre of his military operations, induced him to forego his design of abandoning the service of France. Just then a suitable occasion was presented for removing the constable to the south of France. The Duke of Anjou at that time, by his extreme rigour and excessive exactions, had become very unpopular in his government of Languedoc. In the year 1378, in order to pay the troops which he had collected with the design of laying siege to Bordeaux, he imposed a tax on the people under his government, which amounted to two hundred thousand francs; and, although the enterprise was abandoned, not a denier was returned to the over-taxed inhabitants, who had found great difficulty in raising so large an amount. This heavy tax, and other unpopular acts of his administration, induced the communes of Toulouse and the other cities and towns of Languedoc,

* D'Orronville, *Vie de Louis de Bourbon*, ch. xxxviii. pp. 138, 139. D'Orronville states that Bertrand du Guesclin adhered to his resolution not to resume the sword of his office; and that he was on his way to Spain, when he was induced to lay siege to Châteauneuf-de-Randon; but Morice has shown conclusively that the constable never abandoned the service of France.—*Hist. de Bretagne*, tom. i. p. 1008, note lxv.

in the year 1380, to implore the king of France to remove the duke, and send the constable, Bertrand du Guesclin, in his stead.*

The king availed himself of this application from his subjects of Languedoc to displace the Duke of Anjou, and to remove the constable from Brittany, where he would necessarily come often in conflict with his old companions in arms, to another part of the kingdom, where his services would be more agreeably and as advantageously employed against the leaders of the Free Companies, who had broken out afresh in the provinces of Languedoc, Auvergne, and Limousin.

Among these freebooters the sternest and most cruel of them all was a Breton, named Geoffrey Tête-Noir, who obtained, through the treachery of a servant, the strong castle of Mont-Ventadour, in Auvergne. The Count de Mont-Ventadour and de Montpensier was a nobleman of mature age, of probity and experience, who had passed the period of bearing arms, and who then kept quiet in his castle. He had a squire as his valet, named Pons du Bois, who had long served him to little profit, as the valet thought; so he resolved to indemnify himself for his past services by an agreement with Geoffrey Tête-Noir, to deliver up the castle for six thousand francs, upon the condition that his master was to be put out, without injury to himself or his household. In this manner Geoffrey Tête-Noir came into possession of Mont-Ventadour, from which he harassed and laid under contribution all the neighbouring country.

Amerigot Marcel was another daring freebooter, who gained, by force or artifice, the castles of Caluset, Aloise, and Vallon. With these leaders were joined others of less

* Miguel del Vermes, *Chroniques Béarnaises*, p. 588; Froissart, liv. ii. p. 29.

note, who, when all their garrisons were assembled, could bring together between five and six thousand lances; and they overran the whole country without resistance: for no one was strong enough to oppose them.*

To remedy this state of things, the constable was sent into Languedoc with a sufficient body of men-at-arms. Upon leaving Brittany, to take charge of his new command, he had an interview with the king of France. In a touching allusion to his own situation—for the constable was not without a trace of poetry in his nature—he said to the king, that the eagle, which had been accustomed to the loftiest flights, could no longer soar, since it had lost the best plumes in its wings; and he therefore implored the king to make peace with the Bretons, that the eagle might resume its former flights.†

The constable made no long delay in Paris; and, as soon as his preparations were completed, he set out with his army for Languedoc.‡ A short time after he arrived in that province, he laid siege to the strong fortress of Châteauneuf-de-Randon, situated about five leagues from the town of Mende, in the present department of Lozère. The castle belonged to the English; and it was well supplied with provisions and the means of defence. The constable pressed the siege with his usual vigour; but the fortress was occupied by a numerous garrison, and they defended themselves with great valour. This resistance on the part of the garrison only served to excite the ardour of the constable, who swore that he would not leave the place until the castle surrendered. As the English knew that he was likely to perform

* Froissart, liv. ii. pp. 57, 58.

† Guil. de St. André, v. 3538. The constable here alluded to the eagle which he bore as a device on his shield, and to the Bretons who had abandoned him for the service of the Duke of Brittany.

‡ The constable made his muster of men at Paris, May 8th, 1380.—*Actes de Bretagne*, tom. ii. col. 419.

what he had promised, and as they had no reason to expect either supplies or succour from any quarter, they, at length, asked to treat with the constable for the surrender of the fortress; and they offered to capitulate, if, on a day fixed, they should not be relieved by a competent force from the king of England. For the due performance of this agreement, hostages were demanded by the constable, and delivered up by the garrison.*

On the fifteenth day after the commencement of the siege, the constable, who had taken an active part in the assaults on the castle during the hot July weather, was carried to his bed, struck down with a mortal sickness; and it was soon apparent, to himself and to others, that the end of his career was at hand. When he saw that life was nothing more to him, he prepared himself for his departure from it with firmness, propriety, and resignation. He made his will, which is dated the 9th of July, 1380; and he received with deep devotion the last sacraments of the church. To his sorrowing friends he imparted his final admonitions; but even in those solemn hours his thoughts turned on the siege he was then engaged in, and he could remember that it was the day fixed for the surrender of the castle. To the Maréchal de Sancerre he gave his last orders to require its submission; and he then assembled the leaders of his army around his bed-side, to witness the closing act of his life. When they came, he ordered the sword of his office to be brought, and, taking it into his hands, he said:—

"My lords, among you I have enjoyed the rewards of earthly valour, of which I was little worthy. I must now, in brief space, pay the tribute of death, which spares no one. To God, I beg you, first of all, to commend me. And

* Froissart, liv. ii. p. 93; *Chronique* (Anonyme) *de Du Guesclin*, ch. cxlv. p. 93.

to you, Sir Louis de Sancerre, maréchal of France, who have deserved still greater honours, I recommend my wife and kindred. Commend me also to King Charles, my sovereign lord; and this sword, under which is the government of France, return to him for me; I cannot commit it into the hands of one more loyal or abler than yourself."*

With these words, Bertrand du Guesclin made the sign of the cross, and then breathed his last.

Thus passed away the spirit of an earnest, loyal, and brave man, who found work for him to do in this world, and who did it with his might.

Soon after the constable expired, the garrison of Châteauneuf-de-Randon, who had sworn to deliver up their fortress to him alone, hearing of his death, issued out of the castle, with the captain at their head, and, conducted by the Maréchal de Sancerre, they entered the tent where the body of the late constable was lying, and deposited the keys of the castle on his coffin.†

Bertrand du Guesclin died on the 13th of July, 1380, in the sixty-first year of his age. By his will he had selected the church of the Jacobins of Dinan, "in the chapel of his predecessors," as the place of his burial; but Charles V., who greatly bewailed his death, chose for him a more distinguished tomb. When the king knew that his nephew, Sir Oliver de Manny, and other knights, were conveying the body of the late constable to be buried in his native province of Brittany, he sent word to them to bring it to St. Denis, for there he desired that it should be interred.‡

* D'Orronville, *Vie de Louis de Bourbon*, ch. xxxix. p. 140; *Actes de Bretagne*, tom. ii. col. 288; *Chronique* (Anonyme) *de Du Guesclin*, ch. clxvi. p. 93.

† *Chronique* (Anonyme) *de Du Guesclin*, ch. clxviii. p. 95; D'Orronville, *Vie de Louis de Bourbon*, ch. xxxix. p. 140.

‡ *Actes de Bretagne*, tom. ii. col. 286; *Chronique* (Anonyme) *de Du Guesclin*, ch. clxviii. p. 95.

The grief of the king for the death of his greatest subject was equally shared by the people: for, at every city through which the mournful *cortége* passed, the clergy and citizens came out to meet the procession, with the most sincere demonstrations of sorrow, took charge of the body, and placed it in the cathedral, where the solemn service of the church was performed over the remains, and the procession was followed, on leaving the city, for more than a league. At length the body reached the monastery of St. Denis, where it was buried at the foot of the tomb which the king had ordered to be prepared for himself, amidst the very general and sincere grief of the entire kingdom of France.*

Jeanne de Laval, the second wife of the constable, survived her husband, as he not only made ample provision for her by his will, executed just before his death, but she is said to have conferred the honour of knighthood on André de Laval, by buckling on him the sword which the deceased constable used to wear in his battles.†

Bertrand du Guesclin left no children by either of his wives. He had a natural son, named Michel, who served in Normandy during the year 1379, and who received from the king of France, in the year 1381, the sum of one

* Froissart, liv. ii. p. 95; *Chronique* (Anonyme) *de Du Guesclin*, ch. clxviii. p. 95; D'Orronville, *Vie de Louis de Bourbon*, ch. xxxix. p. 140; Christine de Pisan, partie iii. ch. lxix. Charles V soon followed the constable to the grave; and his death took place at Beauté-sur-Marne, near Vincennes, the 16th of September, 1380, at the age of forty-six years, and in the seventeenth of his reign.

† *Actes de Bretagne*, tom. ii. col. 288; Du Chastelet, *Hist. de Du Guesclin*, p. 273; and St. Palaye, *Mémoires sur l'Ancienne Chevalerie*, tom. i. p. 33, note (14).

hundred and eighty *livres tournois*, as a reward for the services which he had rendered during the war.*

Olivier du Guesclin, brother of the constable, succeeded him as Count of Longueville and in the lordships of Broon and Rochetesson. The name of Du Guesclin is known to have continued down to the year 1660, when Bertrand du Guesclin, counsellor of the parliament of Brittany, espoused, in second nuptials, Renée, the daughter of René Sire de Fretay, and who left a son named Bertrand, the issue of this marriage.†

* Du Chastelet, *Preuves de Du Guesclin*, p. 466; Morice, *Hist. de Bretagne*, tom. i. p. 374. Du Chastelet also states, on the authority of Alonzo Lopez de Haro—*Nobiliario de España*—that Du Guesclin had two natural sons by a servant-girl of the town of Soria, in Castille; one of whom, named Bertrand de Toreuz, was a knight of the order of Calatrava, and commander of Mudela; and the other, whose name is not given, was the ancestor of the Marquis de Fuentes.—*Preuves*, p. 465.

† Morice, *Hist. de Bretagne*, tom. i. p. 374; Du Chastelet, *Généalogie de Du Guesclin*, p. 280.

THE END.

CPSIA information can be obtained
at www.ICGtesting.com
Printed in the USA
LVHW040026180422
716440LV00005B/401

9 783752 595109